Lincoln,
Rocky
& Zeke

Lincoln, Rocky & Zeke

Richard Haddock

LINCOLN, ROCKY & ZEKE

iUniverse books may be ordered through booksellers or by contacting:

iUniverse
1663 Liberty Drive
Bloomington, IN 47403
www.iuniverse.com
1-800-Authors (1-800-288-4677)

ISBN: 978-1-4917-9311-4 (sc)
ISBN: 978-1-4917-9312-1 (e)

Library of Congress Control Number: 2016905449

Print information available on the last page.

iUniverse rev. date: 04/13/2016

"If a free society cannot help the many who are
poor, it cannot save the few who are rich."
John F. Kennedy

"Priests are no more necessary to religion
than politicians to patriotism."
John Haynes Holmes

"A little group of willful men, representing no opinion
but their own, have rendered the great Government
of the United States helpless and contemptible."
Woodrow Wilson

"The best mirror is an old friend."
George Herbert

For
The Fencil Kids

Anita
J.B.
&
Bobby

Robin, Tracie & Lisa

1

The three young men were different in every imaginable way: family backgrounds, educational interests, political leanings. Even their choice of food, music, and clothing further differentiated them from one another. And yet, as they hurtled down the desolate country road on a snowy November night, laughing and joking, they were united by a bond that often shapes young minds and hearts.

That bond was youthful rebellion; a resistance to the path that had been prescribed for them. For the driver of the 1965 Chevy Impala, Rockford Charles Wellington II, that path had been dictated by his father, president of the only bank in tiny Walnut Grove, Kansas. "Rocky" had been groomed since childhood to one day succeed his father in title, power and prestige.

Rocky bore his fate good-naturedly. And why not? He breezed through all his college finance and banking classes, having mastered their content in his years of working at the Walnut Grove bank and from his father's steady council at the dinner table, on the golf course, and in the wood-paneled privacy of the old man's office.

His rebellion would be in replacing his father's folksy way of running the bank with all the new methods, tools and strategies he had learned here at Kansas State University. Like his father, Rocky was tall, blonde and handsome, with light blue eyes and an engaging smile. A fixture at local bars and campus parties, Rocky was popular amongst his classmates, particularly the girls. Always being flush with money helped.

Across from Rocky in the front seat sat Lincoln Archer, also a senior at K-State, enjoying the last year of his liberal arts curriculum before he returned to his father's church in Wichita. Lincoln too had learned his predestined trade from a lifetime of work in and around the church and from the dynamic personality that was his father. But his rebellion was brewing, these past four years having raised questions about faith and religion he had been reluctant to yet discuss with his father.

Unlike Rocky's handsome features and outgoing personality, Lincoln was shy and soft-spoken, with a head of neatly trimmed black hair, sleepy brown eyes and a face that had yet to require shaving, an easy smile and a high-pitched laugh. He preferred reading and listening to classical music to the bar-hopping exploits of his banking friend. But tonight was yet another example of his growing willingness to be coerced into leaving his dorm room for a night of adventure.

In the back seat, fighting to stay awake, Zeke Porter stared gloomily out the window, the snow coming down harder now as Rocky sped through the night. Unlike his two friends, Zeke had no parental guidance or mandates regarding his future. His parents had died in a car accident when he was two years old and he was raised by his maternal grandparents on their tiny wheat farm in western Kansas.

With a background steeped in the soil Zeke initially studied agriculture in anticipation of returning to the farm after graduation. But when both his grandparents died his sophomore year he had sold the farm, using the proceeds to pay for his remaining education and establish a meager nest egg.

His grandparents had been full-blooded Cherokee and he had their physical characteristics: dark eyes, hair and skin, a stocky frame that made him look bigger than his six foot height. He also had an appreciation for the plight of his ancestors as reflected in his grandparent's stories and tales about the "true" treatment of Native Americans that seemed to conveniently escape the history books. After his grandparent's deaths he turned "hippie," letting his hair grow shoulder length and sporting a bushy mustache. With no family legacy to follow, Zeke began to pursue any subject that interested him, changing majors five times before he settled on journalism.

He had a natural curiosity about the truth behind the headlines and he loved research, pointed discussions and uncovering hidden facts. His articles for the Wildcat, the campus newspaper, had made him a bit of a local legend, highlighted by his investigation into the mysterious burning of Hargrove Hall, the dilapidated auditorium that was eventually rebuilt by a company owned by a member of the Board of Regents. The latter's conviction for bribing two students to set the fire caused a local sensation and cast Zeke into the role of a populist muckraker. His rebellion would be against the corruption, ignorance and hypocrisy of the world as he saw it. He reasoned there would be a never-ending abundance of material to work with.

Although he had made a number of casual friends at K-State, Zeke's relationship with Rocky and Lincoln was special. They were a tether to sanity, to shared desires, to having someone you could talk to about the myriad of issues that descended on most college students. There was a thread of common ground between the threesome that had started with their random assignment to a study group for an English Lit' course. That thin thread spooled slowly as they spent more time together and shared the wide-ranging, all-encompassing discussions about life that were fueled by a generous supply of marijuana and its liberation of their fears, passions and dreams.

Beside Zeke in the back seat slept Andrea Jackson, an unplanned addition to the trio of friends tonight. They had shared beers and conversation with her at Jack's, one of the local pit stops near campus, and agreed to give her a ride back to her house in the town of Manhattan, the tiny burg that sat just south of the University. A "townie," a KSU student who had been born and raised in Manhattan, Andrea had been a frequent visitor to Aggieville, the cluster of shops, restaurants and bars adjacent to the KSU campus, since she was fifteen. She was an attractive redhead with a perky cheerleader personality, a glamorous smile and a dynamite figure. Her rebellion was simply to graduate and get the hell out of Dodge, her home life a miserable existence under the thumb of two strict, suffocating parents.

Zeke straightened up and tried to clear his beer-soaked brain. He ran a hand through his mane of hair. "Where the hell are we going, Rocky?"

Rocky's eyes flashed to the rear view mirror. Zeke had seen that wide-eyed look before. Rocky was in full-fledged heat. "Sparrow's Point," he said, referring to the isolated area where couples parked.

Zeke shook his head. "To do what?"

"You kidding me? Andrea there is ready to go," Rocky said with a familiar leer. "You heard her back at Jack's. Let's go see what happens, remember?"

"I think all she was looking for was a ride back to her house," Zeke said.

Rocky belched. "Well, she's going to get a ride alright," he added.

"Shit, you're too drunk to do anything," Zeke said with a laugh. Indeed, in addition to the beers they had previously consumed, they had been passing around a fifth of Jack Daniels and were all well beyond the legal limit of intoxication, particularly Andrea who had chugged from the bottle like a veteran boozer, then promptly passed out. "Besides," Zeke went on, "I'm not gonna stand out in the cold while you force yourself on this girl."

"Hell, you guys can have a turn when I'm done."

Lincoln offered a groan of disgust. "That's groady, man," he said.

"Yeah, Rock," Zeke added, "she's unconscious. How much fun could that be?"

Rocky shook his head and his shoulders sagged. "Shit, you guys could ruin a wet dream." The car slowed down. "O.K., let's get Andrea back home and then maybe you two can grow a pair and we'll go to The Chuck Wagon," he said, referring to the topless bar near Ft. Riley that was strictly off limits to KSU students.

"We get caught there and we'll all be expelled," Lincoln said, alarm in his voice.

"Time to live on the edge, men," Rocky said.

Zeke had already been to the Chuck Wagon with Rocky several times and it always provided an entertaining view of Midwestern culture and personalities: farmers in their cowboy hats and boots, construction workers, soldiers from Ft. Riley, a few daring college students and, of course, the dancers with their glistening bodies and the overwhelming smell of cheap perfume that would gag a maggot. The place had provided fodder for several of his short stories in Creative Writing class. "Sounds O.K. to me," he said.

"Atta boy, Zeke," Rocky said. "At least somebody in the car is interested in having some fun."

Lincoln sighed. "Alright, got nothing else to do tonight."

And so the plan was set. First, the trip back to town to drop Andrea off, then on to whatever adventure the Chuck Wagon would provide. A typical Saturday night search for fun and diversion. Rocky slowed down and turned the car around, then punched the accelerator. "Let's see what this baby will do," he exclaimed, gripping the wheel tightly.

Zeke watched the speedometer climb to the right: seventy, eighty, ninety miles per hour. "Whoa, man, slow down," he said. "These roads are slippery as hell."

"Relax," Rocky said, "this car wasn't meant to drive the speed limit, man."

"Damn," Lincoln said, bracing himself against the dash board with an outstretched arm. The car's engine roared.

They must have been doing close to a hundred when the other car passed them going the opposite direction; a gray and blue blur. "Shit!" Rocky said, glancing in the side view mirror. "Trooper!"

"Slow down," Lincoln yelled, turning to look behind them.

"Bullshit!" Rocky said. "I can't get a ticket. My old man will have my ass." Behind them the state trooper had turned around and was in hot pursuit, red light flashing, siren wailing.

Like most roads in Kansas the one they were on was straight as an arrow, heading due west all the way back to the outskirts of Manhattan and the K-State campus. It was a virtual dead end and they were trapped. Sensing his plight, Rocky suddenly jerked the wheel to the right and the car shot off the paved highway and onto an adjacent farm road, mud, snow and gravel spewing in all directions.

"What the hell?" Lincoln said, bouncing up and down in the front seat.

"I know a shortcut," Rocky said.

"To where?" Lincoln asked, eyes wide.

But Rocky had no answer. He was doing what his inebriated brain told him to do. Run. The Impala bounced along, sliding from side to side. The gravel road bisected snow-covered fields and the headlights revealed rows of trees, windbreaks, that shot by on both sides as Rocky fought to maintain control of the car. Behind them the state trooper slipped farther away.

"He's not interested in wrecking his patrol car," Rocky said, glancing into the rear view mirror. "He'll give up in a few minutes."

Then, out of nowhere the curve appeared, bending sharply off to their left. Rocky was slow to react to the sudden change of direction. The car flew off the road and landed hard in the open field, dragging a barbed wire fence with it. Dirt and snow spewed up all around them, enveloping the car. The Impala bounced and banged along, then suddenly was airborne again. Zeke had that feeling you get as a kid when you fling yourself from a swing at its apex: weightless, your body out of control and falling.

The car pitched forward and slammed down, tossing its passengers all over the interior. The window next to Zeke exploded. Steam boiled from under the hood. The car creaked as if bolts and screws were popping loose. Rocky was slumped against the wheel. Lincoln was up against the passenger door. Andrea was next to Zeke, still asleep and moaning, as if she was having an erotic dream. Zeke felt something ice cold against his side, then realized that water was pouring in the broken window to his left. What the hell?

They had plunged into a pond at the far edge of the field and it sounded like a waterfall as the cold water rushed into the back seat. Zeke reached forward and jabbed Rocky. "Hey! Rocky," then, "Lincoln!" Neither moved. Were they dead?

Zeke forced himself into the cascade of water and wiggled through the open window into the icy pond. It was pitch black except for the headlights of the car shining down into the murky water. He reached back inside the car and grabbed Andrea, pulling her through the open window. She was still out of it. Zeke turned her around and grabbed her from behind, under the chin, as he had learned from his Red Cross training years ago, and pulled her away from the car. Where was the shore? How far away? He swam along, wide awake now, Andrea silently in tow. He reached for the bottom with his feet. It was slippery but he was able to stand. The water became shallower still and he realized he'd reached the shore line. He pulled Andrea up onto the muddy bank and laid her down. She was breathing normally so he turned and waded back into the pond.

"Help!" he heard Lincoln yell and he swam over to the far side of the car. The passenger door was open and Lincoln came splashing out into his arms. "Are you O.K.?" Zeke asked.

"Can't swim," Lincoln yelled, grabbing at Zeke with both hands.

The pond was probably ten feet deep at that point and the car was slowly sinking. "I got you," Zeke said, "relax and quit fighting me." But Lincoln continued to thrash and pull Zeke under. In desperation Zeke yelled, "Rocky's still in the car, damn it!"

That seemed to do the trick as Lincoln calmed down and allowed Zeke to steer him towards the shore. "You can stand up here," Zeke said a minute later, pulling Lincoln into an upright position, then turning back to the car, only the rear end of which was still above water.

As Zeke swam back to the car the entire scene was suddenly bathed in bright lights. The state trooper had caught up with them and had parked on the gravel road, his headlights following the path Rocky's Impala had made across the field right into the pond. The trooper began trudging across the field, backlit by his headlights, his shadow casting an eerie, movie monster-like image.

Zeke dove under the icy water and felt for the driver's door. He couldn't see clearly, but managed to find it. He tried to pull it open. It wouldn't budge. He came back up for air and moved to the open rear window, took a deep breath and forced himself back into the car. It was full of water. He reached out for Rocky and grabbed him by the shoulders, struggling to pull him over the seat, but the guy couldn't be budged. Zeke reached past him and unlocked the driver's door, then pushed against it. It inched open but Zeke was nearly out of breath. He turned and swam back through the open window and to the surface, gasping for air. He took another deep breath and went under the cold water again, this time pulling the driver's door wide open. He reached in and grabbed Rocky by the arm, pulling the dead weight from behind the wheel and out of the car.

Zeke gripped Rocky by the collar of his jacket and half swam, half walked, feet slipping and sliding, up onto the shore of the pond. He laid him on his stomach as the lights from the patrol car illuminated the muddy bank and the steam rising from the three bodies now laying there.

Andrea had woken up. "What the hell?" she moaned.

Lincoln tried to explain the situation to her as Zeke moved to Rocky's unconscious body, turned him on his back, and began CPR. "Rock, come on, man," he yelled.

Zeke pumped Rocky's chest and breathed into his mouth for several minutes. "Come on, dammit!" he yelled. Finally, a gurgling sound gave way to a violent wretch that brought Rocky upright as he vomited the contents of his stomach, not once but twice. He choked, coughed, spit up more water, and gasped for breath. "Take it easy," Zeke said.

Rocky wiped at his nose with the sleeve of his jacket. "What happened?" he asked groggily.

"Your car is now a submarine," Lincoln said.

Rocky turned and stared as the tail lights of his car slipped beneath the water. He hung his head. "Jesus. My father will kill me."

The trooper had finally made his way to the edge of the pond. "Is everyone out of that car?"

"Yes, sir," Zeke said.

"Anybody hurt?" the trooper asked.

"No, we're all O.K.," Zeke answered.

"Good," the trooper said. "Now, which one of you was driving?"

There was a sudden hush, the hissing noise from the hot engine under water the only sound. Zeke slowly stood up, his mind racing against the consequences of what he was about to say. He knew that the truth would probably get his friend expelled and into deep shit trouble with his father. He exhaled heavily and said, "That would be me, officer."

# # #

2

The Manhattan Holiday Inn, nestled conveniently just off the northeast side of campus, was the hotel of choice for parents visiting their aspiring students at KSU. Rooms were clean and cheap and the hotel was within easy walking distance of the football stadium, field house, student union, and dorms. When not overflowing with hordes of proud parents, the University Lounge restaurant, located on the ground floor, was a favorite hangout for students, the free coffee and donuts on the weekends a big hit for those stretching their meager funds.

Lincoln, Rocky and Zeke sat in a corner booth of the restaurant, the only customers at three o'clock in the morning. A short order cook and a lone waitress stared wearily at them across the sea of empty tables. Lincoln was feeling lucky to be alive, Zeke, fortunate to have not been arrested. Rocky was just hungry.

After they had all been taken to the local police station, Rocky quickly closeted himself with the state trooper, a rookie named Jennings, while Lincoln and Zeke replayed their version of events for Andrea. An hour later they were all released with no charges. Andrea's parents picked her up, irate rather than relieved, while the boy's initial trauma had given way to hunger pangs which brought them here courtesy of trooper Jennings.

Rocky was waxing eloquent about how he had negotiated their freedom. "Now Officer Jennings was caught with his pants down, so to speak," he said, eyes wide, hands gesturing as he told his tale. "He didn't have his radar on when he passed us so he didn't know if we were speeding or not," he added with a smirk towards Zeke. "He admitted that he didn't witness the actual crash and all he saw was Zeke pulling my soggy butt out of the pond, a rescue he stood and watched rather than helping with."

The other two drank in the convincing yarn. "How did you know he didn't have his radar on?" Lincoln asked.

Rocky shrugged. "Just played a hunch. So, the question was, what could I do to play to Officer Jennings' weaknesses?" He looked directly at Zeke as he spoke. "I convinced him that, without an official radar reading he couldn't pin speeding on you and, not having actually witnessed the accident, he couldn't charge you with reckless driving."

"Jesus Christ, Rocky, you ran off the road at a hundred miles an hour, drove through a fence, tore up a field and wound up in a fucking pond," Zeke exclaimed. "How can that *not* be reckless driving?"

"For all Jennings knew you could have swerved to avoid a deer," Rocky said, smoothly placing Zeke behind the wheel in his tale. "Anyway," he continued, finger pointed at Zeke for emphasis, "I told him how bad it would look to arrest a genuine hero, someone who had saved all our lives."

"Wow," Lincoln said, shaking his head in wonder.

Rocky poured syrup on his Belgian waffle. "To sweeten the deal I gave him what would have been the fine, which we all know wound up in his pocket, plus, no paperwork for Officer Jennings." He smiled as he cut a piece of waffle.

The other two boys exchanged glances, still amazed at how Rocky had maneuvered his way out of trouble tonight.

Rocky went on. "Anyway, I owe you Zeke. Taking responsibility for driving saved my butt and I won't soon forget that."

"Not to mention saving your life," Lincoln added.

"Well, yeah," Rocky said, as if that was an afterthought.

Zeke smiled, having second-guessed his noble cover up more than once already tonight. What would he have done had he been charged, expelled from school, most of his meager savings depleted by fines or legal fees? "You'd have done the same for me if you had been in my shoes, right Rock?" Zeke said, shooting Lincoln a wry smile. They both knew Rocky's penchant for self-preservation.

"Well, as I was fucking unconscious at the time I guess we'll never know," Rocky said. "Anyway, to move onto more important things, what are you two doing for Thanksgiving?" he said, dismissing the subject of the accident as if it was of no further concern. To him it wasn't.

Lincoln shot a look at Zeke. "We, uh, deliver meals to the homeless," he explained. "It's a busy week for me."

Rocky nodded, filling his mouth with a healthy piece of Belgian waffle. "And you, Zeke?" he asked, cheeks bulging.

Zeke shrugged. "I'll be hanging around school. Got a few papers to finish," he offered, feeling that emptiness in the pit of his stomach as he recalled previous holidays spent alone on campus.

"Bullshit," Rocky said, jabbing his fork in Zeke's direction. "When I talked to my father tonight he insisted you come join us at home this year. My parents are anxious to meet the person who saved my glorious life," he added with a wink.

Zeke weighed the request, the relief of not having to spend another lonely holiday on campus versus the guilt of continuing Rocky's lie face to face with his parents.

"Now, they won't take no for an answer," Rocky said, giving Zeke a stern look, then breaking into a smile. "What do you say?"

Zeke felt cornered, but a tinge of curiosity at being able to meet Rocky's parents swayed his answer. "Sure, Rock. That would be great."

"All right," Rocky said with a broad grin. "The folks will be thrilled."

"Have you told your parents the truth about who was driving?" Lincoln asked.

Rocky shook his head. "Are you crazy? My old man would have come down on me like a safe if he knew I'd been behind the wheel. I told him I'd been drinking and Zeke here volunteered to drive."

Zeke smiled weakly. He still wondered if he had done the right thing.

Rocky flashed a wide smile and turned to Lincoln. "Lincoln, why don't you drive down to Walnut Grove after you do your thing on Thanksgiving and I'll get the both of you laid?"

There was a silent pause as Lincoln considered the offer. "Why wait until Thanksgiving?" Zeke asked, and they all laughed.

"Well, if it isn't the three stooges," came the voice from across the empty restaurant.

They all turned to look. It was Andrea, her muddy hair and soaked clothes from the accident replaced by form-fitting jeans and a purple sweater pulled tightly over her gorgeous figure. Her red hair was shiny and looked like she had just walked out of a salon. She smiled with dark red lips, her eyelids showing just a hint of purple. "Mind if I join you guys or is this a stag party?"

"No, please," Zeke said, sliding to one side to make room. "We thought your parents would have locked you in the basement. Your old man was pretty pissed when they picked you up at the station."

"Yeah, well, it's a drill they're used to," Andrea said with a laugh. "We live right up the street so I snuck out of my room and headed here. This is the only place in the booming metropolis of Manhattan that's open this late so thought I'd get a cup of coffee." She raised her hand towards the lone waitress and gave her a pouring gesture. She turned back to her booth mates. "You guys look like hell," she said with a laugh. "And you smell like dead fish," she added, waving her hand in front of her nose.

Indeed, unlike Andrea, who had obviously had the benefit of a shower, the three guys had only been able to run their clothes through the dryer at the police station locker room and slip them back on. They still smelled of pond water. Hunger pangs had won out over a hot shower; not an unusual choice for college students.

"How are you feeling?" Zeke asked. "You look, uh, great."

Andrea giggled and punched Zeke playfully on the shoulder. "A girl is always thankful for a compliment, especially after a midnight swim in a frozen pond," she said with a grin.

They all laughed. "Seriously, guys," Andrea went on, "like I told you at the police station, I don't remember a thing once we all got in Rocky's car at Jack's." She stared at Rocky. "You didn't cop a feel while I was out cold, did you?"

"Madam, you cut me to the quick," Rocky said, placing a hand on his chest.

"He's not into necrophilia anymore," Zeke added with a smirk.

"Anymore?" Andrea said with wide eyes. They all laughed, then Andrea looked at Rocky. "What's going to happen with your car?"

He waved a dismissive hand. "I'll get my buddy over at Central Towing to go pull it out of the pond tomorrow. I'm sure it's totaled."

"So, you'll get a new one?" Lincoln asked.

"Hell, yes. Can't have the future president of the Wellington National Bank without wheels, man."

There was an awkward silence as the waitress poured Andrea a cup of coffee, then refilled everyone else's. "You guys good?" she asked.

"Yeah," Rocky said, pulling out his water-soaked wallet and handing her a wad of bills. "Keep the change, babe," he said with a wink.

The waitress eyed the money, then smiled. "Thanks, Rocky," she said, pocketing the bills.

"Another fan," Rocky said after she had left.

"Hell," Zeke said, "For twenty bucks I'd be the *president* of your fan club." They all laughed.

"So, Andrea," Lincoln began, anxious to move the conversation back to the gorgeous redhead, "what are you going to do when you graduate?"

"New York, baby cakes," Andrea answered. "Broadway."

"Broadway?" Zeke said.

"I'm a theatre arts major," Andrea said. "You've never been to any of the school productions?"

"Zeke has no sophistication," Rocky said. "The only theatre he's ever been in was a burlesque show in Kansas City."

"Oh, so *you've* seen our shows?" Andrea asked.

"Well," Rocky said, "I've gone to a few. It's a great place to pick up chicks, you know?"

"I'm honored that you're such a patron of the arts," Andrea said with a smile. "Anyway, we're doing Oklahoma next month and I can get you all tickets if you're interested." She looked around the table hopefully.

"Absolutely, we'd be honored," Lincoln said.

"And Rocky, I'll even introduce you to some of the girls in the show if that'll entice you to come," Andrea said.

"You're not interested in me yourself?" Rocky said.

Andrea laughed, but said nothing.

"It's hard to believe you don't find him irresistible," Zeke said with a smile.

"I admit it's a tough call, but if I were attracted to any of you it would have to be the guy who saved my life," she said, patting Zeke on the leg.

Zeke blushed at the comment and her hand on his leg.

"Well, you two ought to look one another up," Lincoln said. "Zeke is headed to New York after he graduates too."

Andrea turned to Zeke. "You a song and dance man are you, Zeke?" she said with a grin.

Zeke smiled. "I'm a journalist."

"Zeke writes for the Wildcat," Lincoln said.

"Wow," Andrea said. "A writer, huh?"

"Investigative reporter, actually," Zeke added.

"That sounds cool," Andrea said, sipping her cup of coffee.

They went on to talk about the upcoming Big Eight basketball season, several professors they loathed, and made jokes about the food at the student union. Finally, Andrea looked at her watch and yawned. "Well, guys, it's been real, but I better get back home and sneak into my room before the prison guards wake up." She started to slide out of the booth, but turned to Zeke. "Thanks again for what you did tonight," she said. "I owe you one."

"No charge," Zeke said. "And thanks in advance for those show tickets. I'm sure you'll be great."

Andrea blew a kiss to the threesome and waved as she left the restaurant.

"You dog," Lincoln said. "That gal's got a crush on you, big time," he said to Zeke.

Zeke waved off the comment. "She's still traumatized by the accident. By next week she won't even remember my name."

# # #

3

The mellow tones of Miles Davis played softly on Rocky's stereo system in his new Impala. He and Zeke were driving west on the road that ran, like a thin black wire, all the way to the horizon. It was early morning and they were off to Rocky's home for Thanksgiving. The drive from Manhattan to Walnut Grove would take a full three hours today as Rocky was treating his new car and his recent escape from vehicular disaster with unusual prudence.

Zeke gazed at the flat surroundings that reminded him of home on the farm, and his grandparents. Being raised by people who were significantly older than he was had been pleasant as a child; they doted on him, coddled him, gave him everything their modest life style permitted. But when he began the traumas of a teenager, the age difference between them created problems.

He chafed at their rules, their curfews, their watching over him like he was a toddler. They didn't understand his music, his rebellious spirit, his disdain for their endless stories about the Depression, the War and how "life was hard and then you died." When he met the parents of his high school friends he saw the comparison in stark contrast: the younger, more relaxed life styles, people who spoke his teenage lexicon, were interested in what he thought about things, treated him like an equal.

His grandparents had spent their lives doing the back-breaking work of wheat farming in western Kansas; one hundred and sixty acres where the work day was dawn to dusk, year round. When they died two years ago within ninety days of each other Zeke at first felt relief, then a growing sadness. He had taken them for granted, spoke harshly to them, failed to appreciate the cocoon of protection and love they surrounded him with until it was gone. They were his only family; no uncles, cousins or paternal grandparents, no distant relatives he could call his own. The sudden realization that he was alone in the world knocked him on his emotional ass. His regret that he had not treated them more kindly tore at him and added to the isolation and loneliness that was his new world.

"So how did it go with the Jesus freak?" Rocky asked, breaking Zeke's reverie. "We haven't had a chance to talk about your phone call without Lincoln being around."

Zeke straightened up in the front seat and took a deep breath. "Well, Reverend Archer is everything Lincoln has told us about him."

Rocky laughed. "A real bible pounder, huh?"

"Yeah, he takes his religion pretty seriously," Zeke agreed, recalling the solemn nature of his conversation with the Reverend the Sunday evening after the accident. "Everything is according to scripture, with a prayer at the drop of a hat."

"Give me an amen," Rocky added.

"Well, like you, Lincoln doesn't agree one hundred percent with the way his old man conducts his business."

"Religion as a business, huh?"

"Same as banking as a religion, don't you think?"

Rocky flashed a grin. "Touche', you smart ass. So did the old man try to convert you?"

Zeke shook his head. "Nope, just thanked Jesus for putting me in the car with Lincoln. Anyway, you know I'm not a very receptive audience when it comes to religion."

"Hell, you're just skeptical about everything, man."

Zeke shrugged. "When it comes to religion I'm still gathering information; haven't made up my mind yet."

"Waiting for the appearance of an angel?"

"Why, Rocky, is that what you are, an angel?"

"That's what all the ladies say," Rocky said with a wink. They drove on a few miles in silence then Rocky said, "You know, it's funny."

"What?"

"The three of us being friends. I mean, it's obvious why you and Lincoln like me; I'm a charming, funny, dynamic sort of guy and you two could use a liberal dash of all those traits, plus, you both hang around hoping for my rejects when it comes to the girls." He turned and flashed a smile. "The question I keep asking myself is why do I like you guys? I mean, you're both just this side of boring, especially Lincoln, and, let's face it, we just don't have that much in common, you know what I mean?"

"It's true that we're honored to even be in your presence, and yes, we're hopeful of gathering the female crumbs you throw our way, not that there have been any to speak of, but I suspect you like us because we put up with your arrogant, conceited, asshole personality where normal people would avoid you like the plague."

They sat in silence a minute then both broke out in uproarious laughter. Rocky jabbed a finger at his passenger. "You see, who but a good friend could talk to me like that and get away with it? I mean, you're wrong on all counts, but I respect your balls, man." He punched Zeke lightly on the shoulder and broke out in another burst of laughter. Then his face got serious and he said, "The truth, old buddy, is that you don't want anything from me; you never take my money, ask for favors, and I can be myself with you. I have to put on an act for my father, my teachers, Robin, and eventually, my goddamned clients, but not you and Lincoln."

"You put on an act for Robin?" Zeke asked, referring to Rocky's fiance'.

"You know what I mean, pretending to give a shit about what's on our registry, what flavor the wedding cake will be, that sort of crap."

"Does she know how incredibly lucky she is to be your chosen one with all those broken hearts you'll leave back at school?"

"Everybody I bless with my friendship knows how lucky they are to have met me. Don't you feel the glow yourself?"

"I'm tingling," Zeke answered with a grin.

Rocky smiled, enjoying the give and take. "So," he said, finally, "are you going to accept the Reverend's invitation and spend Christmas there in Wichita with the holy rollers?"

Zeke sighed. "Hell, it might be an interesting experience, who knows?"

"Not as interesting as this weekend with the Wellington clan."

Zeke nodded. "Are you and your old man going to cross swords about the bank over turkey and dressing?"

Rocky shook his head. "Plenty of time for that after I graduate. No, I plan on doing some hunting, seeing Robin and watching a little football."

"You really plan on putting your old man out to pasture once you settle in at the bank?"

Rocky sighed and looked annoyed at the prospect. "It's the natural order of things, Zeke. You'd never make it in the business world, man."

"Wouldn't want to. I've already seen enough of the underbelly of business. My job will be to show the rest of the world the crap that goes on there."

"You gonna start with me?" Rocky asked.

Zeke laughed. "No offense, Rock, but I think there are bigger fish in New York. I'll get to you later," he added with a smile.

"Well, it's not like I have a choice, man. I've had my career drawn up for me since I was five years old. So has Lincoln. At least you have the freedom to do what you want."

Zeke sighed, his agonizing search for a vocation flashing through his mind. "Sometimes freedom of choice can be the biggest burden of all, my friend."

#

4

Walnut Grove, Kansas, was a typical small, Midwestern town. Main Street was five or six blocks in length, lined by one and two-story brick or limestone buildings: hardware stores, a pool hall, a movie theatre, a jeweler, and the biggest building in town, the towering three story Wellington National Bank, its granite façade giving it the appearance of a prison. The parking spaces along the storefronts were all at a forty-five degree angle, situated astride parking meters and Zeke smiled at the similarity to his hometown of Exeter, Kansas.

"Need to stop at headquarters," Rocky said as he pulled into a parking space out front with the bank's green WNB insignia painted on the curb. "Sorry, but we need to report in to the old man."

"Am I presentable?" Zeke asked with a smirk.

Rocky opened his door. "Not really, but I'll cover for your pedestrian manners and looks."

"I did save your arrogant life, you know," Zeke said as he got out of the car.

"That might be worth something later in life, but today I'm just another junior executive in waiting. Let's go kiss the ring." They headed towards the bank's main entrance.

Inside, the bank lobby was like a mausoleum. The place was dark and deathly quiet, only a low murmur audible. The waxed marble floors squeaked under Zeke's tennis shoes. Rocky shot him a look and rolled his eyes in fake dismay and embarrassment. It was, as Rocky had described, like walking back into the 1930's.

They approached an elderly man situated at a desk at the back of the lobby. The old man stood as the two students approached. "Rocky," he said, extending a pale hand. "Good to see you again, sir."

Rocky shook his hand. "Davis, good to see you again too. Is R.C. in?" he asked, referring to the moniker his father preferred.

The old man glanced towards an elevator behind him. "He's with a customer, but he said to send you up immediately when you arrived."

Rocky nodded. "Oh, Davis, I'd like you to meet my good friend, Zeke. He's visiting for the holiday."

Zeke reached out and shook the old man's cool, wrinkled hand. "Good to meet you, sir."

The old man's hair was neatly parted down the middle and he looked dapper in a dark, three piece suit and red bow tie. "Welcome to our fair city, young man and I do hope you'll have an enjoyable stay."

Zeke smiled. "Thank you, sir."

Rocky put a hand on Zeke's shoulder and moved him towards the elevator. He pressed the up button and they were greeted by a harmonious ding as the doors opened. "I think Davis is going on two hundred years old," Rocky said as the only elevator in Walnut Grove began its ascent. "Been with my dad since they ran the bank out of the back of the old feed store north of town."

The elevator lurched to a stop and the doors opened to reveal a cozy waiting room with a small couch and two facing arm chairs atop a red and yellow Persian rug. Beyond the waiting room were double doors leading into a spacious office. The doors were open and two men stood shaking hands. The one behind the desk was obviously Mr. Wellington, or R.C. as Zeke had learned, and the other was a thin, wiry man wearing overalls and sporting a late season sunburn. "Thank you again for your understanding," the latter man was saying.

"We've both been through this before, Elmer and your word is your bond with me. Good luck with this year's crop."

The farmer smiled and reached for a baseball cap on the table next to where he had been sitting in front of the huge Captain's desk. He turned to leave the office, saw Rocky and smiled. "Welcome home, Mr. Wellington," he said, reaching out to shake Rocky's hand.

"Mr. Richardson, how are you doing? How is the missus?"

"She's doing fine. Thanks for asking."

"Have a wonderful Thanksgiving, sir," Rocky said and the old man headed towards the elevator. Rocky guided Zeke into RC's office. "Father, this is----"

"Zeke," R.C. said, his smile turning to a frown as he ran his eyes over the young man's appearance. "You're not quite as I pictured you."

Zeke felt a little self-conscious with his long hair and mustache. He fit right in on campus, but here everyone was clean shaven with close-cropped hair.

"We're so glad you could join us for the holiday," R.C. went on, recovering from his first impression and gesturing towards one of the chairs in front of his desk. R.C., like his son, was tall and blonde, with a dazzling smile and piercing blue eyes. With the addition of a horned helmet and broadsword, he was the embodiment of a Viking, Zeke thought.

"Thank you, sir, and thanks again for inviting me."

"You're welcome any time, my boy, any time." He turned to his son. "How are you, Rocky?" There was no hug or handshake.

Rocky shrugged. "O.K., I guess. How are you, father?"

"Excellent," R.C. answered, taking a seat behind his cluttered desk.

"Extending another loan to Mr. Richardson, are you?" Rocky asked as he sat down.

A frown crossed R.C.'s face. "As a matter of fact, yes. Summer prices for wheat were down and he had some disease to deal with so, yes. I'm sure he'll do fine in the spring. He's been a good customer for years."

"Seems like a bit of a risk to me," Rocky said, taking his chin in hand as he studied his father.

"Well, you take risks with old friends," R.C. said.

"Like you did with Sam Lowrie last year?" Rocky said.

Another frown from R.C. "It's worth taking a loss occasionally to keep an old customer, to provide a service he can count on. He'll bounce back and when he does he'll remember who took a chance on him when he was down."

"And what if he doesn't bounce back?"

The older man emitted a heavy sigh. "Let's not get into this today, Rocky. We're here to show your friend Zeke a good time." He turned to Zeke. "Zeke, do you hunt?"

"Uh, no, sir."

R.C. looked disappointed, as if this was a serious character flaw. "Well, Rocky and I will be going pheasant hunting tomorrow and you're welcome to join us."

"Actually," Rocky interrupted," I've asked Robin to show him around town while we're hunting."

R.C. smiled. "Well, that's wonderful, although there isn't that much to see, but I'm sure she'll be excellent company. You won't mind spending the day with a beautiful young woman will you, Zeke?"

"It'll be a dramatic departure from his otherwise staid existence," Rocky interjected with a smile.

Zeke felt himself blush. "I'm looking forward to it," he responded, the arrangement already discussed with Rocky on the ride down from campus.

"Well," R.C. said, standing. "I won't keep you boys any further. I've got a meeting in a few minutes and your mother is anxious to see you, Rocky." He shook Zeke's hand again and ushered both boys out of the office, waving as the elevator doors closed.

"I don't think your father approves of my long hair and mustache," Zeke said.

"Hell, neither do I, but it does have the advantage of hiding your ugly face," he added with a wink.

Zeke laughed, knowing Rocky was only half kidding. "From what you've told me, today's loan discussion wasn't an isolated case of disagreement between you two."

"Yeah, father believes the bank is a service, not a business. He takes a lot of unnecessary risks because he's friends with these people. You can't let your emotions sway your business judgment. When I take over things will be different."

"You gonna be a hard ass, are you, Rocky?"

Rocky smiled. "I've got big plans, Zeke. Plans that go beyond this one horse town, but that's way ahead so let's just enjoy Thanksgiving. And tomorrow, well, you get to spend the day with the best looking gal in town." He turned and looked down on his friend. "So keep your horny eyes to yourself, you hear?" he added, slapping Zeke on the shoulder and laughing. "That little filly is all mine."

* * *

If there was an upscale part of Walnut Grove, the Prairie View subdivision was it. Located in the foothills east of town, just across the Arkansas River, Prairie View consisted of a dozen or so "estates," each situated on what Zeke figured to be five to ten acre plots. The Wellington house sat behind a waist-high stone wall with imposing iron gates and an asphalt driveway lined with holly bushes. The holly hedge was a good ten feet high and was drooping with red berries, portending a wet winter according to Rocky. The house was turn of the century architecture, yellow limestone with a green tile roof and pyramid shaped gables that gave the place the appearance of a castle.

They pulled the new Impala into the far end of a three car garage and were quickly in the kitchen. Rocky's mother was overseeing the work of two Hispanic women. "Rocky," she exclaimed with a wide smile, holding her arms open wide. The two Hispanic women added their smiles, but kept working.

"Hey, mom. Happy Thanksgiving," Rocky said, hugging his mother and planting a tentative kiss on her cheek. "Mom, this is Zeke," he said, gesturing towards his guest.

Mrs. Wellington appeared quite a bit younger than her husband, a handsome woman with dark hair, a thin waist and ample bosom. She moved forward with arms wide again. "Of course, I've been counting the days to meeting you. You are quite the hero in this household." She gave Zeke a firm hug and held him by the shoulders, smiling in a motherly way.

Zeke was aware of her pleasant perfume. "Thank you for having me for the holiday," he said.

"Nonsense," Mrs. Wellington said, "the thanks is ours and we are so grateful that, well, you know what I mean."

Zeke nodded and the kitchen went strangely quiet. He moved towards the two Hispanic women, hand outstretched. "Hi, I'm Zeke," he said.

The two women looked embarrassed, wiped their hands on their aprons and shook Zeke's hand, heads down.

"This is Juanita and her daughter Christina," Mrs. Wellington said. "Now," she said quickly, "Rocky, please show Zeke to his room so he can freshen up. Robin will be here any minute."

Zeke's room was a suite downstairs that included a spacious bedroom, full bath and a kitchenette. "This makes my room at school look like a hovel," he said.

"Your room at school *is* a hovel," Rocky said with a laugh. "Take your time cleaning up then join us upstairs for a cocktail."

Zeke bowed expansively. "Very good, sir. I prefer my martini very dry, with an olive."

"You'll get a beer, no olive," Rocky said with a wink.

* * *

By the time Zeke had cleaned up and changed, Mr. Wellington had arrived and the foursome was enjoying a cocktail in the huge corner study when Mrs. Wellington looked out the window. "Robin's here," she said, looking at her son. "Go meet her at the door, Rocky."

Zeke watched as Rocky opened the front door and stood waiting for his "intended." Their less-than-passionate embrace was designed, Zeke thought, to shield Rocky's parents from the normally torrid actions that Rocky had described on their ride down from Manhattan. Rocky took her hand and they walked into the study.

"Robin, this is Zeke," Rocky said.

Zeke had seen Rocky with a number of attractive girls on campus, but Robin was an absolute knockout. She was almost as tall as Zeke, with a model's face; porcelain skin, high cheek bones, full lips and a fantastic smile. Her eyes were green, her brown hair curled down to her shoulders and she had a healthy figure from what he could imagine beneath her conservative skirt, blouse and sweater. She surprised everyone by giving Zeke a big hug. "Anyone who saved my Rocky's life is my best friend already," she said.

Zeke felt a bit embarrassed by the display.

"Here, here," Mr. Wellington said. "Your usual, my dear?" he asked, moving towards the bar.

Robin continued to stare at Zeke. "Yes, thank you, R.C."

Zeke cleared his throat. "So, you're going to be my tour guide tomorrow," he said.

Robin's smile widened. "Well, yes. There's so much to see around here while the men do their dreadful hunting."

"You'll be bored in ten minutes," Rocky said with a smile.

"Not by my guide," Zeke added.

"Aw, aren't you sweet?" Robin said. "Rocky, your friend has exceptional taste."

"Not once you get to know him," Rocky said, punching Zeke on the shoulder. "He's quite the Cretin."

"Actually," Zeke added, "I'm not from Crete, but from western Kansas."

Everyone laughed although Mrs. Wellington didn't appear to get the joke. "Well," she said, "I need to go check on dinner. Robin, will you be joining us?"

"Actually, no thank you, Mrs. W. I'm having dinner with my folks." She turned to Zeke. "I'll pick you up at seven sharp tomorrow morning and we'll have breakfast at Tiny's. That too early for you?"

"No, that'll be fine. Looking forward to the tour."

Robin gave Rocky a kiss on the cheek and was gone. "A lovely girl," Mrs. Wellington said, turning and heading for the kitchen.

"Is there really all that much to see around here?" Zeke asked.

Rocky shook his head. "Not really, but Robin will make it entertaining I'm sure."

# # #

5

Tiny's was in a building that, according to Robin, had at one time been a car dealership. The floor-to-ceiling windows provided a panoramic view of Main Street and the rising sun. The place was packed and noisy, business men in their suits and ties shoulder to shoulder with other customers wearing flannel shirts and jeans. Waitresses that were clad in blue tee shirts that had "Tiny's" emblazoned in bright yellow across the front hustled between tables, coffee pots at the ready. From their booth near the front window Zeke enjoyed the pleasing aromas of bacon, fresh coffee and Robin's perfume. As promised, she had picked him up at seven sharp, all bouncy and energetic while he had struggled to get his eyes open. Two hours earlier, in the pre-dawn darkness, Zeke had heard the rumble of a pickup as Rocky and his father left to go pheasant hunting.

"So you're not a hunter, Zeke?" Robin asked, sipping her coffee.

Zeke shook his head. "I've never had any interest in killing helpless animals."

Robin laughed. "How have you managed to live in Kansas your whole life without loving guns?"

Zeke smiled. "I'm not a typical Kansan I guess. I don't love cars, fishing, or religion either."

Robin seemed unaffected by his self-proclaimed profile. "What *do* you love, Zeke?" she asked, staring at him attentively.

He swallowed another mouthful of coffee. "I don't mean to sound flip, but I love the truth; why things really are the way they are, not how they look on the surface."

"Like what?"

He shrugged. "Pick anything: politics, big business, the economy, education. You name it, I'm interested in what's really going on behind the headlines."

"So you want to be a modern day Ida Tarbell or Upton Sinclair?"

"You know about them?"

"Not a lot, but I read The Jungle. Very disturbing." She held her coffee cup between both hands, elbows on the table. "You couldn't sound more opposite than Rocky. How did the two of you ever become friends?"

Zeke wrinkled his face in thought, recalling his discussion with Rocky driving down from Manhattan. "Good question," he said. "Not sure I know exactly, except that I guess both of us are rebels."

"Rebel? My Rocky?"

"Oh, yeah. He can't wait to do things differently than his father at the bank."

Robin nodded. "And how are you a rebel, Zeke? Is it your hair style; looking like one of the Beatles?"

Zeke was suddenly conscious of the fact that everyone, *everyone* in the restaurant sported short-cropped hair. "Well, at least you didn't call me a beatnik," he offered with a smile. "Rocky says that my mustache makes me look like Emiliano Zapata."

She laughed at the comparison.

"To answer your question though," he started again, "I'd like to think I'm different from today's typical journalist. I'm a skeptic, don't believe much of what's obvious, and am positive if something is too good to be true, it isn't. My bottom line has always been the truth, no matter where it leads."

"So you're not a skeptic, you're a pessimist?"

"Just a realist; no Walt Disney view of the world for me."

She leaned back with a smile. "I like the Walt Disney view of the world. As a little girl I always wanted to be a princess, you know, like Cinderella." She laughed. "I knew it was all make believe, but it made me happy and gave me hope; you know, good things happen to good people, that sort of fantasy."

"You sound like a hopeless romantic. Everything will eventually be all right, huh?"

"It's the old glass half empty or half full isn't it?"

He nodded. "Maybe it's learning to find a balance between the two; nothing is ever as bad or good as it seems."

The waitress brought their breakfasts; two heaping stacks of pancakes with bacon and scrambled eggs. "Ya'll need anything else, Robin?" she asked, eyeing Zeke's long hair with a frown.

"No, Agnes, we're fine, thanks," Robin said. Agnes refilled their coffee cups without asking and was off.

Zeke felt at ease with Robin and his investigative reporter persona took over "So," he said, "tell me all about growing up in Walnut Grove."

Robin sighed. "Not a very exciting story, I'm afraid. My daddy owns the biggest department store in town, so we've always been pretty well off; nothing like Rocky's family, but I've always had pretty much everything I needed."

"How did you two meet?"

Robin looked wistfully out the window. "I've known Rocky since grade school. You could say we've grown up together." She turned to look at Zeke. "Some time during high school daddy had some dealings with the bank and he and R.C. really hit it off. They played golf together, our families started seeing one another socially, that sort of thing. I guess after a while it was kind of expected that Rocky and I would like each other. We started dating and before long we were a thing." She forced a weak smile.

"It must have been tough after all those years together for each of you to go to a different college. Rocky says you're at Kensington. Isn't that an all-girls school?"

"Yes, but being on my own these last four years has shown me a world I didn't know existed."

"That's supposed to be what college is all about; opening your eyes to a lot of things."

She smiled. "Yeah, but I just wanted a chance to be myself, you know?"

Zeke remembered Rocky's complaint that he couldn't be himself around Robin. "You're not yourself around Rocky?"

"You know what I mean," she said. "Everybody needs their own space occasionally. Anyway, it's time to settle down and start our lives together. Rocky's smart and funny and he'll make a great father."

The question came out of nowhere; Zeke's penchant for asking direct questions taking over. "Do you love him?"

Robin looked at him with a curious expression. "Of course. You don't marry someone you don't love."

Zeke shrugged. "Lots of people do. That's why the divorce rate is so high."

She frowned. "I don't like that kind of talk, Zeke."

He reached across the table to take her hand, then quickly withdrew it. "Hey, I didn't mean to upset you. Sorry."

There was an awkward silence between them, the cacophony of the restaurant suddenly deafening. Robin sipped her coffee and worked up a smile for her guest. "So, what will you do when you graduate, Zeke?"

He welcomed the change in topic. "Head to New York I guess. I have a classmate who lives in Manhattan, said I could share his apartment with him while I look for a writing job."

"An investigative reporter, huh?"

"Yeah, I've got a couple of leads up there. We'll see what happens."

"And if that doesn't pan out?"

"Maybe I'll come back here and work at The Pioneer," he said, referring to the local newspaper.

"Nothing to muck rake about around here."

"Oh, I bet there's more going on in a small town like this than you realize."

"Well, I sure haven't seen it and I've lived here my whole life." She smiled again. "Tell me about the accident."

It was another abrupt turn in their conversation and Zeke wondered exactly what Rocky had told Robin about that night. Stick to the story, he told himself. "Nothing much to tell. I wasn't watching where I was going, missed a curve in the road and we wound up in a pond."

"And you pulled Lincoln and Rocky out of the car, saved their lives?"

"Yeah, Andrea too."

"Andrea?"

Zeke thought quickly. "A friend of mine we were taking back to campus."

"Oh, Rocky didn't mention that there was a girl involved. How in the world did you talk Rocky into letting you drive his car? He doesn't even let *me* drive his precious Impala."

"He'd had quite a bit to drink, Robin. It was pretty easy to talk him out of his keys."

"So is Andrea your girlfriend?"

"No, she just needed a ride back to town."

"Do you have a girlfriend, Zeke?"

Zeke shook his head. "No, not really."

"Spend all your time reporting, do you?"

Zeke laughed. "No, just haven't run across anyone who enjoys my weird personality, that's all."

"I bet you meet a lot of girls, hanging out with Rocky."

"What do you mean?" Zeke asked, trying to hide his surprise.

Robin shook her head. "Come on, Zeke. Rocky's quite the flirt. He loves the ladies almost as much as he loves that damned bank."

There was another awkward silence. Zeke choked down his pancake while Robin stared out the window. She turned to look at him and he thought her face wrinkled like she was about to cry. "Are you O.K.?" he asked, lowering his voice.

Robin pulled a handkerchief out of her purse, dabbed at her eyes and smiled. "Sure. Now finish your breakfast and I'll show you all the exciting parts of Walnut Grove."

* * *

She drove him south of town to see the remnants of the old packing house where cattle drives from Texas and Oklahoma once brought massive herds to be slaughtered there and shipped north to Chicago.

The train yard was half the size it had been during the boom of the forties and fifties when freight and passenger trains dominated the land. The flour mill, the refinery and the trailer manufacturing plant had all scaled back from the good old days.

They drove the length of Main Street, seven blocks, Robin pointing out landmarks of the past and present. "There's the theatre where we used to go to Saturday matinees as kids," she said, pointing at the weather-worn marquee. "Twenty-five cents."

There was the Five and Dime, Stark's Grocery, the Medical Arts building, Marvin's Texaco, the dilapidated Western Hotel, her father's department store, Brigg's Hardware and, of course, the towering three stories of granite, the Wellington National Bank. There was a story or childhood anecdote to be told about each establishment.

They drove east of town, back across the Arkansas River and pulled into a small park that sat on the banks looking back at the cluster of squat buildings. "It's not exactly the New York skyline," she said, "but it's home." She opened the driver's door and got out of the car. Zeke followed her and they started down a winding trail that led south through the sparse woods, high above the slow-moving, muddy river.

"What are you doing for Christmas?" she asked, bending to pull a long strand of prairie grass from the side of the path. "Coming back here I hope," she said, turning to look at him.

"Actually, I've got some term papers due and I'm going to take the time to get them done."

She gave him a sorrowful look. "Nobody should spend Christmas alone," she said, taking his hand. They walked on down the path. "Have you done any writing other than for the school newspaper?"

"Actually, I have," Zeke said. "I've written half a dozen short stories, but I don't think I'm good enough to write a full scale novel yet."

"Is that what you want to do?"

He shrugged, feeling a bit uncomfortable with her hand in his. He pulled free. "Eventually. Need to make a name for myself first. Publishers don't exactly cater to unknowns."

"Have you had anyone take a look at your short stories, give you some feedback I mean?"

He shook his head. "No, not really."

She turned to face him. "I'll give you my address at school before you go. You mail some of those stories to me and I'll edit them for you. I'm really pretty good."

He nodded. "Guess it couldn't hurt, huh?"

She smiled. "Every writer needs a sounding board. I don't claim to be an expert, but I've helped a lot of my classmates."

They went on to talk about what it was like to attend Kensington, the school subjects they had in common, and, of course, the wedding.

"So I guess you guys will want to start a family right away or do you want to just raise a little hell first?"

They came to a picnic table and she sat down. "I suppose Rocky will want a son as quick as possible," she said, staring out at the river.

"What do you want?" he asked, sitting down opposite her.

She frowned. "I'm not sure I get a vote on that, you know?" She bowed her head and her shoulders sagged.

"Are you crying?" Zeke asked, getting up and circling the table. He reached out and touched her shoulder.

She stood up and threw herself into his arms, her face in his chest. He didn't know what to do so he just patted her on the back. "Hey, take it easy," he said softly.

She pushed herself back and looked up into his eyes. "I'm sorry, Zeke. It's just that, well, I've had a lot of time to think about getting married so soon. There's a lot I want to do first, but, well, our parents have their own agenda and, of course, Rocky has made it clear what he wants, so I sort of feel trapped."

"I don't think you should do anything you don't want to," Zeke offered, wondering how he had suddenly gotten himself into this situation. He barely knew this girl, yet here he was offering advice concerning her plight, a plight that involved one of his few friends. "Maybe you need to sit down with Rocky and tell him how you feel."

"You don't understand," she said, taking a deep breath. "What's my life going to be like if I don't marry Rocky? He's certainly the most eligible bachelor in town. I don't want to wind up being tied down to some redneck dirt farmer with ten kids pulling at my apron strings.

Rocky will provide for me. We'll be comfortable and, well, I'll find a way to be happy." She looked at him. "You said yourself that a lot of people get married who aren't in love."

Zeke shook his head. "You sure don't want to take my word for something like that. I've never been in love, wouldn't know what it felt like. You should talk to someone who knows something about it."

"Like my mother? Like Mrs. Wellington?" She laughed sharply. "Do you think either one of them really loves their husband?" She scoffed. "Guess you don't know how romance works in a small town, Zeke. You take what you can get and if the richest guy in town fancies you, you better jump on that wagon real quick, take what fate drops in your lap. If you wait for real love you become an old maid."

She reached out and took his hand again, pulling him back up the trail towards her car. "Now don't let me spoil you on love, Zeke. I'm sure a great guy like you will find a wonderful gal and you'll both fall in love. It does happen, you know?"

He was completely flustered. This was not what he had imagined he would find here in Walnut Grove. Yeah, Rocky was a womanizer, but that was just a good looking guy with money sowing his oats, as they said, not someone who would force this young girl to marry him when she didn't love him, an arranged marriage that smacked of the Middle Ages.

"Look," she said as they approached her car. "Try and forget all this. I'm not myself this week. Female issues, you know?" She pulled out a tissue and blew her nose, then took a deep breath and exhaled heavily. She smiled at him. "Now you send me those short stories and I won't pull any punches, I'll tell you what I really think, O.K.?"

He nodded. "Yes, ma'am. And if you ever need to talk about, well, anything, I'll give you my number in Manhattan. O.K.?"

She opened the car door and stood looking at him, then broke into a wide smile. "O.K., Zeke. I'll do just that."

* * *

The first half of the trip back to K-State was spent in silence, the jazz station out of Wichita providing background as both boys reflected on their holiday in Walnut Grove. They pulled into a truck stop in Florence, Kansas, for gas and lunch at the diner there. The hot roast beef sandwich with mashed potatoes and gravy for $2.50 was a local legend. The town of Florence was noteworthy for its distinctive water tower that could be seen for miles and the intersection of two state highways that provided for spectacular wrecks on a daily basis. Indeed, the adjacent wrecker service, body shop and mortuary had a thriving business, particularly when eighteen wheelers were involved. Polaroid pictures of the more gruesome collisions were posted proudly on a bulletin board behind the cash register.

Revived by his hearty lunch, Zeke resumed his reporter mode once they were on the road again. "What do you look forward to the most, Rocky; getting married or taking over the bank?" Zeke asked.

"I knew letting you spend the day with Robin was a bad idea," Rocky said, shaking his head.

"What do you mean?"

"Well, I'm sure she whined about all the time I'm going to be spending at the bank rather than home deciding on wall paper and carpet colors. Am I right?"

"Well, I don't know shit about such things, but she seemed nervous, like any other bride I suppose, about competing with the bank for your time."

"She'll be plenty busy furnishing our house and doing all those wife-y things. I've already explained to her how taking over the bank is going to be a struggle and how she's going to get used to all the time I'll be spending there."

"Yeah, I hear you, only you might want to look at the situation from her perspective too, you know?"

"Jesus, now you sound like my mother."

Zeke threw up both hands in surrender. "Hey, not trying to stick my nose in the wrong places, just playing back a little of what Robin shared with me, that's all."

"So, what else did she share with you?"

Zeke sighed. He had already gone too far, but Rocky had kept the door open. "She's worried about your ambition to move up in the world, to leave Walnut Grove behind. What's that all about?"

Rocky turned to look at his passenger. "Why do I feel like I'm confessing to a priest? Well, if you must know, yes, my goal is New York, Wall Street, the big time. To get there I'm going to have to build the bank up, modernize it, get some recognition. To do that I'll have to literally shove my old man aside. That," he said with emphasis on the word, "is what Robin is really worried about; my old man."

Zeke started to comment, but Rocky was on a roll.

"My old man will be fine. I'll find some honorary role for him, let him continue to attend all those conventions in Chicago he and Robin's father like to go to." He turned and winked.

"Robin's father attends banking conventions? That seems odd."

"Neither one of them goes for the convention itself, dummy. It's the entertainment they go for."

"Entertainment? Like ball games or nightclubs?"

"Jesus, you are a farm boy aren't you? No, they go for the women. Banking conventions are crawling with them; looking for guys like my dad who just want to have a good time and don't mind spending a few bucks, you get me?"

"You mean prostitutes?"

Rocky shook his head again. "Female escorts. Look, my old man works his ass off all year long. He puts in long hours, visits every one of those clod-buster clients of his in their homes, goes out of his way to personally get involved in their lives. He deserves a chance to get out of town three or four times a year and let off a little steam."

"And Robin's father---"

"Look, they aren't just buddies because they do business with one another, they enjoy raising hell together too."

Zeke let the image of the two distinguished middle-aged men he had just spent Thanksgiving with cavorting with women half their age. Like father like son he thought, wondering if Robin knew what her father did when he was away from Walnut Grove. "Who are you going to raise hell with, Rocky?"

Rocky laughed. "You just wait until I get to New York. If you're still there I'll show you what having fun is all about, my friend."

# # #

6

It was like no other church in town. The broad tinted windows, bordered by glinting steel, red brick, and light brown aluminum siding, gave the impression of a mid-fifties art deco office building. Only the gold cross atop the entrance canopy identified it as a church. The place had, at one time, been a bowling alley; a "can't miss" venture to attract enthusiasts from the west side of Wichita. However, after a period of modest traffic the owners gave up, sold all the equipment to a bowling house in Chicago and the building stood empty for several years.

The place caught the Reverend Billy Archer's eye and it soon replaced the old revival tent that had stood for years in the empty field he rented from a nearby farmer. Like most churches in the area, the Church of Hope's congregation were hard-working, straight talking folks of the great plains who believed that they bore the burden of original sin and that their lives must be spent in strictly following the rules of the church, the literal words of the bible, and patiently awaiting the second coming of their Lord. Although the specifics of these tenets varied slightly between the different sects that had grown out of the Reformation, local congregations were commonly God-fearing and serious about their religion.

As he grew up watching and listening to his father's pulpit-pounding sermons, Lincoln found himself drawn instead to the volunteer work that flowed from the church, toiling across the broad spectrum of need, hip deep in the misery, suffering, joy and hope of everyday life. Lincoln's tasks included the manual logistics of the old tent service, then maintenance of the new church building and printing of monthly newsletters. He became familiar with all aspects of life on the surrounding farms and the families he worked alongside repairing barns and fences, hauling hay, planting crops and sharing meals. The rambling discussions that filled these long hours of work led him to realize that what these people really wanted were straightforward lessons from their religion and how to use them in their own lives. No demonic punishments for being human, no shame or guilt or fear. How can I be a better person, a better spouse, parent, child, or neighbor? How can I use love to deal with everyday problems, setbacks and disappointments?

As he grew older, the path that had been formed for him years ago by his father was no longer as clear and desirous as it had been at the beginning. He knew, for instance, that he did not possess his father's eloquence, his command of the pulpit, or his powers of persuasion. Lincoln was frightened of public speaking, terrified in front of a crowd like today's overflow Christmas congregation. He had no gift for crafting a sermon, emphasizing the points that would satisfy the diverse needs of the congregation, that would calm them, inspire them, bring them back next week.

But the strongest deterrent to Lincoln's ascension to the pulpit was his growing lack of faith. As a child he had accepted his father's lessons as fact, had been swept up in the art and music and romance of the story of Christianity.

But by the time he entered college, the friends he made there and the wide open, marijuana-fueled discussions he was drawn into with them had created a different perspective, one that portrayed religion as superstitious, manipulative, dishonest and an anathema for free thinkers, reason and scientific thought. It was indeed confusing for a young man who had been raised within the comforting bubble of belief, and gave him constant pause and doubt, concerns he never had the courage to discuss with his father.

Reverend Billy Archer cleared his throat and smiled from the pulpit out at the congregation. He wore no traditional church wardrobe, dressed instead in a plain tweed jacket, brown trousers and a white button-down shirt, no tie. His face was covered in perspiration from his thirty minute exhortation on faith and obedience. He dabbed at his moist forehead with a handkerchief. It was time for the calm, soothing close to his Christmas sermon, time to remind the congregation of why they were all here this afternoon.

"Friends," he said, "in this time of celebration of our Lord's birth, it is appropriate to witness an example of how his love affects us even today." He drew a breath and exhaled. "I want you to imagine for a moment that you are out driving with three close friends. Suddenly there is a catastrophic accident that places your friends in mortal danger. They cannot help themselves. Only you can help them, yet to help them you must put your own life in peril."

He paused and looked out across the crowd, waiting for the scene he had just painted to be absorbed.

"Instinctively, without hesitating, you move to their rescue, risking your own life not just once, but again and again and yet again." He studied the congregation, their attention riveted on him. "How do we describe this reaction? Adrenaline? Temporary insanity? A total disregard for one's own safety?"

He smiled and looked from side to side, as if gathering his thoughts. "What I have just described is God's love: love of our fellow man, love so strong as to risk losing our life so that others may survive, love that understands that such sacrifices are often necessary in order for God's will to be done. This is an emotion so powerful, so complex that even the young man who used it that night doesn't fully understand what motivated him to act, why he did what he did."

"God had a different plan for these four young people, it was not time for them to perish. So he sent an angel of mercy to guide our hero."

Reverend Archer's voice got louder, his pace faster. "The angel told him what to do, helped overcome his fears."

He paused, smiled, and went on, softer and slower now. "God's love is a force that is within each of us, on the surface in some, hidden deep within others. We need to acknowledge his presence, his power and our need to use his love as often as possible. It is only then that truth, honesty and integrity can emerge; only then that we can begin to be rid of hatred, prejudice, war and fear." He lowered his voice to a whisper. "Only then that our world can embrace the peace that Jesus sought for us all with his life on earth."

The congregation smiled and nodded, breathlessly awaiting the climactic end of today's lesson. "And now," Archer said, "please join me in welcoming the young man of whom I've been speaking, the man who saved those three lives, including my own son. Say hello to Mr. Zeke Porter." He gestured towards the front pew with outstretched arms.

Lincoln nudged Zeke who rose slowly as did the congregation, the latter offering thunderous applause and a craning of necks to see the hero.

Zeke felt his face go hot as he acknowledged the applause, wishing now that he'd made up some excuse to stay back on campus rather than accept the Reverend's offer to appear here today. Lincoln turned toward his friend, smiling and clapping. He leaned forward and lowered his voice. "This isn't quite as good as Rocky's offer to get us laid, but it's as good as you're going to get in a church, man."

Reverend Archer held up his hands and the congregation ended their applause and sat back down. "Let us give thanks to God for blessing young Zeke with the spirit of love; love that Jesus spoke to us about all those years ago. Take that love with you as you leave here today and share it with your family, your neighbor, even the strangers that you meet. That is God's will and that is his message for today."

With that the organist struck up "What a Friend We Have in Jesus" and the congregation raised their heads high and sang the words they knew so well.

* * *

"You know today isn't even the day that Jesus was actually born," Lincoln said as he cut vegetables for the dinner salad.

"Really?" Zeke answered, setting the table in the Archer's dining room. He and Lincoln were responsible for Christmas dinner while

Reverend Archer conducted the evening service. Zeke had been amazed at how skilled Lincoln was around the kitchen, watching him prepare the ham and sweet potatoes, snap the green beans, make the biscuits and cook the chocolate pudding dessert.

"Yeah," Lincoln said, tossing the salad with an oil and vinegar dressing. "It was established by the Christian church around four hundred A.D. December twenty-fifth was chosen as a combination of pagan rituals associated with the winter solstice, and nine months from when religious scholars determined that Jesus had been conceived. And don't ask me how they figured *that* out," he added with a shake of his head. "Over time other pagan traditions that included gift-giving, decorating pine trees and Kris Kringle, alias Santa Claus were folded in."

"Why did it matter when the church claimed that Jesus was born?" Zeke asked.

Lincoln nodded. "You have to remember that the early Christian church sort of made up the rules as they went along, changing the story of Jesus where they needed to make their religion look more attractive."

"Like how?"

"The early Christians were Jews, so the story they told of Jesus' birth followed Old Testament prophecies regarding the coming of the Jewish messiah: virgin birth, born in Bethlehem, performing miracles, being killed, etcetera. Then, as they struggled to grow their church they discarded one of Jesus' own rules and admitted Gentiles. It was the only way to grow and survive."

Zeke surveyed the three place settings on the table, adjusted the water glasses slightly, then moved back into the kitchen. "So nothing about Christmas is true: the date, being born in a manger, the three kings?" he asked.

Lincoln nodded. "All made up; all fiction. Amazing isn't it?"

"And how do you know all this?"

Lincoln took the ham out of the oven to cool before slicing it. "Couple of religious history classes I took."

Zeke pointed at his friend. "Yeah, that professor you told me about; the controversial guy."

Lincoln nodded. "Professor Rawlings, yeah. Anyway, he taught the life of Jesus from a historical, not a religious perspective. Pissed a few people off."

"How so?"

"He basically explained how the story of Jesus' life in the New Testament was written decades after his death by people who never knew him, never witnessed the life they wrote about and how they took license to embellish where they thought was necessary, again to make the Christian church look more attractive. The clincher, the piece of the puzzle that lifted Christianity above all other religions at the time was the resurrection."

"It's hard to beat life everlasting as a selling point," Zeke said. "So Professor Rawlings claimed that the resurrection was another fabrication by the early church?"

"Yes, but he was quick to point out that the whole story of Jesus is as hard to disprove as it is to prove. That's the mystery of faith, he explained. It's up to us as individuals to draw our own interpretation. What's yours?"

Zeke wrinkled his face in concentration, having drawn his own conclusions years ago. "Well, by nature I'm a skeptic. You claim to be the son of God and I want proof." They both laughed. "Anyway, there's just so much about the universe we don't know or understand, so, keeping an open mind, I think anything is possible."

"And?"

Zeke sighed, a bit uncomfortable with his position on the subject in Reverend Archer's home. "And I think that religion is a well-intended attempt to explain the world in a simple, comfortable way. But I also think that there have been many who have manipulated those who want to believe that story. Like you, I think the whole message leaves lots of unanswered questions and is full of loopholes."

Lincoln nodded. "Before I went to college I wondered if my lack of faith was just a reaction to father's belief, you know? Teenage rebellion and all that."

"But?"

"Yeah, once I was challenged to actually think it through without the emotion and the doctrine hanging over my head, well, I have a very different view than the Reverend's."

"And how are you going to reconcile that when you come back to his church after you graduate? That's always been your plan, hasn't it?"

Lincoln glanced at his watch, opened the oven to check on the sweet potatoes. "I'm afraid I'm in the same boat as our friend Rocky. In order for me to feel comfortable in taking over the pulpit I'm going to have to do things totally different than my father." He offered a healthy sigh and a look of true dismay. "It's a battle I don't look forward to."

Zeke thought about Rocky and his plan to push his own father aside at the bank. "I actually envy you both. Sometimes I wish I had a legacy to inherit, you know?"

Lincoln smiled. "No you don't, but nice try at making me think so." They both laughed. "So, you're still planning on heading back to campus tomorrow? Can't talk you into staying another day or two?"

Zeke had borrowed a classmate's car, a kid from New Jersey who had flown home for the holidays. "No, I've got a few papers to finish, a lot of laundry to do, that sort of exciting crap, but thanks. I've really enjoyed my visit and getting to know your dad."

"Well, another couple of days here might just change your mind on that subject. Anyway, promise you'll let me fix you a doggy bag from dinner tonight."

Zeke put his arm around Lincoln's shoulder. "Beats the hell out of cold pizza. Thanks, Lincoln. You're a good friend."

#

7

Like many homes around campus that were used for student lodging, Zeke's apartment house was always in need of repair: flaking paint inside and out, a hot water heater that was too small for the six tiny apartments, and window air conditioners that did little to ease the sweltering heat that often lingered into the Fall. The owner saw no reason to waste money on providing college students with anything but the basic amenities: a few sticks of second hand furniture and kitchen appliances that had been salvaged from the military surplus store at nearby Ft. Riley.

Zeke had long ago commandeered the two room "suite" (a tiny living area/kitchenette and a bedroom) on the third floor that overlooked the campus just a block away. He sat on his bed by the window in the bedroom, watching as the snow came down in slanting sheets outside, driven by a northern wind that created drifts against the few cars on the street below. It was late afternoon two days after Christmas and the campus was deserted. He had grown accustomed to this routine since his grandparents had died, this spending the holidays alone, having the vast sprawling University to himself. It had always been a time of contemplation, of walking the campus and letting his mind wander.

But this holiday season had been different. Thanksgiving with the Wellington clan had painted a complex picture that Zeke had not anticipated. He admired how R.C. had given the desperate farmer a loan, taking a risk based on friendship and "his duty to provide a service" to those who depended on it to survive. He even admired R.C.'s choice of sending Rocky to K-State rather than the University of Kansas, where those destined to become lawyers, doctors or bank presidents normally matriculated. "The young people you have encountered at State," R.C. had repeated for Rocky's benefit over Thanksgiving dinner, "are the types of folks who will eventually be your clients; the farmers, cattle ranchers, people of the earth. Like you, they will have a different way of doing business than their fathers. You need to appreciate that perspective, understand what makes them tick. That will help you do your job better."

The day spent with Robin, Rocky's soon-to-be wife, had been an eye opener too, a revealing picture of life in a small town, the match-making of the well-to-do families, the creation of a pre-destined path and way of life. He had been surprised to learn that Robin seemed disillusioned by her fate, despite Rocky being the best that was available compared to the limited choices other girls in Walnut Grove had. Yet Robin was smart, clever, savvy even. Perhaps her dismay masked a secret agenda; a plan for leveraging her marriage to Rocky for reasons that weren't readily evident.

As they had sat at the huge dining room table enjoying the Thanksgiving spread, Robin's eyes had often found his. He saw a plea in those eyes, a "help me" message that caused him great distress. Was he inventing that look because it was a convenient mirage that fed his loneliness; a desire to have a girl like Robin?

Zeke's often melodramatic view of love and sex had been driven by the movies where the lovers exchanged knowing glances, the love scenes faded to black, leaving the image of what was about to transpire in the imagination of the viewer. It was a chaste, almost Victorian perspective he carried in his brain, a glimpse of a bare leg or shoulder as alluring as any cheesy calendars at the barber shop.

He switched his thoughts to his Christmas visit to Wichita and the Archer's hospitality. He had been uncomfortable amongst the Reverend's constant prayers and quotes from the bible, yet the man had been kind, gentle and so appreciative of Zeke's heroics. Zeke felt Lincoln's discomfort, based on the many discussions they had shared about religion and all the questions that naturally arise when talking seriously on the subject. Like Rocky, Lincoln seemed to have his career defined for him, yet unlike Rocky, who looked forward to assuming his father's role, Lincoln was unsure, frightened even, about his ascension.

Despite the warmth and hospitality there had been a poignant void in the Archer household. Lincoln's mother had died when he was ten, young enough for him to cling to childhood memories of the woman, old enough to understand the tragic impact on his father.

Zeke reached for the bottle of Budweiser on the table beside him and took a healthy swig. His focus on the trials and tribulations of his two friends was a distraction, a diversion from his own situation. With graduation in the spring, unlike many others, he had no job secured, not even a promise or a hint. Yes, he would go to New York City and live with Bernie Richards, his buddy from one of last year's journalism classes. Bernie had convinced him that New York was the place to be if you wanted to write for a living and sharing an apartment was too good an offer to turn down.

He took another pull on the beer. His head hurt and he was weary of worrying about what was next. He had one more semester to live the carefree life of a college student and he had sworn he would enjoy it. He turned and looked out the window again, trying to dismiss the gloom of the gray afternoon and swirling snow. The knock at the door caused him to jump. Who the hell? "It's open," he yelled.

The door opened and the figure was silhouetted against the glare of light from the hallway. "Zeke?"

He stood up. "Robin?" What was she doing here?

She moved forward, into the dim light from the window. Her hair was tucked up under a ski cap, her figure hidden by a thick coat. She held a grocery bag in front of her. "I've had time to go through your short stories," she said. "And we've got a lot of work to do."

#

8

"What in the world are you doing here?" Zeke asked, Robin's presence creating a confusing mixture of apprehension and pleasure.

"Well, good to see you too, Zeke," she said with a smirk.

"No, I mean, shouldn't you still be at home?"

Robin held up a grocery bag. "I've gone through your short stories and have a lot of comments. So, I told my folks I had to get back to campus for a few days to get some things done before next semester."

"A couple of days?"

"Well," she said, pulling one of the manuscripts out of the grocery bag and placing it on his desk, "like I said, we've got a lot of work to do."

"But----"

"Look, you've got some really good stories here; I mean, really great, but every writer needs some feedback and mine comes free." She took another manuscript out of the bag and put it on the desk. "Well," she said with a smile, "I will require a place to sleep and a few decent meals, but the advice is gratis."

Zeke scrambled to accommodate Robin's unexpected appearance and request. "I, uh, well the guys next door are gone. I could jimmy their lock and----"

"Nonsense. I've got a sleeping bag in my car. The floor right here will be fine." She emptied the grocery bag and shot him a smirk. "This won't be the first time you've had a girl sleep over, will it?"

Zeke shook his head. He had been out maneuvered. "I respectfully plead the Fifth Amendment."

"Smart man. Now, let's get to work."

* * *

They worked late into the night, poring over several of his short stories. He was amazed at how thorough she was, how she picked out loopholes, contradictions, pointed out lack of detail, confusing dialogue. Around midnight they walked up the street to Aggieville, found a pizza joint that was still open and discovered how intellectual interchange actually stirred their hunger for food. They ate like a pair of wildebeests.

As they walked back to his apartment she asked him to describe what he had been trying to say in a particular scene in one of the stories. As he gesticulated, waving his hands to make a point and enact one of the characters in the scene, she put her hand in the crook of his elbow to calm him down and help with her balance on the icy sidewalk.

When he had finished she said, "Well, that's really good, Zeke, but it's not what you actually said in the story. If you go back and re-read it, you'll see what I mean."

And so on, Robin's insight providing Zeke plenty of ammunition to revise each and every one of his short stories. He could hardly wait to get started on his revisions, but they were both exhausted and agreed to continue tomorrow morning. She changed into pajamas, unrolled her sleeping bag and settled in on the floor beside his bed. As they lay on their backs, side by side in the tiny dark room Zeke broke the silence. "So, what are you going to do?"

"About what?" she answered, stifling a yawn.

"You didn't just come here to review my writing."

She turned on her side to face him in the dark. "What are you talking about, Zeke?"

"I'm talking about Rocky."

"What about Rocky?"

"Are you going to marry him this summer?"

There was a long silence. "Why would you ask that?"

He sighed. "Because when we talked at Thanksgiving you told me you didn't love him; that you were part of an arranged marriage and you didn't know what to do."

"I said all that?"

He threw back the covers on his bed and swung his feet onto the floor. "You want to talk about it?"

Again, silence filled the room, broken suddenly by the sound of the zipper on her sleeping bag. In a moment she was sitting next to him on his bed, elbows on knees, head in her hands. She began to cry.

He put his arm around her shoulders and pulled her close, feeling exhilarated and simultaneously full of guilt. She turned and put her arms around his neck and they hugged for the longest time, no words spoken, no other movement although Zeke's imagination wrestled with what could have been natural at such an emotional moment.

Finally, she broke their embrace and shimmied backwards until she could lean against the wall next to his bed. She pulled her knees up to her chest. "People get married all the time without love and they manage to survive," she said without much conviction.

"Is that all you want to do, survive?"

"That's what life is all about, isn't it?"

"There has to be more to it than that. How about being happy?"

"It's all relative, Zeke. Every gal my age in Walnut Grove would die to be Rocky's wife, whether they loved him or not."

"But we're not talking about every gal in town, we're talking about you."

She sighed. "Well, maybe I can have a lover on the side, play both ends, you know?"

He smiled. "Walnut Grove is a pretty small town. How would you keep something like that a secret?"

"Why does it have to be a secret? Rocky has his women right now, right, and that's no secret?"

Zeke paused, caught between loyalty to a friend and the truth. "Well----"

"You don't have to cover for him, Zeke. And I know it wouldn't be any different once we're married, so turnabout is fair play."

"You sound resigned to a life of lies and unhappiness."

"Better than most gals. Better than those who'll go through life lonely and miserable, or poor and miserable. There are some who would call me fortunate."

Zeke shook his head. "This is getting way over my head. I'm the last person on earth to give advice on love and marriage."

"You know he's going to ask you to be his best man?"

"What? Me?"

"Don't be too flattered; there aren't many choices for Rocky. He's not exactly popular amongst his peers."

"Really? I thought everyone loved Rocky."

"Well, he knows that anyone who is friendly really hates his guts or wants something from him."

Zeke recalled Rocky's explanation of why Zeke was his friend. "But not me?"

"You saved his life, Zeke. You covered up for him, took the blame for driving his car that night. That means a lot to Rocky." She pointed at him. "Now don't deny it. Rocky would never let anyone else drive his precious car and he'd be the first in line to let someone else take the fall for him. That's just the sort of person he is."

"Knowing him like you do you're still willing to accept him as your husband?"

"You've accepted him as your friend."

That caused him pause and Zeke wondered if the friendship was really that shallow. "Well, I don't plan to spend the rest of my life with him," was all he could come up with.

"Maybe I don't either." That momentarily stopped the conversation. Robin leaned back against the wall. "Look, I'll be comfortable, I'll be taken care of. I'll find a way to be happy."

"But how can you raise a family with someone you don't love?"

She laughed. "Well, don't tell him I said so, of course, but Rocky's not much in the sack." She paused while Zeke weighed this startling revelation. She sighed. "But I've had worse experiences on my back, you know?"

Zeke felt himself blush.

"Oh, dear, I've embarrassed you, haven't I?"

"Uh----"

She reached out and touched his arm. "What about your experiences, Zeke? Had any special moments, any girls that set you on fire?"

"A couple," he lied.

"Any like me?"

And then it happened. Their conversation, the closeness, the intimate discussions gave way to the inevitable. She turned to him and moved slowly, hesitantly, into his arms, her warm mouth finding his. Surprised, he offered no resistance, pulling her closer. They both moaned and when they came up for air several moments later, she said, "Wow, where did you learn to kiss like that?"

He laughed, then pulled her body against his. She guided one of his hands under her pajama top and onto one of her breasts. It was warm and firm and Zeke could feel her arousal. He turned her onto her back, slid on top of her, and looked down into her eyes, small white spheres in the darkened room. She stared back, then pulled his face down to hers with one hand, the other fumbling with the draw string on his pajamas. He felt like his head was going to explode.

"Oh, my," she said in a throaty voice when her hand found its way home.

Suddenly he pulled away, moved off her and scrambled out of bed.

"What's the matter?" she said, out of breath.

"I can't do this," he said.

She turned on her side and reached a hand for him. "Sure you can. Come back to bed."

He shook his head. "No, Robin. This is wrong."

Her bottom lip curled down and she lowered her eyes. The room was silent, then she said, "You're right." She sighed. "This is the wrong time for this."

"There isn't a right time, Robin. You're going to marry my friend. How can I look either of you in the eye if we do this?"

She sat up and slid out of bed. "Guess we got caught up in the moment. I'm sorry I came on to you," she said.

"I'm sorry I let you," he offered.

They both laughed. She put out a hand to shake. "Friends?"

He took it and shook. "Friends."

"Now," she said, climbing back into her sleeping bag. "We could both use some shut eye."

He nodded in agreement and got back into his bed. They both lay on their backs trying to quiet their imaginations, listening to the other one breath until, at long last, they both fell asleep.

* * *

Outside, down on the street in front of Zeke's apartment house, Andrea sat in her darkened car. She had been out cruising the bars in Aggieville and was on her way home when she thought about Zeke; about how he had told her one night at Jack's how he spent the holidays here at school alone. She had come to know him, in the casual way you know someone sitting on the stool next to you in a noisy bar; had decided he was an interesting guy, someone who, like her, would be heading to New York after graduation. Perhaps their paths would cross there, in the city with nine million paths.

She smiled at the thought. She knew that her quest to make it on Broadway would be long and stressful. Why not have a friend to reach out to? His journey would most likely be the same as hers. There must be thousands of people in the city that never sleeps trying to be a successful writer. Anyway, on an impulse she had decided tonight to stop at his place and get to know him even better. Who knows, they might just spend the night talking or, well, she'd just have to see how it went.

As she waited she had seen a couple come around the corner, walking arm-in-arm from Aggieville. She hadn't recognized the girl, not in the yellow glow from the streetlight, but Zeke's distinctive haircut stood out. The twosome had clambered up the stairs to his apartment and the lights went on, then off.

Andrea released a deep sigh. Well, not tonight she said to herself. Maybe I'll just have to wait until we're alone together in New York. She pulled the car into gear and drove slowly away, her imagination creating a vivid picture of what must be going on up in his bedroom.

#

9

The wedding of Rockford Charles Wellington II and Robin Forsythe was the social event of the year in Walnut Grove. As Robin had forewarned, Rocky asked Zeke to be his best man and Zeke had reluctantly accepted. Lincoln was one of five groomsmen, the rest hometown obligations representing various business connections to the bank. Robin had several bridesmaids cut from the same cloth of required commitments, but chose a college classmate as her maid of honor.

One of Rocky's groomsmen who knew his way around Wichita arranged a bachelor party there; a typical scenario involving a strip club, private lap dances for the groom, and bar-hopping in the comfort of a rented limousine. It was a rather awkward evening with most of the groomsmen fawning over Rocky in an attempt to further ingratiate themselves for future business reasons. Zeke spent most of the night exchanging humorous observations and asides with Lincoln, who was stunned into wide-eyed, open-mouthed awe by the parade of gyrating flesh. They were both amazed at the number of dancers who knew Rocky by name.

The wedding ceremony itself was held in the Walnut Grove Presbyterian church with all the attendant blessings on the young couple from God, Jesus, and the surrounding community of friends, supplicants and small town hangers-on.

The reception was at the country club, its grand ballroom decorated festively with blue and white balloons, and an identically colored arrangement of silk flowers at each table. Zeke sat next to Rocky at the head table, exchanging occasional glances with Robin.

When Zeke had awoken from their torrid night back in December in his apartment, she was gone, leaving without an embarrassing goodbye. She had called that night and apologized again for "taking advantage of him" and they had agreed to put the experience behind them and remain good friends. They had continued their relationship long distance, exchanging letters and phone calls back and forth regarding his writing and her comments. Neither spoke again of the events in his room that night, but visions of every moment that evening kept finding their way into Zeke's imagination.

"Robin really likes you," Rocky said, leaning in towards Zeke at the head table.

"What?" Zeke said.

"I said, Robin really likes you. You're probably my only friend that she cares for. Must be your way with words." He looked at his best man as if expecting a confession, Zeke thought.

"Yeah, well, she has helped me a lot with my short stories," he offered.

Rocky nodded. "Well, keep it up, old buddy. She's going to need something to do once I dive into the bank business." He smiled and winked. "Just keep it platonic, you rascal, O.K.?"

Zeke smiled back. "O.K., Rock. She really is a wonderful gal."

Rocky nodded and sighed. "Yeah, everyone keeps telling me that," he said, sounding like he was tired of all the flattery concerning his bride.

The required sequence of events transpired: toasts from best man and maid of honor, a short speech by R.C., first dance, dances with father and mother, etc. After dinner, wedding cake, bouquet and garter toss, Robin found Zeke by the bar and held out a hand. "Your turn with the blushing bride," she said.

He followed her onto the dance floor, feeling like every eye in the place was on him. "It's a lovely wedding," he offered as she guided him into a waltz.

"I'm so happy you could be here," she said, looking up at him.

They completed several slow circles, Zeke struggling not to match her intense gaze. "Rocky says he's glad we're good friends," he said finally.

She moved her body ever-so-slightly against his. "So am I," she said, and he felt himself instinctively respond. "So, when do you leave for New York?" she asked, curling her lower lip down, reminding him of the same expression that night in his room; the expression that kept coming back to him in his dreams.

He cleared his throat, fearful that his nerves would produce a squeaky response. "It's funny," he started, straining to keep their bodies a respectable distance from one another, "I've been waiting four long years to move on with my life, to begin making a mark, you know?"

She nodded. "And yet?"

He smiled at her ability to read his mind. "And yet, next week is right around the corner and, well, I'm kind of scared. I guess I'll be all right once I get to New York, but right now I wish I could just go back to school and continue being a student."

"New York," she said wistfully. "It sounds so exciting. I envy you." She squeezed his hand. "And you'll do fine. You're a great writer and it will only take the big city a little while to realize that." She looked around the room and sighed. "Nothing new or exciting for me here. As of tonight I'll be just another housewife."

"One that every gal in town will envy."

She shot him a resigned look. "Please stay in touch, Zeke. Your friendship is important to me. You'll be like a lifeline."

He nodded. "We'll both be busy starting our new lives, but I'll write when I can. I guess you'll be busy making babies, huh?"

A frown. "Rocky's convinced me we should wait at least a year, give him time to get settled in at the bank. He's got big plans, you know?"

"That's what he tells me. I don't understand all the financial lingo, but he sure knows what he wants to do."

Another sigh. "Rocky's always known what he wants to do. The rest of us just wait for our orders."

"Please try and be happy," he said. "Give Rocky a chance, O.K.?"

She smiled up at him and he felt his heart race. He imagined momentarily that he was the groom today; that it would be him taking her on their honeymoon tonight, then back to the comfortable confines of Walnut Grove, her in their cozy home waiting every evening for his return from work. He felt dizzy. Thankfully the song ended and he walked her back to the head table. "Thank you for the dance lesson," he said, bending to kiss her hand. Her engagement ring nearly blinded him. He stood up, still holding her hand and their eyes met.

"Hey!" came the deep voice over his shoulder. He turned to see Rocky glaring at him through bloodshot eyes, one arm slung around Lincoln's shoulder.

"How 'bout a toast?" Rocky said, slurring his words. "To the guy who shaved my life."

Zeke reached for his drink on the table and raised it. "To the beautiful bride and the beautiful groom." They all laughed and Robin relieved Lincoln of his burden, moving Rocky off towards several elderly guests, shooting a parting glance over her shoulder at Zeke.

Lincoln sipped his drink. "This is quite an affair."

Zeke smiled. "Surely this isn't your first wedding is it?"

Lincoln shook his head. "No, but the ones in my father's church are a bit tamer; no alcohol, no dancing."

"No fun," Zeke added.

Lincoln nodded his agreement. "Speaking of fun, what's the first thing you'll do in New York?"

Zeke took a deep breath and exhaled. "Well, I've got a few dollars saved up so I'm just going to relax and get the lay of the land first, you know? Bernie's got a place for me to stay and I'll take a little while to learn my way around, then start looking for a job."

"Sounds like an adventure to me."

"What about you? Ready to sit down and have that talk with your dad about old time religion?" Zeke asked.

"Not immediately. Like you, I need to get the lay of the land first. I guarantee your adventure will be a lot more fun than mine."

* * *

The reception quickly played out in a predictable pattern: various cliques congregating together; the youngsters, the families, the old crowd. Zeke found himself sitting alone at the head table when the D.J. played Jimmy Durante's version of "I'll Be Seeing You." Older couples made their way slowly onto the dance floor, wrinkled smiles, stooped backs, all nattily attired, gray hair neatly combed and coiffed.

The song brought back memories of his grandmother for Zeke, out on the back porch after Saturday morning chores, doing her ironing and listening to the radio. Whenever this song played she would tell Zeke it had been his mother's favorite. "She used to play it all the time when your dad was overseas," she would say with a distant look in her eyes.

Moments like those caused a yearning in Zeke to have known his parents. He had experienced the same feeling two weeks ago at graduation: all the happy families, beaming graduates, and the isolation he felt at such a momentous occasion in his life. He wondered what they would have looked like had they been there; what they would have talked about. He wondered if they would have been proud of him?

As the last line of the song played he pictured his mother listening to the words, praying that her young husband would return from the war in one piece and that they could resume their lives together. How joyous their reunion must have been, Zeke thought with a smile. Only to have their dreams ended a mere two years later.

And what of his own dreams? Would he live to see them come true? Was there some sort of cosmic balance in play, a long, fulfilling life in exchange for his parent's tragic, abbreviated existence? He stared off across the ballroom, at the couples making their way slowly from the dance floor and took a long, deep breath. He was about to find out.

# # #

10

The newlyweds spent two weeks in Europe, visiting London, Paris and Rome. Robin had never been out of the country and was awe-struck by places she had only seen in books and movies. Rocky had seen all the sites before, having travelled here with his family when he was a teenager. His impatience was not in having to revisit all the tourist attractions, but in counting the days until he could return to Walnut Grove, the bank, and his new life there.

But when they returned R.C. insisted that his son "focus on his bride and establishing their new home" before business matters. "You can get started on making me a grandfather, too," R.C. has suggested with a raised eyebrow.

So Rocky bade his time, suffering through elongated discussions on wall colors, furniture type, period and placement and the million things new brides cherish when furnishing their first home. They had agreed that pregnancy could, despite grandpa's wishes, wait, allowing them time alone as a couple, but Rocky's mind was never that far from his plans for the bank.

Finally the new home was complete with his bride suitably ensconced and Rocky once again felt it was time to begin making his mark at the bank. After the weekly Board meeting that drove him to distraction, he lingered behind to talk with R.C. "I'm concerned about the profile of our reserves," he started.

R.C. looked up with a quizzical expression. "What do you mean?"

"I mean," Rocky said, taking the chair next to his father at the long conference table, "It's ultra-conservative. It's all in low yield treasury bonds."

"Our job is to protect our customer's assets," R.C. began.

"Our job is to maximize our profits, dad. With a better return on our investments we would be strengthening our customer's assets."

"We're not in the business of risking those assets, Rocky. We have an obligation to protect those investments and guarantee a steady return. That's what builds customer loyalty and trust."

"And what if you could offer a more lucrative return? What would that do to your customer's trust?"

R.C. leaned forward on the table, hands folded together. "And what if our investments lost money, Rocky? What if we had to lower the return on our customer's investments because we took unconscionable risks?"

"Dad, I'm not asking you to sink all your money in some fly-by-night stock, but we need to beef up our portfolio or we won't remain competitive. United Federal up in Wichita is offering a full two percent higher return on their savings accounts. It won't take long for customers to notice the difference and move their money."

"I've had most of these customers their whole lives, Rocky. From the first Christmas Day savings programs to financing their home mortgages, to helping them with loans for their farms or sending their kids to college. Our relationship is built on trust, not on a few points of interest."

"People follow the money, dad. Loyalty is one thing, but when the rubber meets the road, they can't afford to stay with the low price spread. You've got to be competitive or you're going to lose your customer base, one at a time. It's inevitable."

R.C. slammed the top of the table with his fist. "I didn't build this bank on being greedy or taking unnecessary risks. You may think I'm old fashioned, but I brought these people through the Depression and a World War by keeping their interest first, not mine. Sure, I could have made more money, taken some risks, but I started this bank with the long term in mind, with surviving and growing so that you, my only son, would inherit a prosperous business, not one that failed along the way because I was greedy."

Rocky shook his head understandably, trying to retain his composure. "Dad, I appreciate all that, but times change, the way business works changes too. That's why you sent me to college, to learn all that and be able to come back here and apply it."

"Rocky, like your other suggestions, let's let this one stay on the back burner for a while. Learn the ropes here, get settled into your job and," he said, raising a finger for emphasis, "pay attention to your young bride. There'll be a lifetime of wheeling and dealing here at the bank but your first priority is that young lady and keeping her happy."

Rocky knew when the limit of R.C.'s patience had been reached. He had said what he wanted, planted several seeds, so time to back off. Like his father said, there would be plenty of time to change things here. Be patient. "O.K., dad. Fair enough. But I've got a lot more ideas and sooner or later we need to discuss them all."

"Get your priorities straight, Rocky, and we'll have plenty of conversations about your ideas."

* * *

Robin stood and looked at herself in the bathroom mirror. She had spent the day in Wichita: new hairdo, pedicure, manicure, massage, waxing and sexy lingerie. She smiled at the result. The new nightgown was white and sheer and hid nothing from the imagination. She sprayed herself with the new perfume from the atomizer on the counter and turned to admire her profile.

In the adjoining bedroom of their new home Rocky was propped up in bed reading the New York Times. It had been a grueling week, most of his energy spent in self-restraint at enduring the old fashioned way his father ran the bank. The articles Rocky read about how modern banks operated just made matters worse, but he would have to be patient, not a trait he had cultivated.

The bathroom door opened and Robin stepped into the room, pausing to drape an arm up against the door jamb. She cocked her head and smiled. The light from the bed lamp caused her nightgown to shimmer. "What do you think of my new outfit, Rocky?" she said.

Rocky glanced in her direction, then back to the newspaper. "Very nice," he mumbled.

Robin moved forward until she was at the edge of the bed. "Maybe you should look a little closer," she said.

Rocky looked up and surveyed the sheer outfit. "You're gonna freeze to death in that come winter."

She moved forward and put a knee on the edge of the bed. "But it's not winter yet," she said breathlessly. Holding his eyes for the moment, she undid the nightgown, then pulled it over her shoulders and let it slide to the floor.

"What the hell?" Rocky asked, pointing between her legs.

"It's the newest fad, Rocky. It's called bikini waxing. Do you like it?" She moved up onto the bed, straddling his legs and arching her back for him to get the full effect.

He frowned and went back to his newspaper.

Robin leaned forward, running her hand up his leg. "Why don't you put your paper down and pay attention to me?" she asked. "You haven't touched me since our honeymoon and I could use a little loving, you know?" She peeked over the top of the newspaper and smiled as seductively as she could manage.

"Robin," he exclaimed. "Not now." He turned the page.

She sat back, her lower lip curling down. "Maybe I should call Marcie and get on your calendar," she said, referring to his secretary at the bank.

Rocky put down the newspaper. "Look, I'm doing my best to move those old codgers at the bank into the current century and, well, it takes all my energy, you understand?"

She leaned forward again. "Well, you wouldn't have to do anything but just lay there; I'd do all the work," she added, blinking her new eyelashes.

He shook his head. "I'm just not in the mood right now. That excuse seems to work for you women, so now I'm using it."

"You women?"

"Oh, don't start in on your feminine rights bullshit. Just put your pajamas on and come to bed. I've got a long day tomorrow."

It was a familiar scenario that had been repeated many times since the wedding night. Despite knowingly entering into a loveless marriage, she wanted affection, not just sex, but recognition that she was his partner. Rocky had never been romantically eloquent, but his total devotion to the goddamned bank was getting old quickly. She deserved at least equal time. She understood all about getting his feet planted in his new position of Vice President, of fighting the old guard to modernize the bank and all of that, but she should be just as important to him as his damned job.

She clambered off of Rocky and picked her cotton pajamas up from the chair next to her side of the bed and pulled them on, then slipped underneath the covers without a word. In a minute Rocky turned off his bed lamp and mumbled good night.

They both lay on their backs staring up into the darkness. Rocky thought about tomorrow's meeting with the Board, cringing at the antiquated procedure, the focus on gossip and anecdotes rather than hard business. Taking over would be a long, slow process, but he was smarter than these yokels, young and energetic and armed with new ideas. It would only be a matter of time.

Robin felt a tear run down across her cheek. Her worst nightmares were coming true. She had known going in that this would be a marriage of convenience, that her vision of a fairy tale romance was a non-starter, but she had been hopeful that she could still make it work. Rocky had managed to fill in the box labeled "get married" on his checklist of accomplishments and now his attention was on other things. She was left to her own devices and her mind searched frantically for an escape from this maze of unhappiness. She closed her eyes and pulled the covers up to her nose. What could she do to get through tomorrow?

# # #

11

In nearby Wichita, Lincoln Archer faced a dilemma ironically similar to that of his friend Rocky. It was Sunday morning and he stood in the back of the converted bowling alley watching the congregation listen to his father's sermon. Lincoln had read the transcript and wasn't paying attention to the words now but to their effect on the assembled group. Their necks were craned, like baby birds awaiting their food, their mouths slightly open, eyes wide. The old man had them mesmerized. They drank in every word as if it were, well, gospel. Lincoln smiled at his play on words.

He had met and talked with a number of the congregation as part of his duties over the years and he knew that, despite the outward appearance of being sod busting yokels, these were intelligent people, with dreams and aspirations as real as any. Law abiding, conservative, outwardly friendly, inwardly religious. But, these were no wild-eyed bible thumpers, though, much more pragmatic. "I don't want to be lectured about sin," one farmer had told him in confidence. "I want to hear about how to get through today and look forward to tomorrow."

Others had expressed similar convictions. They wanted practical, day-to-day advice and counsel. Mix in a few humorous anecdotes and talk about community projects and get it all done in less than an hour. These were busy people with lots to do back on the farm or in the local grocery store or at the fire department. It was a disruption to their other Sunday activities to clean up, get dressed and drive into town. "Make my trip worthwhile," an elementary school teacher had demanded.

It was a no-nonsense, straight-talking, get-it-done crowd and Lincoln was beginning to build an appreciation for their perspective. He listened now to the closing remarks, studying how his father would make the final summation and points of his sermon. He was particularly attentive because later this evening, at the six p.m. service, he would deliver his version of his father's sermon. He was scared to death, of course, having never stood in front of a congregation in the pulpit before.

He could say the words, he supposed, but he worried about his conviction, the energy his father called upon based on his faith and belief.

The first notes of the closing hymn echoed through the cavernous hall and Lincoln made his way towards the exit where he would position himself and greet the guests in his father's house. Again, he smiled at his choice of words. He actually enjoyed these one-on-one situations where a short exchange of "thank you for coming" or "so good to see you again" or "how's your mother doing?" were all that was expected of him. His father would do the heavy lifting, reminding the faithful of upcoming church events, greeting each person by name, and answering questions raised by his sermon.

This evening would indeed be a test and Lincoln wondered, as he shook hands and smiled, whether he was up to it?

* * *

The answer came quickly. Having studied the script for the sermon all week, Lincoln had made numerous changes; replacing a paragraph here and there, inserting a few humorous comments and selecting several members he knew regularly attended the 6:00 p.m. service as subjects of his points in the speech. He deleted all biblical quotations and references to God or Jesus, adding his own home-spun philosophy on how to live one's life and serve your family, your neighbor, and your community. The collection of private admissions on what the congregation wanted to hear was about to be put to the test.

Once he started, once he received his first agreeing nod, once his hands stopped shaking on the rim of the pulpit, Lincoln relaxed. He gained confidence with every word, felt energized as never before.

Even his father smiled at the humorous comments Lincoln had added. Halfway through the sermon Lincoln moved from behind the podium and ventured down into the main aisle where he was able to point to the individuals he would reference in his talk. It turned out to be an extremely popular feature of his "style" and he was swarmed like a celebrity afterwards, everyone delighted with his inaugural sermon and pleasing personality.

"What you said about doing what is right rather than what is easy really struck home with me," one rancher offered.

A wrinkled, frail great-grandmother said, "My father used to tell me to consider how my actions affected other people and now you're saying the same, young man."

"Your father must have been a very wise man," Lincoln replied and the two enjoyed a hearty laugh at the implication.

And so it went for nearly thirty minutes, seemingly every member of the 6:00 service offering congratulations and positive comments about his words. Unlike previous services where he simply stood and greeted the congregation with small talk, now Lincoln felt in command of the moment. The praise was pleasing and he sensed ordinary people believing that he was extraordinary, that his words and messages came from some deep well of experience and wisdom despite his youth. These weren't his words, of course, but comments from people who were not easily moved to praise or flatter.

As he lay in bed that night Lincoln was still exhilarated from his debut. There was a feeling of power at holding an audience's attention, at garnering heartfelt praise for his words. His chest felt like it might explode with confidence. Even his father seemed pleased although he had been unusually quiet at dinner.

Lincoln was energized, unable to calm his thoughts, already planning his next appearance. But as his mind raced and his emotions swelled he had one lingering concern about today's performance: what did his father *really* think?

# # #

12

New York City can be beautiful in the summer. When the largest metropolis you'd ever visited had been Wichita, Kansas, "the city" could also be overwhelming and intimidating. Bernie, his ex-KSU classmate had promised him a place to stay and Zeke now enjoyed a modest basement apartment on Staten Island. Although technically one of the five boroughs of New York, Staten Island was almost like living in Kansas with small, friendly neighborhoods, lots of trees, open spaces and nary a skyscraper. Bernie had suggested that before Zeke launch his quest for a writing job, which Zeke was chomping at the bit to do, he should first take a few weeks to familiarize himself with the city.

As he strolled the avenues and parks, walked across the Brooklyn Bridge, and visited the various museums and other landmarks, Zeke was constantly reminding himself to close his mouth. His favorite locations were the hustle and bustle of Grand Central Station where he marveled at the frantic pace of thousands of people on the go, and the isolation and quiet of Central Park with its joggers, lunchtime walkers and groups of tourists, necks craned to take in the sights. But as he familiarized himself with the city the small nest egg he had brought with him dwindled quickly. His short post-graduation vacation was over. Time now to find a job and finally begin the arduous task of being one of thousands of artists trying to make their way in the big city. As a start he found a job unloading trucks on the weekends at a Staten Island warehouse. Venturing into the city, he landed a job washing dishes and bussing tables at Vito's, a Manhattan restaurant, during the lunch shift, then, following the lead of a co-worker at the restaurant, joined a cleaning crew that emptied trash and vacuumed offices on Wall Street five nights a week.

Juggling three jobs kept him on the move. His room on Staten Island proved convenient to work and transportation, namely the Staten Island ferry. The rent was reasonable and he enjoyed the relative quiet compared to the frenzied cacophony of the city.

His meals were dictated by his work schedule. Breakfast was a bagel and a cup of coffee on the ferry, then he was given lunch at the restaurant and took leftovers the cook would make available as snacks during his nightly Wall Street duties. Midnight meals were from numerous "roach coaches" at the southern tip of Manhattan or from a 24 hour diner on Staten Island that had a Midwestern flavor.

Providing for his basic needs left little time to pursue his primary objective: a writing job. He pounded the pavements of Manhattan in what spare time his jobs permitted, carrying a portfolio of his Wildcat columns and several of his short stories, revised per Robin's helpful comments. He called on every major newspaper, but the results were discouragingly similar. "Not enough experience," or "you really don't know your way around the city well enough to uncover stories," or "we just don't have an opening at this time."

All his efforts, his menial jobs, his hurried pavement pounding, were all aimed at opening that proverbial door of success just a crack so that he could visit his talent on the waiting world. He kept up this merciless pace through the fall, the metamorphosis of the city from warm and welcome to the colors of autumn and the cool, damp nights. Then the winter and it was like being back on the farm: biting winds, swirling snow and sleet, slipping and sliding on frozen sidewalks, feeling like he was traversing Tierra del Fuego as the Staten Island ferry cut her way through the choppy waves of New York harbor.

Despite his arduous schedule he had managed to keep a lifeline back to Kansas via correspondence with Lincoln and Rocky. The former had managed to apparently shake off his stage fright and was now sharing sermon duties with his father and actually enjoying it. Zeke thought back to their meandering conversations in college and how reluctant Lincoln had been to embrace his father's faith. Had he been converted?

As for Rocky, well, the letters from Walnut Grove were from Robin, Rocky being too busy at the bank to compose even a short note. Robin complained that her new husband spent an inordinate amount of time at the bank or taking business trips to Wichita and other nearby towns where he hoped to open branch offices.

As the holidays came and went Zeke managed to take copious notes describing the contrasting worlds he witnessed firsthand: the wild Christmas parties on Wall Street, the ebullient crowds in the restaurant, the homeless begging for a handout everywhere he turned. How could he turn these observations into leads for stories? He overcame his normal shyness, making friends with everyone he met. He kept taking notes, wracked his brain, kept his eyes and ears open. Something would inevitably present itself, he reasoned. The stories were out there; he just had to find them. He didn't mind the hard work, the long hours, but often, late at night lying in bed, he felt the isolation and loneliness of being an observer, not a participant.

Then, in the depths of a bleak and cold February, Robin wrote that she was planning a shopping trip to New York and hoped that he would be available for a lunch or dinner while she was there. Seeing an old friend from back home would be a welcome break from the stress and frenzy of his new life.

* * *

Robin was staying at the Royal Devonshire hotel on the south side of Central Park and she invited him for dinner there on a Saturday night. He left his warehouse job and began his trek north to the city and the excitement of seeing an old friend after all this time. They met in the hotel lobby, he in his weathered winter coat, her in a magnificent slinky red dress she had just purchased that afternoon.

"You look magnificent," he gushed, holding her hands by the finger tips.

"And you shaved your mustache and cut your beautiful hair," she said, reaching out to brush some snow off his shoulder. "You look like a teenager again."

"Thanks, that was the look I was going for," he said with a laugh. He stuffed his gloves in a coat pocket and removed the bulky jacket, then shivered at the sudden warmth of the nearby fire place in the lobby.

"I'm starved. How about you?" she said, taking his hand and leading him towards the ground floor restaurant.

Zeke hesitated. "Yeah, I'm pretty hungry, but not sure I can really afford this place."

She squeezed his hand. "Don't be silly. This whole trip is courtesy of the Wellington National Bank."

He laughed. "Well, if it's on Rocky then I'm *really* hungry."

The maitre' de seated them at a table by the front window and they watched horse drawn carriages heading off into Central Park with tourists wrapped in thick blankets. They ordered drinks and he couldn't take his eyes off her. "Marriage really agrees with you, Robin. You look stunning."

She smiled and reached across the table for his hand. "Always the charmer," she said. "I bet you have half the women in town at your beck and call by now."

He laughed. "Not exactly. Too busy with my various jobs."

She prompted him to describe what he did to make ends meet and he did his best to make his jobs sound a bit more exciting and fulfilling than they really were, making her laugh as he recounted characters and hilarious circumstances he had experienced. "I'm glad to see you still have your sense of humor," she offered.

Their drinks arrived; a vodka gimlet for her, bourbon on the rocks for him. "Cheers," she said as they clinked glasses.

"Cheers," he said. "It's sure nice to see a face from back home. I really miss you guys."

"And I miss you too, Zeke. Life can be pretty lonely some times."

He knew that feeling all too well. "So, how's Rocky doing?" he asked.

She sighed and shook her head. Her face wrinkled into a frown. "Well, if he's not working late he's off on a business trip. He's got big plans but he's meeting a lot of resistance from his father and the Board. He's really frustrated."

Zeke nodded. "Well, Rocky's a smart guy; he'll figure it all out before long."

Another sigh. "I guess. I really don't understand all that he's trying to do but it doesn't leave much time for me, you know?"

He frowned. "Well, once again I don't have any relevant experience, but it seems to me that starting a career is pretty consuming; it takes a lot of time and energy. Here I am trying to get mine off the ground working three jobs and I sure don't have time for a girlfriend, let alone a wife. I think it's just a phase most marriages have to go through." He pointed at her. "What you need is something to focus on while Rocky does his thing at the bank. You ever think about getting a job?"

She laughed. "In Walnut Grove? Are you kidding? I suppose I could get a sales job with my father, but what do I know about tractor tires, work boots or farm clothes? No, I wouldn't be any good at anything like that and I'd be bored to tears."

The waiter arrived with the menus and Robin ordered Chateaubriand for two and a bottle of red wine. "And we'll have a chocolate soufflé afterwards," she said, handing their menus to the waiter.

"Very good, madam," the waiter said with a slight bow, shooting Zeke an envious glance as he left the table.

"Guess he thinks I'm a kept man," Zeke said in a lowered voice.

"Well, for tonight that's exactly what you are, Zeke, so sit back and enjoy yourself. You want another drink?"

They enjoyed their sumptuous meal with the conversation directed mainly at Zeke and his exploits in the "city that never sleeps." When pressed for details about life back in Walnut Grove, Robin always shook her head, saying that was just boring stuff, preferring to hear about his adventures.

"Hey," she said, as they walked out of the restaurant, "you just have to see the view from my room. I'm up on the tenth floor and Central

Park is spread out like a picture postcard." She reached for his hand and pulled him towards the elevators.

He felt a little awkward following her down the quiet hallway, but he was curious as to what a room at this place looked like. When they entered her suite he was amazed. He was used to the cramped confines of his basement bedroom on Staten Island so this had the appearance of a palace. She moved to the far end of the room and pulled the drapes back, revealing, as she had previewed, a magnificent view of Central Park, covered in snow and twinkling lights.

"Isn't this marvelous?" she said, her eyes wide.

"Wow, what a view."

They stood admiring the scene for several minutes, Zeke pointing out several of the landmark hotels and corporate offices that surrounded the park like castle towers.

"You've really learned your way around, haven't you?" she said, turning and moving across the room.

"Well, when you live here you kind of have to know where everything is," he explained.

She opened the mini-fridge. "How about a night cap?"

He hesitated, knowing the long trip back to Staten Island that awaited him. "Well, just one, maybe."

She produced two bottles of Drambuie and poured them into the bell-shaped glasses. "Cheers again," she said, handing him his glass. She downed hers with a snap of her head, then put a hand on his shoulder as she removed her shoes, one at a time. "Got to go pee," she said, turning to head for the bedroom. "Get another drink. I'll be right back."

Zeke nodded and watched her disappear into the bedroom. He emptied his glass and turned to look back out the windows again. So this was how the upper crust lived, he thought. The dinner had been fantastic, he had a bit of a buzz working, and this room, wow. He wondered how much this place cost a night? The movement behind him snapped him out of his trance.

Zeke turned around and almost dropped his glass. Robin stood in the bedroom doorway, completely naked, her eyes boring into his, a hand seductively on one hip, a confidant smile filling her face.

"Robin, what---"

She moved to him, ran her fingers under his shirt collar and looked up into his eyes. He could smell her perfume, feel her warm body pressing against him. "We have unfinished business, you and I," she whispered, her fingers beginning to unbutton his shirt. "And we have all night to catch up," she added.

# # #

13

Reverend Billy Archer and his son Lincoln lived in a modest frame house in the Mountain View development northwest of Wichita. Mountain View was a misnomer for the small group of houses that made up the subdivision. The sweep of land to the west was mile upon endless mile of flat wheat farms, segmented into Kansas' familiar mile square acreage. The nearest mountains were the Rockies, invisible a thousand miles away. They had lived here since Billy purchased the old bowling alley and converted it to a church. That building stood a few miles east, just this side of the Arkansas River that wound its way through the city and south towards the Mississippi.

Moving from the old revival tent to the bowling alley happened right after Lincoln's mother passed away. Her two year battle with a rare form of leukemia subjected her to the torment and ravages of chemotherapy. Billy had never really recovered from the tragedy and Lincoln had been too young to fully appreciate what his parents went through, but poignant memories of his soft-spoken mother lingered with father and son.

Inside their home this cold winter afternoon, Billy and Lincoln relaxed near the blazing fire in the fireplace, both drinking a mug of hot chocolate. It was time, Lincoln thought; time to discuss the conflict that had been building inside him for several years now. He had avoided this awkward conversation with his father about as long as he could.

Since Lincoln's debut sermon back in the summer, Billy Archer had gradually accelerated his son's involvement to the point where the two now split the preaching duties equally. It was a faster-than-planned transition, but Lincoln had warmed to the increased responsibility.

Before Lincoln could start the dreaded dialogue, his father said, "I've been wanting to have this conversation for a long time." Reverend Archer sipped his hot chocolate and sighed, an ironic smile crossing his weathered features. "I'm delighted at how you've taken to the pulpit," he went on. "You've become a fine preacher and the congregation has welcomed you with open arms. I'm very proud, son."

Lincoln nodded. With that preamble the subject of his concerns deepened. He wondered if the issue should even be broached?

"I'm at the point in my life where I need to start slowing down a bit," the Reverend continued. "The fact that you've done so well with the sermons has only hastened my decision." He stared at his son. "It's no secret that my congregations have slowly become smaller over the years. I thought for a while that reflected a trend of folks just not going to church anymore, but since you've taken to the pulpit I see bigger crowds for you every week." He paused and gathered his thoughts, then smiled at his son. "Perhaps it's time for me to step down and let you carry the Church of Hope forward." A worried look crossed his face.

Lincoln had seen the transformation first hand, the steady movement of worshippers from his father's afternoon service to his own in the evening. Lincoln saw it as a reflection of what the congregation had been telling him for some time about what they wanted to hear. He had formed his sermons around those inputs and had discarded the evangelical style of his father. But he had not expected this; his father stepping down.

"But," the Reverend continued, "I sense that there's something bothering you; not the stage fright we dealt with earlier, but something more fundamental."

The door Lincoln had been trying to go through for so long was suddenly wide open. Time to put it all on the line. "I don't think I believe, father," he blurted out.

"Believe what?"

Lincoln cleared his throat. "The whole religion thing; God and Jesus and heaven and hell; I think it's all a fantasy."

Reverend Archer smiled. "Well, you don't have to believe to be an effective preacher, son."

"What?"

"Oh, I guess I believed in the early days, but then life showed me how cruel it could be and I couldn't resolve how so many bad things could happen under the guise of God's supposed grace and caring."

"You mean like mom?"

Billy Archer grimaced. "That was the breaking point for me. If so gentle and kind a person as your mother could be made to suffer like she did then, well, it opened my eyes."

"But how could you go on being a man of the church?"

The Reverend pointed a finger at his son. "Let me tell you a thing or two about religion, Lincoln. First of all, it's plain and simple a business, and it can be a very lucrative business. Do you know what the largest and most profitable enterprise in the world is? The Catholic Church, that's what," he said, answering his own question. "And, just like big corporations, religion has a product and needs to make a profit to stay in business."

"And hope is that product?" Lincoln guessed.

"Fear, Lincoln, fear. Fear that your sins on earth will be punished and, come judgment day you'll be left to toil forever in a fiery hell. And people will swallow any wild, illogical, totally unreasonable guidance from the church or the scriptures in exchange for the promise of getting into heaven."

"But if you don't believe in God----"

"It's not what I believe that counts, Lincoln. It's about all those people who take time out of their busy lives once a week to come and hear someone speak to their fears."

"But if we don't believe, doesn't that make us hypocrites?"

Billy Archer smiled benevolently and said, "Do you think a politician believes everything he says; that there aren't some 'convenient' lies to be told? Or celebrities who pitch a product actually believe their own words? No, son, we're merely actors following a script. Like every other spokesman, we have to deliver our message with conviction, with sincerity, every word tailored to what our audience will buy."

"We're selling religion?"

"Of course we are. Selling religion is like selling any product, Lincoln. You learn what the people want and you tailor your message to them. And you play that message over and over again, imbedding it in their subconscious. Religion is soothing, emotional music, messages of hope and fear, the promise of salvation in exchange for believing the message. Religion's marketing campaign has been so effective over the years that it's driven men to war and to do unspeakable things."

"It's also given hope and comfort and brotherhood," Lincoln argued.

"That's my point, Lincoln. It's what your audience wants to hear. If they want blood, religion can incite them to genocide. If they want compassion, the properly shaped sermon can give them comfort. It's up to you to read your audience and mold your message to their needs and wants. And I believe you've done an excellent job at that," he added.

Lincoln considered the points. "So it's irrelevant whether I believe or not? I'm merely an actor following a script?"

"Precisely." Billy Archer shifted forward in his chair, elbows on knees, his eyes boring in on his son's. "Lincoln, you don't need God in your life to be a good man; to be fair and just and honest. You don't need God to tell you right from wrong, to obey the law, to seek justice. These are all traits you've learned from others, from your education, from your own instincts and observations. We should not waste our time fearing and trying to appease a concept that demands our fealty and devotion yet leaves prayers unanswered and a heartless trail of misery, hatred and depravation wherever he is allowed to exist."

These were amazing words coming from the bible-pounding, fire-and-brimstone preacher. "But your sermons don't reflect any of that, father. You're as God-fearing as any man I've ever met."

"It's what I once believed and what I thought my congregations wanted to hear. I never had the courage to speak from the heart, afraid I'd be rejected and abandoned. But you," he said, pointing a shaking finger at his son, "are not burdened by all that. You have a unique voice and message and the ever-increasing attendance at your services is proof that you are in step with the congregation."

Lincoln sat back and considered all that had transpired in these past few minutes, at a lifetime of withholding true feelings, releasing deep seeded fears and the exhilaration of freeing those fears and beliefs. The room had gone silent as Lincoln's brain tried to walk through all the new doors that had just been opened.

But Billy Archer had yet another revelation to share. He bit his lower lip and let out a sigh, then looked up at his son with a mournful expression. "I've got cancer, Lincoln. It's in my brain and they can't do anything about it. I've probably got less than a year to live."

# # #

14

Zeke thought about Robin every day, the memories of their glorious time together replaying over and over in his mind. They had made love hungrily at first that night, trying to devour one another, then settled into a calmer, gentler, tender form of lovemaking. She had wanted to be held and caressed and fall asleep in his arms. After a late breakfast the next morning they had walked the paths of Central Park, holding hands and talking about what life held in store for them.

She was bitterly unhappy, of course, Rocky devoting all his time and attention to the bank. Their plans to wait on having a baby had become a self fulfilling prophecy as he rarely touched her; too tired or disinterested. Zeke thought that he would have been racked with guilt at having cuckolded his friend but strangely, he had felt no guilt at all. It had been a confusing feeling, but Rocky had been miles away, focused exclusively on his own career, and Robin had been right here, sharing feelings and sex he had only dreamed of. Oh, there had been some hayloft groping with Linda Fullerton back home where she had taught him to kiss and explore their bodies, but being with Robin had been a true sexual awakening. She had been sultry, exotic, adventurous, constantly stroking his ego and making him feel like the most important man on earth. It had been heady stuff and all he thought about as he awaited her next visit.

As they had strolled Central Park that morning their conversation eventually led to Zeke's search for a writing job. Robin had produced a business card from a college classmate that worked for World News right there in Manhattan. "Use my name," she had urged, "Linda will at least give you the time of day." When Zeke had later contacted the woman, she agreed to read his material and was impressed enough to pass it along to one of her bosses, a senior editor, who asked for an interview.

* * *

The editor's name was Edith McLean, a handsome brunette in her mid-sixties who had a reputation for being a shrewd judge of talent, and of being a wily businesswoman. She was candid in her assessment of his work and his prospects. "You're quite a good writer," she said, tossing his portfolio back on her desk. "That makes you about one of several thousand roaming this town looking for work."

He had heard this assessment many times before, braced himself for the inevitable. "Yes, ma'am."

She studied him a second. "But what interests me is not just your writing skill, per se, but your attitude." She nudged his portfolio on her desk. "Your writing reflects a natural skepticism and an apparent unwillingness to accept things at face value. That's absolutely essential for an investigative reporter. And the fact that your work found its way onto my desk shows you have perseverance, another necessary trait to succeed in this business."

Zeke nodded, waiting for the other shoe to drop.

"I can't offer you a full time position at this point, but I can bring you on part time as a stringer. You write me some good stories and we'll see about a full time position."

He couldn't believe it. Here was the break he'd been looking for all this time. "That sounds great," was all he could offer.

"What are you doing to make ends meet right now?" she asked.

Zeke explained his three jobs, but when he mentioned the Wall Street janitorial job her eyes lit up.

"Well, Wall Street is always producing something scandalous. I'm sure a smart young man like you can uncover something newsworthy there, don't you?"

Zeke's brain raced through his notes, the potential leads he had uncovered through conversations with late night workers, the tantalizing reports and memos he had seen as he emptied the trash. Time to accelerate his efforts. "Absolutely. Thank you for the opportunity, Mrs. McLean."

She stood and reached across her desk to shake his hand. "Don't thank me until you've started producing some headlines, Zeke. And call me Edith."

* * *

Like any other field of endeavor, investigative journalism requires a combination of hard work, long hours, patience, trial and error, and a spattering of luck. Being at the right place at the right time didn't hurt either. In Zeke's case that place was Wall Street and his job as a janitor. Before, it had just been a boring job, emptying trash cans and vacuuming offices. But now, with the possibility that his previous snooping could lead to a meaningful job, it was a potential informational gold mine.

Many office workers filled their trash with material they had been working on that day and Zeke had become adept at scanning those reports, charts and memos, looking for something that could provide the lead to a story. He had a photographic memory and followed up anything that looked interesting with painstaking research and fact checking. He memorized names, dates, and figures, noting anything that appeared unusual. He had even struck up a running conversation with workers who were burning the midnight oil, but so far nothing remotely scandalous had surfaced.

His diligence finally paid off as one night he found a financial report in the trash that revealed how a major corporation shielded ninety percent of its U.S. income by claiming that its headquarters were located in Germany. When Zeke discovered that the corporation indeed had an office in Stuttgart, manned by a single person, he had his breakthrough story. Following his instincts, he quickly uncovered six other major corporations utilizing the same scheme.

Then, introducing himself as a "writer for World News," which was technically true, he called several organizations asking for quotes. A spokesman for the IRS exclaimed, "This is a loophole in our tax code that belongs at the feet of Congress and their lobbyists."

"A flagrant twisting of the rules in the name of profit," said one sufficiently outraged Congressman who, Zeke discovered, had voted for the legislation that created the loophole.

A mouthpiece for one of the named corporations contributed his point of view by saying, "We are simply following accounting procedures that are authorized by the U.S. Tax Code and verified by our independent auditors."

In his report Zeke reasoned that even to a financial novice, being able to shield millions of dollars in revenue earned in the United States by having a one person office in Germany seemed unethical.

He triple-checked his facts and sources and filed his report with Edith. She was suitably impressed and, after completing her own verification process, ran the expose as a feature story in the next edition of World News. "I'll get you a handsome stipend for this," she said. "Now go get me another story."

It was a good start but Zeke needed more stories and they couldn't just come from reading the trash on his Wall Street job. As luck would have it, a new addition to the janitorial crew solved Zeke's problem.

Miguel Diaz worked alongside Zeke as they methodically cleaned offices from six to midnight. Miguel was from Mexico and, like Zeke, overeducated for his job as a janitor, having taught college in Mexico City. As they got to know one another Miguel told amazing stories of how he had crossed the border in the false bottom of a truck, spent two years doing day labor as he worked his way across the country to New York, where a cousin had emigrated several years before. He shared an apartment in the Bronx with his cousin and ten other immigrants. "I filed my application for a green card over two years ago," Miguel explained. "I think the INS lost it," he added sorrowfully.

It was an amazing story of struggle, back-breaking work, and constant fear that INS authorities would one day discover him and deport him back to Mexico. "The company you and I work for pays me in cash," Miguel said. "They don't report me as an employee and don't pay taxes or Social Security. I make half what you do and I'm happy to do so, amigo. This is a great country and I never want to go back home, but, like many others in my shoes, I'm being taken advantage of."

Zeke listened carefully to Miguel's story, recorded their conversations in notes he transcribed after work. Emboldened by his previous investigation, he made inquiries to the INS, asking about procedures, responsibilities, and green card application processing. He established several contacts who were anxious to speak out about staggering workloads, mismanagement, and excessive turnover of disgruntled employees. Zeke had uncovered his next story.

One night during a break, Zeke shared his plan with Miguel. "I'd like to do a story on the plight of illegal immigrants," he started, "and how the INS is ill-equipped and unmotivated to process all the green card applications." Zeke could see the fear in Miguel's eyes. "I won't use your name, but the world needs to know what's going on."

Miguel nodded. "Absolutely, tell the story, but I doubt it will help my case."

Zeke smiled. "I've done my homework, Miguel. I've made a few contacts at INS and they located your application and moved it to the top of the pile. You should be receiving your green card in a matter of weeks."

Miguel's face lit up. "You did that for me, Zeke? Just for a story?"

"No, amigo, just for a friend."

Zeke's three part series on the secret world of illegal immigrants and the woeful conditions within the INS was his second "expose" and moved him a step closer to full time status. As Zeke promised, Miguel obtained his green card and, with Zeke's help, eventually obtained a nighttime assistant teaching position at Queen's Community College.

Meanwhile, the trash of Wall Street continued to be a mother lode of stories and Zeke wrote of stock manipulation by brokers, the excesses of executive compensation, other corporate tricks to lower their tax rates, and a revealing profile on a-day-in-the-life-of a typical broker with its pressures, long hours and borderline ethical treatment of customers. These articles convinced Edith that Zeke was now worthy of a full time position at World News and he eagerly agreed to his new job, knowing that his life would now change in many ways.

He moved from Staten Island to a small apartment on the top floor of a Greenwich Village brownstone. He purchased a few basic bachelor furnishings: a bed, a sofa and a television to enjoy during the few hours that his busy schedule permitted. The apartment was nothing exotic, but it was a place to call home.

Zeke kept his late night acquaintances on Wall Street, cultivating contacts that would provide him with tips for future stories. He started frequenting Vito's, the restaurant where he had worked as a bus boy, becoming a regular there for dinner. He kept his friendships with the chef from Paris, the maitre' de, and the aspiring actors who waited tables. He rubbed elbows with celebrities who dined there with their entourages, cops on the beat, city officials, athletes. As before when he had been a busboy, he observed them all with a keen eye, listened to slivers of conversation, remembered every word and detail.

There was news everywhere, but it required extensive follow up, research and an extraordinary amount of pavement pounding. He added to his knowledge of navigating the city, from the Bronx to Harlem to mid-town, around Greenwich Village, the business district, sporting venues, and social events from Long Island to New Jersey. He knew the subway system by heart, every train, every stop. He developed contacts everywhere, people he would do favors for and vice-versa; an information network. He became a New Yorker.

His frantic work schedule did not permit much of a social life other than attending events where his interests were casting his gossip net for story leads and following the conversational scent of the crowd like a bloodhound.

Then one night he stopped in a neighborhood nightclub to have a drink and after settling in at the bar he was shocked to hear a familiar Kansas twang. "Well, I'll be damned," the female bartender exclaimed. "We finally managed to find one another." It was Andrea Jackson, the girl he had pulled unconscious from the pond back in Kansas. She circled the bar and threw herself into his arms, jumping up and down like a cheerleader. "What in the world have you been up to, Zeke?" she asked. "Let me buy you a drink."

They exchanged stories about their mutual trials and tribulations since coming to New York as she fed him drinks. She listened wide-eyed as he recounted his host of jobs and how they led to his reporter status at World News. He listened, fascinated, as she told of her struggles to find a role in a Broadway musical. "I haven't got my big break yet," she added with a smile, "but I've got plenty of gigs singing in places like this. In fact," she added with a dazzling smile. I'm on at eleven. Stick around and I'll dedicate a song to an old friend."

# # #

15

R.C. Wellington had originally chosen the smallest of the four offices on the third floor of the Wellington National Bank building years ago, mainly for the convenience of being immediately adjacent to the elevator. Now that Rocky was a permanent resident, the young, rising star commandeered the old conference room down the hall and had it refurbished.

Like many executives, Rocky's new office reflected the personality of its occupant. He replaced the dark paneling, thick curtains that had always been closed, and ancient carpeting that gave the place the appearance of a funeral home, with a motif of off white accentuated by pastel blues. The wide windows overlooking Main Street were left unadorned, creating a bright, airy atmosphere. His sleek desk was made of glass and brushed steel, bare except for the computer that sat atop its polished surface. Fading pictures of cowboys and cattle drives had disappeared in favor of bold colorful prints encouraging "teamwork," "innovation," and "winning."

Rocky was at his desk by 5:30 every morning, in time to coordinate business with investment houses in Hong Kong and London. He was wheeling and dealing, leveraging contacts he had made in school and in his daily dialogue with firms on Wall Street.

The planned transition from father to son was underway, in Rocky's mind at least, but for R.C. there was a festering sore that was growing, a sore that was about to burst.

* * *

R.C. Wellington strode into his son's office and closed the door behind him. "We need to talk," he said, pulling a chair up in front of Rocky's desk.

Rocky leaned back in his leather chair. "Sure, what's up?"

The old man unbuttoned his jacket, sat down and crossed his legs. "One of the reasons I sent you to college was for you to learn what was happening in the world of finance above and beyond what I've taught you." He studied his son. "That's why I've let you try some of your new ideas."

Rocky studied his computer screen as he talked. "Change is inevitable, dad. You've got to keep up with what's going on in the world or you'll wind up falling way behind."

R.C. waved a hand at his son. "I've always known that, Rocky, but it's the pace of change that bothers me and, quite frankly, most of the Board. They've gone along with your experiments primarily out of loyalty to me."

Rocky's eyes shifted to his father. "And every one of my *experiments* has proven to be a financial success. We've opened branches in six other cities, bought up two smaller banks, modernized our computer system and doubled our profits."

R.C. nodded. "I know, son, and even though I was originally uncomfortable with those decisions I acquiesced, thought you might learn from failure, but each one has proven sound and smart."

Rocky shrugged and lifted both palms. "So?"

R.C. sighed. "But this latest plan seems a bit beyond the pale. We're a commercial bank, not a house of speculation and gambling. I've studied our investment portfolio and it just seems too risky to me. We're not experts in Wall Street manipulations and deals; we've always played very conservative with our investments."

"Dad, I'm not going into this blindfolded. I have strong contacts on Wall Street who provide insight and tips on how to invest. I've done my own research and know what I'm doing. The results speak for themselves," he added.

R.C. shook his head. "You're missing my point. This is not your money we're talking about; this is our customer's money and we have an obligation to protect it."

"We have an obligation to maximize our profits for our customers, dad. To survive means to grow, to expand, to stay ahead of our competitors. The days of sitting back and accepting conservative investments are over. We need to be smart, but aggressive."

"It's just too much too soon, Rocky. I just don't think I can support you here."

Rocky leaned forward, elbows on his desk and leveled his gaze at his father. "You don't have any choice, dad. I've got the support of the Board on this so don't fight me."

R.C. straightened in his chair. "I hand-picked every member on the Board; most have been with me their whole careers. Don't fight me on this, Rocky. I don't want to embarrass you."

"The embarrassment would be yours, dad. Look, these guys are all loyal to you but every one of them is long in the tooth, they're looking to retire. What I'm offering each one of them in exchange for their support is a handsome golden parachute, a nest egg that will make their retirement years quite comfortable. Those packages are only possible because of the profits we've been making on our investments. Loyalty to you is one thing, but nothing tops cold hard cash in their pockets. It's the way of the world, dad, and that world, quite frankly, has left you behind."

* * *

R.C. Wellington left the bank before lunch that day, headed home to what he knew would be an empty house. Thelma was in Oklahoma City visiting her sister and R.C. welcomed the solitude. He needed time to think; to contemplate the results of the plan he had put in place years ago. That plan, of course, was to groom Rocky as his successor; to prepare him for the day when he would take over leadership of the bank and R.C. could quietly step aside. That day, so many years in the preparation, had suddenly arrived.

R.C. had anticipated this transition with equal amounts of excitement and trepidation. The bank had been his life. Every waking moment had been dedicated to its existence. But now that was all moving into Rocky's hands. R.C.'s position had become almost ceremonial and, as Rocky had proven this morning, worthless in terms of exercising any control over the bank's business.

And control was what the presidency of the bank was all about. R.C. had enjoyed that power his entire career; his word was law, he made all the key decisions, and everyone bowed to his wishes. Despite exercising that power with a benevolent hand, he had clearly been in charge.

Now Rocky sought that same power. As R.C. considered the situation he had come to realize that Rocky was not unlike a younger version of himself. Better educated certainly, but basically seeking total control of his world. R.C.'s vision of a gradual transition was proving impossible. There couldn't be two men in charge. Today's encounter with Rocky had been the final straw in deciding to let him assume the sole leadership of the bank. Hell, R.C. thought, he doesn't need my help any more. It was time for the old man to step aside before he embarrassed himself or made a costly mistake.

And just like that, without fanfare or further deliberation, the decision was made. He would meet with Rocky tomorrow, draw up the appropriate paperwork, and be out of his office by the end of the week. No reason to draw this painful decision out any longer. By Friday he would officially be retired.

So what would he do then? He was still a comparatively young, active man suddenly thrust into a sedentary environment. He felt uncomfortable around "old people" his own age. He had maintained his health and did not feel at all like most of his elderly counterparts; stooped, wrinkled, nodding off at parties or family gatherings. He still had a young man's energy, but he was suddenly out of his element in a business that had been his life blood for his entire career.

R.C. moved into the study and poured himself a stiff bourbon and took his drink to his favorite chair. He settled into it with a sigh. This was the way it was supposed to be, right? Passing the torch, father to son, progress, change, a new beginning. Still, it was difficult to digest, to feel comfortable about. Old ways die hard but they must surely die. Change is inevitable. He took a swallow of his drink, winced at the irony of two bitter tastes in his mouth.

Surely there would be other things to do now; things that the hustle and bustle of running the bank had never allowed. Now there would be time. Lots of time. He closed his eyes against the impending fear of a boring existence, of days filled with long stretches of emptiness, of waking each morning with absolutely nothing on his plate for the day. How many books could he read? How much T.V. could he endure? Grandchildren did not appear on the horizon and he worried that he might grow tired of spending every day with Thelma.

R.C. got up and poured himself a double, realized that he had been sitting here for several hours, had managed more than one drink. He made his way back to his chair, with the view out the window across the town where he had been born and where he had lived his entire life. He thought about his father and how he must have felt at this age. The thought added to his sadness and, as the crickets began their evening serenade, R.C. stared blankly out into the growing darkness.

# # #

16

The two old college friends hadn't seen one another since Rocky's wedding. With each busily pursuing their own careers, there had been little reason to maintain the friendship as their paths had never crossed. Until now. Lincoln had contacted Rocky and asked for a business meeting that he wanted held face-to-face. Rocky had assumed that Lincoln was seeking a loan and the President of the Wellington National Bank was fighting to keep an open mind concerning Lincoln's business argument. Rocky didn't have a lot of experience in making loans to churches, but he'd hear his old friend out.

Lincoln arrived early for his eleven o'clock appointment and was shown into Rocky's office after being plied with coffee and donuts in the fashionable waiting room. He admired the spacious accommodations and the panoramic view of Main Street. Rocky stood and shot his cuffs, looking resplendent in a three piece charcoal gray suit and dark blue tie. "Lincoln," he exclaimed, reaching to shake his visitor's hand. "You look great, my friend."

Lincoln returned the handshake. "As do you, Mr. President," he said.

They both laughed, then Rocky's face became serious. "I was so very sorry to hear about your father," he said, motioning Lincoln towards a chair in front of his desk.

"Yes, thank you," Lincoln said. "The flowers you sent were very thoughtful."

Rocky nodded, feeling a pang of guilt that he hadn't attended the services, an emotion that was quickly dismissed. He glanced at his Swiss watch. "So, how are you getting on with your church?"

Lincoln smiled, leaning back and crossing his legs at the knees. "Quite well, actually. I've managed to overcome my fear of public speaking and, if I do say so, deliver a pretty good sermon every once in a while."

"I'm sure you do," Rocky said with a patronizing smile.

"Anyway, I appreciate you seeing an old friend. I doubt you've had a lot of experience in dealing with churches."

Rocky pointed at Lincoln. "You've got me there. Most of the churches in this area tend to finance their projects with fund raisers or by other means. They very rarely incur outside debt. So, what are you interested in, Lincoln? A loan for improvements to your building?"

"Actually," Lincoln said, uncrossing his legs and sliding forward in his chair, "we recently moved into a new facility and we paid for it in cash."

"Really?" Rocky said, trying to picture what sort of paltry accommodations could be acquired on the cheap.

Lincoln reached into his coat pocket and produced a brochure that had a picture of the Church of Hope's new building on the front cover. He handed the brochure to Rocky.

The picture on the front looked like a modern three story hotel, with sweeping arches, tinted glass, a manicured lawn and ornate shrubbery. Opening the brochure, Rocky's eyebrows raised as he looked at pictures of the spacious sanctuary, meeting rooms, kitchen and offices. "Very nice," he said, pursing his lips in admiration. He tossed it onto his desk. "Paid for it in cash, you say?"

Lincoln nodded. "We have a generous flow of revenue from the local T.V. advertisers and our congregation and we don't believe in incurring debt."

"You must run a tight ship, Lincoln."

"Well, just like your bank, Rocky, for my church to stay in business we must show a profit. That's the bottom line of business, right?"

Rocky chuckled. "Yes, but somehow I never applied that to religion."

"I think old time religion is like old time banking; it needs a modern overhaul, wouldn't you agree?"

Rocky smiled. "Absolutely. So, what brings you here today?"

"Well, Rocky, we've got a surplus of cash and I read one of your advertisements in the Wichita papers and saw that you offered consulting services for stocks and bonds."

Rocky leaned back in his chair and templed his fingers under his chin. "We have an arrangement with Morton & Cummings, the big investment firm on Wall Street. It's one of our new services for letting the average man have access to the stock market."

"Well, I confess I don't know much about Wall Street so I figured using the services of an old friend who knew his way around the block was the smartest way to invest our money."

"And how much money are we talking about?"

Lincoln reached into his coat pocket again and produced an envelope which he placed on Rocky's desk. "I'd like to start with a million dollars," he said calmly.

Rocky opened the envelope and studied the cashier's check. This would sure as hell impress his liaison at Morton & Cummings; pulling a million bucks out of a bumpkin church was no small feat.

"I've got big plans for my church and I need a decent return on our investments. Letting all that money sit around at four or five percent is a waste. I may as well keep it all under my pillow, right?"

"Right," Rocky said, still surprised that such a sum could be generated by a small town church. He tilted his head in admiration. "You must give a helluva sermon."

Lincoln smiled. "You ought to drop by one Sunday and take in a service. I'll give you a front row seat."

"Thanks for the invite, but to be honest, I'm not a religious man."

"To be honest," Lincoln said, standing, "neither am I."

* * *

As Lincoln drove back to Wichita that afternoon he thought about all the changes he had made since his father passed away. Using all of the Reverend's basic sermons as a guideline, Lincoln had modified them to suit his own style. First, he removed all references to God, to Jesus, to scripture. There was to be no deity in his product, no reliance on words written two thousand years ago that did little to address the complex problems facing his congregations today. He eliminated all the mystique and superstition and tales of miracles and heavenly signs. His sermons were directed at today's world, today's issues and common sense messages his congregations could understand clearly. He added humor, ensuring that each anecdote or theme had an intertwined joke that would later be repeated at lunchtime around town, at PTA meetings, or in the grocery stores. Word of mouth advertising. Then there was the popular highlighting of individuals or families as part of the sermon, a strategy that everyone in the church anxiously awaited.

On the business side of the equation, Lincoln had hired an office manager responsible for handling church expenses, negotiating sponsors and other means of fund raising. The Church of Hope was run like a business enterprise, with amazing bottom-line success. The church itself had been built at twenty percent of cost, furnished almost for nothing and the amount of donated material for church enterprises was staggering. Potential sponsors lined up at the door, anxious to have their advertisements in the weekly church program and on one of the coveted thirty second spots on the locally televised Sunday afternoon sermons and the subsequent replays during the week.

But Lincoln's proudest achievements lay in what the church did with all that money. They had built and staffed three homeless shelters in town, ten low-cost day care centers, two drug rehab facilities, established college scholarships, and made hefty donations to a host of local charities. Lincoln's favorite initiative was the "Help Your Neighbor" club, where volunteers performed tasks such as babysitting, home and auto repair, tutoring, transportation assistance, and a variety of other chores aimed at helping one another. Lincoln was the face of these church activities, donning an apron to serve meals in the homeless shelters, reading to children in the day care centers, appearing all over town for the "Help Your Neighbor" program, clad in overalls and wearing his trusty tool belt. No task was too trivial or too large to tackle. Lincoln smiled as he recalled the hugs and kisses from all those he and his church had helped. His father would have been proud, and astounded.

###

17

Their dinner dishes had just been cleared away and the housekeeper was busy cleaning up in the kitchen. Outside their dining room window the lush lawn stretched towards the sunset, low on the distant horizon. Rocky took a sip of his wine and cleared his throat. "I had a very interesting talk with an old college friend today."

"Oh?" Robin said, anxious for any conversation that would fill in the void of her day here at home.

"Lincoln Archer. You remember? The preacher up in Wichita. He was at our wedding."

Robin picked up her own glass of wine, vaguely recalling the man. Her memories of the wedding day had been about Zeke. "Yes, how is he doing?" she asked, taking a healthy sip of her Riesling.

Rocky chuckled. "Pretty damned well. He gave me a million dollars to invest for his church."

"I had no idea religion was so profitable," Robin said.

"That's exactly what I said, but he told me all about how he runs his church like a company; cost controls, marketing, a focus on profit."

"Doesn't sound like any church I know," Robin added, Zeke still crowding her thoughts.

"He fed me a lot of mumbo jumbo about love and kindness and taking care of your neighbor."

"That sounds like how your father used to run the bank," Robin said, unable to resist the jab.

Rocky frowned. "Well, that might have been in the old days and explains why the bank never got any bigger than the mom-n-pop operation dad ran."

"I'd say he did alright by you."

Rocky shook his head. "I've turned the bank into a big time operation, Robin, and I had to fight father every step of the way. When it became obvious I knew what I was doing it got to be too much for him. That's why he retired."

She had always liked the old man, wished Rocky was more like him. "I think R.C. retired because he thought the world had passed him by. That's hard for anyone to admit, you know?"

"Well, the world *had* passed him by. He refused to adopt any of my new methods. I had to battle him to get any changes at all. It was exhausting," he added, draining his glass of wine.

"Well, he's pretty miserable now. Your mom says he just sits around the house all day. Maybe you should go see him, give him some sort of position at the bank, you know, a senior consultant or something like that?" Indeed, Mrs. Wellington had spoken to Robin on more than one occasion, pleading for her to talk to Rocky about some sort of role for her husband. Robin had tried, but Rocky had always stiff-armed the idea.

"There's nothing the old man can contribute to the way we run the bank today," Rocky reiterated. "He doesn't understand international finance, new government regulations or how to play Wall Street."

"So, maybe you could teach him like he taught you," Robin offered, trying a different tack.

Rocky shook his head. "He's too stubborn and I don't have the time." He reached for the decanter in the middle of the table, thought better of another drink, and put it back. "By the way, I'm going to New York next week. Would you like to come along?"

The suggestion caught Robin by surprise. She was never invited on any of his business trips.

"You'd be pretty much on your own. I've got a series of meetings in Manhattan, but I'm sure you could find a few stores near the hotel to keep your interest."

Robin's mind raced through the possibilities. It had been months since her last "shopping trip" and she really needed to see Zeke again. "Sure," she agreed. "I could use a break from this place."

"Fine," Rocky said, pushing his chair back. "We leave from Wichita next Wednesday. Pack for a long weekend. Now," he said, wiping his mouth with his napkin, "I need to get back to the bank for a meeting. I'll be late." He bent and kissed her on the top of the head. "Don't wait up."

Robin sat at the empty table listening to Rocky's BMW whir away down the driveway and towards town. These late night meetings at the bank had become more frequent and she suspected some sort of big business deal was in the works. Her mind shifted to the trip to New York and Zeke. She'd have to be more discrete than usual but the thought of lying in his arms again caused her heart to race. She closed her eyes and smiled.

* * *

Rocky turned the BMW onto the dirt road and drove slowly towards the farmhouse nearly half a mile in the distance. The lamp in the living room window was on which meant the coast was clear. He pulled his car up to the back of the house and let himself in through the screen door that led into the kitchen. The floor creaked as he moved past the refrigerator and into the adjacent living room. The lamp that served as his green light shone in the far window. He turned and walked down the hallway that led to the bedroom.

He could hear the soft music through the half open door and he pushed it open to see Beverly Hawkins lying in bed reading a magazine. She was naked, her long blonde hair cascading down over her breasts. Her slim body reflected the evidence of her workout routine; a flat stomach, toned arms, long, sinewy legs. She put the magazine down and turned on her side to face him.

"Bring that thing over here," she said in her throaty voice, motioning towards Rocky. Her eyes were more specific in her request, zeroing in on the front of his pants.

He smiled and moved to the side of the bed. God he loved the way she took charge, made him feel like the king of the world. In many ways he was, of course, but this woman had a way of taking him to another level. He started unbuttoning his shirt, felt the gentle tug on his zipper, then the unfastening of his belt.

"Ooh," Beverly said. "He's ready to play already." She slid to the side of the bed, swung her long legs around on either side of him and pulled him towards her.

Rocky closed his eyes and tilted his head back in pleasure. He moaned, his pulse racing. He reached forward and pushed her back onto the bed. She giggled as he excitedly pushed his pants and underwear down his legs and lunged forward. She smiled up at him. "I've missed you and your friend," she said.

"We're going to make up for that tonight, babe," he said, tossing his shirt behind him onto the floor.

"Why don't you take off your shoes?" she asked, "or is this going to be another wham, bang, thank you ma'am night?"

He paused and slid back off of her, stood up and awkwardly pulled off his shoes and socks, then his pants. "You're gonna have to beg me to stop tonight," he exclaimed.

She took him in both hands and guided him into his familiar position. "Oh, Rocky," she moaned. "Please stop," she joked, pulling his face down to her own.

Rocky felt that uncontrollable surge of energy and excitement that always accompanied his visits here. She moved beneath him, slowly building his pleasure. He had had many women, of course, but Beverly was special. She was married to a local dolt, a fertilizer salesman who was on the road five nights a week and the woman was, to say the least, unfulfilled. They had met at some inane party at the country club and he had been attracted to her immediately. Funny, smart, absolutely glamorous by Walnut Grove standards, she had invited him out to inspect their house for possible refinancing. She had seduced him that night and their arrangement had continued for several years now.

Rocky kept coming back because she was absolutely fantastic in bed and knew how to treat a man like himself. There was no senseless small talk and, most importantly, there were no strings. Like him, Beverly wanted only a good roll in the sack. He would partake of her incredible wares, shower, dress and head home. No lingering, no cooing or spooning, no talk of where this might lead. The perfect arrangement.

But tonight would be different. After a particularly rigorous session Rocky showered, dressed and sat down on the edge of the bed. "We're moving to New York," he said matter-of-factly.

Beverly sat up, alarm in her voice. "What?"

"I'm selling the bank to a Wall Street firm and part of the deal is that I'll be an executive vice president up there. We'll be finalizing the deal next week and we'll probably move within a month."

Beverly sat staring at him. "But, what about us?"

He looked annoyed. "Bev', there never has been an us. You know that. We've enjoyed the sex, but that's it."

"That's it?" she said, her voice rising in anger. "That's it? What the hell am I supposed to do in this one horse town with my moronic husband? You can't just leave me here. I'll go bat shit, Rocky."

"Look," he said, reaching out and putting a hand on her shoulder. "I'll send you some money and----"

"Money?" she said, pushing his arm away. "I'm not a goddamned whore. What good would money do me anyway? You trying to buy my silence, is that it? Afraid I'll ruin your damned career?"

Rocky shook his head. "I'm not trying to do anything, Bev'. This is one of those once in a lifetime opportunities and I just can't turn it down. It has nothing to do with you."

She sat back on the bed, a frown on her face. She lowered her head. "Please leave," she said in a whisper.

"Aw, Bev', don't be mad," he offered.

She waved a hand towards the bedroom door. "Dammit, go," she said.

He stood up and looked back at her. The beauty of her naked body aroused him again. "You want to do it again for old time's sake, babe?" He reached for his zipper.

She looked up at him, anger in her eyes. "Get the hell out of here, you creep. Get out!'"

Rocky shrugged, turned and left the room.

Beverly sat on the bed and listened as the muffled roar of the BMW moved slowly down the long driveway, back to his house on the hill, and out of her life. Her anger continued to boil, hot tears sliding down her cheeks. The bastard wouldn't get away with this, she thought. Nobody walks out on Beverly Hawkins. Nobody.

# # #

18

Robin's hands gripped Zeke's bare shoulders, pulling him slowly back and forth in rhythm with her movements. Then she stopped, holding her breath in anticipation, and her fingers tightened their grip. He sensed she was close and he slowed his efforts and braced himself. Her whole body tensed and she let out a primordial scream, then began laughing uncontrollably. "Oh, my god, my god," she moaned.

He raised his head, his smile a celebration of her pleasure, of being able to satisfy her so completely, so intensely. She gently nudged his shoulders and face away from her, gasping for air and collapsing back into her stack of pillows.

They had spent all afternoon in his Greenwich Village apartment, making love as the rainstorm outside pelted the windows with a sensual rhythm that matched their own.

"My, god," she said in a whisper, pulling him down beside her. "I may never walk again."

He laughed. "You won't need to for a while," he said, stroking her cheek as the rain continued its sensual dance against the windows.

They lay quietly in one another's arms until their breathing returned to normal. "We need to talk," she said softly.

He pulled her closer, kissed her on the forehead. "About what?"

"We're moving to New York," she said matter-of-factly.

He tried unsuccessfully to sit up, but she was holding on to him tightly, as if afraid he would blow away with the swirling wind outside.

"Really? Here to the city?" he managed, straining to look her in the eye in the fading light.

"Well, I'm not sure where we'll live just yet, but Rocky has sold the bank to a Wall Street firm and he'll be an executive vice-president of some sort." She sighed. "Anyway, it's a big deal for him."

Zeke blinked at the unexpected news, his mind racing. "So now we can see each other any time we want," he said excitedly.

She shook her head, stroked the hair on his chest. "With Rocky being here in New York, we'll really need to be even more discrete."

"It's a big city, Robin. We can be together as often as we want."

She put a finger to his lips. "Let's not talk about this anymore right now. Let's just enjoy each other, O.K.?" She kissed his neck and started working her way down his chest. Outside, the rain came down harder and a flash of lightening lit the room for a fleeting moment. Robin pulled him closer, her cheek on his stomach, eyes wide as she contemplated the new life that awaited her.

* * *

"So, what may I do for you today?" Lincoln Archer asked the two men. They were sitting in Lincoln's office in the Church of Hope building in Wichita.

"Well," the man with the thick glasses started, "as we said over the phone, uh, Reverend, we're with World News, the media conglomerate."

"Actually," the other man said, "we're with the cable segment of our corporation as distinguished from the press side with which you may also be familiar."

"Yes," Lincoln said. "Do you know my friend, Zeke Porter? He works for your company."

"Of course," the man with the glasses said.

"Everybody knows Zeke," the other man added.

Lincoln nodded and smiled. He had talked with Zeke earlier in the week, had been alerted to today's visit and purpose.

The two men looked at one another. The man with the glasses cleared his throat and said, "We'd like to talk with you about syndicating your sermons."

Lincoln wrinkled his face as if confused. "What does that mean?"

"We've done a fair amount of research on your church, particularly the local television broadcasts and they're quite popular."

"We've had a good following," Lincoln agreed.

"Well, our research shows that your sermons would be just as popular across a wider audience, Reverend. We'd like to start regionally at first, but we think your messages have a nationwide appeal."

"And exactly why do you think that?" Lincoln asked.

The second man leaned forward in emphasis. "Your sermons are down to earth, Reverend. No fancy vocabulary, no attempt to be cute or trendy. Messages that people can take back home and practice all week. That sort of thing."

"I see."

"So, here's what we're thinking, Reverend. We'd like to syndicate your feature Sunday sermon, the one o'clock session live, then replay it several times later in the week. We have affiliates throughout the Midwest and your message would reach literally millions of people."

"That sounds attractive."

"Well, with syndication it would not only spread your message but would substantially add to the church's revenues."

Lincoln smiled. "Can you be more specific?"

The man with the glasses glanced at his colleague, then said, "Well, we're talking a one year contract, six figures with twenty percent of sponsor revenue."

The other man nodded and grinned, as if this was one of those offers 'you could not refuse.'

Lincoln studied the two men. "I'd have to give this some thought, gentlemen." He stood up.

"Actually," the second man said, "we're on a tight deadline here, Reverend. We'd like to strike a deal today and begin the telecasts next week."

"We already have scores of sponsors lined up just waiting for the agreement," the first man added.

Lincoln sat back down and studied his two guests like they were playing high stakes poker. In reality, they were. "Alright," Lincoln started. "I'd need a three year contract, seven figures and fifty percent of the sponsor revenues. I'd want complete freedom regarding the subject and content of my sermons, copyright and exclusive franchise rights including videos, books and magazines with sole authority regarding interviews, news stories and any other form of advertisements. Oh, and I'd want first right of refusal on the sponsors. It's very important that our viewers are not subjected to some of the ridiculous products that flood our airways today."

The two men forced a chuckle, the one with the glasses shaking his head. "Those are pretty stringent terms, Reverend," he said. "I'm not certain we're authorized to negotiate something so encompassing."

Lincoln stood again. "I'd suggest you get the authority, gentlemen. I'm not trying to be unreasonable, but I've got my church and its reputation to protect. I'm sure you understand my need for terms that are favorable to our cause?"

The two men stood. "We'd ask that you give us twenty-four hours to run this up our chain of command," the first man said.

"I understand how corporations work," Lincoln said with a smile.

"Uh," the second man said, "you don't mind me asking if you're in discussions with any other media company, do you, Reverend?"

"No, I don't mind you asking at all," Lincoln replied with a handshake. "Now, you boys be sure and get back to me by tomorrow, you hear?"

* * *

"This is quite a place," Zeke said, gesturing towards the ocean with his drink.

Robin stood beside him, nursing her glass of wine. They were on the veranda of the Wellington's new home on the western end of Long Island. "Well, it's sure not Walnut Grove," she said with a smile.

"You getting used to being the small fish in a big pond?" he asked.

She laughed. "It doesn't much matter how big or small you are if the pond is empty," she said. "I see less of Rocky now than I did back home. He's got a place in the city and he stays there during the week and he travels a lot more with this new job," she said, her face conveying resignation.

They moved from the veranda down to the swimming pool area. Zeke sensed a mood of unrest that he hadn't seen since their affair began. "So, what about the neighborhood wives or the wives of Rocky's Wall Street colleagues? Made any friends there yet?"

Robin frowned and shook her head. "A couple, but many of them are pretty snooty; they come from old money and went to some Ivy League college. I'm just a country girl from a place these women fly over on their way to Beverly Hills or Hawaii."

"I bet," he said, "when you get to know them, you ladies have a lot more in common than you realize."

She scoffed. "Like what?"

He waved his glass at the lush surroundings. "Well, this neighborhood isn't exactly ghetto living and I'm sure their husbands are away as much as Rocky. And," he said, staring at her, "I bet more than a few of them have lovers on the side."

Robin's eyes widened and she looked around in alarm. They were alone by the swimming pool. "The walls have ears, Zeke," she said under her breath. "Besides," she added, "I'm not really close enough with any of them to have broached that subject yet."

"Is it too soon to broach the subject with me?" he asked. They had not been with each other since the Wellington's move to New York.

She smiled. "Zeke, let me get settled into my new digs first. Being the wife of a Wall Street big shot comes with a lot of commitments and social obligations. I'm just now getting used to my new life. Anyway, you're not exactly in town all the time either."

"When you're an investigative reporter you never know where you're going to be next," he explained. "I enjoy the travelling, but now that you're here I want to stay close to home."

Robin's lower lip turned down, her patented pout. "Aw, aren't you sweet?" She reached out and took his hand.

"Hey, what the hell is going on out here?" came the deep voice from behind them. They turned to see Rocky headed across the patio towards them under a full head of steam. "I leave you two alone for five minutes and you're out here holding hands," he said, anger in his voice and expression, then he broke into a wide smile and jabbed Zeke playfully on the shoulder.

"I was just congratulating Robin on your new digs," Zeke said. "This is quite a place."

"Yeah, it's something isn't it?" Rocky said, waving his hand to encompass the property that led out to the Atlantic.

"Pretty fancy for a hick banker from Kansas," Zeke said. "Congratulations, Rock, you've really come a long way, lovely wife, lovely home."

"Don't forget my new job," Rocky said.

"Oh, of course. What are you now, an executive vice president?"

Rocky shrugged. "Not even sure of my title, but they don't pay me to hand out business cards."

"What do they pay you for?" Zeke asked.

Rocky slung an arm around Zeke's shoulders. "You planning on doing another expose of Wall Street are you?"

"You got anything that might make juicy news?" Zeke countered.

Rocky lowered his arm and his voice. "I know plenty, old buddy, but if I told you all my secrets I wouldn't have a job, you know?" He laughed and punched Zeke on the shoulder again. "Well," he said, looking back towards the house, "I need to get inside and press some flesh. You two can get back to holding hands," he added with his customary wink. "See you later."

They both watched as Rocky strode back into the house and into the throng, laughing and glad-handing. "Do you think he knows?" Zeke asked for the millionth time.

"About us? No, of course not. He would never suspect his best friend."

"I didn't know I qualified as best friend," Zeke said.

"Well, Rocky says it's all pretty cutthroat on Wall Street, so he doesn't exactly bond with those guys," she said, gesturing towards the party in the house. "Old friends are trusted friends, you know?"

Zeke felt a flash of familiar guilt, but his desire to be with her was the dominant emotion. They stood looking at the magnificent view for the longest time, the sun slowly sinking over the Manhattan skyline with a last gasp of orange light. "I'd like to take you somewhere far away," Zeke said. "For a couple of weeks, a month, just you and me."

She turned and looked at him. "Zeke," she said, sounding like a mother trying to lecture her little boy. "You know that's just not possible." Her lip turned down again, accompanied by a sigh. "There's just too much going on in both our lives to think about something like that right now. We might have to cool things for a while until I get my feet on the ground here, O.K.?"

Zeke knew he was treading on thin ice here but he was tired of the cat-and-mouse game that having an affair demanded. He had always pictured an old fashioned scenario of courting, engagement and a church wedding with the first woman he ever loved, not the stress, stolen moments and inability to foresee a future together that their current arrangement dictated. Besides, Zeke knew that he could never provide her with all this luxury and social status and he sensed that, despite her protestations, Robin was beginning to warm to the elite life that came along with being married to Rocky.

Robin turned and extended a hand to Zeke. "Come on, let's go inside and I'll introduce you to the cream of Wall Street. I'm sure there's a story there somewhere for you."

Her hand was warm and soft and Zeke forced a smile. "I'm sure you're right," he said and they started up the steps towards the house together.

# # #

19

Lincoln stood behind the podium, a smile on his face. In front of him sat his congregation, faces uplifted, their own smiles matching his. They were in the spacious Church of Hope building on the western outskirts of Wichita. To Lincoln's left the television camera recorded his every move and word, his message now broadcast on a nationwide basis with a viewing audience in the millions.

His rise to celebrity status had been rapid. It was not all that long ago that he had stood watching his father give sermons in the old circus tent they had rented just a few miles to the west, then the converted bowling alley where he had begun sharing preaching duties with Billy Archer until the Reverend had passed away.

Lincoln had "found" himself in the art of preaching. His messages were simple and straightforward and the feeling of confidence and excitement they brought to his audiences bolstered his ego. He had become an inspiration, a leader whose popularity had been meteoric. And, as his personal fame grew, so did the coffers of the church. Donations poured in from all over the country, often accompanied by a letter and picture. Lincoln used these often intimate pleas as a way to "personalize" his sermons, speaking directly to these people by name on television, much as he had first started selecting individuals in his "live" audience to include in his messages of hope.

One of the facts Lincoln had learned from his nationwide exposure was that the stress of providing for a family where both parents often worked multiple low income jobs was not just unique to the Wichita area, or the Midwest, but was a problem that permeated every corner of the country. Lincoln also learned that poverty was not necessarily caused by a sudden economic downturn, or a company going out of business or trimming costs. Poverty was systemic and provided no easy path to break its vicious cycle. The poor and increasing numbers of the middle class couldn't afford proper health care, couldn't save for the future, couldn't send their children to college, couldn't own a home. Their inability to pursue "the American dream" through dedication and hard work left their children facing the same obstacles. Most struggled just to survive from paycheck to paycheck.

But the biggest revelation for Lincoln was that, despite these appalling circumstances, the government and corporate America didn't seem to care. Laws kept getting passed that rewarded the wealthy and penalized the poor. Corporations retained their enormous profits for shareholders and executive bonuses rather than increasing wages for their workers. It was a shameless example of greed and disregard for the plight of the masses. People were desperate and often turned to Lincoln's homey, down-to-earth sermons as sources of inspiration, calm and hope.

Lincoln didn't spew meaningless promises like most politicians, didn't obscure the issues through economic doubletalk like many CEOs and financial analysts, didn't invoke a deity or scripture to mask problems with false hope or fear. Common sense, practical, candid assessments and solutions, plain talk that made him seem like a lifelong friend. And that was what he had become to millions; their trusted friend.

On cue, the television camera zoomed in on his face, his smile widening. "I want to speak to Sally from Atlanta, Georgia now," he started. "Sally has shared with me her pain and anguish in trying to raise three little girls as a single mother and how it has slowly drained her heart of hope and promise." His face morphed into an expression as serious as his subject and he began his explanation of how the Church of Hope and its message could help Sally.

* * *

The conference room was situated on the top floor of the Morton building, amidst the other gray towers of Wall Street. To the right, the East River glimmered in the early morning sun, the Brooklyn shoreline casting long shadows across the water. Gazing uptown, Rocky could just glimpse the spire of the Empire State Building. To his left, the waters of the Hudson River flowed into New York Harbor at the southern tip of Manhattan. He smiled and turned his attention back to the dozen men seated around the long conference table. This was the quarterly meeting of the Executive Committee, the presidents of the seven major divisions that constituted the hierarchy that was Morton and Cummings.

The man at the head of the table, resplendent in a gray suit and purple paisley tie, turned to Rocky. "Rocky, why don't you update the committee on your division's activities?"

Rocky Wellington nodded, picked up the remote controller and clicked the first slide of his presentation onto the screen at the end of the room. "As you all know I've been exploring international investments with a focus on technology. My primary area of interest has been the Japanese automotive industry. Japan has long centered its sales on domestic consumption, but has most recently begun exporting on a global scale. They have proven to be highly competitive due to their use of technology such as robotic assembly lines and fuel efficient engines that far surpass those produced here in the United States."

"Not to mention their advantage in labor costs," the distinguished gray haired man to Rocky's right said.

"Yes, but in two ways," Rocky explained, clicking to the next slide. "With the use of robotics they require less labor and they assemble in teams that move with each car rather than the stationary approach Detroit has used for years."

"And they don't have a union to deal with," a man at the far end of the table added.

"That's not as much a factor as the government subsidies that help keep their overall costs down," Rocky replied.

"That will never happen here," another director quipped and there was laughter of agreement around the table.

"So why hasn't Detroit taken advantage of these technologies?" another director asked.

"It's like trying to turn an ocean liner around on a dime," Rocky explained. "Detroit will need a complete retooling of its material and assembly process to begin producing fuel efficient cars. The culture there still believes that the American consumer wants big, bulky gas guzzlers."

"So Japan has leapfrogged Detroit and is ahead of the consumption curve?" another director asked.

Rocky nodded. "They have made significant inroads here and will continue to hold market share for as long as Detroit remains stubborn and keeps its head in the sand." He went on. "Our investments in Honda, Toyota, Mitsubishi, and other Japanese automobile companies have outdone the performance of domestic companies ten to one." The group stared at the screen which showed the comparisons. Everyone smiled.

"We're the only firm on Wall Street to have seen this development emerging and Rocky has spearheaded our investment and growth here quite successfully," the chairman said with a grin.

"Here, here," another director interjected, followed by similar words of praise from others around the table.

"But there's more," the chairman said, turning to Rocky.

"Yes, sir," Rocky said with a smile. He pressed the red button on the controller. "With the rise in crude oil prices around the world we've exploited the massive increase in spending from the OPEC nations, specifically Saudi Arabia and its burgeoning interest in computer technology."

"I hear they're trying to automate everything," a director added.

"Absolutely," Rocky said, "and we're zeroing in on the computer services companies who are winning their major contracts. There are a number of domestic firms, but quite a lot from the U.K., Germany, India and France. Most aren't as well known as the American companies, but they have a long-standing presence in Saudi," Rocky explained. "They know the culture and have relationships with the royal family which is critical, but also a keen understanding of the local procurement policies."

"Bribery," a director interjected and the group chuckled.

Rocky unbuttoned his suit coat and continued. "Yes, it's a less subtle form of marketing, but it's absolutely mandatory to do business in the country. It takes years to build these relationships and newcomers face formidable opposition to enter the inner circle. That's why we've invested in companies with long established credentials and ties to the Saudi decision makers." He gestured towards the screen. "The companies we have invested in have established a foundation of contracts that will help restructure the entire Saudi economy and these contracts are all multi-year with non-competitive extensions guaranteed with customer satisfaction."

"With the profits we will see from our investments here," the chairman said, "our revenue flow will increase significantly and with the positive impact that will have on our balance sheet, our stock price will increase dramatically."

"That means more capital to work with and," the director next to Rocky said, "bigger bonuses for all of us."

"Here, here," came the chorus with all smiles aimed at their rising star. Rocky beamed and nodded his acceptance of their praise. His boyhood dream of wheeling and dealing on Wall Street had come to fruition. He had finally escaped the minor leagues and become a rising star in "the show." A long way from arguing with his father and the small minds at the bank in Walnut Grove, Rocky considered. But he was only getting started.

# # #

20

Being an investigative reporter responsible for producing a weekly column turned out to be more demanding than Zeke had ever imagined. Unlike his days of leisurely putting together a monthly story for the college newspaper, here in the Big Apple he was inundated with rumors, gossip and other leads that required endless fact-checking, interviews, verifying multiple sources, and pulling in all relevant information that gave depth and color to the story. The toughest part of the job was often paring down this mountain of data and selecting the two or three leads he had the time and interest to pursue. Every week. It was daunting, but incredibly exciting and challenging.

He quickly built a reputation as an avid listener, an indefatigable researcher, and, much like a scientist, he followed the evidence and the facts to the truth of the story. His column was entitled "The Truth, No Matter Where It Leads." His reporting was never mean spirited, he could be trusted with "off the record" commentary, and he presented every viewpoint on any subject. Throw in a dry sense of humor, a keen appreciation for history and local color and the result became a growing readership anxiously awaiting his column every Friday. He was popular, well paid, and couldn't wait to get up in the morning and see where life would take him. The stuff of dreams.

Zeke formed a network of contacts, informants, and other sources of leads that sent him off in a hundred different directions, into every aspect of life in New York. He found himself at high society cocktail parties, mingling with the city's movers-and-shakers, while also interviewing the homeless in soup kitchens and shelters. City Hall, Yankee Stadium, Wall Street, a Harlem nightclub; every place where interesting people gathered to celebrate, demonstrate, and provide the basis for a story. A story that would be read vociferously by the demanding New Yorker who wanted to be informed, entertained, shocked and moved. Every week.

Zeke's typical day began before sunrise so that he could mingle with stevedores on the docks, subway riders, early birds at Rockefeller Center, people on the move towards a thousand different destinations at Grand Central Station. Today had been another such day with time spent talking with doormen, joggers and dog walkers around Central Park, attending a union meeting of sanitation workers in Brooklyn, a jaunt into the Bronx to interview a legendary jazz musician whom everyone believed had died a decade ago, and several hours traversing the halls of Gracie Mansion in search of political tidbits.

When he finally arrived at his Greenwich Village apartment late this warm summer night he realized he had missed dinner, so he set about making a sub' from the meatball leftovers from Vito's last night. The knock on the door surprised him. He looked at his watch, wondered who in the world this could be? When he opened the door the young woman threw herself into his arms.

"I got the part!" Andrea Jackson shrieked. "I got the part!" She squeezed him around the neck, then kissed him full on the mouth. "All because of you," she added with a broad smile.

"That's wonderful," Zeke said, slowly undoing her arm lock around his neck. "Come on in and tell me all about it." He was aware of the lingering aroma from her perfume.

Andrea could barely contain herself as she removed her purple scarf and winter coat. Zeke took them both and hung them on his coat rack near the front door. "It's great to see you again." he said, motioning towards his living room.

"It's great to see you too," Andrea said. The apartment was filled with the pleasing odor of tomato sauce from the meatball sandwich. "Oh, I've interrupted your dinner," she said. "I'm so sorry."

"No, no," Zeke said, "I was just throwing together a snack. Why don't you join me?"

"Thanks. I'm not particularly hungry, but I could sure use a drink."

Zeke smiled. "I'll find us a bottle of wine. Now, sit down and relax," he said, motioning towards the overstuffed couch that was the central piece of furniture in his living room. He went to the kitchen, cut the sub' into two pieces and carried both on plates into the living room. "Here," he said, "half is yours. I'll go get the wine." He paused and looked at her. "Red or white?"

"Yes," she gushed.

* * *

Despite her disclaimer of not being hungry, Andrea managed to wolf down her half of the sub' in between an excited description of her recent success. "When you brought Tyler Jones to the club to hear me sing I never thought I'd ever hear from him," she said, accepting her second glass of wine.

"But two days later I got a call for an audition for his newest musical. I was scared to death. Turns out there were about a dozen of us and the few I heard while waiting were really good."

"You were obviously better," Zeke said.

Andrea smiled and shook her head, still amazed at her good fortune. "I guess. Anyway, the very next day I got a call back and I figured, wow, I made the first cut, you know? But when I showed up at the theatre I was the only one there; I was shown into Tyler's private office."

Noting his upraised eyebrows at the comment, she reached out and took his arm. "No, I didn't have to try out on his couch if that's what you're thinking."

Zeke shrugged. "Well, it did cross my mind. I thought that was how things worked in show business."

Andrea laughed. "Zeke, honey, just about every director I know on Broadway is gay, so no, I got the part with no strings attached." She laughed again and drained her glass of wine.

"I'm sorry, I guess Broadway is one area of the city I don't know much about. I didn't mean to insult you."

She slapped him playfully on the shoulder. "Well, the boys who try out might have a different path, you know?" She let out a hearty laugh, but then her expression turned serious. "Anyway, he offered me the chance to play Julia, who is the female lead. It was a terrific break; you rarely see an unknown given that sort of opportunity."

"You must have really impressed him."

"Well, I made it through rehearsals, then we took the show to Connecticut and it got great reviews. Anyway, we're opening next month, so I just had to thank you for getting Tyler to come hear me at the club. Without that break I'd still be tending bar."

Zeke refilled her wine glass. "I met Tyler at an art exhibit here in the Village and he told me all about his new musical and how he was looking for a new talent. When you appeared out of nowhere that night at the club I thought, wow, there might be a fit here."

Andrea smiled and drank her wine, more slowly now. "I've wanted to thank you since I first got the part, but I waited until it was all final. Then I realized I didn't know where you lived."

"Well, I used to be in a rat hole over on Staten Island until I got my job with World News, but how did you find me?"

Andrea winked at him. "You're not the only person who knows how to dig for information, you know? I've got a few contacts too. Anyway, I read your column every week. You're so funny and I've learned so much about New York City and its people. Is this all you were hoping for when you left K-State?"

Zeke nodded. "It's a lot harder than I thought it would be, but like you, I was amazed at how quickly it all suddenly happened. I was lucky enough to get a contact at World News and well, she took a chance and gave me the break I needed."

"Just like me," Andrea added.

"Funny how that works, isn't it?"

Andrea got up and walked slowly to the bank of windows on the far side of the living area. "We've come a long way since that night in the pond back in Kansas, haven't we?"

Zeke studied her shapely silhouette framed by the window, recalled how magnificent she had looked that night in the Holiday Inn restaurant in her tight purple sweater and form fitting jeans. He stood up and joined her by the window. In the distance the top of the Empire State Building was bathed in bright lights. "Sometimes it does seem like only yesterday I was drinking beers with you at Jack's," he said.

She turned and looked up at him. "There's going to be a cast party after opening night next month. At a place called Vito's."

"Vito's? On fifty-third street? I used to work there as a bus boy."

"Really? Well, I don't have a date and I was wondering, well, would you like to go with me? I mean, I think there's lots of interesting stories about the folks on Broadway, and you said you don't know much about that scene."

He smiled. "Andy, of course I'd be honored to accompany Broadway's newest star to the party, but surely there's some guy you know in the cast that—"

She shook her head. "You and I would be the only people there from Kansas; it would make me feel great to share my good fortune with someone from back home, particularly the guy who saved my life."

He lifted his drink towards her. "It's official then, the two hicks from Kansas will take Broadway by storm. Just don't ask me to sing."

She bobbed up and down, her magnificent smile filling the room. "You know," she said, "I've probably had too much to drink, but ever since I've been here I kept wishing that somehow, some way, you and I would cross paths."

He smiled at the coincidence of two friends from Kansas actually meeting here in the city of millions. "It is amazing that we ran across one another isn't it?"

She raised her glass of wine to him. "Babe, it's gotta be karma."

# # #

21

Back in the Gilded Age of the late eighteen hundreds, rumors persisted concerning a secret organization, composed of the leading industrialists of the time: Rockefeller, J.P. Morgan, Carnegie and others, whose purported goal was to use their money and influence to dictate the economic, political and social destiny of our country.

Whether this secret cabal, known as The Ten, actually existed or was able to exercise such profound influence remains a matter of conjecture, but the concept continued to be fodder for storytellers and conspiracy theorists alike.

In its current manifestation, The Ten involved a secret fraternity of Congressional and business leaders who shared common goals, interests and ambitions not unlike those of their illustrious Gilded Age counterparts. Simply put, The Ten remained wedded to the god of the free market and rejected any forces of government, labor or social movements that unnecessarily gummed up the machinery of capitalism.

Under the leadership of the senior senator from Ohio, a man with the unlikely name of Sam Adams, The Ten had taken steps to realize the implementation of their dream. Their membership included those in key positions of power; in the Congress, the courts, the intelligence and defense communities, Wall Street, and, of course, the corporate world. The missing piece in their intricate puzzle was someone who could serve as the visible embodiment of their secret dream, someone who could be manipulated and controlled, yet appear to be his own man to the general public. What they sought was a President of the United States.

Unlike many of the situations they could influence, electing a president required the involvement of the general public; the fickle, ignorant, unsophisticated masses. To be successful, their candidate had to appeal to these people, be viewed as "on their side." With such a man in the White House, The Ten could enjoy nearly a decade of coordinated control over the country, more than enough time to imbed their dream into legislation, laws and the shallow minds of the electorate.

With all the other pieces now in place it was time to select their candidate.

* * *

The huge conference room seemed empty with only four men sitting around the table that normally seated the twenty members of the Board of Directors. To Rocky's right sat Roger Smook, the President and CEO of Morton and Cummings, and a charter member of The Ten. To his left sat the Chairman of the Board, R. Winston Johnson, and directly across from Rocky sat Lester Filmore, the company's Washington liaison. At the far end of the room the remnants of the buffet breakfast were being whisked away by the wait staff.

Smook waited until the last of the waiters had left the room before he spoke. "I appreciate you all coming in on a Saturday," he said. "Unfortunately, getting our respective schedules to coincide forced today as the only time to get together."

The three other men nodded. Saturday morning meetings were indeed unusual, what with the long hours of the standard work week demanding recovery and relaxation over the weekends.

Smook turned to the dapper man across the table. "I've asked Lester to fly in from Washington and give us a report on recent developments in gridlock city."

Everyone chuckled at the reference. Politics in Washington had indeed turned into the most non-productive period in history, anything forwarded by the administration immediately tabled by the opposition and vice-versa. There was no common ground, compromise was not in their vocabularies, and national problems continued to mount with no resolution in sight.

Filmore grimaced and pushed his empty cup and saucer away from him, as if he needed more arm room to speak. He had a deep, rich baritone voice that was soothing, yet commanding, speaking in a slow, measured manner reminiscent of an old southern gentleman. "This is not for public consumption just yet," he started, pausing for effect, "but Darren Lockwood plans to announce his retirement this month. He won't be running again next fall."

Lockwood was the senior senator from New York and Chairman of the powerful Senate Finance Committee.

"We all know how well Darren has represented our interests and how successfully he's fought the oversight zealots," Filmore intoned, his eyes moving between his three colleagues.

"His votes have allowed us the latitude we need to pursue our interests without SEC or White House interference," Smook added.

"It's more critical than that," Filmore said with a frown, not keen on being interrupted. "Congress is filled with dolts who don't even know how to balance their own checkbooks, let alone understand the inner workings of free market capitalism. Their votes on many matters are clouded by ignorance, political ideology and downright stupidity. Darren served as a schoolmaster for many of these morons, patiently explaining the pros and cons of various monetary and international finance policies. His influence was profound regarding our interests and his absence will be a huge blow to common sense in Washington."

"Which brings us to the subject of our meeting here today," Smook said. "We need to identify someone we can back for Darren's seat. Someone who understands what's important to those of us on Wall Street; who can represent those interests as well as Darren has over the years."

R. Winston Johnson chimed in, "Lester, describe what we'd be looking for in a candidate."

Lester nodded. "First we need someone who's well known here on the Street, someone with a reputation for financial awareness, someone the Street and our supporters can back fully."

"That narrows the field," Smook interjected.

Lester went on, again annoyed at being interrupted. "We need someone younger, there are far too many gray hairs in D.C. so youth will be an important criteria. We also need someone who's fit and handsome, being a good looking guy will enhance his candidacy in this age of celebrity."

"And having an attractive wife will be important too," Smook added.

"Yes, a young, sexy spouse is a major plus in D.C., someone who can get those old codgers to wet themselves,"

Filmore agreed. "Finally, we need someone who can claim to have represented the small guy on Main Street. That will be important to the upstate vote with lots of farmers and small business owners there."

Smook turned to Rocky. "You know anybody that fits that profile, Rock?"

* * *

"They want you to do what?" Robin asked. They were sitting on the patio of their Long Island home, overlooking the Atlantic.

"Run for the U.S. Senate," Rocky said, picking up his tumbler of bourbon.

"But you've never been interested in politics."

"I know, but they've made it sound intriguing. I can make a difference in Washington, educate those clods on what sort of legislation will help the economy."

"But what about your position at the firm?"

Rocky nodded. "If I'm unsuccessful at winning the seat my old job will be waiting for me. In fact, Smook suggested a special bonus for being a team player."

"Do they really think you have a chance? You're not exactly a known figure in politics."

"That's a big plus with the disdain for the current Congress. Being an outsider will give me legs and Smook assures me that I'll have the financial backing of the Street."

"It sounds too good to be true."

Rocky took a sip of his drink. "I've told them I'll think about it, discuss it with you, but I can't really see a downside." He turned to face her and winked. "What do you think, babe? Want to be the best looking woman on Capitol Hill?"

# # #

22

The twenty-fifth floor conference room at World News headquarters was a narrow, windowless affair lined on both sides by floor to ceiling bookcases. The place resembled a landfill; shelves jammed to overflowing with a decade of accumulated books, magazines, memos and a half-eaten sandwich or two. The room gave off the musty odor of a library mixed with the pungent smell of rotting roast beef.

Zeke and his boss Edith sat on opposite sides of the long conference table watching the television at the end of the room. They had both been glued to the election coverage, specifically the race for the Senate in New York. Rocky Wellington had just accomplished a surprising victory and would be on his way to Washington.

Zeke, of course, had learned of Rocky's surprise candidacy from Robin, who swore him to secrecy until Rocky made his official announcement. Once the campaign began, Zeke kept his coverage at arm's length. The voters of New York would decide who would be their next U.S. Senator without the benefit of Zeke's opinion on the matter.

When Rocky appeared at the podium of the Ritz-Carlton hotel in downtown Manhattan, with Robin at his side to claim victory, Zeke swallowed hard. She was beaming, waving, seeming to love the spotlight.

"Well," Edith said, muting the television, "his campaign was extremely well organized and he had the financial backing of the Street, but that's what won the election for him," she added, gesturing towards the television where a close up of the smiling couple filled the screen. "She's a knockout."

Zeke's mind was still racing over the personal impact of this unexpected development. As surprised as he had been about Rocky's candidacy, he had never given him much of a chance of succeeding. But now? How would this affect Zeke's relationship with Robin?

Edith leaned back in her chair. "Time for you to take your gloves off and renew your friendship with young mister Wellington, don't you think?"

Zeke snapped out of his trance. "Uh, yeah; he promised me an exclusive interview if he won."

"Well, your instincts to stay away from the campaign were correct. There was no controversy, no other candidate who ever presented a viable challenge. The election was given to him on a silver platter," Edith went on, her eyes flashing back to the ongoing celebration on television, the ballroom filling with balloons and confetti.

"Yeah, he never took anything but a generic stand on any major issue," Zeke replied. "It's amazing how indiscriminant the voters were. What the hell did they vote for?"

"His gorgeous wife would be my bet," Edith said dryly.

Zeke nodded his silent agreement.

Edith turned to face her colleague, a serious look crossing her face. "This is all perfect for what I have in mind for you, Zeke."

"And what's that?"

Edith lowered her voice and leaned closer to the table. "This is not for publication, but Luther Dell will be retiring next year and I'd like to start working someone new onto his show; someone who can eventually take over for him as host." Luther Dell was the senior executive reporter for World News, his weekly hour long program, The Bottom Line, one of the most watched television shows in the country. "I'd like for you to be that person, Zeke, and an interview with this old friend might just be the perfect way for you to start."

"My own segment?"

She smiled, but then her face became serious again. "At first, yes, but I have to warn you that adding a twenty minute T.V. slot every week to your other responsibilities will be tough as hell." She studied him for a second, then said, "But let's see what you come up with and go from there. Reacquaint yourself with our newest political star. Let's find out the *real* truth behind his success."

"You smell something here?"

"I *always* smell something, honey. Now go find out what it is."

* * *

A strange noise woke Robin up. Her eyes opened slowly and she struggled to remember where she was. There had been dinner and a lot of wine and, oh yes, the glorious, wonderful sex. She turned on her back and looked off across the darkened expanse of the bedroom. Through the open door she could make out the figure of Zeke in the kitchen, busily preparing breakfast. She closed her eyes and drank in the invigorating smell of freshly-brewed coffee.

Eyes wide open now, she watched as Zeke moved across the kitchen attending the toaster, the stove, and cutting up fruit. She laid back and smiled, her bare skin luxuriating against the smooth Egyptian cotton sheets she had bought for him, her memories of last night causing her to blush. Their affair was an exciting, pleasure-filled adventure, but with Rocky's career taking its unexpected turn, her life, including her relationship with Zeke, was bound to get more complicated.

Zeke's job was already taking more and more away from their times together, as were her duties as a new senator's wife. She was becoming impatient with these constraints and even though the sex was terrific, there was something still missing in her life, something else she wanted. She had warmed to being a Wall Street wife; living in luxury, buying anything she wanted, the glamor and excitement of living in New York. And now, the amazing new world of Washington politics and power. But despite the elaborate trappings of both lives, she was still Rocky's side car, still his satellite, still "the little lady." She longed to have a spotlight of her own, to be the central figure at dinner parties, to be the darling of the press and not just for her looks. The thrill and allure of an illicit affair had begun to fade in favor of greater accomplishments, *her* accomplishments.

Her thoughts were interrupted by the man clad only in his boxer shorts standing in front of her. "Here you go," Zeke said, holding a steaming cup of coffee out to her.

She propped herself up with a pillow and took the cup with a smile. "You really know how to take care of a girl," she said, taking a tentative sip.

"Girls are one thing," he said, sitting down on the edge of the bed, "but satisfying a sensual, provocative, sexually demanding woman is something else."

She uttered a purr, more of a growl, and reached out to stroke his bare leg. He smiled and stood up. "Not now, tiger. I've got pancakes on the griddle." He slapped her on the thigh. "Come on, rise and shine."

Her lower lip curled down. She knew his routine. After breakfast they would lay in bed together reading the papers, then she would arouse his interest and, well, it was always so good in the dim light of morning, particularly with the gloomy, snowy day outside.

"When does Rocky get back?" he asked from the kitchen, sliding a stack of pancakes onto her plate.

She slipped out of bed, pulled on his bathrobe and walked to the table by the dining room windows. "Next Friday," she said, sitting down and admiring the spread of food. "He's got a couple of meetings, a few dinners, and he's closing on our townhouse in Georgetown."

"What do you think of D.C.?"

She shrugged and picked up her fork. "Kind of dreary this time of year, but Rocky says things will pick up in the spring."

"I would think that as the wife of a new senator you'd have lots of social obligations?"

She sighed. "Yes. I'm not into all that gossip and smiley-face bullshit, but Rocky absolutely loves it. Well, I'll do my part. After all, he *is* my husband."

Zeke broke several eggs into a bowl and beat them with a fork before pouring the yellow concoction onto the griddle. "It's still hard for me to believe that Rocky is a senator. For someone with no political background it's just remarkable."

Robin sighed. "Yeah, I know, but Rocky said there was a plan in place and he just happened to fit the profile of who they were looking for."

"A plan?"

Robin shook her head. "I don't pretend to know any details, I'm not really all that interested and Rocky, well, he's super-secret about all this, but yes, he claims there's a group who developed this plan that he's now a part of and he's sworn to secrecy about it."

"Really?"

"Yeah, the group sounds a bit like the Shriner's, wearing funny hats and having secret handshakes, that sort of silliness."

"Interesting," Zeke said, sensing there was more to this than just an elderly fraternity. He piled the scrambled eggs onto a plate, turned off the griddle and took a seat across from Robin. She helped herself to a generous portion of the eggs.

Zeke smiled. She had a voracious appetite after a night of sex and he watched her eat, wondering once again how all this had happened. He had been confused about his feelings for her ever since their first night together. Guilt mixed with a generous dose of lust. The relationship, dangerous from the beginning, had become even more so now with Rocky's emergence on the national political scene.

But other things were changing; he could sense it. Robin seemed distracted, as if she was having second thoughts about their affair. Earlier discussions about divorcing Rocky had all but disappeared and yes, their times together were less frequent, but that was as much his fault as hers, his job having become more demanding than ever.

His thoughts were interrupted as Robin pushed back from the table and stood up, then turned and walked slowly back towards the bedroom. As she reached the door she undid his robe, slipped it off and tossed it onto the bed. She looked over her bare shoulder at him and smiled.

He smiled back, immediately aroused. She had a magnificent body, smooth and firm and curved in all the right places. The glare from the snow outside outlined her figure like a backlit stripper as she moved slowly to the bed and stretched out on it, her eyes beckoning him.

Zeke left his breakfast unfinished, stood up and headed for the bedroom.

* * *

The klieg lights were arranged in a semi-circle, all aimed at the leather couch that faced the fireplace. The Georgetown home of Senator and Mrs. Rockford Charles Wellington was modest by comparison to their Long Island estate, but the townhouse was well appointed and convenient to work on the Hill. The freshman senator was making good on his promise of an exclusive interview if he won the election.

Zeke sat next to him on the couch, waiting for the cue from his director. "First of all, Rocky, congratulations on your election. You've come a long way from our days in college together."

Rocky smiled, looking relaxed in an open-necked white shirt and blue blazer. "Well, I guess we've both come a long way since those days back in Manhattan, but yes, sometimes I have to pinch myself when I'm sitting on the senate floor."

"A lot of people find it amazing that a newly elected senator with no prior political experience has already been appointed to several key committees by the tradition-rich senate. How do you feel about that?"

"Well, I'm honored, of course, but I think it's fair to say that Congress in general is looking to infuse itself with new blood in an attempt to change its image with the public."

"That seems like a noble objective assuming, of course, that newcomers like yourself have a different attitude and perspective than those in Congress who have created such a negative public image, but let's concentrate on you. It's no secret that you have had powerful backing from your former colleagues on Wall Street, and some might question your objectivity in dealing with the interests of Main Street America in the senate. How do you answer those critics?" It was a powder puff beginning, designed to give Rocky room to repeat his campaign mantra before Zeke started asking hard questions.

Rocky looked past his host, straight into the camera. "I believe I bring a balanced view to my responsibilities here in Washington, Zeke. I served the interests of the working man and woman during my banking days, and every American who has a retirement plan has a vested interest in how well Wall Street performs, so I think my experience in both areas will allow me to represent the broad cross-section of my constituents."

"But isn't it true, senator, referring to your comment about your time on Wall Street, that the segment of American society that benefits most from the stock market's success is the upper echelon of the population? After all, the retirement plans of most Americans are comparatively meager, given the public's penchant for having to spend rather than save. Wealthier citizens, on the other hand, have the luxury of surplus cash and the ability to hire professionals to guide their money into the higher yield investments."

"Well, the investments of those wealthier citizens in the stock market causes its value to rise, and that benefits everyone who owns stocks."

"So, the rich getting richer is good for everyone?"

"It's always been that way, Zeke. Capitalism is predicated on upward mobility, of people like you and me who came from comparatively humble beginnings to utilize our respective skills and hard work to better ourselves, socially and economically. It's what makes this country great."

Zeke side-stepped Rocky's "humble" beginnings comment and said, "Well, rags-to-riches is an attractive story to tell, but the truth is that the mobility you speak of has been sharply declining for many years. The middle class is on the verge of disappearing as the number of poor in this country continues to grow. The gap between the ninety-five percent who are the supposed backbone of our economy and the five percent at the top has widened dramatically."

"That's a bit of a distortion, Zeke. It's true that the gap has widened but there's an explanation that goes beyond the rich get richer claim. There has been a shift in demographics that's been caused by the massive influx of immigrants. They tend to be under-educated and unskilled in the higher paying types of job opportunities that exist here. They are poorer, by and large, and their presence by the millions statistically lowers the average wage and widens the gap you spoke of."

"That argument might have some merit, but some of those who don't have the extra cash to 'invest' look at those who do as greedy, exploiting their position to reap whirlwind profits while the average family struggles to make ends meet. Is this disparity fair?"

"Capitalism is fueled by class distinction. If everyone earned the same no matter what we'd discourage initiative and risk taking. The problem you're describing is not a class problem, but a globalization problem. American workers are being underbid by those in other countries. This has led to the outsourcing of millions of jobs and we've been woefully unprepared in anticipating this shift and providing retraining of our work force."

"What do you, as a representative of the people, do to address this problem?"

"It's a real challenge, Zeke. There are so many varied interests in this country, each with their own agenda and priorities that getting consensus and compromise has become very difficult. Objectives are often at cross-purpose to one another. What we need to do is unleash the ingenuity and inherent capabilities of capitalism to allow American business to reach even greater heights. As business prospers it makes life better for all Americans."

This was a classic doubletalk non-answer and caused Zeke to frown. Before Zeke could ask his next question, Rocky took advantage of the pause.

"Look," Rocky said, holding a hand aloft, "we need to let the economy stabilize, to broaden and expand, to adjust to the forces of globalization. People need to be patient and recognize that these cycles often take years. You don't turn this economy around on a dime. Progress takes time."

More generic doubletalk, Zeke thought. "I think the element of patience you speak of is inversely related to one's economic status, but, as you say, progress takes time. So, Rocky, give us a specific example of legislation you will back that will demonstrate your support of the ninety five percent, the average working American."

Rocky pointed at his host and smiled. "I'm glad you asked me that question, Zeke. Yes, the currently proposed Minimum Wage Bill represents the type of legislation I'll support that will benefit the average worker."

Zeke looked surprised. "That's quite a departure from your party's position on the subject. Their claim is that raising the minimum wage will be a burden, specifically on small businesses that will have trouble absorbing those higher labor costs."

"There's a fundamental economic truth that is being overlooked by that argument, Zeke. It's a fact that over seventy percent of our economy in this country is driven by consumers, you and me spending our money on goods and services. Now, it stands to reason that if you give all of us more money, we're going to spend most of it. Now this spending benefits all business, big and small, it fuels our economic growth and, as the economy prospers, it encourages the five percent to invest. Investment further spurs economic growth and adds momentum to the surge created by consumer spending, all driven by a higher minimum wage."

Zeke started to make a comment, but Rocky wasn't finished.

"What most opponents of a higher minimum wage fail to take into account is the bigger picture. Now if businesses don't provide a wage that allows workers to do more than just survive, guess what happens? Many of those same workers become eligible for government assistance: welfare, food stamps, free meals at school, etc. So the question is this: should taxpayers be responsible for footing the bill for these assistance programs or should the business world accept lower profits to provide a substantive wage?"

"But won't some smaller businesses have to close because they can't afford to pay the higher wages?"

Rocky nodded. "A few, yes, but every business in this country is faced with adjusting to fluctuating costs whether that be payroll, rent, raw material, insurance and they make adjustments including accepting a lower profit margin. Those that are creative and flexible will adjust and survive, those that don't will fold their tents. This situation is true no matter what the issue; it's the Darwinian rule of business. It's the heart of capitalism."

"Well, as I said earlier, this represents a departure from the fundamental position of your party and it's interesting that a junior member of Congress would have such an outspoken approach."

"I think my position represents a new movement within my party to broaden our platform to address changing circumstances and to attract more of the ninety-five percent voting bloc."

"I applaud your attitude and wish you the best of success in your new venture, Rocky. Thank you for taking the time to talk with us here tonight and I hope you'll invite us back as time and events permit."

Rocky reached forward and extended his hand. "It's always a pleasure to talk with you, Zeke, and I look forward to many more conversations in the future."

Zeke swallowed hard, but his next point was in his script, a must-ask question. "Perhaps next time we can include your lovely wife, Robin."

Rocky smiled. "Yes, I'm sure your viewers would love to see her beautiful face rather than my ugly mug. We look forward to you arranging that as soon as possible."

# # #

23

T he four men sat around the T-shaped desk configuration in Lincoln Archer's office. A small rectangular conference table had been placed perpendicular against the front of the Reverend's desk, an arrangement he had borrowed from his father's experience in the Navy where space aboard ship was at a premium. Space was not an issue in Archer's office, but the arrangement afforded an intimacy for discussion, planning and strategy. The three Deacons that constituted the Board had become a bureaucratic necessity as the administrative side of church business expanded.

Lincoln's office bore no vestiges one would expect in a church; no religious paintings or icons, no crosses, not a bible in sight. With its wall of tinted glass, plain paneling and dark furniture, it looked more like the office of a corporate executive; a role into which the church's financial success had thrust "the preacher of the people."

Today was the weekly meeting to review the inputs from the congregation: letters, e-mails, phone calls where church members expressed their opinions, asked questions, and made requests for favors, charitable assistance and other uses of the church's vast financial resources. This composite of input was often used as fodder for Lincoln's subsequent sermons, a practice that kept him close to the needs of his followers.

The meeting had been going on for an hour and a familiar trend was presenting itself. "Here's a letter from a single mother of two in Nebraska," one of the Deacons said, waving the letter in front of him. "She works sixteen hours a day for minimum wage and struggles to pay her bills, feed her kids or spend any quality time with them. It's another cry for help, for advice on where she can turn."

"Here's one from a factory worker in St. Louis," another Deacon said. "Hasn't had a raise in three years, struggling to support his family, has no savings, lives from paycheck to paycheck. And yet," he went on, his voice rising, "the senior management of the firm he works for just got bonuses totaling over twenty million dollars this year. How is this fair?" he asks. The Deacon read on. "People like me are the reason the company makes a profit in the first place and yet the rewards go to the guys sitting in headquarters, guys who have never seen the inside of a plant or spent a day working on the factory floor."

"These letters are typical of the hundreds and thousands we get every week, Reverend," another Deacon said. "The people are looking to you for help, Lincoln."

"You read every day of some corporate CEO or Wall Street banker getting millions of dollars in pay or bonuses," the first Deacon said, anger in his voice, "while literally millions of hard-working Americans are living from payday to payday. Those people are getting angry, are getting tired of working so hard and living like vermin while these fat cats get fatter."

"Your people want to hear from you, Reverend," the second Deacon repeated. "They're watching their livelihoods disappear right in front of them while big corporations don't pay any taxes, defense contractors build weapons of war that even the Pentagon doesn't want, and Congress doesn't appear to even want to try and solve any problems. Hard-working people are looking for someone to speak for them." He looked towards the man behind the desk.

Lincoln shifted uncomfortably in his chair. "What these people want goes beyond the nature of my sermons," he said. "They're looking for someone to address economic and political conditions that I can't control."

"Reverend, it's no longer about your hands-on ministry; you working in the soup kitchens or helping a farmer rebuild a fence or personally delivering meals to the elderly. Your message goes beyond your friends and neighbors here in Wichita. The people across the country you have reached with your weekly sermons feel that you are on their side, understand their plight, will speak out on their behalf," the first Deacon suggested.

"But, you can't get too political in your sermons," the third Deacon warned. "We'd lose our tax-exempt status and get caught in a cross-fire from every religious group in the country."

"And yet the people are restless," the first Deacon pressed. "They look to Reverend Archer for practical solutions to their problems. You must speak out, Lincoln."

Lincoln Archer studied the faces of his closest advisors. They were right. He must speak out. He must give advice and counsel to those who were demanding it. Events had conspired to force his hand. It was time to step out of the comfort of spiritual guidance and into the spotlight of political activism. He pushed back from his desk and stood up. "I'll address all your concerns in Sunday's sermon."

* * *

Lincoln Archer chewed on his problem most of the week, weighed the pros and cons of the advice from his Board, searched his own heart. In the end he decided to do what he had done for years, to speak his mind as honestly and candidly as he could. As he stood at the podium the following Sunday, the struggle he had endured all week seemed to lift from his shoulders as he spoke.

"I have been overwhelmed," he began, "by the sincerity and openness of the many letters and messages I have received from you all, tales of despair and hopelessness, financial ruin, family heartache. They touch me deeply and I'm flattered that so many of you have sought my opinion on such important matters."

He paused, having chosen his words carefully as he prepared today's sermon. "Your plight has weighed heavily on me and, to be honest, has kept me awake at night searching for the right things to say today. As sometimes happens when I wrestle with a difficult problem, the answer came to me in a dream. Let me tell you of the dream I had this week."

He paused again, conscious of the television camera in the distance and the millions of viewers behind it.

"In my dream it was this coming Wednesday and a dramatic event was taking place. Those of you who have written me so earnestly seeking guidance made a collective decision. That decision was to demonstrate your value to our country, to the day-to-day conduct of business in America and how much your contributions mean. For, in my dream, on this coming Wednesday, the backbone of our nation, the people whose efforts make our economy work, took the day off."

"Bus drivers, short order cooks, janitors, sanitation workers, teachers, construction workers all took the day off. Small business employees, pizza and newspaper delivery folks, department store workers, government employees that labor in low-level obscurity all took the day off. Those that harvest our food, process and ship it, deliver it to your local market, stock the shelves, check you at the register all took the day off. Excluding those who provide safety and health care, everyone whose life has been negatively impacted by the inactions of government, by the greed and avarice of big business, took the day off."

The audience had begun to murmur, to voice approval of the Reverend's message with a nodding of heads and a spattering of applause. "And do you know what happened when all these valuable members of the unrecognized masses took the day off? This country, in all its glory and economic superiority, ground to a halt. The daily flow of commerce, the conduct of business, of government, of life in your neighborhood, stopped in its tracks. Just for that one day, this Wednesday."

"And what happened as a result of this peaceful day of protest? The answer did not come to me in my dream, but I can envision an awakening, a realization that things as they are today must change; that those who reap the financial benefits of your hard labor must share those benefits. Indifference to your financial plight must end with action and problem solving aimed at making your life better."

"These might be viewed as wishful, even fanciful outcomes to the events in my dream, but similar peaceful protests have led this country to great social and economic advances, advances that would not have seen the light of day without the actions of concerned citizens."

By this point the congregation was on its feet, cheering every word as if they were attending a political rally. In a manner of speaking, that was exactly where they were. Lincoln Archer had never waxed so eloquent, spoken so fervently from his beliefs. In his mind he wasn't making a political statement, merely reflecting the angst and frustration of those he served, suggesting, via his dream, a dramatic demonstration of the power of the masses, rising in common cause.

"This Wednesday was not a revolution in my dream; it was a peaceful demonstration of concern and a message to those in power. To be truly great our country must serve its most disadvantaged as well as its most wealthy and powerful. Those at the bottom of our economic ladder do not seek unwarranted equality with those at the top, merely the opportunity to climb those rungs and to share in the country's wealth proportionate to their contributions."

The congregation grew more enthusiastic, but the greatest impact was on the television audience, many of whom found themselves standing and applauding in their living rooms.

"I don't claim to be clairvoyant or prophetic in any manner," Lincoln went on. "Merely to share with you the thoughts that cloud my mind and surface in my dreams. Perhaps together we can better your lives and send a powerful message to those who control your collective destinies."

# # #

24

The television news commentator stared at the camera with a serious expression. "We've been following this story since last Sunday when the Reverend Lincoln Archer, in his nationally televised sermon, recounted a supposed dream where a 'national day of protest' was held with the suggestion that disgruntled workers should boycott their jobs for a day. The Reverend's message apparently gained traction as workers all over the country have been organizing and mobilizing for today's protest. Spokespersons for the various worker groups claim that millions of people have stayed away from work, protesting a variety of issues from government stalemate to minimum wages to Wall Street greed. For the impact of this worker protest, let's turn first to our associate in New York City, Sandy Williams. Sandy?"

The reporter's image, microphone in hand, gave way to the scene behind him: an empty Fifth Avenue surrounded by the gray canyon-like walls of skyscrapers, pieces of trash whirling about the desolate scene. "Yes, Jim, I'm here in an almost empty Times Square and it's like a science fiction film about the end of the world. Transportation systems are completely out; no subways, buses or taxis to be seen. Restaurants, hotels and other businesses are closed, the absence of cooks and waiters and other hourly workers leaving managers helpless to conduct business on their own. There are no sanitation crews out and about, no delivery trucks, no bustling crowds filling the sidewalks. We have seen a higher-than-normal level of police, perhaps anticipating a threat of looters in a nearly empty city. This is like nothing I've ever seen, an entire city brought to a standstill. There are no protestors carrying signs or staging any sort of demonstration that we've seen, just the stark absence of people during what is normally a crowded, noisy rush hour. Back to you, Jim."

"Thanks, Sandy. For a report on how this protest has affected our nation's capital, let's turn to our reporter in D.C., Ryan Williams."

"Good morning, Jim. I'm standing here on the west side of the Capitol building, looking down Pennsylvania Avenue into the heart of the District and it's like a ghost town." The camera zoomed in on the vacant stretch of road, stoplights performing a futile function with hardly any traffic to command. "Like Sandy reported from New York, there is a complete absence of public transportation which has forced thousands of government workers to remain at home so we're not able to ascertain how many of them are actually participating in this worker protest. Troops from nearby Ft. Myer in Virginia have been brought in to support District law enforcement as, like in New York, there is a fear of looting, but so far no evidence that is actually happening." The camera panned back to reveal another man beside the reporter.

"I have with me Mr. Robbie Danucci who is a courier for a D.C. law firm. Mr. Danucci, what do you hope to gain from participating in today's protest?"

Danucci, astride his bicycle, shot a determined look at the camera. "I work twelve hours a day for minimum wage and it just ain't enough to take care of my family. I'm like all the other working slobs here in the city just trying to make a living, you know?"

"And you hope that staying away from work today will call attention to your plight?" the reporter asked.

"Yeah, and that maybe some of those fat cat lawyers I work for, the guys who live in their big houses and drive their Mercedes, will cut me some slack and raise my pay. It ain't like they have to give up their yachts or expensive suits; all I want is a fair shake. I work hard too, you understand?"

"Thank you, Mr. Danucci. Back to you, Jim."

"Thanks, Ryan. We're going to take you now to Wichita, Kansas, where our reporter Don Avery has made his way to the source of today's protest. Don?"

A downpour with rain drops so big they could be heard splashing off the reporter's wind breaker caused him to squint into the camera and speak louder than normal. "Yes, Jim, I'm here in Wichita, Kansas, outside the Church of Hope whose Reverend Lincoln Archer was the undisputed spark that set today's protest in motion. His Sunday sermon where he recounted a dream he had about such a protest was enough to set the ball rolling. Reverend Archer is with me here today and Reverend, we thank you for enduring this downpour to come out and speak with us."

Lincoln stood on the covered walkway between the main church building and the nearby administration facility, flanked by two Deacons. The reporter had caught Lincoln coming out of the main church and requested a minute of his time. "Yes," Lincoln said as the rain came down harder, "this is a typical Midwestern summer storm and is long overdue. We've been in the middle of a draught and this rain will help our farming friends tremendously." He flashed a wide smile at the camera.

The reporter nodded and shoved the microphone closer to his subject's face. "Reverend Archer, your sermon last Sunday basically called for today's massive protest and the power of your message was very clear. Is it a coincidence that this demonstration of working class Americans comes at a time when the minimum wage legislation is before Congress; a law which would benefit those same workers?"

Lincoln smiled as a flash of lightning lit up the surroundings. He held up a finger to await the subsequent boom of thunder. It came and the group flinched in response. Archer then said, "First of all, I'm not in the protest planning or organizing business; my message last Sunday was merely a response to the tens of thousands of letters I have received where the people of this country expressed their outrage and frustration on a variety of issues."

"But your so-called dream was, without a doubt, a call to action."

The rain splattered off the microphone held out to Lincoln. He leaned closer to it. "That was the response, yes," he almost yelled to be heard. "But the organization of a variety of working groups was done spontaneously. My words may have inspired this action, but I was in no way involved in its implementation."

"So you see no correlation with the Minimum Wage Bill in Congress?"

One of the Deacons leaned forward past Lincoln towards the microphone. "Reverend Archer is not a politician nor does he have political motivation in his sermons. He was merely speaking out for the plight of his congregation, most of whom are working class citizens."

The reporter looked annoyed at the interruption. He moved the microphone closer to Lincoln. "But it does seem that those same workers will be looking to you for guidance, or maybe another dream, to tell them what to do next."

Lincoln held up a hand to stop the Deacon from interjecting again. "I think we'll all watch and wait to see what actions will be taken by this country to address the working class problems that have existed for some time now. Nice talking to you," he added as he began to move down the walkway.

"Thank you, Reverend. And now to our roving correspondent, Roger Davis, who has a different perspective on today's protest. Roger?"

The sudden absence of the noisy downpour was like moving out of the cacophony of rush hour traffic into a library. "Thank you, Don. I'm here at the home of Raymond Stillwater, the senior senator from Illinois who also heads the powerful Senate Appropriations Committee. Senator, how do your colleagues respond to this work protest, particularly as it applies to the upcoming vote on the Minimum Wage Bill?"

The senator's white locks were carefully coiffed, not a hair out of place. His ruddy complexion showed signs of makeup and his hand tailored suit fit perfectly. "Well, Roger, we certainly support the rights of people, particularly in the numbers participating in today's demonstration, to voice their concerns. There are a multitude of complex problems facing our country and it goes without saying that simple, immediate solutions, although they might be popular, are very difficult to translate into legislation when Congress is so diverse in its opinions and perspectives. We understand the frustration of many

Americans, but realistically, the types of changes needed to spur our economy are the type that take years to craft, negotiate and legislate. There is no quick fix."

"But the Minimum Wage Bill, if enacted, would be an immediate benefit for the workers who are protesting today."

A scowl crossed the senator's face, perhaps a reaction to being asked the same question a number of times already. "As I have said before, raising the minimum wage will harm businesses at all levels, but particularly small businesses who cannot afford to absorb those higher expenses."

"But surely the argument that these increased wages will flow immediately back into the economy is a powerful incentive on a national level?"

The senator shook his head. "Those types of expenditures would be temporary and would not contribute to the required investments that would help our economy recover. Turning our economy around requires prudent, cautious policies that are long term in their effects, not Band-Aid fixes like increasing the minimum wage. Long term policies take time to have their effect and we must all be patient in allowing them to unfold." He smiled broadly at the camera, obviously pleased with his response.

"But certainly you understand that time is not the ally of the average worker who is living from paycheck to paycheck, desperate to feed and clothe their families? This seems to be the type of situation that Reverend Archer alluded to in his sermon."

The senator's smile disappeared and his face clouded in anger. "I find it difficult to see how a man of the cloth can retain his church's tax exempt status while taking obviously political positions and I will encourage the IRS to examine that status closely."

"But, Senator----"

"Thank you, Roger, but I have a meeting to attend and I shouldn't keep my colleagues waiting. Good talking to you." The senator flashed an expensive smile at the camera, shook the reporter's hand and was gone.

Roger turned toward the camera, his face reflecting the frustration of getting another canned non-response to his questions. "And there you have our input from Senator Raymond Stillwater of Illinois, a response that's certain to frustrate those who are participating in today's protest."

* * *

"That was an unmitigated disaster," Senator Sam Adams from Ohio said. He and two other members of The Ten had just watched the interview with Senator Stillwater.

"Raymond got way off message with his attack on Reverend Archer," the senator from Texas added.

"The old fool is on the wrong side of this battle," Adams said. "We can't ignore thirty million votes," he added. Indeed, Lincoln Archer's "day of protest" had caused an estimated thirty million workers to stay at home.

"What are you suggesting?" the senator from Virginia asked.

"Look," Adams started, "we've got an election coming up and our standing with those folks who are protesting today is very shaky. We need to weigh in and convince them we're on their side."

"But how do we do that?" Texas asked. "Our side of the aisle has seen to it that The Minimum Wage Bill is dead in the water. That isn't going to buy us a single damned vote from these workers."

Adams pointed at his colleague. "Exactly. Look, we've already positioned our boy on this minimum wage issue. He's made good press, particularly amongst blue collar workers. He's got momentum. It's time to call in our chits and get the party to rally around him."

Texas was more forceful. "We'll have to convince our most stubborn colleagues that if we give a little ground on this single issue it will go a long ways towards winning the next election. It's a damned no-brainer, actually."

"Like you said," Virginia offered, "it's hard to ignore thirty million votes, but can Rocky pull this off?"

Adams smiled and nodded. "With our help and his ego, that shouldn't be a problem."

* * *

"Lincoln, what the hell were you thinking?" It was Zeke on the phone and he was unusually agitated.

Lincoln had been expecting the call. In fact, he had already been contacted by scores of concerned members of his church. "I suppose you're calling about my 'dream' sermon and today's day of protest?"

"Of course I am. Do you realize what a position you've put yourself and your church in?"

"Look, it was just another sermon addressing the plight of my congregation. I'm not concerned about the Church of Hope's tax status with the IRS."

"Well, you should be. When your sermons start addressing political issues, you become the target of critics all over the country. Not only does that include the businesses your little dream has affected today, but now there's a renewed focus on you by religious leaders everywhere."

"You talking about Cardinal DuPont?" Lincoln asked, referring to the Archbishop of New York who had written several Op Ed articles criticizing Lincoln's 'godless sermons.'

"Well, he's been the most vocal, but every clergyman who's seen your popularity grow has become your enemy."

"Zeke, I had nothing to do with organizing today's protest. I really did have such a dream and I was merely repeating it. I had no idea so many people would take it seriously and act as they have. I'm as surprised as anyone."

"Well, you've created a hornet's nest and a lot of people will be after your hide for a variety of reasons. You really should retain a lawyer."

"I'm not guilty of any crime."

"And what if the IRS comes after you? What if any number of businesses sue you for what today has cost them? Whether you're guilty of a crime or not, you need to be prepared to defend yourself."

Lincoln sighed. "I am passionate about the plight of the working men and women of this country, Zeke. Most of my sermons are drawn from their calls and letters. Obviously my subconscious wrestled with those issues and caused the dream I had. There's nothing nefarious or illegal about repeating that dream. Don't I have free speech like everyone else?"

"Of course you do, but there's such a thing as incitement to civil disorder. Just because you didn't mobilize these workers, you planted the idea in their heads. You're not just some loud mouth at a bar, you're a national figure with a vast following. What you say makes a difference to millions of people. No, you didn't set fire to the building, you just suggested it would be a good idea."

Lincoln exhaled heavily. "Look, I can't undo what I've said, can't undo what's been done today. If this protest results in some form of positive action that helps the working people of the country, then I've done my duty as someone who sympathizes with their problems and has, however unwittingly, advanced their cause."

"O.K., I hear you, but the uproar over this isn't going away. At least promise me that if this gets out of hand you'll make an appearance on my show, let me give you the forum for explaining your actions."

"Zeke, with respect, I don't need a forum. I've got my pulpit and, as you've suggested, a national audience who listens to what I say. I don't owe anyone an apology for my words, and if certain parties want to take me to court, they know where I live."

Zeke held up a hand of surrender. "Alright, I hear you, just remember, I'm on your side and I have an audience as well. Between the two of us we can get your message to an awful lot of people. I'm with you on this if you'll let me be."

Lincoln nodded. He knew Zeke was simply trying to help a situation that could, in all reality, get ugly. "I appreciate your concern and your advice, Zeke. Let's stay in touch."

"Back at you, my friend. Take care of yourself."

Lincoln hung up the phone and sat staring at it for several minutes. His dream, as he had told Zeke, *was* real. He had never thought it would result in so many million workers reacting the way they had today. He smiled. Wouldn't his father be amazed at how the once shy son, terrified of public speaking, had emerged as someone with such power and influence? It was one thing to speak to the daily drama of local farmers, quite another to impact the lives of millions of workers across the country. Should he be cautious of where this could lead him, as Zeke had warned? Or should he follow his instincts and continue down this path? He laughed to himself. By next week this day of protest would be forgotten, and with its passing, the country minister from Wichita would fade from the national news as well. I've had my fifteen minutes of fame, Lincoln thought with a smile. And to be honest, it felt pretty good.

# # #

25

The speech on the floor of the U.S. Senate caught most everyone by surprise. In the course of the debate on the Minimum Wage Bill, Rocky Wellington, despite opposition from his own party, spoke strongly in favor of the proposed legislation. In words scripted by others, Rocky waxed eloquent about the plight of the economy and the need to divert money into the hands of the workers, much as he had said in his previous television interview with Zeke Porter.

It was a defining moment for the young senator and unseen forces began their carefully orchestrated campaign to sway key members of their party to support the bill and its advocate. Short term sacrifice would benefit long term goals was the theme; gaining the working man's future vote was more important than granting a modest raise in the minimum wage. It was a gamble, but The Ten were counting on their considerable influence, plus the emerging dynamic personality of their hand-picked star.

* * *

The news broke around lunch time later that week. The vote was close but demonstrated the influence that Rocky and his senior colleagues had on the august body that was the U.S. Senate. The Minimum Wage Bill that had been DOA since it was passed by the House, was narrowly passed by the Senate. That evening, most of

America was glued to their television sets to watch Zeke's interview with Washington's emerging hero.

"Senator Wellington, what has been achieved here today in passing the Minimum Wage Bill is truly amazing. It's no secret that when the bill was passed and moved over from the House it had virtually no support from your party's side of the aisle in the Senate. How in the world did you change so many minds?"

Rocky was resplendent in a charcoal gray suit and blue tie that matched his eyes. "Well, Zeke, the credit goes to my colleagues. I was just a spokesman for what has become a paradigm shift in attitude."

"How did this come about?"

"Well, contrary to popular belief, my party is sensitive to the plight of the average worker in this country. A stable, productive work force is the key to our economy and when that stability became threatened it was easier to convince many senators that this bill needed to be passed."

"The predominant criticism of the bill claims that raising the minimum wage actually harms corporations and especially small business in that they must absorb these now mandatory labor costs. How did you combat this argument?"

"It's an outdated position created by 1950's economic thinking, Zeke. The country has changed dramatically since those days and my party has evolved in its understanding of this new dynamic."

"I must admit, from our previous discussions, your position on this issue has been consistent, senator."

Rocky nodded his agreement, then said, "What some of us have seen coming is a tipping point. Worker unrest is at an all time high and the creative forces of capitalism have not kept pace with their changing needs. If the 'stay away from work' protest that was staged last month had spread we would have seen an unmanageable shock to our economy. Businesses of all sizes would have been adversely affected. Passing this legislation will now allow American businesses to adjust, stabilize and move forward. I think we've averted a crisis and the strength of our economy will rise to the occasion."

"Do you think this legislation will cause our old friend Lincoln Archer to have another dream?"

Rocky smiled. "Actually, I believe Lincoln and I are simpatico when it comes to the future of the workers in this country." He turned to face the camera. "Don't forget, as a small town banker I dealt with the plight and interests of the working man every day. I understand their concerns, their needs and what they consider to be in their best interest. I also have been fortunate enough to have the same understanding and sensitivity to the interests and concerns of corporate America. I think my overall background allows me to define positions of compromise and problem solving that may be unique on Capitol Hill. I believe that is why my colleagues chose me as a spokesman for this important legislation."

"Senator, you've now become a very visible icon for both sides of the class struggle that many see as predominant in this country today. Some would even say that your new popularity is brilliant politics. Do you have other legislation you will sponsor or support and if so, what are we looking at; immigration reform, tax reform, environmental issues?"

"Zeke, I appreciate your investigative reporter instincts, but quite frankly, my main objective is to see this current legislation implemented and to use my experience to further the interests of our great country."

"Senator, thank you for your time and congratulations on your role in this amazing story."

* * *

The two men sat in front of Lincoln Archer in the latter's Church of Hope office. "We appreciate you taking the time from your busy schedule to see us here today," Roger Jones said.

Lincoln nodded. "What can I do for you gentlemen?"

Jones cleared his throat and leaned towards his host. "We feel that you, as much as any person in this country, stand for the rights of the working man."

"We too represent the interests of the working man," Jimmy Angeles said. "Roger here represents the farm workers of our country," he went on. "I speak for the manufacturing sector and the rights and interests of the many service industry personnel in our nation."

"Many of the same people I hear from each week," Lincoln said.

"Exactly," Jones said, jabbing a finger at Lincoln. "Your 'dream' sermon spurred passage of the Minimum Wage Bill which benefitted all of our membership and we're eternally grateful."

"My role was insignificant but I thank you nonetheless for your compliment," Lincoln replied.

"We think you understate your influence, sir," Jones said. "Anyway, as you know, the business community in general and the people in Washington have had a detrimental effect on organized labor these past few years. We've not only seen our combined membership decline drastically, but our ability to negotiate wages and benefits for those remaining is at an historic low."

"The working men and women in this country have lost their power," Angeles added. "We have no clout in Congress anymore; there aren't enough of us left to represent a meaningful number of voters, and our ability to deal with corporate management is non-existent. We're at the mercy of big business, lobbyists, and a political machine that is hopelessly broken."

"Your voice and message have become a beacon of hope for the working people of this country, Reverend, and we're here today to ask you to get even further involved," Jones said.

"In what way?" Lincoln asked.

Jones smiled and shot his colleague a glance. "We're forming a super union," he started. "Workers United. Unlike unions of the past that represented a particular segment of industry, we will have a union whose members represent the entire working class of this whole country; not just those working for minimum wage but all the workers who have slipped from the middle class through the greed and dysfunction of corporate and political America."

"By making membership generic we will eventually enjoy the largest block of voters in this country; we will demand legislation that will bring back the middle class, give those in poverty a chance to legitimately pursue the American dream, and close the gap between the rich and the rest of the country," Angeles added.

"If this shift in wealth does not happen," Jones said, "we will see life become intolerable for a huge segment of our society. We will see continued unrest and frustration, particularly with a Congress that listens only to special interests and an elite class that flaunts their obscene wealth in the face of those who are struggling to survive."

"This country cannot continue to operate efficiently as long as these issues go unresolved," Jones added. "We're at a crossroads and we fear the results will be turmoil."

"A revolution," Angeles said, grim-faced.

The room went silent as the ominous words settled.

"I too fear where we are headed as a country," Lincoln said finally. "But I'm not exactly sure what you think I can do about it. I'm only one man."

"We know you are old friends with Senator Wellington," Jones said. "You two seem to have a symbiosis of empathy for the working man and he has magically been able to work miracles on Capitol Hill."

"Well, one piece of legislation, despite the political dysfunction you describe, is hardly a miracle, but yes, Rocky and I are old friends."

"Since your day of protest dream and the publicity associated with the passing the Minimum Wage Bill, our membership has taken off. If this response continues we're talking nearly one hundred million workers joining Workers United," Angeles said, his face alive with excitement.

"We want to begin forging legislation that will raise the well being of millions of Americans," Jones chimed in.

"We're not only talking improved wages, we're talking affordable health care, shared corporate profits, improved working conditions, job training and, most importantly, a union that represents most Americans, not just the special interests that have created such a mess and has Congress tied in a knot," Angeles said.

"Sounds very ambitious," Lincoln said.

"We only charge a dollar a month for dues. With the membership we anticipate, that's a hundred million dollars a month," Angeles said. "That will buy a lot of clout on Capitol Hill."

Jones said, "If we don't see a change in how capitalism now works we're going to see the end of our democracy as we know it."

"This is not just a question of economics, this is an ethical issue," Angeles added, "a moral cause that must be undertaken by those of us who care more about our country than our personal pocketbooks or our political party."

Lincoln guessed the true meaning of the meeting. "I'd be happy to provide you an introduction to Senator Wellington if that is what you'd like," he offered.

Lincoln's two guests exchanged glances. "That would be gracious of you," Angeles said. "He needs to understand that this super union will descend on Capitol Hill with a force that has never been seen before. A hundred million voters will begin demanding the types of legislation we just described and powerful factions will resist mightily," Angeles emphasized.

"If Senator Wellington is truly on our side as we believe he is, he needs to know that he'll have a hundred million voters behind him," Jones said.

"But we are unknown to the Senator. Rather than cold calling on him, even with your introduction, we would prefer that call be made by a spokesman for our union, a leader with national recognition, someone with the respect and admiration of the workers," Angeles added.

"And someone who is personal friends with the Senator," Jones said. "And that person is you, Reverend Archer. We want you to be the face of our cause."

#

26

After Zeke Porter took over as host of "The Bottom Line," the weekly news program added to its established popularity and became the most watched show on television. The Sunday night telecast was eagerly viewed by millions, anxious to share the revealing, and often provocative stories that Zeke and his team of investigative journalists had uncovered. Although most of the stories dealt with fraud, corruption and waste, there was always a human interest piece that provided a positive balance to the otherwise discouraging revelations of wrong doing.

But tonight's featured segment was strictly political although, to Zeke, his guest made the story quite personal. He smiled at the camera and began the interview. "Some months ago I sat with Senator Rocky Wellington of New York and discussed his support of the Minimum Wage Bill that appeared headed for defeat in the Senate. As you will recall, Senator Wellington was instrumental in getting the bill passed by Congress, a stunning reversal for his party."

Zeke turned towards his guest. "Although Senator Wellington deserves much credit for his role in this historic legislation, the true initiative for the bill started with our guest tonight, another old friend of mine from college, Reverend Lincoln Archer, whose dream about a national day of protest was the spark that began the groundswell of support for this bill. Apparently buoyed by the success of that legislation, Reverend Archer has assumed a new role as the spokesman for the newly established Workers United super-union. Reverend

Archer is here tonight to explain this new organization and his new role. Lincoln, welcome."

The Reverend was dressed casually in slacks and a sports coat and shook Zeke's hand vigorously before leaning back in his seat next to the host. "Thanks, Zeke, and thanks for giving me this opportunity to voice our concerns and our intentions."

"Reverend, this union spokesman position is quite a change for you. How did this transformation happen?"

"Well, Zeke, as you know I've always been a voice for the working class in this country. My sermons have been aimed at helping them cope with life's daily ups and downs and how the Church of Hope might assist their struggles. But as I have learned, it's one thing to preach about how to solve problems, it's quite another to actually solve those problems and that's we hope to do."

"What sort of problems?"

"The problem of economic fairness, Zeke. The average worker in this country has, for the most part, been abandoned by corporate America and their elected representatives in government. The goal of the union is to present a consolidated, powerful voice to create legislation that will better the lives of most workers. That goal can be achieved by better wages and benefits, a fair portion of the enormous profits achieved by corporate America, and the ability, through that economic redistribution, of restoring the American dream once again for most of our citizens."

"Doesn't this equate to socialism, Reverend?"

"Absolutely not. Socialism deals with eliminating the private means of production and distributing all the wealth of the state equally to every citizen. It's a transitional state between capitalism and communism. What we want instead is a restructuring of the capitalist model to more fairly share corporate success with the workers. Those workers at the very bottom of the economic ladder would be able to lift themselves back into the middle class and could once again realize their dreams of owning a home, sending their kids to college and having a secure retirement to look forward to."

"And is it the hope of this union that, by the mere force of numbers, it can push legislation that would accomplish this economic fairness?"

"Yes. This is not something that corporations or Congress will do without great resistance. But a hundred million voters will be tough to ignore."

"Reverend, this seems like a dramatic departure for you. Some will see this move as shifting from religion into the world of politics. How do you answer that claim?"

"As you know, Zeke, I'm not a religious man or a political one. My sermons have tried to show how love, understanding, patience and doing the right thing are more powerful weapons against poverty and ignorance than any religion or political belief. Speaking for the union will help me expand that message into meaningful acts that will assist workers everywhere. That's not politics, that's compassion and love."

The host turned toward the camera. "We asked Senator Wellington to join us today but he had other commitments, but I ask you Reverend, do you think that your new role will allow you to leverage your friendship with Senator Wellington to achieve your goals?"

"Well, I would hope that, as an astute politician, Rocky will see the handwriting on the wall and help us change the face of our economy. We believe our momentum is unstoppable and we welcome his, and other political leader's support."

* * *

Rocky was working late in his senate office on Capitol Hill, but he had taken time to watch Zeke's show. His old friend Lincoln, despite his disclaimer, was fast becoming a national political force. As spokesman for Workers United, he could lift his folksy sermons to address social issues of every ilk, and the hundred million workers would follow his lead and advice right to the polls.

Rocky knew that to align himself with Lincoln and support his cause would be a shrewd political move, but supporting some of the progressive legislation that Lincoln would champion for the union could create friction for Rocky within his own party. He had no personal sensitivity or allegiance to the workers, but their sizeable block of votes were just too powerful a voice to be ignored.

The phone on his desk rang. Rocky picked up the receiver. "Hello?"

"Hello, Rocky. Did you watch the Bottom Line television show with Reverend Archer?" Senator Adams asked.

Adams had taken Rocky under his wing since the latter's election, providing guidance, advice and counsel to the younger man. He had seen to it that the junior senator was appointed to several important committees, and made certain that he and his lovely wife were active in Washington's social circles where they met key members of the party, business leaders, and media who were anxious to make the young, handsome man and his attractive wife national celebrities. The couple's popularity sold newspapers, television sponsors, and had enormous political capital.

"Yes, I just finished watching, sir."

"Good. I think it would behoove you to remain close to this man, particularly as regards the profit sharing legislation he's going to champion."

"As part of your plan for my future?" Rocky asked.

The senator from Ohio smiled. The bastard was smarter than he had thought. "Well, yes. By aligning yourself with this legislation you could build on your success with the Minimum Wage Bill."

"As a champion of the working man?"

"And as an ally of big business by keeping a nationwide strike off the table."

"Do you suspect that's Workers United's next move?"

"Perhaps your Reverend friend could enlighten you about that."

Rocky nodded. "I'll arrange a meeting with him ASAP."

"Actually, we'd like to meet with you first; this weekend. I'll have my office send you the details. It will be local and I think you should set aside several hours. We have a lot to talk about."

"Should I bring Robin?"

The senator paused. Clever bastard, he thought. "No, as delightful as that would be, but there'll be time to bring her up to speed later. And Rocky?"

"Yes?"

"I wouldn't tell anyone about our little get together. Not even Robin for now."

"Of course, Senator. Whatever you say."

"That's an attitude you'll need to keep, young man. See you this weekend."

"Yes, sir. Good bye."

Rocky leaned back in his chair and studied the view of the Capitol building out his office window. Apparently he and Senator Adams had the same thoughts regarding the importance of Reverend Lincoln Archer, but there was more to this weekend meeting than a profit sharing bill, no matter how important that might be. Rocky smiled and let his imagination take flight.

# # #

27

A subset of The Ten met regularly every month to discuss current issues, report on the status of ongoing tasks, and assign future actions. The meetings were held at different locations each month, rotating amongst members as hosts. This month the gathering was being held at the Middleburg, Virginia, country estate of the CEO of the country's largest computer firm.

From a distance, the twenty-five room "main" house resembled a medieval fortress: maroon brick and dark mustard stucco topped by a green tile roof with matching trim, doors and window sills. Set squarely in the middle of five hundred rolling acres of "horse country," the home afforded maximum privacy from prying eyes and ears. The massive garage easily accommodated the collection of automobiles from today's six attendants, the ensemble of expensive transportation resembling a high-end showroom in Monte Carlo. After a catered barbeque cookout on the patio, the group got down to business in the spacious library.

"It is time," the senator from Ohio started, "to shift our plan for Rocky into the next phase." He looked around the room at the other members assembled there. They all nodded. "His success in getting the Minimum Wage Bill passed has him well positioned with the workers and our corporate allies alike."

The CIA official picked up on the point. "The press has portrayed him as someone who can negotiate compromise, who can bring both sides together. We all know that the truth about that power sits in this room right now, but Rocky's image in that regard is golden."

Ohio nodded and went on. "We will soon have before us this Corporate Profit Sharing Bill. The worker's union drafted virtually every word and the House will undoubtedly pass it next week."

"We should seize the opportunity to get Rocky firmly in the middle of this new legislation," the senator from Virginia said. "He could make it the central theme of his candidacy announcement."

"I'm a little worried that his ego is so big we'll have trouble controlling him," the governor of Texas said.

"You'll all get a firsthand look at that issue very soon," Ohio said, checking his watch. "I've invited Rocky to join us here this afternoon. I don't think we'll have any trouble getting our boy to do exactly as we wish."

There was a mumbling of understanding. Although not privy to the details, members of The Ten were aware that the senator from Ohio employed teams of private investigators and even government agents to uncover information he often used to "persuade" others in obtaining support for his many objectives. Everybody had skeletons in their closets and Rocky must not be an exception.

"Well, Workers United has signed up a hundred million members so far," the CEO offered. "If this Profit Sharing Bill were to pass it would be a direct indication of their power to influence votes."

"And if Rocky were to be perceived as the man who made that happen, it would position him favorably for the upcoming election," Virginia said.

"We've got to find a way to make the bill acceptable to our corporate friends," Texas said, looking at the CEO. "Mandatory distribution of profits back to the workers will be a tough sell."

"Well," Ohio said, "I've got an ace in the hole we can use that I'll talk about later, but the main message is that if we can pass this bill with Rocky being seen as the one who made it happen, it will be a great kickoff to his campaign. We can ride that success right through the election, gentlemen." He raised his drink and everyone followed suit.

"We really need to get his wife more involved," Texas said. "She's a goddamned knockout and having her at his side will be a big plus." He paused, then said, "She'd sure as hell get my vote."

Everyone laughed.

"She was the difference in his senate campaign," New Jersey added with a smile.

"Well, she's about to become the most famous woman in America," Ohio said.

* * *

Robin couldn't believe her ears. "They want you to do what?" she asked.

"Run for president," Rocky replied.

"You're kidding, right?" Robin asked with a laugh.

"Absolutely not. They're dead serious and why not? Think about it. First they get me to champion the Minimum Wage Bill so I'm a hero to the average worker and to big business by avoiding a strike, and now they want to use me in the same way on this Corporate Profit Sharing Act. I'm being positioned for the upcoming primaries as their candidate of choice."

Robin shook her head. "But, you're a junior senator with just a few years of experience."

"I know, I know, but my inexperience is in my favor. I'm not one of the old boys and I've already shown how I can drive legislation through the gridlock."

"But that wasn't just your doing. Lincoln Archer helped make that happen."

"But I'm the person that the public thinks pushed it through the Senate," Rocky said, repeating the argument that The Ten had provided him. "It doesn't matter what the truth is, what happened behind the scenes, when the country talks about the Minimum Wage Bill it's my face that shows up on the news and in the papers." He smiled and motioned for her to sit down. "Now, let's talk about you and how much of an asset you will be."

Robin sat down and waited. She had been reluctant to be involved during Rocky's senate campaign, but when the limelight began to shine on her, her perspective changed. Reporters were literally all over her, anxious to get a quote, a smile, an opinion. She enjoyed the rallies, the fund raisers, the interviews. She was no longer the dutiful wife of the banker from Kansas, she was a celebrity in her own right. This could be more of the same, on a much bigger stage.

Rocky sat down beside her. "Look, you're a beautiful, smart woman who can hold her own at any cocktail party or fund raiser. With you at my side during the campaign, the cameras will zoom in on you and American men everywhere will fall all over their dicks. They don't give a shit what I have to say; I'm the guy with the gorgeous wife. They'd love to see you in the White House and on the news every night."

"Will you want me to give speeches?" she asked, having warmed to the task during the senate campaign.

"Well, of course," he answered. "And you can have a complete new wardrobe."

Robin smiled, her mind racing through where all this could take her. "And my role is to get the votes of all the horny men in America?" she asked.

"Every red blooded American male will go to bed at night with visions of you dancing through their skulls. You could become America's next sex symbol, babe." He smiled at her. "You may think this sex angle is a joke, but nobody votes for ugly old white men whose wives are wrinkled and sagging in all the wrong places. Appearance counts for more than you think."

"But what about policy and platforms and where the country is supposed to be going and all that?"

"Everybody says the same bullshit, Robin. The election will be blah-blah-blah to most people. They'll vote on what they see, not what they hear."

Robin let out a heavy sigh. "They say that the presidency is a thankless job that kills men. Are you sure that's what you want?"

He shot her a look of bewilderment. "The chance to be the most powerful person in the world; to have armies and helicopters and Air Force One and travel all over the world in luxury? Jesus, are you kidding me? Who wouldn't want that job?"

"It all sounds too easy, Rocky."

"Trust me. I'll have the backing of the most influential people in this country and the votes of every working man and woman. I can't lose."

* * *

Senator Rocky Wellington gripped both sides of the podium and stared out into the bright lights, a wide smile on his face. He wore a gray suit with a purple tie, the colors of Kansas State University, a flag pin prominently displayed on his suit lapel. Directly behind him, Robin stood, appropriately attired in her white skirt and sleeveless purple blouse, smiling and waving to members of the audience who called out her name.

Rocky reached to adjust the microphone, smiled again, and said, "Thank you all for being here this afternoon as I know you'd really prefer to be in class or sipping a beer over at Jack's." The crowd laughed and applauded.

Rocky wasted no time, his announcement a foregone conclusion. "I have returned to my alma mater, a place of fond memories, to announce my candidacy for the office of President of the United States."

The crowd, mostly KSU students, cheered wildly, waving signs that said "Rocky's Our Man," or "Win With Rocky." In the front row of Snyder Auditorium, the assembled press corps recorded the event for their respective newspapers, magazines, or television news shows.

"I won't bore you with a long speech," Rocky went on. "We'll save that for the campaign." More laughter and applause. "I would only say that it's time for a change in Washington, time for fresh ideas to guide our country, time for someone who appreciates the unique perspectives of both the working man and Wall Street, and time for someone who can negotiate compromise in a way that will begin to resolve the many problems that face our divided country today."

He turned to the side and raised an arm towards his wife. "And someone who will bring beauty and grace to the White House, my lovely wife Robin."

Robin stepped forward and waved to the crowd, many of whom were on their feet applauding, taking pictures, and waving signs that read, "Robin For First Lady."

"It's great to be back on my old stomping grounds," Rocky said, putting his arm around Robin and pulling her close. "And we both look forward to your support in the Fall," he added, the nomination a forgone conclusion in Rocky's mind. The Ten would see to that.

The handsome couple moved from the podium to leave the stage, both waving and smiling. The audience continued to shout and cheer and applaud. It was a seminal moment in American politics and they were all thrilled to be a part of it. Thus the first of many such appearances with brief, to the point speeches, with plenty of time allocated to posing for pictures, smiling and shaking hands with adoring supporters. The momentum had started and would continue to build right through election day. America had found its celebrity couple to lavish their attention on, the issues becoming secondary in their minds; just as The Ten had foreseen.

###

28

"R everend, your efforts have been responsible for adding millions of workers to the union. Now it's time to use their leverage on this Corporate Profit Sharing Act," the dark-skinned man said.

"I think you give me far too much credit," Lincoln Archer said. "I'm just a volunteer who's made a few T.V. appearances and written a couple of Op Ed pieces."

The dark skinned man waved his hand at the comment. "Nonsense. The membership looks to you as their leader, to give them guidance. Now we need for you to call for a general strike that will last until Congress passes the Corporate Profit Sharing Act." He pointed his finger at Archer. "The bastards on the Hill need to know that we'll be aware of every damned vote that's cast. Those that vote against us will be out on their ass when the election is held. Those that cooperate will get our support."

Lincoln shook his head. "I agreed to this spokesman position as someone who could simply advocate the worker's plight and the purpose of the union. You can't ask me to recommend a strike that would bring the country to a standstill."

"So, maybe this strike is another of your dreams. We need to show the power of our membership and get immediate results; no promises that can be reneged on later. Call your senator buddy and let him know what's going to happen. If he wants our support for president he's going to have to deliver on this legislation."

"I really don't think we can get away with blackmailing Congress."

"Are you kidding me? What do you think they've been doing to us all these years? They promise everything on earth during their lying campaigns, then when they're elected they do what the big corporations want, not what they promised us to get elected. That's blackmail by any other name. It's time to turn the tables."

* * *

The attractive blonde sat across from Zeke in his World News office in Rockefeller Center. She had walked in off the street, found her way to his office and introduced herself. "I have to say, it's been a long time since I've run across anyone from Walnut Grove, Kansas, here in New York," Zeke said, settling into his desk chair. "I suppose it's nearly impossible that you don't know Rocky Wellington?"

Beverly Hawkins smiled. "Well, I suppose a lot of folks outside of Walnut Grove know him now," she said, "but Rocky and I had, well, a special relationship."

"Oh?"

She leaned forward. "I don't want to be indelicate, but I also don't want to be misunderstood. Rocky and I had an affair for several years."

Zeke chuckled. "I'm sure that a lot of young ladies could make the same claim, Beverly. Rocky was quite the lady's man before he was married."

"Our affair was while he was married."

That tidbit got Zeke's attention. "I see. While he was living in Walnut Grove?"

"Yes. But when Rocky got his offer to move to New York he broke it off. Left me to rot in that hell hole."

"And you haven't seen him since?"

"Oh, I tried, but Rocky's become skilled at avoiding me." She sighed. "You see, things have not gone very well for me since those days. My husband and I divorced, I kicked around here and there: Kansas City, St. Louis, finally here in New York. I don't have a lot of skills, Mr. Porter, it's been a tough life. I tried to call Rocky, hoped as a big shot on Wall Street he could help me find a job, but he never returned my calls. I guess having anything to do with an old screwing buddy isn't exactly acceptable in his social circles."

"So why have you come to me, Miss Hawkins?"

"Rocky made me promises back when we were younger," she started. "Said he would help out, you know, financially?"

"And has he?"

Beverly shook her head. "Not a damned dime." She looked at Zeke imploringly, a sad expression causing her blue eyes to open wide. "We were in love, Mr. Porter, yet he was trapped with Robin, had to marry her, he said. Told me we could still see one another, had to be discrete, hinted that he had big plans, wasn't going to hang around Kansas much longer, and when he left he'd take me with him."

The alleged scenario caused Zeke's affair with Robin to flash through his mind. "And you believed that? He was happily married, Miss Hawkins," he added, knowing that Rocky was only happily married to his own career.

She laughed sharply. "Come on, Mr. Porter. I know better than that. Hell, they didn't even have sex for the longest time. He was too damned into that bank. And me," she added with a crooked smile.

Zeke recalled Robin's description of her sex life with Rocky as infrequent and unexciting. "So, I repeat, why are you here today?"

She drew a deep breath. "Well, it's hard to believe that Rocky is running for president. It's almost a dream, maybe a nightmare, I don't know. Anyway, I'm damned certain he wouldn't want me to suddenly show up and tell the world what I know about him."

"It's not unusual for people to come out of the woodwork and claim they've had an affair with a presidential candidate, Miss Hawkins. It would be his word against yours and, no disrespect, but I believe the public would side with Rocky."

"What if I had proof?"

"What sort of proof?"

"I had his son, Mr. Porter. From what I understand a simple DNA test could prove he was the father."

Zeke sat back in his chair. "And why did you wait until now to reveal all this, and why to me?"

"When Rocky took off for New York I figured I had been left at the gate. He was off to be a big shot and there was no way he was going to honor his promise to me. After all, I was just a small town whore he used for his pleasure. Anyway, I found out I was pregnant and that ended my marriage. My husband was impotent, so when I started showing he threw me out. I was on my own. I figured, hell, that's the way life can be, you know, so I just plowed ahead and did the best I could. It wasn't easy, but my baby and I managed."

She paused, gathered herself and continued. "But things got tight, Mr. Porter. I couldn't support us both on what little I was making, plus, moving from city to city just wasn't a good life for my little boy." She hung her head, shoulders slumped and sighed.

Zeke waited, trying to decide what parts of this story, if any, he believed.

Beverly looked up, her face scrunched up and her eyes watering. "I had to put my boy up for adoption. It was the only fair thing for him." Tears were rolling down her cheeks now. Zeke offered his handkerchief. She took it, wiped her eyes, then blew her nose.

"Does your son know that Rocky's his father?"

"Not a chance. I told him his old man ran off when he got me pregnant, which just happens to be the truth." She forced a smile. "So I figure now it's time to reach out to Rocky one more time."

"Blackmail?"

"I prefer to think of it as child support; getting what was due me a long time ago. Hell, he's got plenty of money, won't miss a few dollars. If he were to own up to his responsibilities I could try and find my boy, spend time with him, give him the things I couldn't before." She looked at Zeke hopefully. "And maybe I could hang up my waitress shoes and have a normal life."

The story, if true, was both tragic and explosive. But Zeke, true to his nature, was skeptical. "You say your affair lasted a couple of years?"

"We got together at my place almost every week." She explained how her husband was on the road all the time. "Started when Rocky was in college and ended when he moved to New York."

Rocky was always pointing out girls on campus that he had seduced, frequently describing the encounters in lurid detail, yet he had never mentioned being with a married woman. "I'm assuming you used some form of protection all that time, so how did you manage to get pregnant?"

Beverly smiled. "You're good at digging for details, aren't you? Well, to tell you the truth when Rocky told me he was heading to New York, leaving me behind, I was mad as hell. I fumed and stewed over things but, after I calmed down I came up with a plan. I called him a couple of weeks later, said I understood, didn't want to stand in his way, all that crap, then invited him to come over for one last taste of paradise, you know?"

"And he agreed?"

"Honey, I was the best lay west of the Mississippi." She shot him a smirk. "Still in the top three this side even today." Zeke felt himself blush. "So, damned right he agreed."

"So you went off your birth control, hoped to get pregnant and trap him?"

Beverly shook her head. "You could write a helluva romance novel, Mr. Porter. That was exactly what I did. We spent three days together and I nearly wore him out, you know what I mean? Anyway, about the time he was settling in up here on Wall Street was when I found out I was pregnant."

"That's when your husband threw you out?"

She sighed. "Yeah, poor dumb bastard. Anyway, that's when I started trying to contact Rocky, let him know what he'd done."

"But he refused to talk to you?"

"Not a word; not a phone call; nothing. I even came up here to New York, tried to see him at his office, but security there was better than what you have here. His secretary would see me coming and call the guards. I didn't have much money to keep hanging around so I gave up, went to Kansas City to live with an old friend while I had the baby."

"How long have you been back in New York?"

"Got a lead on a job here a couple of years ago. Was scratching around, living like a dog and, what the hell, old Rocky becomes a U.S. Senator. Unbelievable!"

"Did you try and contact him then?"

Beverly shook her head. "Too damned busy staying alive. I worked two jobs, was almost always exhausted. I figured he was always down there in D.C. anyway, so I just kept my head down, paycheck to paycheck, you understand?"

Zeke nodded. He certainly understood the strain of working multiple jobs to keep afloat here in New York. "So now that Rocky's a candidate for the presidency you figure you've got some leverage, huh?"

"Yeah, that's a good word, leverage."

"Why come to me?"

"I don't know much about politics, but if I had showed up out of nowhere again and tried to see Rocky I'd be looking over my shoulder every night. People like me are expendable. Hell, if I was to fall into the East River or be found in a dumpster somewhere nobody would give a damn, right?"

"So you're afraid that Rocky would harm you or your son if you went public with your accusations?"

"Happens every day is what I understand. Now, if you were to take my message to Rocky, kind of serve as, what do you call it, an intermediary, then I'd be more comfortable with the arrangement. I don't want to sit face to face with the bastard anyway. I just want what's due me, Mr. Porter."

"And how much did you have in mind, Miss Hawkins?"

She leaned back, her eyes searching the ceiling, tongue edging out of the corner of her mouth. She leaned forward and stared directly into Zeke's eyes. "I figure a million dollars even would be just about right."

* * *

Edith McLean's office was a reflection of her personality: prim and proper, everything in its place. Zeke wondered if her apartment was as neat and organized. A meeting here, rather than in the conference room or his own office indicated a recent visit with Carl Sinclair, the owner of World News, and some form of pronouncement regarding Zeke's upcoming priorities.

"The Bottom Line" had soared to the top of the ratings with Zeke's flair for identifying stories that piqued the public's interest, outrage or funny bone. For his part, Zeke's segments on the show had ranged from an expose on America's prison system, to wildly popular stories about Wall Street chicanery, climate change, black market human organ trading, the plight of the world's 50+ million refugees fleeing war, disease and terrorism, a series on Congressional Medal of Honor recipients, the Olympics, and interviews with leading personalities around the globe.

He had also dipped his journalistic pen wherever his interest drew him and the public had responded by eagerly reading his syndicated column ("The truth no matter where it leads"), every week. His views were respected, his opinions admired and he began to suffer the curse of celebrity, unable to negotiate his old haunts around the city without being mobbed for autographs.

He had come a long way since that fateful day so many years ago when he sat here in Edith's office, proud of his humble collection of college articles and short stories, thrilled beyond belief that she would take a chance on him. Zeke smiled as he recalled those salad days of struggle and adventure.

He had truly found his niche in life; exploring the best and the worst of the human species. It wasn't the subject matter of the stories that necessarily interested him, it was the people. He had met every walk of life, every possible representation of the human race and whether they were friendly or hostile, interesting or dull, he found something entertaining in them all. He had truly found his passion in life and his three Pulitzers reflected how good he was at his chosen profession.

The door behind him opened and Edith walked briskly to her desk, sat down and smiled at him. "Are you still friends with Rocky Wellington?" she asked.

Zeke wondered where this question had come from? He laughed. "As far as I know."

Edith nodded enthusiastically. "Good. We want to take advantage, rather Carl wants you to take advantage of that friendship and devote a segment a week to his presidential campaign," she said.

"As part of a series on all the candidates?"

"No, Carl doesn't give a shit about any of the others. He wants a focus on Wellington; a positive focus."

Zeke shifted uneasily in his chair. "But that's not objective, Edith."

"Carl is not interested in objectivity, Zeke. He wants Rocky Wellington in the White House."

Zeke shook his head. "I can't do that, Edith. Even a profile on all the candidates doesn't interest me. This campaign will be dull and uneventful. It's not something I want to focus the show's attention on. There are too many other important issues to air."

Edith shot him a frown. "In this country there's nothing more exciting and dramatic than a presidential campaign, Zeke. You know that. Why the hesitation?"

"Like I said, this campaign is open and shut. Rocky has the backing of corporate America, Wall Street and is a hero to the workers of this country. The opposition has no one who can hold a candle, so I predict no controversy, no excitement, no news story worthy of a segment a week."

"What if I told you Carl insisted?"

Zeke sighed. "He's never levied a demand on me before. Why now?"

Edith shook her head. "It doesn't matter what his reasons are, Zeke. He's the goddamned owner and we do as he says."

Zeke leaned forward, elbows on knees. "Look, Edith, the truth is I'm too close to Rocky. As you know our relationship goes back to college. I just can't provide an objective perspective. You want someone else on the staff to do it, O.K., but I would be too biased to give an accurate picture of the man."

"What about his wife?"

Zeke sat back. "Robin? What about her?"

"She's the real story of the campaign. Perhaps a focus on her rather than Rocky would be of more interest to the public."

"And to Carl?"

"Well, he *is* a man and she's a beautiful woman."

"No, I want to focus on things that are more important than this campaign. It's a simple beauty contest with no drama, controversy or excitement. If my refusal costs me my job, then----"

Edith held up the palm of her hand to Zeke. "Don't be ridiculous. Carl may be stubborn, but he's no fool." She sighed. "Let me talk to him. I'm sure he'll be disappointed, but I personally admire your integrity."

That last word caused Zeke to flinch and close his eyes. Integrity. Just repeating the word in his mind caused a bad taste in his mouth. Although his journalistic integrity was beyond repute, his personal integrity had been tarnished by his affair with Robin and it gnawed at him every day. His mind raced against his dilemma. As he walked back to his office, he realized there was something he had to do, something that had been brewing for a long time.

# # #

29

They met at the southern end of Central Park, just off Columbus Circle. From his vantage point on a bench he watched her glide towards him. She was absolutely gorgeous; every curve he knew so well accentuated by the chic tan pant suit, her hair flowing down over her shoulders, her wide, inviting smile as he stood to greet her.

"What a beautiful day," she said as she removed her sunglasses and kissed him on the cheek.

"Almost as gorgeous as you are," he replied.

"Flattery will get you me," she said with a wink.

He gestured east towards The Pond. "Let's take a walk."

"Sure," she said. "It'll stimulate our appetites. I've got reservations at Tavern on the Green," she added, referring to the restaurant on the edge of the park.

He nodded, resisting the urge to take her hand. They moved down the path side by side, the late morning sun highlighting the dark green of the grass and trees and the clear blue of the sky and its reflection in the lakes. "We need to talk," he said, looking straight ahead.

"Ooh," she said, smiling. "Serious."

"Yeah, it is," he replied. "It's about us."

She stopped and turned to face him. "You're not going to ask me to leave Rocky again, are you? We've been through that, Zeke."

He stopped, head down, then slowly raised his eyes to hers. "Yes, we have, and you've always chosen to stay with him. I've gone along with that all these years, hoping that one day you'd change your mind and we could really be together; not stealing minutes here and there. It's not the life I want with you, Robin."

"Are you saying you don't love me anymore?" There was anger in her voice and a hint of fear.

He put a hand gently on her back and nudged her forward, feeling the tension there. "Of course I still love you; that's what makes this so difficult. You've made it clear that you'll never leave Rocky and I understand, I just want more out of my life; a chance to be with you all the time. But now you've got an opportunity to be the First Lady, as close to being that childhood princess you dreamed about as you'll ever get. I can't deny you that."

"And what does that mean exactly, Zeke?"

He stopped. "You belong with Rocky and I don't want to complicate your life, so I'm ending our affair."

"Just like that? After all these years?" She looked at him, her eyes wide. "There's someone else, isn't there?"

He shook his head. "No, there's no one else. It's just time for us both to face reality. It's over, Robin."

"That's bullshit, Zeke. It's just your guilt flaring up again. What knowledge of our affair would do to Rocky has always gnawed at you. Does his friendship mean more to you than us?"

"That's not a fair question. I've always loved you, Robin."

She pulled a strand of her hair back off her face and studied him, her eyes intent. "Jesus, Zeke!" She walked to the nearest bench and sat down hard, her back to him.

Zeke sat down beside her. He waited for a young couple to pass by, then lowered his voice. "We always meet when and where you want, share a few hours, then there's nothing in between until you want to see me again. All our relationship boils down to is the sex. You've never needed anything more, but I do. Now I finally see we'll never have the kind of relationship I want, so it's time to end it. Each of us can move on with our lives."

She pulled a handkerchief from her purse and dabbed at her eyes. They sat in awkward silence for a moment or two, her back still to him.

Finally she said, "It sounds like you've given this a lot of thought. Have you been this unhappy for a long time?"

"I've loved every minute we've spent together, Robin. I've only been miserable when we've been apart and that's been way too many times."

She said nothing, just dabbed at her eyes with her handkerchief.

"You need to be free so you can commit yourself to Rocky and his campaign. Without you by his side, he doesn't have a chance of winning."

She turned to face him. "Now you sound like his damned advisors. They want me to do interviews and even make speeches."

"Smart people. You would be the most glamorous First Lady that's ever been in the White House."

She smiled. "There's enough bullshit in you to make a good politician." They both laughed, then her face grew serious. She reached out and put her hand on his. "What do I have to do to change your mind, Zeke? We can still make this work. Even First Ladies can have affairs." Before he could answer she opened her purse and pulled out what looked like a credit card and held it out to him. "I've got a room at The Plaza," she said. "Let's spend the afternoon there and I'll remind you why you'd never want to leave me." She lowered her head and looked up at him through long, sensuous eyelashes; that sultry look that melted his heart and stoked his fires. Then she clicked her teeth at him, her gesture that suggested she was ready to devour him. "Let's skip lunch, baby," she said, her eyes boring into his.

He felt the pressure building in his head, his pulse quickening. This was the most difficult thing he had ever done in his life, but deep inside he knew what he was doing was right. "No, Robin. I've made up my mind. Don't make this any harder than it already is."

She stood up abruptly and threw the room key at him. It fluttered around like a butterfly and fell to the ground. "You're making the biggest mistake of your life, Zeke."

He sighed. "Well, maybe it is a mistake, but I don't think so. I'm sorry."

"Oh, you'll be sorry, alright. You're a fool." She spun on her heel and stormed away, never looking back.

Zeke leaned back on the bench and watched her walk away, anger in her quickened stride. She disappeared from view and he closed his eyes, the built up tension flowing from his body like sweat off a distance runner at the finish line. He was unbelievably relieved, yet his heart ached. He really did love her, but he couldn't continue a life in the shadows filled with guilt and the never-ending fear of discovery. He wanted a real relationship.

He opened his eyes, certain that everyone in the park was looking at him. It was the familiar feeling of paranoia he always felt when they were together. No more. They were both free now and he knew Robin would make the most of that freedom. He would be forgotten as she got swept up in the glamour and excitement of presidential campaigning. She would be a star, the celebrity status she had always sought.

Zeke bent down and picked up the hotel key from the ground. Perhaps she was right; he was a fool. Deep down inside he had always known she would never leave Rocky. But even in those moments when he had dreamt of them being together he was filled with insecurity and doubt. Would the newness of being together every day have eventually worn thin, Zeke wondered? Would she have left him for someone more exciting, more adventurous, more daring?

He fingered the hotel key and slid it into his coat pocket, a final memento of a time in his life he would never forget and a decision he would always question. He missed her already and the longing he knew would descend was like a door slammed in his face. He would survive this, he said to himself. He would survive this.

* * *

The two men looked like FBI agents: close-cropped haircuts, sunglasses, square jaws. Their black suits were off the rack, worn atop starched white shirts and plain blue ties. Robin had been expecting them, prompted by Rocky's explanation that they would be briefing her on campaign protocol.

She welcomed them into her Long Island home, showing them to the living room. Rocky was in D.C., plotting campaign strategy. "Thank you very much for seeing us Mrs. Wellington," the blonde man started, accepting Robin's invitation to sit on the couch.

"You're quite welcome," Robin said. "Might I offer you some coffee?" she said, gesturing towards a tray on the table beside her.

"Nothing for me," the blonde said.

"I'd love a cup," the other man said. "Black."

Robin poured a cup and handed it to him. "Sure I can't get you anything?" she asked the blonde.

The man shook his head. He was all business. "I hope your husband explained our purpose here this morning?"

"Not in any detail. Something about campaign protocol. Are you here to tell me what to wear and what to say?"

The blonde pulled out a small notebook and pen. "We're here to make certain suggestions that will be advantageous to your husband's campaign."

"It's standard procedure," the other man offered.

"Of course," Robin said, anxious to make her appropriate contributions. The thought of what it might mean to be the First Lady had dominated her dreams.

"Let's start with your cause," the blonde said.

"My cause?"

"Every First Lady has a cause: a charity, a disease, a human rights issue," the other man volunteered.

Robin's mind raced. She had never really been a do-gooder, never championed a particular cause or right. "Well, when we lived in Kansas I did volunteer work on the reservation," she said tentatively.

"The reservation?" the blonde man asked.

"There's an Osage Indian reservation a few miles from home. I used to go down there and help with the clinic and the dining hall. It was only once a month, but maybe---"

"That would be perfect," the other man said. He turned to the blonde. "We'd have to find a reservation close to D.C., but we could work that angle, what do you think?"

The blonde nodded. "Yeah, that could work. Anything else?" he asked Robin.

Robin shook her head. "Not really, sorry."

The blonde jotted something in his notebook. "Let's talk about getting pregnant," he said matter-of-factly.

"What?" Robin said with a laugh.

"Do you and your husband plan a pregnancy any time soon?" the other man asked.

"I would think that's a private matter between my husband and me," Robin answered, indignation in her voice.

"Mrs. Wellington," the blonde said patiently, "with respect, but as President and First Lady, you will have no private matters. Everything, and I mean everything, is open to an adoring public. Now do you plan a pregnancy?"

"Why don't you ask my husband?" Robin said.

"Actually, we already have," the blonde said.

"Well, why don't you share our plans with me?"

"We convinced him that it would be a good idea after the primaries," the other man said. "We'll need you on the campaign trail, but announcing that you're pregnant right before the election would attract a lot of votes."

"Well," Robin said, "what are we waiting for? If getting knocked up would buy a few votes---"

"Mrs. Wellington," the blonde said, holding up a hand, "we're only here to make suggestions that would assist your husband in his campaign."

Robin exhaled heavily, barely able to contain her anger. "Well, what else have you got to suggest: I dye my hair, take up skiing, learn Spanish?"

"Actually," the other man offered calmly, "all of those are good suggestions, but we only have one more that we feel is absolutely essential."

Robin folded her arms across her chest and stared at him. "Of course," she said sarcastically.

"We want to make certain there is nothing that the opposition will uncover that will, shall we say, disrupt your husband's chances in the election."

"Such as?" Robin asked.

"We've been following you for several years, ever since your husband began work here in New York."

"Really?" Robin said, her eyebrows raised.

"We're not here to judge you," the other man said.

"Judge me about what?" Robin asked, alarm now laced in her voice.

"About your affair with Zeke Porter," the blonde said.

Robin looked confused. They had been so careful. How in the world? "What do you mean?"

The other man produced an envelope and spread half a dozen pictures on the table. They were pictures that left no doubt as to the romantic adventures of Robin and Zeke.

"How in the world?" Robin said, hand raised to her mouth.

"We're very thorough, Mrs. Wellington," the blonde said. "Although it took an extraordinary amount of work to uncover what we have. You've been very discreet. Unfortunately we have enough here to cause your husband great harm, politically."

Robin sat in silence, her world racing around in her mind. "Does my husband know?"

"No, ma'am. Only our employers."

"And who are they?" she asked, not able to take her eyes off the pictures. She picked one up and studied it.

"We can't, of course, divulge their identities. Let's just say they have your husband's best interests at heart."

She glared at them and tossed the picture back onto the table. "So, what is this? Blackmail?"

The blonde managed a smile. "We have nothing to gain from exposing your affair, Mrs. Wellington. Quite the opposite. We're actually on your side. Well, your husband's side. We want to see him elected."

"Then why are you telling me this?"

"Because we want you to stop the affair. Immediately."

The blonde man leaned forward, his face serious. "If you continue, you risk someone uncovering your situation and that will all but end your husband's chances of being elected. Do we make ourselves clear?"

Robin closed her eyes. She was angry. Angry at their affair having been discovered, angry that it was now being used as a political football. She tried to steady her nerves, gain control of her emotions. Visions of living in the White House, adored by millions, championing some cause that would make her front page news flashed through her mind. Losing Zeke and even having a baby were a small price to pay for the fame and fulfillment she had always sought. Zeke had actually done her a favor. He was already old news. She opened her eyes and said firmly, "You won't have to worry about that issue any more. I'll take care of it immediately."

# # #

30

"So, what's this all about, Zeke?" Rocky demanded. "Normally, you'd have to go through my campaign manager to get an interview and then you'd have to submit your questions in advance and----"

"I appreciate you circumventing your procedure, Rocky," Zeke said. "But this is a very private matter and I didn't think you'd want to bubble it up your chain of command, so, naturally, this is all off the record."

The two men were in Senator Wellington's new house in McLean, Virginia. The cozy townhouse in Georgetown had become too small for the entertaining demanded of a fast-rising political star. Through the glass doors of the family room Zeke could see the swimming pool and the team of workers mowing the vast lawn and manicuring the shrubs. Rocky moved to the bar at the end of the room. "Want a drink, Zeke? This all seems rather serious, or at least, mysterious, so a stiff one might be in order?"

"Sure. Bourbon, rocks."

Rocky fished a few ice cubes out of a silver bucket on the bar counter and dropped them into a glass, filled it half way with Jack Daniel's, then did the same for himself. "Sometimes I wish we could go back to our college days, you know? No responsibilities, no stress, plenty of women." He walked back across the room and handed Zeke his drink. "The good old days, huh?"

"Seems like a million years ago, Rock."

Rocky settled into his chair with his own drink and held it aloft. "Cheers, old buddy."

"Cheers, Rock."

The senator took a healthy swig of his drink and leaned back in his chair, crossing his legs. "Now, what's so important?"

Zeke wondered if this was going to be a complete waste of time, but he had made Beverly a promise he would bring her proposition to Rocky. "Do you remember a woman named Beverly Hawkins? Back in Walnut Grove?"

Rocky wrinkled his nose as he pondered the question. "Hankins?"

"Hawkins. She said she knew you back then."

"Well, hell, Zeke, I knew lots of women back then. You know that," he added with a laugh.

"This one claimed you had an affair, Rock. While you were married."

"To hell you say? An affair, huh? Shit, Zeke, I can't remember every small town gal I might have banged back then, but I sure don't remember anyone named Beverly."

"Said she lived a few miles out of town. Her husband was some sort of salesman; on the road a lot. Said you two had a pretty torrid affair for a couple of years. She claimed you told her you were going to leave Robin, move to New York and take her with you."

Rocky laughed. "Boy, she must have been quite a piece of ass if I promised all that." He studied his drink a minute, then looked up. "No, I messed around a lot in college, can't count the number of women I had then, but once I got married, that was it."

"So you don't remember her at all?"

Rocky shook his head. "She might have been a customer at the bank or something, but no, Zeke. Why, this gal wanting some publicity now that I'm running for president?"

"Something like that."

"Sounds like my word against hers, don't you think?"

"Well, she claims you got her pregnant, Rock. Says you owe her child support and a stipend to live on."

Rocky laughed. "Shit, Zeke. I thought you had more moxie than that. Damned woman comes out of the woodwork, claims I'm the father of her child after all these years. Smells like day old fish to me."

"She says she's tried to contact you several times, but that you always refused to see her."

"Do you realize how many people off the street claim to be an old friend or have a complaint or advice or just want to say hello? Keeping those kinds of people away is what I pay my security people for."

"Well, she's prepared to take you to court, Rock and use DNA testing to prove you're the father."

"Unless?"

"Wants a million dollars and she'll go away."

Rocky drained his drink and shook his head. "Until she spends that million, then she'll be back for another taste. No thanks, Zeke. Tell whoever this gal is to go to hell."

"You sure there's nothing to this, Rock? Some little fling you might have had, forgotten about?"

Rocky leaned forward in his chair. "When you get to be my age you tend to remember your carousing days in detail, but I never heard of Beverly what's-her-name." He shook his head. "A million dollars. Jesus. I suppose there'll be a few of these falling out of the sky before it's all over. Fame has its drawbacks, my friend."

"Well, if these vetting people are as thorough as I've heard, they should have uncovered Miss Hawkins by now, don't you think?"

Rocky smiled. "Not if she's a phony, Zeke."

Zeke shook his head. "Well, I'll pass your message to Miss Hawkins, but I have a feeling you haven't heard the last from her. She seemed pretty determined."

"I appreciate the heads up. I'll sit on this until she makes her next move and then I'll probably have to let my people know what's going on so they can deal with it. I'd appreciate you being as honest with this woman as possible in terms of her barking up the wrong tree."

"And you're prepared to go to court and subject yourself to a DNA test?"

"I think we're a long way from anything that dramatic, Zeke. Not something that fits neatly into my campaign, you know?"

"Rocky, one last time. You're absolutely sure you couldn't be the father of this woman's son?"

"Absolutely, Zeke. Absolutely."

"Well, that's good enough for me; we'll just have to see how Miss Hawkins reacts."

"I wouldn't get yourself too involved in this, Zeke. Pass along my message and get as far away from this woman as you can. It could get very messy."

Zeke nodded and stood up. "Understand. Now, not to waste my few minutes with you, how is the campaign going from your perspective?"

Rocky laughed. "You've got investigative reporter blood in your veins, don't you? Well, it's no secret that I've put a lot of emphasis on getting this Corporate Profit Sharing Act passed as proof that I can bring both sides of the aisle together again."

"The legislation Lincoln is pushing?"

"Yeah, just like the Minimum Wage Bill, but this time he didn't have a dream," he added with a laugh.

Zeke hesitated, then asked. "So, how is Robin adjusting to presidential campaigning? The press seems to love her."

Rocky smiled. "Well, she was rather reluctant at first, but I think the thought of being the First Lady has caught her imagination. They've bought her a whole new wardrobe for her public appearances and the campaign plans to use her good looks to my advantage. She's really got the makings of a solid teammate."

Zeke swallowed hard. "Well, it sounds like Robin is finally going to step out of your shadow."

Rocky nodded. "I think she's going to really enjoy the campaign and I'm sure you'll be at the top of our guest list at the White House." He held out a hand to shake.

Zeke knew that crossing paths with Robin was inevitable and he struggled with how he would handle that awkward situation. Somehow, having ended his affair with her was like a cleansing of sorts. In time the guilt would fade as would his feelings for Robin. It was still difficult to look Rocky in the eye, but Zeke did just that as he shook Rocky's hand. "Well, there's an awful lot of ground to be covered before that happens, but I'll be pulling for you both, old friend."

# # #

31

The television studio set was sparsely decorated, three leather chairs surrounding a coffee table containing a pitcher of water and three glasses. The rest of the set was bare, a black backdrop behind the trio of participants. It was the weekly edition of "The Bottom Line," and Zeke had just welcomed his television audience and turned immediately to the subject at hand.

"In view of the current debate over the sharing of corporate profits and the pending legislation, I have asked two opposing viewpoints to present their cases on our show," Zeke said. "With me tonight are Professor Jeremy Rivers, Chairman of the Wesley School of Business at Harvard University, and Marilyn Sloan, who is the president of the Fairness in Taxation Association of America. Welcome to you both."

Rivers and Sloan both nodded their acceptance of Zeke's welcome to the most highly watched show on television.

"Professor Rivers, in view of corporate America's staggering level of profits, is it fair, under the current tax code, that most corporations pay almost no tax?"

Rivers was nattily attired in a grey herringbone jacket, white shirt and red bow tie. His disheveled hair and dark, horn-rimmed glasses gave him the stereotypical professorial appearance. He spoke as if addressing a room full of students, making his points with jabbing gestures and a gaze that alternated between his host and the television camera. "When corporations make record profits it is good for America; it reflects a strong economy and provides funds for stockholder dividends, research and development, and other investments that lead to growth.

Corporations are simply following tax code legislation that allows them to minimize their tax bill, legally."

"We understand that Business 101 argument, Professor, but the question is whether or not this system is fair, given the wide disparity between corporate profits and the constantly shrinking income of those who work for the corporation. Marilyn, what are your thoughts?"

Sloan was a handsome woman, mid-fifties, with brown, shoulder length hair and a pleasing smile. She wore a dark blue pant suit with silver accessories. Her eyes remained on the host as she spoke. "I believe this discussion should go well beyond arguments over the fairness of the tax code, but should center more on the very essence of the corporate structure and the mindset that suggests that what is good for General Motors is good for America."

"Why is that old catch phrase not relevant in your thinking?" Zeke asked.

"As someone who's served in an executive management capacity in several of our larger corporations, I can tell you that the goals and incentives imposed on me did nothing to benefit my fellow employees or the public in general. Achieving higher and higher profit and revenue goals put bonus money in my pocket, but never concerned itself with quality or product safety or anything that was inherently beneficial to society as a whole."

"It seems to me," Professor Rivers interjected, "that a successful corporation not only provided you with hard earned bonuses and other benefits, but more importantly, it provided jobs for thousands of employees, employees whose salaries were fed back into our economy, spurring even more growth and economic success."

Marilyn's voice was tinged with irritation. "My point is that the goals I was forced to pursue weren't aligned with a modest growth in revenue and profit each year. They had to be stretched beyond reason and that led to achieving those goals by any means possible. That often meant lower salaries for the workers or reductions in staff, avoidance of quality and safety measures, elimination of training programs and other activities deemed detrimental to achieving corporate financial objectives."

"Well, it's been a while since you were out there in the business world," the Professor argued with a condescending smile, "and you have to realize how competitive things have become in just the last few years. Technology and worldwide business models have accelerated the need to improve and upgrade processes and procedures at an unheard of rate. To remain competitive in today's world requires constant pressure on management to improve their market share and profits. Without achieving those goals year after year the company falls behind the competition and eventually dies. That, in turn, leads to a displaced workforce and a number of other negative implications for society in general. The need for excessive pressure to achieve these goals comes with the territory today."

"I'd like to explore that thesis further," Zeke said. "When you apply what you call excessive demands on performance, don't you run the risk of creating the need for shortcuts, bending the rules and achieving these goals at any cost?"

"Exactly," Marilyn Sloan said. "Look at corporate advertising as an example. The phrase *caveat emptor* was created for a reason. It warns the consumer that what you hear and see regarding a product should be treated with skepticism, whether it's an automobile or a prescription drug. Just remember that the purpose of the advertisement is to get you to buy that product and that basically means anything goes; absence of meaningful details and unsupported claims and other advertising gimmicks are the norm. It's a manifestation of the lengths corporations will go to achieve their goals. It's misleading and dishonest."

"*Caveat emptor*, indeed," Zeke said. "Let's return our discussion to the original point, that being what many are calling excessive profits and the inability of most workers to benefit from those profits. The tax code question aside, is it fair that corporations get to keep those profits while the workers that have created them receive less and less in terms of take home income each year?"

"Well," Marilyn said, "the obvious answer is no. When executive compensation has gone up over three hundred percent in the past decade while take home pay for the average worker has actually declined, there's an imbalance there that needs reconciliation."

"You have to compensate executive talent appropriately or they will flee to the competition," the Professor said. "One can argue that the collective workers made those profits in the first place, but that is an erroneous claim. Workers are, in most cases, interchangeable; that is, the jobs they perform are compartmentalized and highly structured. Over time, and with the appropriate training, those jobs can be performed by anyone. The executive managers in a corporation, on the other hand, are the ones who control and direct those resources, who introduce innovation and cost-cutting procedures, who create 'a better mouse trap', and who guide those workers towards corporate goals. They are the ones who truly create the profits we're talking about, not the average worker."

"That argument may well be true," Zeke said, "but the question remains, is it fair? How long can this imbalance go on without blowback from the mass of workers who are struggling to make ends meet while watching the corporate executives buy yachts, homes on the Riviera, and expensive works of art? How long before this boils over?"

"I think we're close to the boiling point right now," Marilyn said. "You're obviously familiar with the efforts of Reverend Lincoln Archer and his campaign to increase worker benefits. The overwhelming support he is receiving from the workers is a powerful political force. But revising the tax structure for corporations is just one step. How do the workers gain their logical share of corporate profits? How do we introduce fairness into a world where that word is not part of the daily lexicon?"

The producer gave Zeke the high sign and the camera zoomed in on the host. "I'd like to continue our discussion, but unfortunately we've run out of time tonight. I'd like to thank my guests, Marilyn Sloan and Professor Jeremy Rivers for their time and thoughts here tonight. Goodnight and please join us next week."

The klieg lights went out and aides appeared to remove the microphones clipped to the three participant's clothes. Zeke leaned forward to address his two guests. "We really didn't have enough time tonight to adequately address the issue in my opinion. Would you two be available in a couple of weeks to resume this discussion?"

"What further points would you like to address?" Marilyn asked.

Zeke nodded. "To add more objectivity to the discussion I'd like to suggest that each of you switch sides in your argument. Some creative thinking from the opposite side of the debate would be healthy and might even wind up with some common ground solutions. What do you guys think?"

The two guest contemplated the suggestion. Finally Marilyn said, "I think it's a brilliant idea and it will certainly challenge my ability to see the other side of my perspective. I'm in. What about you, Professor?"

Jeremy nodded, the serious expression on his face slowly transforming into a smile. "I think it's a classic academic exercise, but it might just set an example for those who are actually engaged on the front lines of the battle."

"Precisely my hope," Zeke said.

# # #

32

T he framework for House Bill (H.R. 215), the Corporate Profit Sharing Act, had originated within the bowels of the Workers United lobby group and had been sponsored by an enthusiastic coalition of pro-union representatives in the House. Sensitive to the mood of the workers of the country and their now-powerful voting bloc, the House passed the bill and sent it on to the Senate for ratification.

Convinced that the bill would be defeated in the Senate, Workers United threatened a nationwide strike if that happened. Fearing that the repercussions from the strike would be placed on their shoulders, and, with an eye towards the hundred million votes represented by the union, Senator Adams called for a late night meeting in his office. As always in such tumultuous circumstances, he saw the situation not as a potential disaster, but as an opportunity to advance The Ten's agenda.

* * *

Senator Sam Adams' office in the Dirksen Office Building on Capitol Hill was a corner suite, reflecting his seniority and related power. Along the far wall, black-framed pictures of the senator with various sports figures, celebrities, and other luminaries were carefully aligned. Behind his expansive desk, citations, awards and other self-promoting memorabilia were also displayed as in a museum. After everyone had settled into their chairs and the leather couch near the door, Senator Adams started the meeting.

"Let's start with an analysis of the bill's merits and its downside, then I'd like to advance our thinking beyond the obvious here," the senator from Ohio began. "Brad, why don't you start?"

The senator from Virginia nodded. "The bill's main features are actually quite straightforward," he started, the twenty pages of legislation lying in front of him. "A mandatory redistribution of fifty percent of corporate profits back to the workers."

"The union's position is that those profits will get put directly into the hands of the workers, who will spend that money and bolster the economy," the senator from New Jersey added.

"It's bald, unfiltered blackmail," the senator from Texas exclaimed, looking like the sheriff who was ready to raise a posse and gallop off after the varmints who had robbed his town's bank.

"We obviously have the votes to defeat this bill, but what are the long term effects of pissing off a hundred million voters?" New Jersey added, tossing his glasses onto his copy of the bill in exasperation.

"We're missing the point here," Ohio said, fed up with the now stale arguments that had been hashed and re-hashed on the Senate floor. "Workers United has offered us a gift on a silver platter."

"Gift?" Texas asked, a look of confusion on his leathery face.

"This is just like the Minimum Wage Bill situation," Ohio explained. "It has the full support of the House, but stands to be defeated without a champion in the Senate."

The office was silent for a second then, "Rocky," Texas said, jabbing a finger at Ohio.

"Yes, Rocky," Ohio said, wondering why the obvious was obvious only to himself. "If we position him as the advocate for this bill, make it appear that getting it passed was his doing, he'll once again be the hero in averting this strike and championing the worker's demands."

"The agent of compromise," New Jersey said with a smile.

"Exactly," Ohio said, "and just in time for the election. We couldn't ask for a better agenda."

"But how in the world do we sell this to our corporate supporters?" Kansas asked. "They sure as hell won't cater to the idea of how to spend their profits."

"I've already explained that at our last meeting," Ohio said, his frustration beginning to show at having to repeat himself. "If we give those union bastards an inch they'll be back with another threat to strike any time they want," Kansas argued.

"Part of the compromise," Texas said, "is to get an iron-clad commitment from the damned union that they won't strike while the terms of the bill are in force."

"They'll never go for that," New Jersey said.

"We give them enough to make them happy, they'll sign up for anything," Kansas said. "Believe me, this strike may sound like a great idea for the union, but they don't have enough money to keep all those workers afloat for any length of time. The pressure to end the strike will grow and grow. If we wait them out we'll get a deal we can live with."

"Not sure we've got the leverage to test that theory," New Jersey said, shaking his head.

"Look," Ohio interjected, "we've obviously got to avoid a strike, but to do so we have to leave the full profit sharing language in the bill. It's the cornerstone of the legislation and a deal breaker if we try and take it out."

"But how do we sell that to the block of senators we need to convince to have enough votes for passage?" Kansas asked.

Ohio sighed and lowered his voice. "Let me explain one more time what's really going to happen here," he said.

Everyone leaned forward in anticipation.

* * *

"This could get ugly, Zeke," Lincoln Archer said over the phone. "You might be the only person who could arbitrate a discussion between Rocky and me."

"I'm not sure he would agree with that, Lincoln."

"Actually, he already called me and suggested the idea. He's willing to participate in a secret sit down between the three of us."

"I'm sure there are plenty of other people out there who are more knowledgeable on this subject. I'm not an economist or a politician, Lincoln."

"Precisely, Zeke. As a reporter you can be objective and see both sides. Rocky and I are too vested in our own perspectives to do this alone. Let's try this secret meeting and see how it goes. Look," he added, "if we're successful you can write about it and have a best seller. If the meeting falls apart, it never happened."

"You're more of a politician than you think, Lincoln."

Lincoln laughed. "I don't know whether that's a compliment or an insult, but if you say you'll do this, it doesn't matter."

Zeke had no desire to become involved in a political imbroglio, but he realized he might be the only man in the country who could legitimately serve as an objective arbitrator between these two participants. "I'm honored that you two think I can make a difference, so how can I say no?"

# # #

33

Each man came to the meeting on the Corporate Profit Sharing Act (CPSA) with different objectives and guidance. Lincoln represented the interests of Workers United who sought the full profit sharing provisions of the bill as originally drafted by their lobbying firm in Washington and passed by the House. Their leverage was the threat of a nationwide strike that would cost the corporate world a small fortune and bring the wrath of the country down on the Senate.

Rocky came to the meeting with the assurance from The Ten that he could agree to the full provisions of the House bill as a starting point, but that he would need some concessions they could use to pacify the corporate crowd. What The Ten really sought, more than the mere passage of legislation, was to make Rocky the hero of the moment as another catalyst to his campaign.

Zeke saw his role as an objective outsider who just happened to be personal friends with both the negotiators. He would help assure that the discussions remained calm and friendly, and he could present arguments from both sides of the issue. But the avoidance of a crippling strike and the rise of worker's rights were paramount in his thinking.

To further his role as a moderator, Zeke chose his apartment in New York as a "neutral site," and the three men met there with the intention of staying until an agreement had been reached. All phones were turned off, the television unplugged, the refrigerator stocked with beer and snacks. It was like their college days when they would get together to argue the issues of the day.

"You guys remember Professor Watkins at K-State?" Zeke asked after everyone had a beer in hand.

Lincoln shook his head while Rocky took a long draw on his beer.

"Well, the last edition of the Wildcat had his obituary. The old guy finally bought the farm."

"You still read that paper?" Lincoln asked.

"Have to keep up with the old alma mater," Zeke said.

Rocky smiled. "All I remember about that cranky old bastard was that he had a good looking daughter, a cheerleader as I recall."

Lincoln pointed at Rocky. "Yeah, she was a looker in her little uniform."

"She looked better out of her little uniform," Rocky said with a grin.

Lincoln looked shocked. "You mean—"

"Rocky made his rounds through the cheerleading squad while you and I were burning the midnight oil in the library," Zeke offered.

"Hey," Rocky said with a tinge of mock indignation in his voice, "I was in the library too." He paused and took another sip of beer. "There was a couch up on the sixth floor where I studied female anatomy."

* * *

The negotiations went on all day and into the evening, Rocky and Lincoln arguing their various perspectives, Zeke interjecting comments to keep the discussions on topic and aimed at resolution. Point by point the two sides reached compromise until, near midnight only one issue remained that kept the two sides apart, Rocky's need for a "carrot" to appease his ultra-conservative colleagues in exchange for the agreements he had already made in their name.

Weary, disheveled, with bloodshot eyes and exhausted brains, the three men sat in a silent stupor struggling to create yet one more idea. They were so close, but needed one more burst of inspiration. Suddenly, Zeke sat up straight, a renewed look of energy in his eyes. "I've got it," he exclaimed.

* * *

"Rocky, this might just work," the senator from New Jersey said. "This new wrinkle to allow the corporations to deduct their profit sharing payments to the workers as a business expense is pure genius."

Rocky offered his best humble expression, unwilling to volunteer that it had been Zeke's idea. "Reverend Archer assures me that this provision, and all the terms in front of you will be acceptable to Workers United."

"Well," Ohio said, "this is a great accomplishment, Rocky, but from now on we'd prefer you run something this important by us first."

"Yes, sir," Rocky said, knowing that the specifics of the meeting had been reviewed, one on one, with the Ohioan before Rocky suggested the meeting to Archer. It was yet another ploy, enacted in front of others, to illustrate the senior senator's command of the situation. The senator from Texas said, "Well, we don't want to discourage the boy's initiative, but you're right, Senator. Nonetheless, Rocky, you've been able to strike a grand compromise on this bill. It will make you a hero to the workers, and you need to take full credit for the expensing of profit distributions to pull our corporate colleagues back into the fold."

"Yes, sir," Rocky said, glancing at Ohio who gave him a subtle nod.

"This will effectively eliminate the tax on corporate profits," Virginia said. "How do we make up for that lost revenue?"

"If you look at page 5, paragraph 4, Senator," Rocky said, "you'll see the clause that increases the tax on those making more than $500,000 per year. That will cover the revenue shortage quite nicely."

"Our wealthy friends will be furious," Virginia said.

Ohio nodded, "That's true, but we have a long term solution to that problem," he added, eyeing Virginia, who nodded his understanding of the behind-the-scenes strategy that would be employed later.

"How many votes do we need?" Kansas asked.

"Probably ten or twelve in our chamber," Texas answered.

"I'll fly this by Charlie, but I'm sure the House will see this version of their bill as an improvement," New Jersey said. "This could be a winner for all of us."

"Well," Ohio said, "our objective in this whole exercise has always been to underscore Rocky's ability to achieve compromise." He smiled at Rocky, who smiled back.

"The country certainly can't afford a prolonged strike and the longer this situation goes unresolved the more ornery all parties will become," Texas said. "The time for this to fly might just be right now."

Ohio turned to Rocky and patted him on the shoulder. "I think Rocky's given us a great place to start. Let's go to work and get those votes."

* * *

The news anchor sat awaiting his cue. The show's theme music started and the director pointed at him. "Good evening," the nattily attired man began. "Monumental news out of Washington tonight as both houses of Congress have passed the Corporate Profit Sharing Act that establishes a landmark process for sharing corporate profits with workers and averting a possible nationwide strike. For more on this breaking story we go to our correspondent on Capitol Hill, Morgan Rivers. Morgan?"

"Yes, Jim, today's vote in the House on their original legislation as modified by the Senate requires corporations to distribute half of their profits back to workers in the form of cash bonuses, stock and stock options, and in exchange those corporations may deduct, as a business expense, those employee distributions, thus eliminating their overall corporate tax burden. This is seen as a significant victory for Workers United, whose spokesman, Reverend Lincoln Archer, is with us now from Wichita, Kansas. Reverend, good evening."

"Good evening, Morgan." Lincoln sat behind his desk in his Church of Hope office. He looked weary, dark circles under both eyes and the hint of a twenty four hour beard. After negotiating the details of the new bill with Rocky and Zeke in New York, he had then travelled to Washington the next morning to review the results with Workers United management. After getting their approval he stayed in D.C. long enough to review a draft version of the Senate bill, then flew back to Wichita, arriving here mid-day, only to be swallowed up by church business. He was exhausted.

"Reverend, today's passage of this historic legislation signals a fundamental shift in how corporations in this country keep their books and how they distribute their record profits. You must be very pleased with the outcome?"

Lincoln nodded, his bloodshot eyes reflecting a hint of satisfaction. "Yes, Morgan, this is a victory for workers everywhere and avoids a nationwide strike that would have crippled our economy. The workers in this country have risen as one to demand their share of the bounty corporations have enjoyed and the extra money they will have in their pockets will help rebuild the middle-class and pull thousands of families out of poverty."

"Reverend, to offset the loss of tax revenue from the corporate world, the bill calls for an increase in the tax rate for the wealthiest of Americans. Do you consider this shift of tax burden justified?"

Lincoln offered a wry smile and a sigh. As Rocky predicted, both houses of Congress had added amendments by the score to the bill. In order to "sell" the wealthy tax rate increase, a well hidden change to the inheritance laws was inserted that gave the wealthy greater relief in terms of passing their fortunes on to their families. In addition, funds were added for numerous back-home projects, pork, that bypassed normal budget allocation procedures, skirted debate, due diligence and other parliamentary procedures. Business as usual in Washington. "Well, Morgan, I believe this part of the bill reflects the national mood that our wealthiest citizens have enjoyed their good fortune on the backs of the workers and raising their tax contribution to the overall good is long overdue."

"Well, Reverend, with this success behind you, what's next; immigration reform, environmental issues?"

Lincoln offered a tired smile. "We're just going to relax and celebrate our victory with this bill. It's been quite a struggle, we've sent our message, and it's time to sit back and enjoy the benefits of all our efforts."

"Thank you, Reverend, and now for the other side of this story, let's turn to the man who orchestrated the compromise on the Hill that made this bill a reality, Senator Rocky Wellington from New York."

The scene shifted to Rocky's office on Capitol Hill. "Senator, congratulations on your part in this landmark legislation."

Unlike Lincoln, Rocky appeared well rested and energetic. He was decked out in a dark blue suit and matching tie and makeup had hidden the strain of the past few days. He offered a wide smile. "Well, thank you, Morgan, but I was just a facilitator here. Tribute belongs to my colleagues who supported this bill, both in the House and the Senate."

"The most important message here, it seems, is that, with a facilitator such as yourself, compromise is still possible on the Hill and problems can indeed be solved as opposed to the hopeless gridlock we've witnessed in recent years."

"Well, that's generous of you to give me so much credit, Morgan, but let's not overlook the importance of this bill to our overall economy and national mood. This legislation provides benefits for both sides of the aisle and both sides of the labor/management paradigm. The bottom line is that the overall effect is good for our country: more money in the hands of the workers, lower overall taxes for corporations, and an improved working relationship in Congress for the future."

"Senator, many political observers are citing your work here as a demonstration of leadership that has been missing in Washington for some time now. Care to comment on that?"

Rocky smiled, his presidential campaign already in full swing. He struggled to appear humble. "Well, like Reverend Archer just said, it's time to celebrate today's victory and we'll let tomorrow take care of itself."

# # #

34

The three men sat in the Ohio senator's spacious study in his Great Falls, Virginia, home. Outside, the leaves had begun to fall from the hundred year old sycamores that lined the back of the property. Down the sloping hill behind them lay the Potomac River, rushing from its origin in West Virginia south and east towards the Chesapeake Bay. Rocky was here to receive more guidance from the senator regarding his fast-moving campaign.

Since making the formal announcement of his candidacy, Rocky had been whisked through a series of briefings, interviews, fund raisers and other engagements designed to carefully expose the candidate to a nationwide audience. As he sipped his coffee he wondered what role the stranger sitting next to him, introduced only as Jack, would play in the meeting?

"Rocky, the polls are leaning heavily in your favor at this point, primarily due to the passage of the Corporate Profit Sharing Act and your perceived role there," the senator began.

"Perceived?" Rocky said.

"Well, we're playing up your involvement for obvious reasons, but you need to understand the bigger picture we have in mind."

Rocky had always believed that he had been *the* reason the CPSA had passed. A perceived role? Christ! He nodded, careful to hold his tongue. "Okay," he said amicably.

The senator pulled a huge brown cigar from the humidor beside him and examined the tip. "Once you're elected we plan on implementing a totally different agenda than what you've been espousing on the campaign trail." He produced a cigar cutter and snipped the end from his selection.

"How different?" Rocky asked.

The senator clicked a thin silver lighter and carefully set his cigar ablaze. He took a long puff, blew the smoke out, then re-examined the tip of the cigar. "We have managed to hold off our business base on the CPSA with the promise of a reversal once you're in the White House."

Rocky inhaled the rich aroma, wondered why he and Jack hadn't been offered a smoke, then tried to dismiss the insult. "A reversal?"

"Yes. First of all we're going to have the Supreme Court invalidate the CPSA. The provision for dictating that companies distribute half their profits back to the workers will be found to be unconstitutional."

"But, that's the backbone of the law," Rocky argued.

The senator held up a well-manicured hand. "And it's dead, Rocky. It's a promise we made to the business community and it's just the start of our grander plan."

"But how do you know the Supreme Court will rule that way?" Rocky asked.

The senator smiled. "Let's just say we have some influence over there. Now, once that is reversed we expect a hostile reaction from Workers United and their lobbying group."

"I would think so," Rocky said, shaken. His mind raced through the implications of what he had just been told.

"So, when you and I are through here this morning, I want you to spend some time with Jack here," he said, nodding towards the stranger. "He's going to ask you some very personal questions and I want you to be completely forthright with him. We don't want any skeletons you might have emerging on the eve of the election." He paused and smiled at Rocky. "We've all got our secrets, Rocky, but we have ways of making them go away, so don't hold back anything. We're particularly interested in anything you might be able to tell us about your friend Lincoln Archer."

"But—"

"We simply have to discredit the man," the senator went on. "Without his voice the labor movement will revert to being chaotic and leaderless. It's critical that his influence be diminished or eliminated."

"To what end?" Rocky asked.

The senator put his cigar in the ashtray by his side, then leaned forward in his chair, elbows on knees and lowered his voice. "Rocky, with you as the spearhead, we're going to privatize virtually every function of the Federal government. It's clear from the mire of bureaucracy, waste and corruption that exists that there has to be a better way to run this country. And that way is capitalism, Rocky. Surely a well run business enterprise focused on cost control and profit can provide services better and cheaper and our approach, your approach as president, will be to incrementally transfer government tasks to the private sector. It's time that the experience, technological knowhow and business acumen that has made this nation great is given an opportunity to rescue us from the mire and ashes of too much government involvement in our lives."

Rocky was speechless. This was such a reversal from the prompting and guidance he had received in his campaign for the Senate, and in his work on the two landmark bills he was using as the foundation for his current run for the presidency. "So, you want me to paint one picture now, then turn one eighty once I'm elected?"

The senator pointed at his student. "You're a smart man, Rocky. Now, we've obviously got a lot more to talk about, but I want you to spend some time now with Jack. After you two are done, you and I will resume our little talk over lunch." The senator reclaimed his cigar and stood up. "I'll leave you two alone. Remember Rocky, no stone unturned."

* * *

Rocky noticed that Jack had said absolutely nothing so far, hardly expressing any reaction at all to the dramatic plans that had been outlined for implementation once Rocky was in the White House. Was that because Jack had been privy to those plans beforehand? Exactly who was this guy? The man appeared to be in his forties maybe, stocky build, bald, with dark eyes and an expressionless face.

"My job," Jack started, pulling out a notebook from his jacket, "is to follow up on the background investigations that were done before you ran for the Senate and, of course, that were done before you announced your candidacy for president."

"I assume," Rocky said, "that nothing nefarious was uncovered or we wouldn't be sitting here?"

"Let's talk about Reverend Archer," Jack said, ignoring Rocky's question.

The candidate took a deep breath and exhaled heavily. "Look, Lincoln is a friend of mine and I don't have anything derogatory to say about him."

Jack pressed on, undeterred by Rocky's protestations. "You've been friends with him since your college days, is that right?"

Rocky sat back in his chair with a sigh. "Yes."

"Tell me about him back then. What was he like?"

"I don't know; he was a typical college student, just like me."

"And what did typical college students do back then; what was the nature of your relationship?"

Rocky shrugged. "We hung out together, did a little bar hopping, talked about things."

"What sort of things?"

"You know, what most college kids talk about: school, what we'll do after graduation, politics, religion, that sort of stuff."

"And these conversations were aided by beer, pot, other drugs?"

Rocky shook his head. "We smoked a little dope, yeah, everybody did." He flashed back to those days and smiled. "We drank a boatload of beer too. Will that be used against me?"

Jack seemed unaffected by the details Rocky had provided. "Reverend Archer's father was a minister, is that right? A bible thumper, I've been told."

"Yes, but I never met him."

"And what sort of influence did he have on Lincoln?"

"What do you mean?"

"I mean, it seems that Reverend Archer is anything but a bible thumper, so why didn't he follow in his father's footsteps?"

"I don't know, you'll have to ask him. All I know is, when we talked religion, which wasn't all that often, it struck me strange that Lincoln didn't believe in god."

Jack's eyebrows arched. "And yet he wanted to be a preacher?"

"Well, as you said, he's taken a different tack than his father, so maybe it was a compensation for the old man's evangelical approach, I don't know."

"Do you believe in god, Senator?"

The question took Rocky aback. "Uh, well, of course I do."

"Then why haven't you been to church in years?"

"Well, I, uh how the hell do you know that?"

"It's my business to know things like that, Senator. Now answer my question please."

Rocky's mind raced, back to canned statements he had rehearsed when running for the Senate. "My wife and I prefer to do our worshipping in private," he said. "Going to church always draws unwanted attention and is a distraction to other worshippers."

Jack nodded. "Perfect," he mouthed as he made another note.

They talked for another hour, Jack scribbling in his small note pad and asking questions about Rocky's other college classmates, about his relationship with Robin, personal questions like why they didn't have children, their financial status, his parents, friends and associates back in Walnut Grove and in New York. Jack asked about friends who were homosexual, bank clients who might hold a grudge, any Wall Street dealings that might prove embarrassing. He was direct, often rude, but thorough.

"And what about your friend Zeke Porter?"

"What about him?"

"What was he like in college?"

"Look, Zeke saved my life. You're not going to get anything negative about him from me."

"Tell me about how he saved your life."

Rocky took a deep breath and exhaled, then recounted the fabricated story of how, too inebriated to drive, he had let Zeke take the wheel, the chase from the State Trooper, crash into the pond and Zeke's heroics. He saw no reason to undo the façade they had all lived with all these years.

"That's quite a story," Jack commented. "So, do you have any lingering obligations to Mr. Porter, what with him saving your life and all?"

"Like what?"

"I don't know, maybe you've promised him exclusive interviews or inside information. You could be an investigative reporter's dream."

"You mean provide him with leaks or tips on White House dealings? Don't be ridiculous. I wouldn't do that for anyone, not even my best friend."

Jack nodded, his face expressionless. "One final area, senator," he said. "Talk to me about your affairs."

Rocky swallowed hard. "Well, to be honest I had a lot of relationships in college."

Jack waved his hand. "I'm only interested in extra-marital, Senator."

There was an awkward silence as Rocky gathered his thoughts. The bastard seemed to know everything; might as well tell him the truth. He closed his eyes and sighed. "Yeah, there was one; a nut job named Beverly Hawkins."

# # #

35

Lincoln Archer had just finished his "prime time" sermon, the one o'clock Sunday service that was broadcast nation-wide. He stepped down from the pulpit and descended into the well of the Church of Hope for one of the more popular segments of his weekly performance: greeting and talking with members of the congregation.

In the front row were two young men who stood out from the crowd, dressed in bib overalls. Simon and Silas Thrasher, age nineteen. They appeared fresh from farm work of some sort, and were both gigantic, towering over those around them. Despite meaty arms and broad shoulders they looked like young boys in the face with rosy cheeks and soft blue eyes. Archer was drawn to them.

"Hello, friends," he said, extending a hand.

The brother to the right, Silas, took Archer's hand in a firm grip and held on. His face flushed and he yelled, "Judas!"

The other brother, Simon, pulled a pistol from one of his pockets and yelled, "Blasphemer!" and started firing at point blank range. The pop-pop of the gun filled the church. The congregation stood motionless, mouths open, eyes wide. What was happening?

Silas held Archer's hand in a vice-like grip until his brother had emptied his weapon. Silas released his hold on Archer, who fell in a heap onto the floor. Pandemonium ensued. The congregation shrieked and moaned and yelled. The television cameraman struggled to keep the scene in focus. Members of the congregation surged towards the two brothers and tried to subdue them. As they effortlessly shrugged off their would-be captors, the brothers shouted, "Traitor! Heathen! Belzebub!"

The two assailants didn't try to escape, but stood calmly watching the fallen Reverend, now lying in a pool of blood. Several men shouted that they were doctors and fought their way through the crowd, kneeling to tend to the unconscious Lincoln Archer. He did not appear to be breathing.

* * *

The news reports were somber, accompanied by videotape of the incident from the televised sermon. "Reverend Lincoln Archer, noted preacher of the Church of Hope in Wichita, Kansas, and spokesman for the Workers United labor union, was shot multiple times at point blank range during his Sunday sermon. Twin brothers Simon and Silas Thrasher, of nearby Garden City, Kansas, were eventually subdued and arrested by Wichita police. Reverend Archer was taken to Wichita General where he is in surgery at this time, having sustained multiple wounds."

"The two assailants are in custody and claim that Jesus commanded them to punish Archer for his godless sermons. More on this story from our correspondent in Wichita, Carolyn Davis. Carolyn?"

* * *

Lincoln Archer underwent emergency surgery, riddled by shots that had punctured a lung and his stomach, flesh wounds to his right shoulder and wrist, and a bullet lodged in his neck near his spinal cord. He had lost a significant amount of blood and, after surgery, was placed in ICU, his condition listed as critical.

Zeke Porter rushed from an assignment in Chicago and arrived late that night. As Zeke stood looking at his friend through the ICU window, shocked at the tubes, wires and other apparatus providing life support, Lincoln's surgeon explained that, "We were able to remove the bullets from his wrist and shoulder, they obviously weren't life threatening, but because of his weakened condition, the surgery to repair his stomach and lung was quite dangerous."

"What about the bullet in the neck?" Zeke asked.

The surgeon nodded. "Required a separate procedure. Despite the precarious location near the spinal cord, the operation was straightforward. He was quite fortunate a small caliber weapon was used, otherwise there would have been significantly more damage and he might have bled to death on the way to the hospital."

"How long will he be unconscious?" Zeke asked.

The doctor grimaced. "Could be quite a while. His body has experienced significant trauma. It all depends on how strong his will is."

Zeke nodded. "It won't be long then. Thank you, Doctor."

* * *

Zeke stood vigil over his friend for the next five days, sleeping in a chair outside Lincoln's ICU room. He turned the waiting room down the hall into a command center, calling the Wichita police, friends, contacts and sources in an attempt to piece together the mystery of Lincoln's attack. On the sixth day, Lincoln awoke and, after preliminary observations by a team of doctors, was cautiously upgraded from critical to serious. After several more days of observation he was moved to a private room where Zeke sat by his bedside, exhausted but relieved that Lincoln had miraculously survived this point-blank attack. Over the next few days he gave Lincoln short snippets of information he had learned this past week from the doctors and other sources he had called from the hospital.

"There's quite a battle going on outside the hospital," Zeke said. "Your followers want justice while the religious crowd is saying god was punishing you for deserting him. It's quite a story."

Lincoln stared off out the window of his room, apparently deep in thought. He turned to his old friend, his voice hoarse and weak. "Doesn't it seem ironic to you that these two brothers, supposedly good Christians, found it alright to attempt murder in the name of their Lord?"

Zeke pulled a piece of paper from his pocket and unfolded it. "This might explain their motivation," he said, then read from the flyer. "Anyone arrogant enough to reject the priest who represents the LORD your god must be put to death. Deuteronomy 17:12." He handed the flyer to Lincoln. "Then there's your name and the address of your church plus the claim that your godless sermons are leading your congregations to hell."

Lincoln studied the flyer then handed it back to Zeke. "Where did you get this?"

"It was apparently sent to many churches in the area," he replied. "They found a copy in Simon Thrasher's pocket according to the Wichita police."

Lincoln shook his head. "But who would distribute something like this?"

Zeke leaned forward, elbows on knees. "Well, let's review your list of enemies, old buddy. First, you have all those businesses that lost money during your worker's 'day of protest.' Then there's every major corporation in the country who now has to share their profits with their workers."

"But you and Rocky helped shape the CPSA. Aren't you in danger too?"

Zeke shook his head. "The people you have pissed off the most are the other churches who have lost members of their congregation and their associated donations to your church, and finally, religious zealots everywhere who are offended by your godless sermons." He sat back in his chair. "Seems you've single-handedly alienated half the country," he added with a smile. "I never knew you had it in you."

Lincoln stared at the ceiling over his bed. "I didn't either." He cleared his throat and turned to look at his friend. "Do you think these brothers acted alone or could someone have put them up to it?"

"A contract on you? Possibly, but the Thrasher boys claim their hatred of you had been building for some time. They said that the flyer was a message from Jesus to act."

"So who printed the flyer?"

Zeke shrugged. "I'm looking into that as are the police." He smiled. "By the way, your old buddy Cardinal DuPont has proclaimed that god spared you for a purpose so now maybe you'll include him in your sermons."

Lincoln stared at the ceiling. "From what the doctors have told me it *is* a miracle that I'm alive."

"Well, first of all, your would-be assassins used a twenty-two caliber pop gun. Anything bigger and we wouldn't be having this conversation, a miracle from god or not. Second, brother Simon wasn't much of a marksman; he managed to miss your heart, brain and major arteries from less than a foot away. And finally, you were only ten minutes from this hospital and the trauma team that saved your life."

Lincoln considered the facts, his brain struggling to make any sense out of the attack.

Zeke stood up and stretched. "By the way, while you were out of it you had a visit from Rocky. As you might expect, there was quite a press frenzy; the reuniting of old friends, revisiting the legislation we worked on together, resurrection of gun control as a campaign issue, etcetera. Anyway, Rocky flew through here like a tornado, posed for pictures with doctors and nurses and expressed his thanks for their hard work in saving your life. It's too bad you missed it all; you would have enjoyed the drama."

Lincoln smiled. "Had my own share of drama, thank you very much."

"Well, now that you're out of danger I'm going to dig a little deeper here, make sure there aren't other nut jobs waiting in the shadows. You just concentrate on resting and getting better."

Lincoln turned in his bed to better face his friend. "The doctors say I can get out of here next week."

Zeke nodded his understanding. "How about I arrange for you to get out of town then? Some place you can recuperate for a while and just relax?"

Lincoln took a deep breath and released it, started to speak, but Zeke cut him off.

"I've already spoken with your Deacon Walsh and he'll fill in for you in the pulpit as long as you need."

"But what about your T.V. show?" Lincoln argued.

"We're in between seasons and I can write my column from anywhere. I'll rent a place in Jackson Hole. We can relax, forget about the outside world, and just get you back on your feet. How does that sound?"

"Sure, that sounds good."

Zeke bent over and kissed his friend on the forehead. "You get some more rest. I'll make those arrangements for you."

"Thanks again, Zeke."

The door to the room closed behind Zeke and Lincoln lay back in his bed. He was very tired but his brain would not rest. Despite the fact that someone had printed and distributed the flyer, Lincoln dismissed any thoughts of conspiracy that Silas and Simon had been hired to kill him. Professional killers do not commit their crime in public with no planned escape. No, these brothers had acted out of religious fervor. But what had he said in any of his sermons to provoke these two men? Why would supposedly Christian men think it was alright to take another man's life? Lincoln knew the answer, of course. There were many other references in the bible to killing the non-believer other than the one in the flyer, but surely sane men could not take such words literally? Maybe there was something deeper at play here, some troubling event in their lives that had led them down this path? Lincoln tried to consider what that could possibly have been, but he couldn't concentrate. He closed his eyes and, his body drained of energy, fell asleep.

# # #

36

The Sedgwick County jail sits among a cluster of government buildings at the intersection of West Central Avenue and West Wichita Street, a stone's throw away from the Little Arkansas River, a branch of its mother that winds its way through downtown Wichita. Lincoln Archer checked in at the reception desk on the main floor and was escorted by a guard down two flights of stairs to a holding area for his meeting.

He had just returned from a week of recuperation at Zeke Porter's Jackson Hole retreat; the two old friends relaxing and solving the world's problems. During their rambling discussions Zeke had shared his opinions about Rocky's campaign and chances of becoming president, while Lincoln had vowed to return to the pulpit despite his apparent list of enemies. But first, there was the matter of the Thrasher brothers.

In a small conference room in the sub-basement Simon and Silas Thrasher sat silently waiting, handcuffed by wrist and ankle to the metal restraining ring on the floor in front of them. Their orange prisoner uniforms were stretched tight across their oversized bodies and they shifted uncomfortably in the tiny plastic chairs. Lincoln was admitted to the room and took a chair opposite them.

The boy's father had retained a lawyer who, in conversations with Lincoln's Church of Hope attorney, had agreed to this off-the-record meeting. An armed guard stood in the hallway, watching the room through the window in the door.

Across the small conference table, the men who had tried to murder him sat with their heads down. Lincoln cleared his throat and said, "I would have come to visit you earlier, but it's taken me a while to recover from my wounds."

The two brothers sat impassively, each staring at the floor in front of them.

"I'm here to talk about why you tried to kill me," Lincoln said, "and to forgive you."

"Only god can forgive," Simon said, lifting his head and his eyes to focus on Lincoln. He was an enormous young man with calloused hands, a thick neck and soft blue eyes.

"Well, I believe it's important for humans to be able to forgive too. Not to lead to salvation, but to make this a kinder, gentler place to live."

"I don't want to talk," Simon said suddenly, pulling at his chains. He looked at his brother, then returned to staring at the spot on the floor in front of him. Silas was a mirror image of his twin brother, nineteen, as Lincoln had learned, from a small farm in Garden City, Kansas.

"Many of my congregation believe in god just as you two do," Lincoln went on, "so I think I understand your anger and where it came from."

"Do you?" Simon shot back.

"None of us can ever know for certain that god exists," Lincoln continued. "Those who do rely on their faith, those of us who don't seek a different truth."

"I don't know what all that means," Simon said.

"My theory is that god reveals himself to only some people and those people have faith, faith based on their belief that god exists. That's why there are so many different religions in the world; god has revealed himself in different ways to different people. How did god reveal himself to you?"

Simon's forehead furrowed in confusion. "What do you mean?"

"How did you come to believe in god?"

There was an ominous silence, then, "Reading the bible, I guess."

Lincoln nodded. "Well, I've read the bible too, and it leaves me with a lot of questions. I'm one of those whom god has chosen not to reveal himself to yet. He's created doubt for me and my journey is to keep examining myself and others to find the path to the truth."

"What path?"

"Love. Love is the true meaning of life and I've been put on a path to try and convince others that their day-to-day existence should be built around it, not necessarily what it says in the bible or what you may have been taught by other religious leaders."

"Don't make sense," Simon said.

"Life itself sometimes doesn't make sense. But you don't have to believe in god to love your neighbor or forgive him his wrong doing or do something to help him with his daily struggle."

"That's god's job."

"O.K., but only through all of us. We're the ones who can help a neighbor rebuild his barn, round up his stray cattle, harvest his crop before the storm. It's up to us to act, not to depend on a miracle or god's personal attention. He's got to be a pretty busy fellow, right? We've got to do our part."

"I guess," Simon mumbled.

"He's a blasphemer," Silas said suddenly, his meaty face red with anger. "He's insulted god and our religion."

"Perhaps god has chosen me to explore and explain life in a different way than your religion. Isn't that possible? And who are we to question god's motives or ways?"

Silas looked defeated. "Whatever," he said, rolling his eyes.

"So, here's the thing, boys. I'm the first to understand religious zeal and passion, to understand what upset you. But I'm also a man of peace and love and you've given me a chance to practice what I preach."

"How's that?" Simon asked.

"I not only forgive you, but I'm not going to press charges against you."

"Fat lot that will do for us," Silas said.

"Your act was done in a place of worship, boys. By your presence in my church you had sanctuary."

"My dad's lawyer is saying premeditated murder is what they'll charge us with, don't matter where it happened," Silas said.

"Well, the mayor, the D.A. and several judges are all members of my congregation, so I have a small amount of influence in this town and I plan to use it. I'm not going to press charges. I don't want you to spend your lives in jail."

"Ain't got a chance of working," Silas said.

Lincoln pushed his chair back and stood up. "Give me a little time to see what arrangements I can make. We will all survive this and be better for the experience." He reached for Simon's hand.

Simon stared at Lincoln's outstretched hand and blinked as he thought about what the man had said. He slowly raised his arm, chains rattling, and shook the Reverend's hand. Silas kept his head down, eyes avoiding Lincoln's.

"Go pray to your god," Lincoln said, "and I'll use love and compassion and forgiveness to work for your freedom."

The two brothers sat silently as Lincoln walked out of the room, the thick door closing with a clank behind him. "What do you think?" Simon asked his brother.

"He's crazier than a shit house rat," Silas said.

# # #

37

"The Negotiations" was Rocky Wellington's hastily ghost-written book about the secret meeting to negotiate the details of the Corporate Profit Sharing Act (CPSA). The book became a nationwide best-seller and a shrewd political coup. At every campaign event Rocky was inundated with requests to autograph his account of the historic event, his smiling face adorning the book's cover.

As one of the three participants in the now-famous meeting, Zeke resisted the "suggestion" from his management that he devote a segment of The Bottom Line to his version of the get together, claiming that to further publicize the details on his show would create the sort of political bias that he had wanted to avoid since the beginning of Rocky's campaign.

World News management acquiesced to Zeke's position, but, wanting to take advantage of his prominent role in Rocky's book, decided to publish a collection of Zeke's columns. The company would get its pound of flesh one way or another. Zeke requested that all of the proceeds go to several local New York City charities and the company included this commitment as part of its advertising campaign for the book. The book proved popular and Zeke agreed to a limited book signing tour.

At the kickoff event in Manhattan, Zeke signed books for five hours, the line of admirers seemingly never ending. As the line dwindled late in the afternoon an attractive blonde woman slid her copy of the book in front of him. "Could you sign it for Beverly?" she asked.

"Certainly," Zeke said, opening the book to the front page. Inside there was a three by five index card with the words: "Tony's Pizzeria; six o'clock." Zeke looked up into the wide eyes of Beverly Hawkins, the woman who had claimed that Rocky Wellington was the father of her child. Zeke scribbled "Best Wishes" and his name, then nodded and smiled as he handed the book back to her. "There you go, Beverly. Thanks for coming today."

* * *

Tony's Pizzeria was conveniently right down the block from the book store and Zeke made his way there after the signing ceremony. He was early and ordered a beer while he waited. He had, of course, passed along Beverly's demands to Rocky, who adamantly denied being the father of her child. Her request for a million dollars had been laughed at, Rocky dismissing her threat with the same air of confidence he had employed to brush off his car accident all those years ago in college.

At ten after six Beverly appeared at the door, spotted him across the room and walked instead to the counter where she ordered and paid for a slice of pepperoni pizza and a Coke, then walked calmly to the table next to Zeke's and sat down.

Their tables were only inches apart and she had situated herself opposite him so that they could talk. "I think I'm being followed," she said, unfurling her plastic silverware from its paper napkin.

"Right now?" he asked, discretely looking around the room.

She stared at him, eyes bloodshot. "Haven't seen him today, but when I come and go to work there's definitely somebody following me."

"What does he look like?"

She shrugged. "Never got a real good look; tall guy, white, wears a ball cap and sunglasses."

Beverly cut a piece of pizza, holding it aloft on her fork. "So what did his lordship say about my offer?" she asked, chewing the piece, but never taking her eyes off Zeke.

"What would you expect?"

She nodded. "So, maybe I need to raise the stakes a bit."

Zeke lowered his voice to a whisper. "Beverly, I have to warn you, no matter how legitimate your claim might be, you're stepping into some deep political shit here. Some very influential people have invested a lot in Rocky's candidacy and they won't allow something like this to get in their way."

Beverly hissed, "Christ, I know that, Mr. Porter. If I wasn't desperate I wouldn't have contacted you at all. This is my only shot, the only time in my life I've had a leg up on things, and I can't just sit back and let the opportunity pass. Even if it means taking a chance or two," she added.

"How can I help you, Beverly? I delivered your message to Rocky and he denies even knowing you."

"Do you think this guy who's following me works for Rocky?"

"I don't know, Beverly. I didn't tell Rocky anything about you living here in New York, so how could he find you? I didn't even know how to do that myself."

She leaned forward and lowered her voice. "You tell that bastard if he doesn't come through I'm going to give you an exclusive about this shyster politician who's fathered an illegitimate child. See how that fits in his campaign."

"Beverly, I'd need more than just your word on this. We're talking a major expose with repercussions we'd never be able to control."

She leaned back, pushed her paper plate away. "Mister Porter, I ain't got no other options right now. I'm living like a rat with no prospects."

"Assuming you're telling the truth Beverly, how does Rocky know you won't blow through the money and come back for more, particularly if he's elected president?"

She nodded. "Legitimate question. You running interference for him?"

"I'm more concerned about your wellbeing than his, Beverly. Give me something to work with."

Beverly looked down at the table, obviously weighing her next words carefully. She looked up, a tear in the corner of her eye. "Desperate people do desperate things, Mr. Porter."

"You haven't answered my question, Beverly, and it's a question Rocky will surely ask."

She slowly pulled an envelope out of her purse and laid it casually on the table. "In here is a lock of my baby's hair," she said. "You run them DNA tests and it'll be proof positive that Rocky's the father." She took a deep breath and released it. "I gave my baby a different name when I turned him over to the foster home. That name is in here." She paused, the emotion of the moment taking its toll. Her voice wavered and her eyes filled with tears. "You can give him this envelope when I've got my money. The threat of something happening to my son will be enough to keep me quiet the rest of my life."

Zeke picked up the envelope and studied it. "You're quite the negotiator," he said.

Beverly dabbed at her eyes with her napkin. "Maybe you can write a book about it one day," she said, her voice returning to its normal strength. She leaned forward. "Meantime, you let that prick know I'm serious and getting more desperate every day."

# # #

38

They met on the western side of the East River, at the Manhattan entrance to the Brooklyn Bridge. Zeke's series of columns about interviews he had conducted on the bridge had sparked an interest in Andrea, who had never been on the bridge, so he volunteered to be her guide today. As they worked their way up onto the pedestrian crosswalk, Zeke explained how the bridge architect, Jonathon Robling, had died before construction started and how his son, Christopher, took over as chief engineer.

Zeke pointed up at the limestone and granite tower as they walked underneath it. "These towers rest on bedrock," he explained. "The one here on this side goes down about 75 feet while the one on the Brooklyn side about half that."

"How did they build the parts that are underwater?" Andrea asked.

"They built caissons, like huge inverted boxes, then piled rocks on top to sink them onto the river floor. The caissons were filled with pressurized air and the workers dug through all the dirt and muck on the river bed until they hit bedrock. Then they built the tower foundations until they were above water level. It was quite an operation."

"Sounds like a miserable job," Andrea observed.

"Dangerous too. About a hundred workers died while at least that many suffered from the bends, coming up out of that pressurized environment too fast."

"Like SCUBA divers?"

"Exactly. Christopher Robling was incapacitated by the bends and had to supervise the construction of the bridge from his apartment up there in Brooklyn Heights, using his wife Emily as a surrogate engineer." He pointed across the bridge towards the far shore. "Can you imagine a woman in those days supervising all those men, and with absolutely no background in engineering, yet she gained the respect of the workers. When the bridge was complete, she was the first person to cross it."

They moved along towards the center of the bridge, being passed by joggers, bicyclers, people on their way to and from work. Zeke spotted an empty bench and they both sat down, facing New York harbor.

"That's quite a romantic story," Andrea said, "the Roblings building the bridge together like that."

Zeke nodded, deciding not to go into the engineering details he had absorbed over the years, but to observe how the skyscrapers that lined the river dwarfed the bridge towers. "Not too many people know that these towers were at one time the highest structures in the Western hemisphere."

"It's like you were born and raised here," she said, a look of admiration filling her face. "You know so much about the history of the city."

"It's necessary to write an interesting column," Zeke replied. "New Yorkers are proud of their history and most other readers find those details interesting."

They had been meeting like this for some time, on the rare occasion that both had a free day, taking in a ball game, Coney Island, museums and other sites. The more Zeke got to know her, the more he liked. She was funny, smart, and playful. She seemed to like him too, calling during the week to see how he was doing, asking about the latest hot story, and passing along all the Broadway scuttlebutt.

Zeke pointed to the west where dark storm clouds had suddenly appeared from behind the skyline. "We better head in," he warned. They both got up and started walking briskly towards the end of the bridge, but it was too late. The rain came suddenly and seemingly in buckets. In a few minutes they were both soaked to the skin. Zeke hailed a cab. It was just a short drive to his place in Greenwich Village and when they clambered up the stairs they were giggling like school children, looking like the proverbial drowned rats.

Once inside they shared more laughter looking at one another in the hall mirror. "I love what you've done with your hair," he said.

She pulled the wet strands off of her face. "I'll have you know I worked all morning on this new style," she said. "What did it take you this morning, two minutes to create that hideous pompadour?" She reached out to touch his hair but her wet shoes slipped on the floor and she started to fall.

Zeke caught her, pulling her close, their faces inches apart. They stared into each other's eyes. "Thanks," she said in a whisper, caressing his cheek.

"You're welcome," he whispered back. She inched closer, trembling slightly as her breathing quickened, then she closed her eyes and kissed him. They had kissed before, the simple peck on the cheek version, but this one was warm and wet and passionate. They both groaned and pulled one another even closer.

This moment had been building slowly as they shared time together. They had become close friends, enjoying one another's sense of humor, Midwestern roots, and their mutual energy and joy in doing their jobs. A romance was inevitable.

Finally, they slowly broke apart, their eyes still on each other's. Andrea began to unbutton her blouse. "I think I could use a hot shower," she said seductively. "Care to join me?" she asked, looking over her shoulder at him as she moved towards his bathroom.

Zeke struggled with his soaked shirt, finally pulling it over his head and tossing it on the floor. She was already half undressed as she disappeared into the bathroom.

* * *

The jazz music filled the air, a soothing compliment to the conversational buzz, laughter and clink of ice cubes in glasses. The distinctive smell of marijuana competed with exotic perfumes and the pleasing aroma from the breakfast buffet in the kitchen. Andrea Jackson looked out across the sea of bodies and spotted Zeke near the front door of his brownstone apartment, still greeting people as they arrived. She smiled. He had become the perfect companion, attending many of her Broadway performances as he had tonight, then serving as unofficial host at restaurants, bars and other gathering places for the post performance celebrations.

She had had a schoolgirl crush on him since that night so long ago in the freezing pond outside Manhattan, Kansas, when he had saved her life. That incident had been fate in her mind, and when their paths crossed here in New York, she firmly believed it was indeed karma at work.

Back in those early days she sensed that there had been another woman in his life, but she didn't care. She didn't want a permanent companion then, merely someone she could spend time with to avoid the crushing loneliness that can overwhelm a person here in the biggest of cities. They could just be friends and that was alright. Her career didn't leave time for a serious romance anyway.

So, their relationship had proceeded slowly, a brunch get together, a visit to Central Park, and then that glorious day they had been drenched by the downpour on the Brooklyn Bridge. As they slowly evolved into "a couple" she introduced him to the rich experiences and diverse personalities of Broadway; he took her to all his haunts, showed her the New York he had discovered in doing his job. Eventually, she sensed that the other woman had disappeared from his life and Andrea had him all to herself. What had started as simple infatuation had morphed into a deep, satisfying love for them both.

"Great show tonight," the voice from behind Andrea said, breaking her reverie.

She turned to see Stanley Roberts, the Broadway critic, who had already written several glowing reviews of the show and her performance. "Thanks, Stan. I really think the gang is coming together."

Stan was a caricature with a wild uncombed mane of white hair, oversized horn-rimmed glasses, and a portly belly upon which he always rested his martini. "Well, you're the star, Andy," he said, using her nickname. "You set the standard and they try to match it."

"You're very kind, Stan. I'm just thrilled to have the opportunity. A lot of people don't think I've paid my dues, to have a starring role so young, you know?"

Stan took a sip of his drink. "They said the same about Ethel Merman and Barbra Streisand, my dear." He moved closer. "I've seen them all and you're just as good as the best of them. I don't say that to blow smoke up your lovely behind, but because it's true. Your potential is unlimited and I'm the one who feels fortunate to have, more or less, discovered you."

She reached out and took his arm. "Stan, you're making me blush. Please, don't stop."

They both laughed and took sips from their drinks. "You know Sigfreid is here tonight?" he said, referring to the famous Broadway director. "I think he's got his eye on you for his next show."

Andrea finished her drink with a snap of her head. "Well, one show at a time, huh, Stan? I'm having too much fun to be thinking of what's next."

Stan motioned across the room towards Zeke. "On and off the stage, my dear?"

Andrea's smile broadened with the comment and she caught Zeke's eye. He headed in her direction.

"Stan, how are you?" Zeke said, reaching to shake the critic's hand.

"I'm delicious, my good fellow, but not as scrumptious as you two."

Zeke put his arm around Andrea and pulled her close. "She's quite a gal, don't you think?" He leaned close and kissed Andrea on the cheek.

"You make a great couple," Stan said. "Hang on to each other, there's a storm a brewing."

"You know something I don't, Stan?" Zeke asked with a grin.

"Thirty years more of living in this incredible city is all. For every high like you're experiencing there's always a downer somewhere lurking. It's life, you know, so stay close to one another." He raised his martini glass and headed off into the crowd.

"Sometimes he can be like a fart in a space suit," Zeke said.

"Oh, he means well," Andrea said. "He's had his own roller coaster, you know?"

Zeke's face turned serious as he flipped through the ups and down that had marked Stanley's life. "You're right, he's been a good friend to both of us. He thinks the world of you."

"You too, Zeke. He admires you." Andrea hesitated. "Well, I guess all the gay guys in town admire you, in a way," she added, running her fingers through his hair.

"Am I going to have to throw cold water on you guys again?" Rita Summers said as she walked up to the couple. "Jesus, you can't keep your hands off one another. You want me to clear this place out so you can have some privacy?"

They both laughed. Rita was a Broadway star in her own right, just as vibrant as Andrea despite being twenty years her senior.

"You know how it is after a big night like tonight, Rita?" Andrea said with a giggle.

"You mean, being horny as hell, honey?"

They all laughed. "I was thinking more exhilarated at having a hit show," Andrea said. "But horny works too," she added. They all laughed again.

"Well, good luck with both emotions, honey," Rita said with a wink. "You're doing quite well on both fronts," she added, reaching out and pinching Zeke's cheek. "You keep this guy as far behind the curtain as you can, okay?"

"Pay no attention to the man behind the curtain," Zeke said, mimicking the line from the Wizard of Oz.

* * *

Zeke felt her slow, deep breathing and knew she was asleep. Andrea was up against him on the big overstuffed couch in his living room where they had been watching late night T.V. together. The party had broken up early as most of the crowd had a performance or other job tomorrow so, after a few minutes of cleaning up the place, he had suggested they retire to the couch and relax.

The low hum of audience laughter was the only sound in the darkened room. Zeke adjusted himself on the couch, his arm around Andrea, and stared unseeing at the television. They were living a dream, the two of them; each a rising star in their respective fields, each finding the other's companionship deeply satisfying.

The contrasts between his relationship with Andrea and his affair with Robin were striking. Robin had used her financial position to demand and get what she wanted; Andrea came from humble beginnings and lived meagerly until her big break on Broadway. Her idea of a fun evening was to go to a baseball game or see a movie or cook dinner for them, then watch T.V. Robin had preferred the opera or symphony, dinner at the Plaza, or charity events where she could mingle with the other rich and famous. He now knew that breaking it off with Robin had been the most courageous and fortuitous move of his life.

Another muted laugh came from the television and Zeke found the remote controller and turned the set off. Through the tall windows on the far side of the room he could see the Empire State Building uptown, its top floors bathed in Christmas colors of red and green. He and Andrea would go shopping for their own tree tomorrow, the first he would have had since his last Christmas on the farm with his grandparents when he was nineteen.

He thought of that Christmas, how he had chopped down a tree for them and he and his grandmother had decorated it; how, as she had done every year, filled his stocking with childhood delights of butterscotch candy, baseball cards, and bubble gum like he was five again. To her, he always would be. Christmas morning oatmeal, after chores, tearing open simple gifts, the looks of joy and pride they had given him. He was still their little boy in a way and he wondered if his grandmother's tears were from happiness or from the tragic death of her daughter?

All Zeke had were a few aging photographs of his parents from their wedding day to remember them by. He never knew their desires, their hopes, what they thought about him. No memories of being hugged or kissed or held by them. His grandparents provided plenty of affection, but there had been no Boy Scouts or Little League or Friday night dances at the high school for him. Work on the farm precluded all of those childhood indulgences and it added to his sadness that they might have all been enjoyed had his parents lived.

Still, despite the relative unhappiness and loneliness of those teenage years, his reporting career had exposed him to stories far, far worse than his own and he had gradually been able to put those years in perspective.

Next to him, Andrea stirred. "Where are we?" she asked, looking around the darkened room.

He pulled her closer and kissed her. "Right where we want to be," he said softly.

#

39

The number of deaths per day in New York City, on average, was one hundred fifty two. The main causes were heart disease, cancer and pneumonia, mainly among the elderly. Of the 152 deaths, six were homicides. Zeke knew all this because one of his regular rituals was to scan the obituaries in the paper. This routine was not out of any morbid curiosity, but Zeke found that the obit's provided a rich mosaic of life's accomplishments, failures and historical events. More than once he had followed up on the thread of such a story to form the basis of a column or television news segment on The Bottom Line.

But this morning his scan was abruptly stopped when he came across the announcement for Beverly Hawkins. "My god," he said.

"What?" Andrea Jackson asked, pouring herself a cup of coffee.

"Beverly Hawkins, the woman I told you about that claimed to have had Rocky's son. She's dead. Died earlier this week, no cause of death given."

"Is there a service?"

"Yeah, yesterday, St. Luke's in the Bronx."

"You don't think----"

"Foul play? Anything's possible. She was a threat to Rocky though." He shook his head. "I just can't believe that Rocky would----" His voice trailed off as he considered the possibilities.

"Didn't you meet with her after your book signing?" Andrea asked.

"Yeah," Zeke answered, recalling how Beverly claimed she was being followed. She had given him an envelope with a locket of her son's hair for DNA testing and the name she had registered him with Social Services when she turned him over for adoption.

"But the only way to tie Rocky to that hair sample is to get DNA from him, right?" Andrea asked.

Zeke pretended to be speaking into a microphone. "Excuse me, Senator Wellington, could I take a DNA sample so we can prove that this illegitimate child is actually yours from an extramarital affair you had years ago?"

Andrea sat down next to Zeke at the kitchen table, a worried expression on her face. "If her death was political, aren't you worried that you'll be a target if you start snooping around?" she asked.

Zeke smiled and patted Andrea's hand. "That just makes my investigation more challenging," he said.

* * *

The next day Zeke went to the parish church, St. Luke's, where Beverly's service had been held. There was no record of mourners who had attended and the priest who had officiated said he recalled that the sanctuary had been empty during the service. No blonde haired young boy. No one.

When he went to the local precinct asking about Hawkins' cause of death he was told her file was unavailable. "Sealed," the desk Sergeant said bluntly.

"By whom?" Zeke asked.

The Sergeant shrugged. "Above my pay grade, pal."

A search of Social Service offices in New York using the name Beverly had provided for her son turned up empty. "Even if he had been registered here in New York and you had his correct name," one of the social workers told him, "there is the issue of privacy. We wouldn't be permitted to reveal the name of the adopting family or of the real mother. I'm sorry."

As he often did when reaching a dead end, Zeke shifted his focus to other projects, knowing that time would eventually offer him a solution. His solution arrived quicker than most, only a week later.

* * *

Zeke was working in his office when a secretary brought a young lady to his door. "Zeke, this is Sergeant Stephanie Lowery. She says she needs to talk to you."

Zeke stood up. "Of course, what can I do for you, Sergeant?"

The young woman looked about nervously, prompting Zeke's secretary to excuse herself and close his office door behind her. Sergeant Lowery was a stocky woman, mid-fifties perhaps, with short, graying hair and a serious expression. "I thought I recognized you when you came to the station," she said, taking the chair Zeke offered her. "I watch your show all the time. The story you did on a week in the life of an NYPD street cop really was super."

"Thank you. It's always good to meet a viewer. So, what can I do for you?"

Lowery pulled a manila envelope out of her jacket and placed it on Zeke's desk. "Beverly Hawkins' file," she said.

Zeke fingered the envelope. "I thought this had been sealed?"

Lowery nodded. "By the Justice Department," she said.

"Why?" Zeke asked.

"You read through it, you'll see why." She stood up. "And you've never seen me before," she said, turning to leave the office.

"Thank you," Zeke said.

The Sergeant opened the door and paused there. "Once you see what's in there you won't thank me. It's pretty ugly." And then she was gone.

The file on Beverly Hawkins contained a report of an "accidental" death by asphyxiation, the gas heater in her cheap apartment leaking fatal fumes. That was not an unusual occurrence in the Bronx tenements. But two things were very unusual: (1) there was no autopsy, SOP in deaths adjudged accidental to determine if alcohol, drugs, or other factors may have rendered the victim unconscious before the effects of asphyxiation took its toll, and (2) the most suspicious, a notation that a mid-level official at DOJ had demanded that Hawkins' file be sealed "for national security purposes," an explanation that defied logic had anyone bothered to ask for specifics.

Zeke discovered that the aforementioned DOJ official had worked on Rocky's senatorial campaign and now, as an aide to the current senior senator from Ohio. The dots of evidence were all there, they just hadn't been connected yet; a secret trail that might have silenced someone who could have created unwanted waves for Rocky's presidential candidacy. Was such a thing possible? Zeke shook his head at his own absurd question.

# # #

40

As the primaries unfolded it became abundantly clear that Rocky enjoyed the advantages of money, organization, and message. His advertisements had a Hollywood flair about them and they were selectively aimed at audiences that his campaign's computers had targeted. His opponents were a weak collection of political hacks and each was exposed regarding their lack of vision, experience or ability to sway a national audience in the presidential election.

Rocky's message was simple and clear: he was the only candidate who could bridge the divide between big business and the workers of the country. He had demonstrated this prowess through his yeoman work on passage of the Minimum Wage and Corporate Profit Sharing legislation and he had, due to his propaganda machine, become an icon for compromise and reason applied to solving complex national problems. He accrued the necessary delegates well before the convention and The Ten saw to it that his presidential campaign was already in high gear by the time he was officially nominated.

The election became a foregone conclusion when the opposition nominated Hector Williams, an obscure Congressman from Utah who championed a policy of accelerating our fight against terrorism, shifting his attention to the nuclear threat of Russia rather than the myriad of groups roaming the Middle East. He enjoyed lukewarm support from hawks and other war-mongers, but his campaign was doomed before it even started.

Rocky's campaign cast Robin as a prominent figure and she warmed to the attention, appearing at most of Rocky's campaign stops, subjecting herself to multiple interviews, and even making a few speeches of her own. The media, as expected, focused on the handsome couple, their appearances at fund raisers, rallies and other public gatherings garnering as much mileage as Rocky's platform and agenda.

Shortly before the election Rocky's campaign unveiled its secret weapon, announcing that Robin was pregnant. Public attention and commentary shifted to her wellbeing and the anticipation of a baby in the White House. Robin refused to cut back her appearances on the campaign trail and was treated with the reverence often afforded expectant mothers. Her "glow" became as much a part of the campaign dialogue as Rocky's claim to be the "instrument of compromise and progress."

With the election a seeming slam-dunk, Zeke continued to focus his attention on other matters outside the campaign in selecting the subjects for his weekly news program.

The election was indeed a landslide and the country settled into the holiday season, awaiting the incoming Wellington administration, the hope for a "new beginning" in Washington, and the First Baby.

# # #

41

Zeke felt the mounting pressure of an awkward situation closing in on him. The circumstances were innocent enough; dinner with old friends, except two of those friends were a woman with whom he'd had a lengthy affair and her husband, who just happened to be the newly elected President of the United States. As Rocky passed around pictures of Junior, Zeke discretely scanned the table in the White House dining room. Andrea sat across from him, uttering the appropriate "oohs" and "ahhs" as she looked at the pictures. To her left, Lincoln's date for the evening, ballet star Elizabeth Becking awaited her turn. "He looks so big," Andrea gushed, addressing her comments to the source of Zeke's discomfort, the beautiful First Lady.

"Yes," Robin replied from the far end of the table, "he's got Rocky's build."

"A football player, Mr. President?" Lincoln asked with a smile.

"Well," Rocky said, returning the smile, "he does have some pretty good moves now that he's started to walk."

The pictures worked their way around the table and back to the president. "Enough parental chest thumping," he said, raising a hand towards the waiter at the far side of the room. "Let's have some dinner." The six-some enjoyed a meal of Maryland crab cakes and a lively conversation about college days, humorous anecdotes about the presidential campaign, and a few secrets about life on the New York stage. As the dinner dishes were cleared Rocky announced, "For dessert we're having chocolate souffle'. Robin says it's your favorite, Zeke," he added with a hand on Zeke's arm.

Zeke felt the heat of everyone staring at him and he risked a glance at Robin, who shot him a look reminiscent of their first night together in New York all those years ago. Rocky's hand on his arm was like a heavy weight. Zeke managed a weak smile.

"So tell us, Elizabeth," Robin said after the group had finished dessert and coffee, "how did you and Lincoln meet?" She smiled at Elizabeth who gave Lincoln a longing stare.

"Actually," Elizabeth started, turning to the First Lady, "we met in the bar of our hotel just this afternoon. Andrea here played matchmaker with us and I'm so glad she did." Another broad smile at Lincoln, who reddened but managed a smile of his own.

"And Andrea, how did you meet your handsome escort for the evening?" Robin asked, looking at Zeke rather than the object of her question.

Andrea looked at Zeke, then said, "We met in a bar too. A place called Jacks in Manhattan, Kansas, a long, long time ago."

"Yes," the president said, "and Zeke here saved every one of us from drowning all those years ago. He was quite the hero."

"Well," Robin said, "we're honored to be in the presence of a genuine hero. Well done, Zeke."

"Well done, indeed," the president said, standing and patting Zeke on the back. Everyone else stood up. Rocky said, "Robin, why don't you show the ladies around downstairs while we men enjoy a cigar. We'll meet you in the Oval Office after your tour."

Robin smiled and bowed her head. "As you wish, Mr. President," she said with a laugh. She gathered her two female guests and started toward the elevator to show them the tourist sites of the executive mansion's main floor.

The three men chose their cigars from a humidor in the corner and Rocky poured them all a healthy serving of Glenfiddich. "We can't smoke downstairs so we'll have to puff these babies up here," Rocky said, motioning towards the living room area that overlooked the South Lawn. It was a pleasant night so they went out onto the veranda. "Great view, but the Secret Service will come running if we spend a lot of time out here. Some nut with a rifle was actually caught down on the mall a month ago and he wasn't hunting deer."

"You're still on your presidential honeymoon," Lincoln observed. "You haven't done anything to piss anyone off, yet," he added with a smirk.

"Every decision a president makes pisses somebody off," Rocky said. They all puffed on their cigars and enjoyed the warm night and the view. After a few minutes, Rocky led them back inside.

They settled into large chairs around a marble-topped coffee table. It had been some time since Zeke had enjoyed an opportunity to talk face-to-face with the new president, following his political fortunes like everyone else, on television and in the newspapers. Tonight would be a chance for a more personal exchange. "So, Mr. President," he started, "has it been everything you imagined, being the leader of the free world?"

Rocky smiled, then drew on his cigar, letting the smoke drift slowly from the corner of his mouth. "There's nothing free about this job," he said. "My daily schedule is made for me weeks in advance and I'm booked solid from seven in the morning with my security briefing to sometimes midnight or later with state dinners and having to entertain buffoons like you two."

"Compliments are accepted no matter what the source," Zeke offered, raising his glass of scotch.

"I'm serious about lack of control, guys," the president went on. "My speeches are all written for me, I'm told what my policies are, who I should like and dislike; I think one day I'll be told when I can go to the bathroom."

"Don't you think it's been like that for past presidents?" Lincoln asked.

"I think the job is a helluva lot more complex today," Rocky answered. "I don't even know how many advisors I have, but every one of them has an agenda, an input for me to consider or follow. Then there's the goddamned fund raising. It seems like half of every day is spent on the phone calling one asshole after another asking for money. I feel like a hooker trolling for Johns."

"Didn't you get those phone calls when you were on Wall Street?" Zeke asked.

"You're not going to write another expose, are you, Zeke?" the president asked with a grin.

"Do you have some inside dope for me, sir?" Zeke asked.

"Buy low, sell high," Rocky offered.

They all laughed, then Lincoln asked, "Do you get to spend much time with Junior?"

Rocky frowned. "Not as much as I'd like. Thankfully he's not talking yet, so I don't have to put up with another opinion." They all laughed. "He's back in New York with his nanny. Robin will go up there tomorrow and bring him back with her next week."

"And how is Robin dealing now with the two men in her life?" Lincoln asked.

Zeke almost choked, realizing quickly that Lincoln was referring to Junior as the other man.

Rocky shot Zeke a look. "She's doing great. She just loves being a mom." He puffed on his cigar.

"Well," Lincoln said, raising his glass, "here's to the first one of us to be a father. How does that feel, Mr. President?"

Rocky smiled and stared off across the room. "I'd never thought I'd say this, but being a father is the most important thing I've accomplished in my life." He looked at his two companions. "The little guy has really changed me."

"Being raised in the White House will be quite an experience for him," Lincoln said. "Maybe let him see what politics is all about."

Rocky shook his head. "Not a chance. I'm not going to make the same mistake my old man made with me. Junior's going to have a choice about what he wants to do with his life."

"And what if he chooses politics?" Zeke asked.

Rocky grimaced. "Let's hope he's smarter than that."

* * *

Zeke and Andrea were back in their hotel room later that night. Andrea was taking her earrings out and studying herself in the vanity mirror. "I think Liz and Lincoln hit it off pretty well, don't you?"

"Is she seriously as big a fan of his as she admitted tonight?" Zeke asked.

"Oh, yeah, she thinks he's wonderful, standing up for the common man and all. Her father worked in a steel mill so she's sympathetic to the plight of the workers." She turned to face Zeke. "Plus, wine makes her hornier than hell, so I imagine she's showing Lincoln first position right about now."

"Let's hope they work their way through all the positions tonight," Zeke said with a smirk, rubbing her bare shoulders as she undid his tie. He bent and kissed her. "Lincoln could use a girlfriend. It was great of you to introduce them."

"I'm a matchmaker at heart and Lincoln is such a great guy. I really hope they like each other. It would be fun to double date."

"I think their respective schedules would make a romance difficult," Zeke said.

"We've worked through it," Andrea said.

"Yes, but we both live in New York. Commuting from Wichita would be a stretch." He held up a hand. "I know, not if they like each other. Well, let's see how their first date goes before we march them down the aisle."

"Always Mr. Practical," she said.

"Always the hopeless romantic," he countered, kissing her gently on the lips.

"I figured something out tonight," she said, turning so he could unzip her dress.

"What was that?"

Andrea caught his gaze in the mirror. "You and Robin."

"Me and Robin?"

Andrea turned to face him. "She was the one, the one you were seeing before you and I started dating."

Zeke said nothing.

"I could see the way you two avoided looking at one another tonight, how she had you seated as far away from her as possible. Am I right?"

Zeke stroked her cheek. "Yes you are, but that's all ancient history."

She stared up at him with a smile. "Details, lover, details."

Zeke sighed and described first meeting Robin in Walnut Grove, then the awkward night they had spent together in his college apartment.

"So, she tried to seduce you?"

"Yeah, but I wrote it off as just a moment of weakness for us both. Anyway, I had moved to New York, was working three jobs, busting my ass and, all of a sudden she comes up on a shopping trip. We had dinner, she invited me up to her room then wound up standing naked in front of me. 'Time to continue where we left off', she said." He frowned. "I was lonely, a little drunk, and morally weak, I suppose."

"Don't beat yourself up. You were just human."

Zeke shook his head. "I can forgive myself for what Robin and I did with one another," he said. "But I still feel guilty about deceiving Rocky."

"From what you've told me about him, he all but drove her to you."

Zeke lowered his head. He had wanted to confess all this to Andrea, but never seemed to find the right time. He sighed. "We saw each other, on and off, for years. She told me how unhappy she was with the marriage, Rocky always at work, that sort of thing. I suppose I was a distraction for her."

"And she ended the affair because it was a threat to Rocky's political career?"

Zeke frowned. "No. I ended it."

"Why?"

He frowned. "I realized she was using me; I was just a convenience." He reached out and stroked her cheek. "Besides, I had found someone else."

Andrea smiled, then said, "So, do you still love her?"

Zeke looked down at the woman who had changed his life. "I suppose I might have thought so at the time, but since you and I have been together I know what real love is."

She pushed herself up against him. "That's a great answer, babe. You sure you aren't a politician?"

He laughed, but Andrea's inquisition wasn't over. "Does the president know about you and Robin?"

Zeke shook his head. "I doubt it. If he does, he's a helluva actor."

Andrea smiled up at the man who had made her life complete. "Isn't that what politicians are; good actors?"

They smiled at one another then Andrea's eyes widened. "Almost forgot," she said, moving towards her purse on the bed. She pulled out a paper tissue, holding it up like a trophy. "Do you remember when I excused myself tonight, had to go potty?"

Zeke nodded. "Yeah?"

"Well, there I sat in the presidential bathroom, looking all around like a tourist, you know? Suddenly, I get this urge to find something I can take as a souvenir. Well, the towels were out, too big, no room in my purse for presidential toilet paper, but right there on the counter was a hair brush. I picked it up, saw the presidential seal on the back." She slowly opened the tissue, revealing a clump of blonde hair. She smiled at him. "Perfect for DNA testing."

He took the tissue and studied the contents, then smiled at her. "You'd make a helluva investigative reporter."

She smiled back. "I know."

#

42

The story broke around nine o'clock Eastern time, too late for the evening news, but in time to interrupt network broadcasts. The president's son, Rocky Junior, had drowned in the swimming pool of the presidential couple's Long Island home. The president and his wife were in New York City for a fund raiser and the toddler had been in the care of a nanny at the home. Police reported that the nanny, Francesca Ramirez, was playing with the child beside the swimming pool when the young boy fell into the water. Ms. Ramirez, who could not swim, nonetheless jumped into the water in an attempt to save the child, eventually pulling him out of the pool and frantically calling the assigned Secret Service agent who was patrolling the perimeter of the property. His resuscitation efforts were unsuccessful and the child was pronounced dead on the scene when local EMTs responded to the 9-1-1 call. The president and first lady were notified concerning the accident and rushed home to the scene.

Later that evening a subdued president spoke to the assembled press corps, expressing his gratitude for the outpouring of sympathy he and his wife had already received and thanking local paramedic personnel and the Secret Service for their efforts. It was reported that the first lady was in shock and had been sedated. The president said that his son would be buried in the Wellington family plot in Walnut Grove, Kansas, in a private ceremony.

Three days later, a grieving nation watched as the "private" burial was televised live, Rocky Junior interred in the simple plot alongside his grandparents. The first lady, obviously in grief, remained stoic during the short ceremony, but the president was inconsolable, head bowed, shoulders heaving. Zeke and Lincoln were there, but were only granted a short word of condolence as the Secret Service kept the few invited guests at a distance from the mourning parents.

The First Family returned to Washington that evening to find the White House awash with flowers and cards from mourners and well-wishers. The president had his schedule cleared for two days, then issued a statement again thanking those who had sent their support and sympathy and stating it was time for him to return to his duties. "My wife will take some private time to mourn and try to adjust to this terrible tragedy."

It didn't take very long before the machinery of Washington returned to its normal give and take, gossip, bickering and posturing. Even the death of a child could not deter the ebb and flow of politics.

* * *

The legal challenge to the CPSA had wound its way through the lower courts during the long campaign, arriving on the doorstep of the Supreme Court just as the Wellington administration was busy with appointments, filling West Wing positions, and sorting through the administrative remnants of their predecessors. Media focus on that busy first year of activity, then the death of the president's young son had kept the progress of the case as back page news.

As the time for the Court's decision drew nigh, legal experts and pundits split along ideological lines, each side predicting a victory. The word came down early on a cold spring morning as an east coast rain storm soaked the nation's capital. The court split, five to four, to overrule the lower court ruling, stating, in part, that "while Congress has the Constitutional right to levy taxes, specifying how profits were to be distributed fell outside the definition of taxation" and the legislation was deemed un-Constitutional on those grounds. "Furthermore," the ruling continued, "all associated provisions of the Corporate Profit Sharing Act, including how the corporate payments of profits can be deducted as legitimate business expenses are hereby deemed null and void as is the accompanying provision of the law that increases the tax rate for individuals earning more than five hundred thousand dollars per year." None of the "pork" that had been added to the bill was affected by the court's decision.

The corporate world lauded the ruling as fair and just, while Workers United lambasted the decision as "caving in to special interests," and "shameful," imploring its membership to hold fast until union leadership could determine the appropriate course of action.

Union members, now exceeding a hundred million, were shocked. Most had already received their initial "bonuses" as their respective corporations concluded their fiscal years and distributed fifty percent of their profits back to their workers. That money, as predicted, had been, for the most part, plowed back into the economy, and financial indicators reflected a recovering economic picture. Now, outrage over the decision was wide spread and talking heads predicted everything from another law suit to revolution.

Reaction from politicians was, not surprisingly, along party lines, but the corporate world reacted in a harsh manner, declaring that previous bonus payments would be recovered through deductions from ongoing payrolls and that all stock and stock options distributed by the CPSA were rescinded. Workers United plotted massive strikes and other campaigns of protest. The situation was about to get ugly.

In a carefully orchestrated plan, millions of workers participated in crippling strikes against the companies who had used the court ruling to dismantle the previous profit sharing system. The results were devastating as a major part of the economy ground to a halt. Striking workers brought airlines, mass transit systems, trucking, rail and seafaring transportation to a standstill. Manufacturing facilities across the country shut down. Gas stations ran out of fuel, grocery stores ran out of food, and even those who were not part of the striking union began to suffer the consequences of the strike.

Corporations responded by hiring "scabs", non-union workers from the willing ranks of the unemployed who attempted to keep the various industries running. Striking workers marched through the cities in protest, forming picket lines outside plants and factories to keep the scabs from taking over their jobs. These confrontations rekindled memories of the bloody strikes of the twenties and thirties where strikers skirmished with scabs and armed thugs hired by the corporations attacked strikers with baseball bats and crow bars. In several major cities local authorities responded with police to keep the demonstrations as peaceful as possible, but the police soon found themselves overwhelmed by the sheer number of protestors and their adversaries. State governors mobilized their National Guards who, with divided loyalties, many of their families and friends amongst the strikers, were minimally effective in keeping the protests under control.

Caught in the middle of this growing national meltdown, Lincoln Archer, as the spokesman for Workers United, had struggled with exactly how to try and keep the strike peaceful, yet somehow bring it to a successful conclusion. The situation appeared to have gone beyond words. The longer the strike continued, the more entrenched the two positions became. Revolution was not all that far-fetched a concept in the minds of many.

The president appeared to be weighing his options until, on the eve of the strike's second week, he scheduled a televised briefing to the country from the oval office.

* * *

"My fellow Americans, good evening. The recent decision by the Supreme Court to overturn the Corporate Profit Sharing Act and the ensuing actions by corporate enterprises across the land to rescind the Act's provisions comes as a major disappointment to millions of workers. As a member of Congress who co-authored the original version of this bill and helped with it passage, I too, am personally disappointed with this turn of events.

Despite my personal feelings though, as your president, I have an obligation to uphold the laws of our land, to protect and defend the Constitution, which is the basis for our democratic society. I ask that all of you who are protesting this decision, swallow your disappointment, cease your involvement on the strike lines and return to work. Your current actions are creating great harm to our country, its economy, and, in the long run, yourselves.

I am asking that this strike end immediately and we must, as a country, begin to undo the harm that has been done. If these strikes continue I will have no recourse but to order military units of the DoD to engage, disperse the strikers, and allow the alternate work force hired by the corporations to try and return our economy to a productive status.

We will not tolerate lawlessness, anarchy or civil disobedience to disrupt our economy and its vital importance to all Americans. Please heed this warning with the seriousness that underscores its urging. Thank you and good night."

* * *

Immediately after completing his national broadcast, Rocky returned to his private conference room and joined the call that had just been placed to Lincoln Archer.

"Mr. President, how can I help?" Lincoln asked.

"I trust you just heard my request on television?"

"It wasn't as much a request as an order, Mr. President."

"Well, call it what you will, I would appreciate your support in reinforcing my message. These workers will listen to you, Lincoln, and I hope you'll take to the air as I did and encourage them to follow my lead."

"And what do I offer them in return, Mr. President? What do I tell the workers you'll do to make this right?"

"As much as I disagree with the court's decision, I'm bound now to uphold it, Lincoln."

"Then maybe there's new legislation that can address the issue?"

Rocky looked across the small conference table at the senator from Ohio who was listening on another line. The senator shook his head.

"I'll make some inquiries on the Hill, but Lincoln, I have to tell you, the mood there is very different from when the CPSA was originally passed. The corporations and their lobbyists have made their wishes known and Congress will be reticent to subvert the Supreme Court's decision."

"That's very disappointing to hear, Mr. President."

"I understand, but you've got to help me restore order, Lincoln. Help get those people back to work, we'll let the dust settle from all this, then we'll relook at what's possible."

"With respect, Mr. President, the workers enjoy leverage at this moment that they will lose if they end the strike and return to work."

"You don't know that, Lincoln."

"Yes, I do, and so do you, sir."

"I'm sorry you feel that way, Lincoln."

"Mr. President, you leave me no choice in this matter than to defend the people I represent. Starting tomorrow I will join the strike and lead the workers in standing for what is rightfully theirs. Our membership will hold fast to their beliefs. Big business and Washington have ignored the workers far too long and it is time for the pendulum to swing in their direction."

"Lincoln, I appreciate your position, but I hope you appreciate mine. I warn you that being on the strike line may get very ugly with the DoD directive I've just issued. These troops have been given the order to break this strike by whatever means necessary."

"And the workers of this country have vowed to re-establish themselves economically by any means necessary, Mr. President."

"Lincoln, I'm sorry it has come to this, but mark my word, I will uphold the law no matter what. It's my job and I intend to execute it fully."

* * *

"I have just spoken with the President," Lincoln reported, "and he's going to fight us every step of the way, Zeke. I thought Rocky was a different man than the one I just talked with, but I'm going to join the strike tomorrow and I was hoping you'd cover it for your news program."

"Of course I will," Zeke replied. "Where and when?"

"We've planned a massive march on Washington," Lincoln said. "We'll start with the Supreme Court, then move to the Capitol, and finally the White House. The more publicity we get the stronger our message will be."

"And what exactly is the message, Lincoln?"

"We want the corporations of this country to reinstate the CPSA despite the Supreme Court ruling. It's not a violation of the law to voluntarily re-institute the provisions of the original law and return half their profits to the workers."

"And I guess you'd want Congress to pass a separate bill that would allow the profit distributions to be allowed as a fully deductible expense?"

"As I understand it, that's within their authority."

"Yes, it is. Alright then, I'll bring a film crew to Washington tomorrow, but Lincoln, I'm going to be objective in my coverage. There's always two sides to any dispute. I can't just present your side alone."

"I wouldn't expect anything else, Zeke."

# # #

43

The nation's capital braced for its biggest crowd since the previous presidential inauguration. In an ironic twist, many of the workers who had attended the latter in enthusiastic support of the new president were now massed to protest his suggested use of martial law to quell the ongoing strike.

The march was led by Lincoln Archer, with Zeke Porter and a mobile television crew at his side. The crowd was estimated at nearly a million and, although boisterous, was peaceful. With the steps of the Supreme Court as a backdrop, Zeke reported that, "I'm here with Lincoln Archer, spokesperson for the Workers United labor union. Lincoln, what exactly does the union hope to accomplish with this massive display today?"

An ocean of faces served as a backdrop to Lincoln. "Zeke, we're here to raise our collective voices in outrage at the action that started here at the Supreme Court. The lawsuit that made its way here to the Court was initiated and heavily funded by corporate dollars and we're concerned that the Court was unduly influenced by the power of the corporations in rendering its decision."

"But every decision the Court makes is disputed by those who are on the losing side of the rulings. Do you have any proof that there were any direct ties between the Court and money from the corporate world?" Zeke asked.

Lincoln appeared annoyed at the question. "I believe that investigative reporting is your domain, Zeke. I'm merely here to represent the people who have been adversely effected by this decision.

Our legal system has once again favored the corporate world at the expense of the working man and we're here today to say enough."

"Tell our viewers why you plan to march across the street to the Capitol building."

Lincoln nodded. "We believe that Congress should immediately pass legislation that would reinstate the profit distribution tax deduction."

"And you think if they do it will influence corporations across the country to voluntarily reinstitute the profit sharing program that the Supreme Court found unconstitutional?"

"Well, it's not unconstitutional if they voluntarily recreate the profit sharing system."

"Otherwise this strike will continue?"

Lincoln nodded and gestured towards the crowd behind him. "The working men and women of this country are now in an economic corner with their backs against the wall. They have to use whatever leverage they have to reinsert themselves back into the mainstream of this economy. The raising of the minimum wage was a good start and the initial passage of the CPSA was a major step out of the economic shadows."

"Well, the strike has had its intended effect. The economy is becoming more sluggish every day, but I question just how long the union members can continue to go without a paycheck? I know Workers United is providing some limited funding for the strikers but how long can the workers go without basic necessities?"

"The Church of Hope, together with other charities, are providing on-site food kitchens for the striking workers, plus we're delivering a basic food package every week to each union family. The will of the workers is strong and they're prepared to sacrifice for the long term."

"And what do you say to the millions of Americans who are not on strike; the non-union members who are suffering from this strike?"

Lincoln stared straight into the television camera. "Working men and women everywhere are being shortchanged by an economy that rewards and protects the wealthiest, to the point of greed and avarice, while the average worker strains to get from paycheck to paycheck, assuming they even have one. The economy can no longer continue to prosper for just the smallest percentage of the population while penalizing all the rest."

"And what is the purpose of your march to the White House once you leave Capitol Hill?"

"We believe President Wellington is on the side of the working class in this country. His previous efforts with the Minimum Wage and CPSA bills showed his concern for the situation I've described and we seek his strong leadership in regaining what we've lost."

"But the president has made it clear that before any action can be taken the strike must cease. What do you say to that?"

"We say it's time for the president to take the first step. Gather the corporate leaders of this country and convince them to voluntarily reintroduce the profit sharing program. Use his influence with Congress to restore the tax deductions that will be favorable to business. These are both steps he can take in good faith to try and reestablish the momentum we had taken from us."

"But surely you understand that those steps will take time; they can't be accomplished overnight?"

"Of course. We understand the machinery of Washington and corporate bureaucracies very well. What we're asking for is the president's commitment to both of these demands."

"And if he were to make such a commitment would that end the strike?"

"That would be up to the union, but a step in that direction would certainly have my support."

* * *

After Lincoln made a similar statement on the steps of the Capitol building, the mass of humanity moved like a swarming army of ants across Capitol Hill and spilled out down onto Pennsylvania Avenue, headed for the White House. Atop the news van, Lincoln and Zeke led the way, the crowd surging after them.

Inside the White House, advisors clustered about the president in the cabinet conference room adjacent to the Oval Office, each offering their own solution to the growing dilemma outside. "The workers have the leverage right now," an advisor offered in an ominous tone. "The strike is crippling the country and it's getting worse every day. If you can make just enough of an offer to meet their demands in exchange for ending the strike, we'll have won the day."

"You've got to stand firm, Mr. President," the senator from Ohio said, scowling at the advisor. He turned back to the president. "Before you take any action this strike has to end. Call their bluff. Let's see how long these workers can continue to go without a paycheck."

"You've got to send a stern message," the four star general agreed. "Let my boys break up this protest, make a few key arrests and we'll turn the tide."

"Without Archer the workers don't really have a voice," an aide said. "Arrest him and the air will go out of their balloon."

Outside, the noise from the growing crowd could be heard through the thick walls and bullet proof glass in the West Wing. The group turned their attention to the bank of television sets at the far end of the room. There, Lincoln Archer, bull horn in hand, was directing his demands towards the White House.

"Mr. President, I call on you in the name of the workers who have made this country great. A tremendous injustice has been perpetrated, a wrong that can easily be righted by your actions. Use your considerable influence with the corporate community and let the workers of this country share in the bounty they have helped create with the sweat of their brow. Use the power of your office to motivate Congress to introduce legislation that will allow these distributions to be deducted as business expenses. The American people turn to your leadership to guide us out of this dilemma. These principles are why you were elected, Mr. President. We await your response."

The mass of people filling Pennsylvania Avenue from one end to another let out a loud cheer, waving union placards and homemade signs.

Inside the West Wing, the four star general spoke again. "Mr. President, if you give in to this strike that's all you'll see the rest of your time in office. These people need to be taught a lesson, that the law is the law and you can't shut down the country just because you don't agree with it. I've got tanks and aircraft poised. Give me the word and we'll break this thing up in ten minutes."

Outside the crowd awaited a response from the president. Lincoln turned to Zeke. "Thanks for covering this march, Zeke. All the other news organizations refused; pressure from the administration I guess."

"I got a call from the White House last night," Zeke said. "They asked me not to get involved and when I refused they not-so-politely suggested I might never see the inside of the White House again." He smiled. "I told them I'd already seen it and it was over-rated."

Lincoln patted his friend on the back and smiled.

"Hey," someone yelled, "the president's on T.V."

* * *

Rocky Wellington looked tired and stressed, his normal smile replaced by a tight-lipped grimace. "My fellow Americans, we have reached a crisis situation that goes beyond a mere conflict of words and ideas. The nationwide strike has not only harmed our economy, but it has reached into the personal lives of each and every American. It has placed our national security in jeopardy. It cannot continue.

I ask, once again, for a cooling off period, where the grievances of the worker's union can be addressed in a calm, logical manner. Negotiations must replace the chaos this strike has created. To that end, I ask the members of the worker's union to return to work immediately. First and foremost, we must repair the economic damage that has been done and stabilize our economic situation as a country.

To underscore the seriousness of these current circumstances, if the strike does not end immediately, I will institute martial law across the country, using the armed forces of the United States military to reestablish order. Citizens who threaten the operation of our corporations will be arrested. Those who choose to return to their jobs will be protected by our military, as will those non-union members who have been employed as a stop-gap measure. The strike must end, now. Workers must return to their jobs, now."

As the President continued there were mumblings amongst the crowd that nothing had been said about a commitment to negotiate their demands. The crowd's mood, hopeful at first, was turning ugly.

# # #

44

A squad of Marines approached the flatbed minivan that had transported Lincoln, Zeke and his television crew down Pennsylvania Avenue. A sergeant spoke, "Sir, the president wishes to meet with the two of you ASAP. We're here to escort you into the White House."

Lincoln looked at Zeke, who nodded. "Could be the start of negotiations," Zeke said.

The two men agreed to the request and Lincoln announced calmly that he had been summoned to a meeting with the president. The crowd, sensing a capitulation, cheered. Lincoln and Zeke marched off surrounded by the Marine squad, through the gate that led to a West Wing entrance.

The two men were led down a hall and into an empty office. They sat together on a small couch and waited. Ten minutes later the door opened and the president entered the room. Both visitors stood up. Rocky waved a hand. "Guys, please sit down."

Rocky sat heavily in the desk chair and sighed. He stared at a painting of George Washington on the opposite wall as he spoke. "It seems improbable as hell that the three of us, buddies since college, are sitting here today astride this keg of dynamite." He leaned back and stared at his guests.

"As you can imagine, I'm being offered advice and council from ten different directions." Both guests nodded. "But here's what I think." He tried a smile but it didn't work, the result being a twisted expression on his face. "Lincoln, you are, whether you accept the role or not, the leader of the workers." He held up a hand against the expected protest. "They will listen to you. They respect you. They *believe* in you.

We've got to buy some time for things to develop here. Trying to achieve what these workers want cannot happen overnight. Surely you both understand that? But, just as important is the undisputed fact that this strike must end immediately. It's crippling our economy and putting us in a position from which we might never recover. I'm getting the hell beat out of me by the corporate community and the Pentagon is ready to drop bombs on the demonstrators to show them what a tough guy I am! Do you believe that?"

The two guests glanced at each other.

"So, here's what I want you to do, Lincoln. You need to go back out there and, in the strongest terms possible, tell the workers to end the strike, go back to work, and give us time to address their concerns."

Lincoln cleared his throat. "Mr. President, you have to understand that no matter what I might say, it is the union membership that controls what actions they take."

Rocky raised both hands in exasperation. "But you have tremendous influence over these people. They'll at least consider what you say."

Lincoln shook his head. "It is you that has to make the first move, Mr. President, you that has to show them your good faith."

Rocky slammed the desk with his fist. "And that is exactly what I'm being told by my advisors; let *the workers* make the first good faith move; end the strike, then we can move forward." He exhaled in exasperation. "Zeke, do you have anything to offer here?"

Zeke nodded. "I can only tell you that the mood of the workers is one of distrust. They believe there was some sort of conspiracy in passing the original Corporate Profit Sharing Act, then having the rug pulled out from under their feet by the Supreme Court. They now believe that you were an active participant in that conspiracy. You've burned that bridge of trust in their minds."

"Do you two think I was personally involved in a conspiracy as you call it? Do you think I'm that devious and unscrupulous?"

There was a moment's silence. Finally, Zeke said, "Personally, no, but I do believe there were things going on behind your back, things you may still not be aware of in that regard. We've certainly got a lot of previous history to support things being done without a president's permission or knowledge."

"Well, that's the longest back-handed compliment I've ever received," Rocky said with a shake of his head.

"So, where do we go from here, sir?" Lincoln asked.

The president hung his head. "I don't honestly know. I need time to think and I don't have much left." He looked up. "Lincoln, you go tell your people whatever you must, but I'm going to try like hell to negotiate for their demands. If the strike goes on, so be it. I'm doing all I can."

"Yes, sir," Lincoln said.

The president stood up. "The Marine squad will escort you back outside the gates," he said, extending his arm towards the door to the office. The two men shook hands then Rocky said, "Zeke, could you stay behind a minute?"

"Yes, sir," Zeke replied as Lincoln opened the office door and was greeted by the Marine sergeant who had escorted him into the West Wing. The door closed.

"A drink?" Rocky asked, heading towards the liquor cart in the corner of the room.

"No, I'm fine. Thanks," Zeke said.

The president poured two inches into his glass and returned to his chair. He took a strong sip, winced, then looked at Zeke. "Let me tell you how this is going to play out, Zeke. Lincoln is now in the custody of the U.S. government and he will be charged with sedition for his role in inciting this strike."

"What?" Zeke said, wide-eyed.

The president continued. "We have plenty of places where he can be held until he decides that speaking as I have requested is in his best interest." He shook his head. "No, he isn't going to be tortured or anything like that, just given time to reconsider his position."

Zeke stood up. "But that's coercion," he objected. "You can't avoid due process, Rocky."

Rocky stood up and raised his voice. "I can do whatever the hell I feel is necessary. That's what needs to be done to save our country from economic destruction, dammit! The workers are being unreasonable to expect miracles overnight and Lincoln is the only person who can convince them otherwise. Don't worry, he'll sit in solitary for a few days and realize my suggestion is the smart thing to do."

Zeke shook his head. "There's no way you're going to get away with something like this."

"And I suppose you'll run right out of here and make it the lead for your news report tonight?"

"It's my duty."

"Your duty, my ass!" The president leaned forward, eyes wide. "Was it your duty to screw Robin behind my back all those years and still look me in the eye like we were friends?"

Zeke felt his knees go rubbery. He and Robin had always been so discrete and he knew that Robin would never confess to the affair, her current status was too important to her.

"Why, Zeke, for the first time in your life you're speechless," Rocky said.

Zeke bowed his head trying desperately to come up with something to say. "We never meant to hurt you. Robin was terribly unhappy," he offered in a soft voice.

"And you seriously thought I'd never find out? Don't you think a lot of people dug into my background when I was pushed into running for the Senate, and now this office?"

Zeke began to recover his composure. "So, they're using that knowledge as blackmail to get you to do what they want. Is that it?"

Rocky shook his head. "Another damned conspiracy theory, some cabal of evil men who manipulate the president and run a shadow government? It would make a helluva movie, wouldn't it?"

"What's the truth here, Rocky? How much has been dictated to you and by whom?"

The president finished his drink. "You'll never know, Zeke. Actually, you know too much already. You're a very dangerous man."

"The truth is *that* dangerous, Mr. President?"

"You have no idea what the real truth is, Zeke. No fucking idea."

"Try me."

The president smiled. "Trying to call my bluff, huh? Well, let's start with why I was never afraid of this whore Beverly Hankins, Hawkins, whatever, who claimed we had an affair and I fathered her child."

Zeke looked confused. "What does that have to do---"

"The reason she was no threat to me, Zeke, was that I had a vasectomy while I was in college. I didn't want any goddamned kids so I took precautions. Her bullshit story about me fathering her child was physically impossible."

Zeke knew that was a lie. He had the hair sample Beverly had given him from her son and the hair from the brush Andrea had lifted from the White House bathroom analyzed. The two were conclusively father and son. But Zeke held his tongue, believing that card might best be played later.

Rocky went on. "Of course Robin knew I was sterile, you rube. That's where you came into the picture. It was decided that her being pregnant was a great strategy for the election, so she decided she'd use you as a surrogate."

"But Junior---"

"Junior was your kid, you fool. And you thought you were pulling the wool over *my* eyes. Robin played you like a grand piano."

This was totally unexpected. Zeke felt his brain begin to spin.

"How does it feel to have been the sucker in all this, Zeke? How does it feel to have had a kid you never saw, never held, never played with? Hurts like hell, doesn't it?"

Zeke hung his head, his brain on overload. "I, I don't know what to say."

Rocky laughed without humor. "You think you know so much; always in search of the truth. Well, take that little spoonful of truth and see how it tastes."

But Zeke had no rebuttal, no comeback. He was stunned and confused.

"I originally thought of putting you in one of our black sites and throwing away the key, but I've never forgotten that you once saved my life. That's worth something, I guess. So, here's the deal, Zeke. This administration is going to make some very unpopular decisions over the next few years and we don't need you peeking under our tent looking for wrongdoing." He jabbed a finger at Zeke. "It would be wise for you to keep your reporting away from D.C. politics. You understand?"

Zeke instinctively reacted. "There's no way I'd do that. I won't look the other way for anybody; not even the President of the United States."

"The choice is yours, of course, Zeke. But let's just say that I've got people keeping a close eye on Andrea. She could fetch a pretty penny on the black slave market, sold to some Middle Eastern sheik to join his harem, never to be heard from again. They like redheads, you know?"

"You've gone mad," Zeke said.

"Madness to some is reality to others, Zeke. I choose to be on the side that sees the world for how it is, not how I want it to be. The sooner you adopt that as your perspective the easier life will be for you. And," he added, "every time you stick your nose in my business, I'll just add to the time your friend Lincoln sits rotting in prison. It's your choice." The president motioned toward the door to the office and Zeke, furious at what had transpired these past few minutes, walked slowly towards it.

"Oh," the president said, "give my regards to Andrea."

# # #

45

In front of the White House the demonstrators became anxious about the whereabouts of their spokesman. Where was he? What were he and the president talking about? Was there an agreement to end the strike? When would the announcement come?

Somehow, word spread slowly through the crowd that Lincoln had been seen in the company of several Marines, escorted to a black sedan behind the White House and driven away. For his safety, some wondered? What was about to happen? Meanwhile, off to the west a fleet of olive drab deuce and a half trucks made their way slowly up Pennsylvania Avenue and heavily armed troops spilled out, taking positions outside the wrought iron fence perimeter of the executive mansion. They stood, bayonets fixed atop automatic rifles, aimed menacingly at the protestors. The soldier's grim expressions masked an inner fear that they would have to execute the command they had been given should things get out of control.

In the White House briefing room, the same anxiety had energized the press, long overdue for something to report. What had happened to Zeke Porter? Had he been part of the discussion with the president? Were they still talking? When would there be a news release? The room became as noisy and frantic as the crowd outside.

When the White House press secretary eased his way into the room, everyone scrambled for a seat. The man, obviously nervous, held a single piece of paper. He cleared his throat and began the prepared statement regarding the fate of Lincoln Archer, arrested and charged with sedition; inciting riot and civil unrest. He would remain imprisoned until he agreed to cooperate with the government and speak out for ending the strike and allowing negotiations to commence.

Meanwhile, Zeke was escorted from the West Wing by two Marines, the trio headed towards the crowd massed on Pennsylvania Avenue. Zeke was outraged by Rocky's threat to harm Andrea and keep Lincoln in prison. He knew Andy would not be intimidated, but he also knew that Rocky was deadly serious about keeping Lincoln incarcerated if Zeke started a reporting crusade against the White House.

But underlying his normal reporting instincts was the bombshell possibility that he had been Rocky Junior's father. He quickly reconstructed his calendar in his mind and discovered, to his shock, that his last intimate meeting with Robin was almost exactly nine months before Rocky Junior was born. He recalled Beverly Hawkins' tale of going off her birth control to "trap" Rocky by getting pregnant. My god, he thought; what if Robin had done the same thing with him? What if he had been Rocky Junior's real father?

Out on Pennsylvania Avenue word of Lincoln's fate had transformed the peaceful crowd into a mob of enraged workers and supporters. Chants of "justice" began to build and the crowd starting pressing towards the White House gates. The soldiers along the fence tensed, but held their ground.

Then, above the din of the crowd, a single shot rang out. The soldiers thought that the shot had come from the crowd and they responded as they had been instructed to in such a circumstance, protecting the grounds and those inside the White House. They fired back. The pop-pop of gunfire sounded like a long string of firecrackers going off. The front row of protestors fell in a wave and the crowd, shouting and screaming, pressed forward. Another volley of shots felled a second wave, then another until, in a panic, the rest of the crowd turned and began running away. Hundreds were injured as they fell and were trampled. Tear gas followed the retreating protestors and in a matter of minutes they had dispersed, running down side streets and in every direction in fear of their lives.

Zeke struggled to make his way to his television crew on the flatbed truck, directing their coverage of the horrendous scene as he tried to capture the moment with a shaken voice. "This is like a battlefield," he reported. "Pennsylvania Avenue is littered with bodies, there is smoke everywhere, people moaning and crying. The crowd has fled in fear, the troops are ashen and shaken at what they have done. This is a disaster."

The final count was eighty-eight dead, a hundred seventy-five wounded. Fearing a national riot, the White House announced that another presidential address would be televised within the hour.

* * *

The president sat behind his desk in the Oval Office, a determined look on his face. His eyes were bloodshot and his hair uncharacteristically mussed. He looked into the television camera. "We have witnessed today a horrible result of the differences that divide our country. Nearly a hundred Americans are dead, shot by U.S. soldiers protecting the White House. This is an unacceptable price to pay for a situation that could have been handled peacefully.

Earlier today I met with Mr. Lincoln Archer, the spokesman and unofficial leader of the Workers United protest and begged him to speak to his followers, to end this crippling strike that affects all Americans, and to give the government the time necessary to address the worker's concerns and demands. Mr. Archer made it clear that he would refuse to request an end to the strike until the worker's demands had been met.

Today's tragedy, and indeed, this entire strike could have been avoided through the tried and true method of negotiation and compromise. Instead, the workers, spurred on by Mr. Archer, began today's protest march, a move that benefits no one and harms us all.

As a result of today's events I am taking several steps to insure that there are no further confrontations. First, I have instructed General Rogers, the Chairman of the Joint Chiefs of Staff, to deploy U.S. military troops to major urban areas to initiate martial law, impose curfews, and quell any further disturbances. Secondly, I am nationalizing the corporations that have been shut down by this strike and returning them to full operation with non-union workers and military personnel.

Thirdly, the Federal employees who joined the strike in sympathy are hereby fired. We will not let our economy and our government services continue to suffer as a result of this strike. To do so would endanger our national security and as your president, I will not allow that to happen.

Finally, I have detained Mr. Archer until he agrees to use his influence to compel the workers to return to their jobs. Only then will I begin negotiations with corporate leaders and members of Congress to address the worker's grievances. This was a terribly difficult decision as Mr. Archer is a long time personal friend, but this nation's safety and well-being have been entrusted to me and that responsibility outweighs any personal friendship.

These may all seem like drastic steps, but we are facing ominous results if these measures are not implemented immediately. I hope that these actions will be temporary and that we can restore order and return to business as usual as quickly as possible. I ask for your support, your cooperation, and your prayers as we embark on this perilous road. Thank you and god bless the United States of America."

The television technician signaled that the broadcast was over and Rocky slumped in his desk chair, exhausted by the accumulated tension and stress of today's events.

Behind the television camera the senator from Ohio nodded at his puppet. Getting the armed forces involved was a brilliant move. Not only would they shoot any asshole who wanted to demonstrate further, but by placing them in key government agencies to replace fired Federal workers, the ground would be plowed for turning over the function of those agencies to private enterprises. It would take time, require some tricky legislation and clever contracting, but The Ten's plan was about to be realized. With the military and this president firmly in control, the public and their weak-willed representatives on the Hill would be putty in their hands.

The lesson of what happened to those who opposed this administration, whether it had been Lincoln Archer or the mass of striking workers, would be firmly imprinted in everyone's minds. No more strikes. No more worker demands. No more protests. And once the dust had settled and everyone had become used to how things were going to be, The Ten could begin the transformation of this country from a top-heavy, bloated, hopelessly bureaucratic government locked in constant political stalemate and gridlock, into an efficient, smoothly running commercial enterprise. The dream was just around the corner and the senator from Ohio smiled.

# # #

46

Solitary confinement can rot a man's soul. It's not necessarily the boredom, the endless pacing of the eight-by-twelve windowless cell, the bland food, or being cut off from the events of the outside world. What haunts your dreams, causes you to talk to yourself, and creates a certainty that madness is but an instant away, is the absence of human contact.

Twice a week Lincoln Archer was escorted silently to a shower stall a mere twenty feet from his cell where he was allowed to bathe. The single guard never uttered a word during the fifteen minutes that Lincoln was free from his cell. Five nights a week Lincoln was led, again by a silent guard, to a small interior courtyard where he was free to exercise, or, as he did most nights, simply breathe deeply of the cool air and stare at the moon and stars for thirty minutes.

He was not allowed to watch television, read newspapers or magazines or learn what was going on in the world racing past his solitary existence. The only book he was allowed to have was a battered copy of the bible. So of course he read it; cover to cover, over and over.

He often wondered if there truly was a god and that he was being punished for not believing. Nevertheless, he found a certain comfort in reading the book every day; it was his entertainment, his connection to the world, and he read aloud as if in conversation with the many characters portrayed there. He was sure he was going mad.

He had been told that all he had to do to be free was to agree to what the president had demanded of him; convince his followers to end the strike and go back to work. A simple word to any of his guards would allow him to do just that. But every day, as he went over and over the reasons for the strike and the sacrifices the workers had already made, he knew that he must stick to his convictions. The strike would eventually bring negotiations and gains for the workers. There was no way he could agree that it should end.

Besides, the strike must surely be over by now. If his crude record-keeping was accurate, it had been nearly six months since he arrived here. Certainly something had been settled by now. But if that was true then what good was he to the president? If he had no value to offer he might remain, just a step away from insanity, in this living hell forever. Men like Lincoln, no matter how important or recognized they might be, like the causes they stood for, were sometimes quickly forgotten. Footnotes in history. Time marches on. He might never go free.

He recalled the night he first thought he had gone mad. He had been here about two months and was enjoying his half hour of freedom in the tiny courtyard. The moon was full and as he stared up at it he considered the fact that it must look the same to people everywhere; a white sphere that hung in the sky like a Christmas tree ornament. As he looked up into the night he saw a face in the moon and, to his amazement, it began to talk to him.

The face told him he had been a fool to lead the workers; that they had taken advantage of him and now, when he really needed their support, they had abandoned him. The face stared down at him with scorn and pity. He tried to speak, couldn't come up with anything to say but a weak, "Help me." But then the face was gone and he was alone once again.

That had been months ago and Lincoln soon realized that talking to the moon was not a sign of insanity, but could be a release of feelings and emotions that no one else was around to hear. With the moon as his audience he relived pleasant memories aloud, revisited conversations with friends, repeated sermons, tried to imagine what was happening to the world outside; each session ending in the tearful conclusion that his life was over. Hope was beyond his imagination, as distant as the stars.

He wondered what had become of Zeke? Was he in prison too? He might never know and the uncertainty of Zeke's plight, like his own, had gnawed a giant hole in his perspective on life and fairness and the love he had preached. He thought of Liz, his companion at the White House dinner who had become more than just a date. Their relationship was just beginning to blossom and now, he wondered how long she would wait for him? With his life unwinding around him Lincoln felt the walls closing in.

So it came as quite a shock when, without warning or explanation, he found himself standing outside the entrance to the Hazelton maximum security penitentiary in the clothes he had worn the day of the protest march in Washington, waiting as he had been instructed. He folded his arms around his sides against the morning chill and drank in the sweet smell of freedom. Somewhere in the distance a rooster crowed and Lincoln smiled at the welcome sound. Then it was quiet again and he strained to hear another sign of life.

The early morning fog was still heavy but the eerie silence was suddenly broken by the distant sound of an engine. As the sound grew louder Lincoln could make out the dim glow of lights moving toward him. The car moved slowly up the single lane road that ran like a thin gray line out of the trees towards the entrance to the prison. The car glided to a stop just a few feet away and the driver got out and moved around the hood of the car.

From where he stood Lincoln could not make out the face of the driver, but as the man moved toward him he recognized the unmistakable gait of Zeke Porter.

Lincoln instinctively moved towards his old friend, slowly at first, then he broke into a sprint. The two men who had shared so much together stood, wrapped in each other's arms. Both cried softly. Finally, Zeke held Lincoln back at arm's length and smiled. "Let's get you out of this place," he said.

* * *

"You've lost a lot of weight," Zeke said as he turned the car around and drove away from the prison.

Lincoln turned to look back at the high chain link fence, the concertina wire and the gray walls of the prison, trying to imagine where his cell had been. He turned back to Zeke. "That's what a steady diet of lobster and filet mignon will do to a man."

Both men smiled. "Why have I been released?" Lincoln asked.

"I petitioned Rocky consistently to let you go," Zeke explained. "Although we never talked, it was my impression that he was being pressured to let you stew a while before he pardoned you."

"It's not a bad strategy," Lincoln said, shaking his head. "I'm lucky I didn't lose my mind in that place." He paused. "Maybe I did."

Zeke glanced at his passenger. "I can only imagine," he said sadly. "Anyway, Rocky finally relented and I was called last night to quietly come and get you this morning. No press, no news conference, no publicity."

Lincoln smiled at his old friend. "You're the first human voice other than my own that I've heard in six months," he said, voice cracking.

Zeke reached across the seat and took Lincoln's hand. "It's all over now. You're free."

"And what exactly does that mean? What has happened while I've been in here?"

Zeke proceeded to tell Lincoln about the confrontation in front of the White House, how Army troops had killed nearly one hundred protesters.

Lincoln sat back in shock. "That's horrible. My, God." He looked out the window, his eyes moist. "Because of me," he mumbled. "Because of me."

"Don't be ridiculous, Lincoln. A bunch of nervous young soldiers panicked. It wasn't your fault any more than it was mine. I was there too, you know?"

Lincoln shook his head sadly, tears running down his face.

"Anyway, that scared the hell out of the union leadership, because the very next day they ended the strike," he said. "Everybody went back to work, the troops stood down and things returned to normal. Well, to the way it had been before the strike. Profit sharing is still dead, no activity in Congress to revise the tax code, plus, all the Federal workers who joined the strike were fired."

Lincoln shook his head.

"But instead of reinstating those workers, the government created commercial contracts for those agencies and awarded them to private industry. Major government functions are now being performed by corporations."

As he wiped at his eyes Lincoln noted the "Welcome to Maryland" sign as the car sped east. He must have been in West Virginia all this time.

Zeke went on. "Ironically, many of those Federal workers who had been fired were hired by the corporations to perform their old jobs."

Lincoln turned to look at Zeke. "With lower salaries and less benefits I suppose?"

"Right, but what choice did they have? The corporations immediately began boasting about how they had cut costs for those services and become more efficient. It's exactly what the small government crowd has been wanting for generations."

Lincoln considered what had transpired during his incarceration. "And what about you, Zeke? What has Rocky done to you?"

Zeke sighed. "Rocky warned me not to be critical of his administration and all the things they were going to do. He threatened to have bad things happen to Andrea and to keep you in prison the rest of your life if I didn't go along with his demands."

"Well, I'm out so you must have done as he asked," Lincoln said, his expression one of shock.

"Other than petitioning for your release, I've avoided anything to do with D.C. politics. The Bottom Line has focused on all the other things going on in the world."

"Sounds like a smart approach."

"Well, it worked. There's plenty of other reporters who have created problems for Rocky's administration. I secretly fed many of them leads and they have done the rest. Meanwhile, in addition to my daily petitions, Andrea and Liz mobilized their show business friends to lobby Capitol Hill and the White House for your release. I think Rocky finally got tired of all the attention you were getting. You had become an unwanted sideshow to his greater agenda."

Lincoln studied the dash. "I don't know what to say. I owe you guys so much."

"Well, members of your church ran ads across the country demanding your release. Like I said, I think Rocky decided to get you out of the news and take the heat off himself. There's a lot more to tell you, but there'll be time later."

Lincoln leaned back in the seat and closed his eyes. "Yes, I need a while to recover from staring at four walls for six months," he said.

"I've made arrangements for the place in Jackson Hole you stayed before, or I have access to an apartment in Georgetown if you like."

Lincoln opened his eyes and stared at his friend. "I think as far away as I can get from Washington would be preferable." He sighed. "Rocky really did a number on me, Zeke. There's no way I'll ever go back to prison. I'll lose my mind."

Zeke nodded. "I hear you and, no, you haven't lost your mind, but I'll get a doctor to come take a look at you. I want to make sure you're O.K., my friend."

Lincoln stared out the window as the rising sun melted away the fog and the greenery of western Maryland flooded his senses. "So tell me, how is Liz doing?" he asked.

* * *

They stopped at a Mom N Pop restaurant outside of Frederick, Maryland, and Lincoln was overwhelmed by the breakfast. "This is the greatest meal I've ever had," he exclaimed, shoveling the food into his mouth as fast as he could.

The gray-haired old waitress appeared behind him, refilling his coffee cup. "I'll pass on the compliment to the chef," she said with a wink.

"Listen to that," Lincoln said, tilting his head to one side.

"What?"

"The sounds of human beings." Although there were only five or six other people in the restaurant the sound of their conversations and laughter must have been deafening to one who had just spent six long months in silent solitary.

Zeke nodded his understanding.

"You know, the time I spent in Jackson Hole before was really restorative. I'd like to take you up on your offer to go there again," Lincoln said.

Zeke sipped his coffee. "I've got the corporate jet waiting at Dulles," he said. "It's time for two old friends to relax and catch up, so I'll come with you and hang out a few days myself if you don't mind the company."

Lincoln smiled. "That would be most welcome, my friend."

* * *

The trip from Dulles Airport to Jackson Hole took about three hours and was spent mostly in silence. After a few stiff drinks the rhythmic hum of the engines put Lincoln to sleep. Zeke studied his friend, tried to imagine the horror of his incarceration, decided that his imagination couldn't quite duplicate the day-to-day loneliness and fear Lincoln had experienced.

As the Lear jet started down for its landing Zeke stared out the window at the white blanket of snow that spread as far as he could see. Maybe a few days of reflection and strategizing with his old friend would give them both an answer as to what to do next with their lives.

# # #

47

The two old friends sat at the kitchen table in the cabin Zeke had rented, drinking coffee and watching the snow come down outside. Lincoln folded the last section of the newspaper and tossed it on the table. "Still nothing," he said.

Zeke shook his head. "Patience, my friend. As I told you, the conditions of your release were that it was to be done quietly, with no publicity and with a twenty-four hour gag order on contacting anyone. The White House wants to choose when and where they'll leak the story."

"So they can put their own spin on it?" Lincoln said with a frown.

Zeke looked at his watch. "We've only got a few more hours until the gag order expires," he said. "If they haven't made an announcement by then, you can call Liz and your church."

Lincoln nodded his understanding and sighed. "Not to be narcissistic about it all, but I would have thought the press would have been following my situation more closely."

Zeke smiled. "Except to a few of us who kept working on your behalf, your story soon became old news. I called the White House repeatedly asking for a meeting with Rocky to protest your incarceration, but I never got to first base, so I started submitting anonymous letters to a host of newspapers questioning the authority of the administration to detain you."

Lincoln frowned. "It seems the government can wave due process if it suits their needs."

Zeke nodded. "I also met with leaders of your union to try and launch a campaign for your release, but the administration had sufficiently intimidated them. They were scared to death to speak up. Your freedom was sacrificed for their own self-preservation."

Lincoln sighed with the realization that the people he had fought so hard for wouldn't fight for him. "Freedom was something I once took for granted," he said, studying the slanting snow out the window. "But being in prison is more than just being confined, it's the isolation, the lack of human interaction that's terrifying. It truly is cruel and unusual punishment."

"You've endured a lot, my friend. But now you're free and able to get on with your life."

Lincoln turned to face his friend. "Maybe Cardinal DuPont was right; being the spokesman for Workers United was a political power trip for me. I mean, I'm proud of what we tried to do together, but it became so much different than my preaching. It became about me; being the leader, the spokesman, the star. Power like that is an aphrodisiac. I understand why so many seek it and hold onto it so fiercely."

He paused, gathering his thoughts. "I want to go back to the way it was when I started the Church of Hope; not just helping people with my words but with my hands." He raised both hands and looked at them. "Working on food lines, helping to repair a farmer's fence, visiting members of my congregation in the hospital, taking food packages to the elderly. Being out there among the people meant so much to me then and I want to regain that feeling."

Zeke smiled. "That seems like a wise decision." He paused, deciding to proceed cautiously with a subject he had put off discussing until now. "Not to be pessimistic, but from my perspective your union cause was always facing an uphill battle anyway."

Lincoln sipped his coffee. "What do you mean?"

"Think about it, Lincoln. There's always been an economic gap between rich and poor. Roman patricians and the mob, European royalty and peasants, American robber barons and working class immigrants. What we're seeing today is nothing new, it's simply history repeating itself. Ancient royalty has morphed into the corporate world in economic terms and corporations are the winners almost every time there's a fight with the workers. Today's corporations are where the money is and where the power resides." He leaned forward, elbows on the table and looked at his friend. "Having said all that, you were an important voice of hope for the workers. Now it's time to pass the torch to someone else."

Lincoln nodded, his expression twisted in thought. "You're right, of course. I am itching to get back to work, and to see Liz," he added with a smile.

Zeke said, "Liz and I have talked several times a week. I had no idea you two had been seeing so much of one another."

"Not as much as we'd like. It's tough to carry on a romance long distance." They sat in silence a moment, then Lincoln said, "What about you, Zeke? Will you go back to writing about Washington politics now?"

Zeke sighed. "I don't know. I feel like I've betrayed my beliefs by curbing my criticism of the administration. The truth no matter where it leads has become a hollow platitude," he added with a frown.

"It seems like Rocky put you in a no-win situation, threatening Andrea and keeping me in prison forever if you didn't comply with his demands. You did what you had to do, for us."

"To be honest," Zeke said with a smile, "national politics have become predictable and boring: endless stalemates, petty arguing, displays of ignorance that would be humorous if the issues weren't so serious. Solving problems through debate and compromise has somehow become less important than following blind ideology." He shook his head.

"But?"

Zeke nodded. "But there are so many more important issues to cover: human rights, genocide, global warming, terrorism. They make our political squabbling seem petty by comparison."

"This may be the last political observation I ever make, but I think that religion is at the heart of all those issues: fanatics using scripture as justification for murder, for ignoring science, for treating women and children like they were disposable possessions. It's hopelessly intertwined in all of them."

"Speaking of religion, your old friend Cardinal DuPont has written several articles where he claimed that your imprisonment was a punishment from God."

Lincoln smiled. "Do you think he'll also give God credit for my release?"

* * *

After dinner that night Lincoln tried to reach Liz, but was told she was in rehearsal. He left the cabin's phone number and asked that she call him ASAP. He would call his church tomorrow, after he and Liz had made arrangements to see one another. Pleasure before business. Returning to the couch in front of the fireplace, he picked up his drink and took a sip.

Zeke did the same. "It sounds like this relationship with Liz is pretty serious," he said.

"We were certainly moving in that direction before my little sabbatical," Lincoln answered. "So when are you going to make Andrea an honest woman?"

"We're in no hurry, but it's definitely in our plans," Zeke said with a smile.

Lincoln studied his old friend. "There's something I've always wanted to ask you."

"Go ahead."

"Did you have an affair with Robin?"

Zeke laughed. "Now where the hell did that come from?"

"I've always been suspicious. Every time her name came up in conversation you always got this look in your eyes. Then there was the dinner at the White House and how you two avoided one another."

Zeke nodded. "You're very perceptive, but it was over some time ago."

"Does Rocky know?"

"Afraid so," Zeke replied with a grimace.

"Did you love her?"

"You ask the same questions Andrea did."

"Well?"

Zeke drew a deep breath. "Robin was in love with her ambitions, not me."

"But were *you* in love with her?" Lincoln pressed.

Zeke studied his hands, then said, "Overwhelmed and infatuated, but too much guilt and anxiety and worry mixed in to call it true love."

"Have you and Rocky made peace with all this?"

"I'm sure the affair damaged his ego, and I still feel guilty about it all, but he's had a lot more important things on his mind. To answer your question, we've never really talked about it."

"But will you?"

Zeke stared into the fire. "There will probably be a time and place, yes, but not right now. My first priority is to get you re-connected with Liz."

As if on cue, the phone rang. Zeke smiled. "There she is. Now, try not to overwhelm her with your charm."

# # #

48

The president was on a fund-raising trip to Chicago and the meeting was scheduled for late at night in his suite at the Remington Savoy. Zeke was escorted through a service entrance, up a freight elevator, and into the presidential suite. Secret Service agents stood guard outside and several presidential aides were concluding a meeting with Rocky. The president sat spread eagle in a chair beneath a Norman Rockwell painting of a country doctor giving a freckle-faced boy a shot in the posterior.

The hushed conversation with his aides quickly ended and Rocky struggled to his feet. "Give us the room, will you, boys?" he said and his aides scampered, eyeing the newcomer suspiciously.

"I don't know about you, Zeke," the president said, moving to a glass table filled with bottles of alcohol, "but I need a drink." He grabbed a bottle of Wild Turkey and poured two glasses, handing one to his guest, then motioned towards the cluster of overstuffed furniture that constituted the living area of the suite.

Rocky looked exhausted, his black bow tie undone and dangling, his eyes bloodshot. Tinges of gray were now visible around the edge of his blonde hairline. He plopped into a chair in the corner and kicked off shoes that shone like black glass. "Giving speeches for people I never met gets old," he said in an exasperated tone. "Comes with the territory, I guess."

Zeke sat down on the couch facing the president. For nearly six months he had tried to arrange a meeting with Rocky in an attempt to free Lincoln. Now that Lincoln was out of prison Zeke wondered why he had finally been allowed a sit down with the president.

Rocky took a strong pull on his drink and studied his guest. "I have to say, Zeke. You've really got a set of balls on you."

"Excuse me?" Zeke said.

"Calling the White House every day, making speeches on your show each week, getting all those letters and e-mails sent to me, the letters to the editors. You took some chance, you know? I could have been serious about Andrea disappearing and Lincoln staying in prison the rest of his life. Not to mention what could have happened to you."

"Lincoln is my friend and I did everything I could to set him free," Zeke began, "and nobody can frighten Andrea; she's the one with the balls."

That got a sharp laugh from the president. "Yes, I guess you're right about that. Anyway, how is Lincoln?"

"He's gone back to preaching love and kindness and left the union spokesman position behind. Said he wants nothing to do with politics ever again."

Rocky nodded. "Smart man. It's a nasty business." He paused, studying the floor in front of him. "You know, if I would have had my way I'd have just let him sit in prison a week or two then let him go." He looked up. "But my *advisors*," he added, finger quotes raised with both hands, "insisted on six months. They said after that long he'd think twice about making any more trouble for us."

"Well, the strategy worked; like I said, Lincoln is back in the pulpit and out of politics for good. Being in solitary really messed with his mind, Rocky."

The president grimaced and reached for his drink. "I know and I'm sorry as hell. He's my friend too, you know?"

"Maybe you should tell him that face to face, Mr. President."

Rocky nodded slowly. "Yes, one day I will. But let's talk about you for a minute." Rocky sipped his drink, then pointed at Zeke. "I know you've got some sensational shit about me and this Hawkins woman that you want to dangle in front of me as a threat, but, believe me, that train has already left the station."

"You know she's dead?" Zeke asked.

Rocky looked pensive. "Of course I do. There's a chain of evidence, fabricated of course, that brings that decision all the way back to my desk. They've got me painted into a tight little corner, don't you see?"

"And you know that your son with her was put up for adoption?" Zeke asked.

"*My* son," Rocky said, his voice breaking, "is dead." He stared at the Rockwell painting across the room then said softly, "They're both my sons I suppose, both lost to me." He looked at Zeke. "I'm sorry I had to mislead you into believing Junior might have been yours, Zeke, but it was all part of the plan to discredit you."

Zeke heaved a silent sigh of relief. Although being Junior's father had always been a possibility, it just made no sense, didn't fit into Robin or Rocky's carefully orchestrated world. "Was that another suggestion from your advisors?"

"Yes, but I think there was an element of personal revenge involved for what you and Robin did."

"And what have you done to punish her?"

Rocky chuckled. "Hell, Zeke, she's had to be married to me all these years. Anyway, we don't need to go down the road of regret for any of us; just accept my apology for misleading you."

Zeke nodded, amazed that Rocky could be so cavalier about being betrayed by his wife and friend.

But Rocky's mind was on other things. "You know, when I sought this office I thought I knew all about the seamy side of politics: the back room deals, the blackmail, dealing with low lives you can only imagine. And I also knew that whatever I tried to do as president there would always be a large number of people who disagreed with me, but I never thought that people would be killed over those decisions. No amount of political give and take is worth people dying, Zeke."

"Not to wave the flag, but there is a price to be paid for free speech," Zeke said. "Those protesters did not die in vain, nor did Lincoln spend all that time in prison for nothing. They were all willing to fight for their principles."

"Principles," Rocky said with a grunt. "Not sure what that word means anymore." He stared down into his drink, then emptied it, ice cubes rattling in the glass. The president got up, moved to the bar and poured himself a refill. He moved back to his chair and sat down heavily. "I'm sure that as the turmoil of this past year dies down, you'll get back on your game, searching for truth and justice and all that crap." He looked apologetic for his last remark, leaning forward and patting Zeke on the knee. "And that's O.K. You can rally the workers around the flag, write patriotic articles about fairness and doing the right thing, convey your disappointment and outrage nine ways from Sunday." He sipped his drink and stared off across the room, then back at his guest. "What I'm trying to tell you, Zeke, is that, despite all you and Lincoln's efforts and sacrifices, nothing has changed and never will. Big business and its money runs this country and guys like us, hell, we're just actors in a play. Somebody else writes the script, we do what we're told or they find another player to run out on the stage."

"That's a sad condemnation of democracy," Zeke said.

"Isn't it now?" Rocky answered.

"So, the White House won't try and put a lid on anything I write or say about your administration?"

"Hell, say anything you want, Zeke. This is a free country, you have freedom of speech, use it, but you'll never get anywhere fighting them. It's not that they'll try and censor you, but it's just that your words will never cause anything meaningful to happen. It might make you and a few others feel good that you've got whatever off your chest, but, as they say, words are cheap."

Zeke sat in silence, recalling his words to Lincoln about the history of rich and poor and how ancient royalty had evolved into corporations.

"And now," the president said, slipping his shoes back on and standing up, "if you will excuse me, I need to go get briefed on what I'm supposed to do tomorrow as the leader of the free world. I'm sure you can find your way out." He paused and stared sadly at his friend who had stood in deference to his departure. "Thanks for dropping by. It's good to see an old friend again. I don't have many left." He reached for Zeke's hand and shook it. "You take care of yourself, you hear?"

# # #

49

The senior senator from Ohio carefully trimmed the tip of his Cuban, examined it, then set it aflame with his ivory encased lighter. He puffed several times, examined the now burning tip and nodded in satisfaction. "Getting these at a reasonable price will be just one of the benefits of lifting the embargo," he pronounced.

Sitting across from him in the spacious library in the senator's Great Falls home, Rocky nodded, but his mind was elsewhere. He had just endured a dinner-long diatribe listing The Ten's plans for his second term: continued commercialization of government functions, another "adjustment" to the tax code to provide relief to wealthy donors and corporations, and killing immigration reform as it would provide millions of new voters for the opposition party.

"Now," the senator started, reaching for his cup of coffee, "let's talk about your first series of campaign trips."

"I'm not running," Rocky said matter-of-factly, staring down into his own cup.

"What did you say?" the senator asked, his cup suspended half way to his lips.

Rocky drew a deep breath and turned his gaze to his host. "I said, I'm not running. Four years of this bullshit is enough."

The senator sat his cup and saucer down. "Is this some sort of a joke, Rocky? If so, it's not very funny."

"It's not a joke. I'm out. You can find some other errand boy to do your bidding."

The senator was confused. This apparently was not a joke. "Rocky, what has gotten into you? Where the hell did this come from? Are you ill?"

Rocky nodded. "I'm sick alright; sick of being a front for you and your gang. I don't have a say in any major decision and I disagree with most of what you've told me to do. I'm used to being my own man and I'm weary of your arm being up my backside."

The senator leveled his gaze at his guest. "Have you discussed this madness with Robin?"

Rocky sighed. "No, but there's nothing she can say that will change my mind."

The senator offered a thin smile. "Oh, I think you're wrong there, Rocky. She's grown quite fond of being the First Lady." The room was silent as each man sized up the other. "Maybe," the senator said in a low voice, "you need some time off, maybe a fund-raising trip to Hawaii or an extended stay up at Camp David. A chance to unwind and get this all out of your system."

Rocky slammed his fist onto the arm of his chair. "Didn't you hear me? I'm out, dammit!"

The senator leaned forward, elbows on knees and lowered his voice. "Rocky, this is insane. It upsets all of our plans and we simply won't sit still and let you do that. We've groomed you, paved the way for you, twisted arms for you and suddenly you want out?"

Rocky's voice hissed through his teeth. "And you've killed for me, Senator. I'll never get that fact out of my head."

"And I'm sure, Rocky, that you wouldn't want that unfortunate fact tied back to you if you force us to do so. And you know we will."

"That would do you as much harm as it would me because I'll turn over every unscrupulous rock I'm aware of and the press and the opposition will have a field day and you'll be destroyed."

The senator leaned back in his chair and studied the president. "This is going to get very ugly, Rocky, and a lot of it will be out of my control. This decision will piss off a number of very powerful people and they'll want your scalp for it. I can't be responsible for the backlash. You're not only ending your political career, you're condemning yourself to a lifetime of humiliation. Men don't just walk away from this job without being labeled a quitter. Is that how you want to be remembered, Rocky?"

"Hell, I'll be out of office six months and I'll be forgotten. We both know that. All the focus will be on the next guy who's stupid enough to take this job. I'm going to be free from this bullshit once and for all."

"Rocky," the senator said in a conciliatory tone, "you can't leave us in the lurch like this. We didn't plan on someone else running. And," he went on, "once you make this announcement you'll be a lame duck; we won't be able to move our agenda forward an inch."

"I don't give a damn about *your* agenda, senator. And there are plenty of eager beavers out there who would jump at the chance to be your candidate, just don't look for me to endorse anyone."

"Rocky, there is so much more we could accomplish in your second term."

"And what about what *I* want to accomplish? Where do my beliefs and objectives come into play?"

"Rocky, I admit it's been a struggle to keep you on message, but it's not too late for you to have a historic impact on this country."

"Save me the sales pitch, senator. I'm done with being a hypocrite, a liar and a charade. Good luck at finding someone who's been as good at it as I have been. Now," he said, standing up, "I need to get back to the White House and tell Robin what's going on."

"I don't envy you that task, Rocky, but there's still time to change your mind. Go ahead and discuss things with Robin. I'm sure she'll weigh in with a different perspective than what I've presented."

"Oh, I think your perspectives are pretty much the same, senator. It's terribly difficult to let go of power and admit that this has all been a lie." He moved towards the door. "Thanks for the dinner, Senator."

* * *

"You're going to do what?" Robin said, her eyes wide.

"I said, I'm not running for a second term. I'm finished."

"Are you mad?"

Rocky smiled. "That's becoming a popular question."

"Seriously, are you crazy, Rocky? What in the world is wrong with you?"

He reached out to put a hand on her shoulder. "Look, you wouldn't understand. You don't deal with what I do every day."

She brushed his hand off her shoulder. "And you don't understand how important all this is to me."

"Oh, I understand all right. You're in your glory with all your state dinners and causes and having your own staff to do your bidding. Being a celebrity has always been your dream, but it's turned into a nightmare for me so it's over."

Robin's face flushed with sudden anger. "I'll leave you so fast your head will spin. Let's see how far your career can go without me at your side."

"My career is over, Robin. I'm finished, with or without you."

Robin raised a fist then held it there, her arm shaking. "Damn you! It's always been about you!"

"Go ahead," he said, spreading his arms in front of her, "if beating me up will help you feel better, have at it. I deserve it."

"Wait a minute," Robin said, lowering her fist. "What do they have on you? What dirty little secret are they prepared to reveal if you don't do what they want?"

Rocky shook his head. "There is no smoking gun, Robin."

"Not for you maybe," Robin said, panic in her voice. She looked at him, tears in her eyes. "I had an affair with Zeke, Rocky. They have pictures."

The room went eerily quiet for a long moment, then Rocky said softly, "Yes, I've seen them."

"You knew?" Robin said, eyes wide.

"Christ, Robin," Rocky said, "I'm the President of the United States, of course I knew."

Robin was too stunned to speak.

Rocky sighed. "I'm just sorry that my wanting to be president caused you to end it."

"I didn't end it, he did," Robin said.

That was one detail Rocky wasn't aware of. He took a deep breath and exhaled. "Well, they won't risk revealing anything like that for fear I'll tell the world what I know about their dealings." He looked at her. "These are ruthless, calculating men, Robin."

Robin scoffed derisively, wiping at her tears. "Hell, you knew that politics was nothing more than lies and deception and unsavory bullshit. I thought that's what appealed to you about it. That and the damned glamour and power. And now----" The tears were running down her cheeks. She fell back onto the edge of the sofa, hands covering her face. "I don't deserve this," she gasped. "You owe me, Rocky."

"I owe you?"

She lowered her hands and stared up at him, her eyeliner smeared, her eyes bloodshot. "Alright, we both know I married you as my ticket out of Walnut Grove, but once that happened, once you made it into the big leagues I became important to you. You would never have had all this," she said, waving her hands about the room, "without me. And now you want to throw all that away. This is my life too, Rocky."

Rocky nodded. "I wanted out of Walnut Grove too and that required total focus on the bank, but once we had made that break and had Junior I thought things would change; that we would change, but you were already gone, Robin."

She laughed sharply. "Don't tell me now that you grew to love me, Rocky." She shook her head and wiped at her eyes. "Well, I've never loved you; never. But this isn't the end for me, Rocky. I've become famous in my own right. I am somebody now and, unlike you, I will play that fame to my advantage. You're the one who'll wind up a loser."

Rocky bowed his head and nodded. "I gave you everything you ever wanted, Robin. Everything." He paused and drew a breath. "Even my best friend," he said sorrowfully.

#

50

Zeke hadn't been in Walnut Grove since Rocky and Robin's wedding. Like most small towns, little had changed since that time so long ago; a new fast food joint or two maybe, nothing noticeable. The one exception was the towering gray corner building on Main Street that had once been the Wellington National Bank. It was now Dillon's Department Store and the once drab looming façade had been transformed with the aid of a large neon sign and colorful window displays.

The town's most famous son had returned two years ago to live here in quiet obscurity after leaving the White House. The results of Rocky's decision to forego an almost assured second term had been cataclysmic. Shaken by his sudden choice to step down, Rocky's party was left in chaos, no clear candidate to replace him. The Ten had taken great pains to groom Rocky and accelerate their agenda during his second term. All that planning had been thrown out the window and The Ten, not used to events escaping their control, had been both stunned and angry.

Speculation as to the real reason Rocky had chosen not to seek certain re-election ran rampant. The "official" reason given by the White House was mental exhaustion and having never recovered from the death of his infant son. These were both plausible reasons to the general public and the press.

As the senator from Ohio had predicted, Rocky's remaining days in office had been completely non-productive. Lame duck became a kind description for the moribund White House as the administration began to exhibit flat line tendencies.

Rocky's abrupt departure from public life not only ended his political career, but his marriage. Robin, incensed by his voluntary removal of her cherished position as First Lady, quickly divorced him. She followed her own calling, showing up at Hollywood parties, charity events and celebrity gatherings all over the globe, a different man on her arm for each occasion. She became a paparazzi favorite, appearing on the cover of tabloids and on television celebrity watch programs. The glamorous and popular ex-First Lady eventually took up with a German billionaire industrialist and the two became regular members of the international jet set, Robin spending his money like it was her job.

All of these events rushed through Zeke's mind as he cruised slowly along Main Street and onto Presidential Lane, headed for the ex-president's home of self-imposed isolation and humility. His thoughts turned to Robin. He wondered, from time to time, if, in her rare quiet moments, she ever thought about him. He doubted it. Bits and pieces of their time together sometimes replayed like scenes from a movie in his dreams. Zeke smiled, his relationship with Andrea having forced those dreams deeper into his subconscious.

He drove on to the end of the block and Rocky's home. As he pulled up to the gate a Secret Service agent approached the car, checked his identification and directed him to a parking place near the flag pole in the center of the circular driveway. At the front door another agent greeted him. "The president is expecting you," he said, motioning Zeke down a hallway and towards the back of the house.

"How's he doing today?" Zeke asked.

The agent shrugged. "O.K., I guess. Except for sleeping, he spends most of his time in here playing games on his laptop," he said, opening the door to the sun room.

Rocky was barefoot, attired in a blue and white bathrobe with the presidential seal on the breast pocket, sitting in a recliner that overlooked the back yard. Pale, scrawny legs poked out from beneath the robe. Through the glass doors Zeke could see a swimming pool and a dense stand of trees that were backed by a high black chain link fence. "Mr. Porter is here, sir," the agent said, glancing at Zeke and closing the door behind him.

Rocky turned and waved, then struggled up out of his recliner. He moved towards Zeke, arm outstretched. "Zeke, how are you?" he asked, shaking his guest's hand.

"I'm fine, Mr. President. And you?"

Rocky waved a hand of dismissal. "Nobody calls me that any more. Rocky will be fine. Want a drink?"

"I'll have whatever you're having," Zeke said, nodding towards the glass on the table next to the president's recliner.

"Bourbon it is," Rocky said in a slightly slurred voice. He moved gingerly towards a bar at the far end of the room and poured his guest two fingers in a presidential tumbler, then handed the glass to Zeke. "Cheers, my friend. Come have a seat." He gestured towards an overstuffed chair that sat opposite his recliner.

Rocky looked tired, his face drained of color, his hair turning white. He looked thinner than their last meeting and his voice had weakened to a gravelly whisper. "I've been reading your columns and your show on Sunday night is about the only television I'll subject myself to," Rocky said, sitting heavily in his recliner. He retrieved his own drink and took a sip.

Zeke settled into his designated seat. "Thanks, there's never a shortage of issues out there to deal with."

Rocky looked down into his glass. "Yeah, I suppose." He looked up, his eyes bloodshot now in the direct sunlight. "I guess I don't keep up like I should. Except for your show I mean."

"I'm honored that you watch it, sir."

Rocky nodded but said nothing.

Zeke studied his host, memories of their tumultuous times together flashing through his brain. "So, what do you do with yourself all day? The agent said you spend a lot of time right here in this room."

Rocky sighed. "Yeah, it must be boring as shit for those guys. They try and talk me into going for a ride in the country or getting out of town for a while, but I'm content to be right here."

"Doing what exactly?" Zeke spotted a laptop nearby.

Rocky pointed a finger at Zeke and laughed. "Always the investigative reporter, aren't you?" He looked out into the back yard and his face grew wrinkled, as if he were trying to solve a complex math problem. "Doing a lot of thinking, I guess. About what could have been, what should have been, you know?"

"I do a lot of that myself," Zeke said.

"Do you?" Rocky got up and refilled his glass. "I'd say you're in a pretty good place in life, Zeke. You've come a long way from being a dirt farmer back in Exeter."

Zeke nodded. "I guess so." He hesitated, wondering if enough small talk had transpired to get to the meat of their get together. "So, Rocky, you want to tell me why you've finally decided to see me after all this time? Why you left the most powerful job in the world to sit around and do this?" he added, gesturing about the sun room.

"Wow," Rocky said, "you really go right for the jugular, don't you?" Both men stared at one another. "Alright," Rocky said, "let's just say I got fed up with doing what I was told rather than what I thought was right. If that sounds cliché, then so be it, but that's the reason, pure and simple."

"But you've always been a fighter, Rocky; always convinced people to do things your way."

Rocky stared at a spot on the floor. "Yeah, well, sometimes you meet your match, you know?" He looked up and frowned. "Sometimes you wind up against forces that are so much smarter and stronger than yourself."

"That doesn't sound like the Rocky I know."

The ex-president shook his head. "The Rocky you knew should have died in that farmer's pond all those years ago. Everything I've done since has been bullshit."

"Jesus, Rock, you built you father's bank into a regional power, became a giant player on Wall Street, a U.S. Senator and President of the United States. I hardly call that a bullshit resume."

"Let me tell you what's bullshit, Zeke," Rocky said, jabbing a finger at his guest. "I drove my father to do what I'm doing right now, sitting here drinking and wallowing in what I'm going to do with the rest of my life. I played the game of high stakes bait and switch on the Street and parlayed my dubious expertise there and Robin's good looks into a political career. The rest was done for me by others. I just sat there and went along for the ride until I couldn't stand it anymore. Along the way I lost my son and my wife."

Rocky furrowed his face in concentration. His voice was suddenly calm and measured. "So I've been sitting here all this time feeling sorry for myself and all of a sudden it struck me; despite my sorry-ass perspective I've had a unique experience, been an insider at the highest levels of power, seen all the behind the scenes bullshit that goes on, you know? At best my story is a warning for anyone who wants to follow in my footsteps, at worst it's a classic soap opera." He leveled his stare at Zeke. "Like to help me tell that story to the world?"

So that was why Rocky had orchestrated today's meeting, Zeke thought; his memoirs. Zeke had actually considered this task as one of several possibilities for their meeting today; had already warmed to the idea. Unearthing a cache of national behind-the-scenes anecdotes was an investigative reporter's dream. "I'd be honored to work with you, Rocky, but I might be a little too close to the story."

Rocky emptied his glass and grabbed Zeke's and headed to the bar. "Yeah, I guess the subject of Robin might be a bit awkward to describe." He refilled both glasses and handed one to Zeke.

Zeke swallowed hard. "We both betrayed you, Rocky."

"You did me a favor, Zeke. You kept her off my back and on hers," he added with a chuckle. "Sorry, I don't mean to make light of it all, but she wanted more than what you had, more than what I had as it turns out. She left us both high and dry."

Zeke shook his head. "I can't bring myself to judge her, Rocky. I hope she's found the life she always wanted."

Rocky grunted. "Well, it'll take her a while to run through this Klaus fellow's money, but I truly don't give a shit, Zeke." He moved towards his recliner. "But what about you? How is Andrea?"

Zeke's face broke out in a wide smile. "She's doing great. We're very happy."

Rocky nodded, his face serious. "Does she know—"

"About Robin and me? Yes, we've been totally honest with one another."

Rocky smiled. "You better marry that gal before she gets away."

"I plan to," Zeke said.

Rocky stared out the sliding glass doors into the back yard a moment, then turned and sat down. He leaned forward toward Zeke. "Alright, now tell me what's going on with the Reverend."

"Lincoln?"

Rocky nodded.

"Well, he's become a different man now that he and Liz are married. She's retired from the stage and joined him in his church work. They both seem happy and content."

"Yeah," Rocky said with a thin smile, "I was surprised to get an invitation to their wedding." He sighed. "Guess I wasn't ready to face him yet. Besides, with my Secret Service entourage and the press I would have been an unwanted distraction." He paused, a look of envy crossing his face. "Good for them both." He sipped his drink and said, "I feel horrible about what we did to him."

"You ought to talk with Lincoln about that. He's a very forgiving guy."

Rocky raised his head, his eyes watering. "Perhaps I will one day."

The knock at the door startled Zeke.

"Yes?" Rocky said.

The door opened and a Secret Service agent appeared. "Sorry to disturb you, but it's time for your medication, sir."

"Medication?" Zeke asked, looking at Rocky.

"Just some stuff for my heart," Rocky explained, struggling to his feet. He moved to a desk in the corner and picked up a plastic pill dispenser, checking the day of the week, lifting the lid and emptying the pills into his hand.

"Not to be your mother, Mr. President, but is that medication and Jack Daniels a good mix?" Zeke asked, glancing at the agent for confirmation.

"Actually," Rocky said, popping the pills into his mouth and chasing them with a swig of bourbon, "it's the best combination I can think of," he added with a wink. "Thanks, Matt," he said to the agent.

"Anything else, Mr. President?" the agent asked.

"You want something, Zeke?" Rocky asked. "A sandwich, a snack of some sort?"

"No, thanks, I'm fine," Zeke said, holding up a hand towards the agent.

The agent nodded and left the room, closing the door quietly behind him.

"You have a heart condition?" Zeke asked.

Rocky shook his head. "Had a mild heart attack last year. They put in a stent and said I was fine, no damage. Just have to take these damned pills the rest of my life."

"That's a pretty well kept secret."

"Yeah, well, since I left office nobody gives much of a shit about me anyway, so keeping it out of the news was easy."

Zeke nodded.

"Well," Rocky said, standing up, "I'm supposed to take a nap after my pills so I better do what I'm told. It's been great of you to come down and see me. I know you're a busy guy."

Zeke stood up. "Never too busy to visit with an old friend." He held out a hand to the ex-president.

Rocky shook his hand. "Despite all the shit I've been through in this life, the more I thought about it, it's better than the alternative you saved me from all those years ago in that damned pond. But even if you hadn't saved my sorry ass, you'd still be my friend. Great to see you again." He reached out and embraced Zeke, slipping something into his guest's coat pocket.

Zeke returned the embrace, shocked at how frail Rocky's body was beneath the bathrobe. "Back at you, Rocky. Back at you."

The ex-president smiled weakly. "You give me a call when your time frees up and we'll get started on those memoirs. I've got a lot to say."

"It should be a helluva story, Rocky."

Rocky winked at his old friend. "So, Zeke, who do you think Hollywood will choose to play me in the movie?"

# # #

51

A week later Zeke was rummaging through the clothes in his closet looking for a misplaced receipt when he felt something metallic in one of his jacket pockets. To his surprise what he pulled out of the pocket was a computer memory stick. He stared at it, wondered where it had come from? When was the last time he had worn this jacket? Then he remembered. It had been on his visit with Rocky. He replayed their embrace as he had been leaving, how the president's hand had brushed against the side of his jacket. He thought nothing of it at the time but now his curiosity was piqued. Zeke moved quickly to his laptop and inserted the memory stick into the USB port on the side. What he saw on the screen amazed him.

* * *

During the course of his presidency, Rocky had managed to make electronic copies of an enormous collection of classified government documents, e-mails, reports, and notes from various private meetings. He identified the secret members of an organization known as The Ten and how, from their various positions of power and influence, they controlled most of the financial, political and judicial agendas in the country. Their members included two Supreme Court justices, various members of congress, senior officials in the military, intelligence and law enforcement communities, and a who's who of corporate CEO's and Wall Street bankers. The group's leader and Rocky's primary liaison with The Ten, was the senior senator from Ohio, Sam Adams.

Zeke knew many of the members, had a few on his show from time to time, but he was shocked at the highly coordinated, secret and often illegal aspects of The Ten's day to day activities and their apparent plot to shape the country's future in their neo-capitalist image. The collection of documents also illustrated how Rocky had been identified, groomed, and utilized as a pawn to help implement their vision until he balked and refused to run for a second term as president. There was enough evidence of national security violations, obstruction of justice, bribery, collusion and other violations to send most of The Ten to prison. It was a blockbuster assemblage of information and Zeke had already concluded that it would take a monumental effort just to verify.

Two weeks later Zeke travelled back to Walnut Grove, armed with a list of questions and concerns regarding the vast amount of information the ex-president had provided on the computer memory stick.

After welcoming him, Rocky uncharacteristically suggested they leave the house and go for a ride around town. With two Secret Service agents in the car behind them, Rocky directed Zeke to the same riverside park where Robin had brought him all those years ago when he first visited for Thanksgiving. The trees in the park were much taller now and there were new benches and tables, but the river still flowed brown and the dirt path that had snaked its way high above it was now a smooth strip of asphalt. Rocky asked the Secret Service agents to remain behind so that he and Zeke could have some privacy during their walk.

"I'll walk on well ahead of you, Mr. President," the first agent said. "Matt will stay here by the cars."

Matt nodded and lighted a cigarette, seeming to enjoy being out in the fresh air for a change.

Rocky and Zeke waited a minute to give the other agent time to move down the path. When he was about fifty yards away they started their walk. "You finally get tired of hanging around the house?" Zeke asked with a smile.

Rocky nodded. "I'm pretty sure the house is bugged," he said.

"The Ten?"

Rocky nodded. "I was warned not to do anything stupid after I left office, so guess they're just making sure. I wouldn't be surprised if these agents worked for them."

Zeke glanced back at Matt who stood staring off at the river. He turned back to Rocky. "So, what prompted you to collect all that information you gave me?" he asked.

Rocky sighed. "I realized back when I was a senator that my political career was completely out of my control. Every move I made, every speech I gave was dictated to me by The Ten." He stopped, turning to gaze across the river at the modest city skyline. "I went along with it because I was caught up in all the excitement and supposed power of the position." He turned to face Zeke. "And when they dangled the presidency in front of me, well, they had me."

"But then it got worse?"

Rocky continued down the path. "Much worse. They started telling me to do a lot of things I just didn't want to do, some things I knew were illegal. It became intolerable, but I kept thinking I could find a way to outsmart them, you know?"

"From what I read you didn't have much of a chance. The Ten was everywhere."

"These people don't just influence legislation that favors big business, Zeke, they control the entire country. The only aspect of our society they don't have under their thumb is Workers United. I gave you enough evidence to expose their whole organization. You've got the scoop of the century."

Rocky stopped and sat down on a bench that faced west across the river. "At first I thought their motivation was money, you know, but most of these bastards inherited or made their fortunes long ago. No, their quest is power, Zeke, the ability to manipulate and control people and events on a grand scale. It's like a real life monopoly game to them, but their plan is to destroy the integrity of government, denigrate the working people of our country and undermine what democracy is supposed to be."

Zeke sat down beside him. "Well, you're right, it's quite a story, but there's a bit of a problem with what you gave me, Rocky."

"And what's that?"

"All the illegal things you did because of The Ten, and Beverly Hawkins," he added.

Rocky sighed and leaned forward, elbows on knees. "Yeah."

"Tell me what happened with her."

Rocky leaned back and crossed his legs, ankle on knee. "Simple, really. During the presidential campaign I was grilled by a guy who was looking for anything negative that could be used against me. That was right after Beverly had approached you with her blackmail scheme, so I gave the guy her name, explained the whole situation. He said the matter would be taken care of. I figured they'd either pay her off or scare the hell out of her, never thought they'd---"

"But Rocky, the material I read makes it look like you were in on the decision to kill her, that you were involved in covering it up, getting her police file sealed for national security reasons."

Rocky shook his head. "It isn't true, Zeke. Sure, I gave the guy her name, but after that I forgot about it. When she died I was told it was an example of what happened to people who 'got out of line.'"

"They could make a case that you were right in the middle of the whole scheme, Rocky."

"I know. I know."

"And if we expose The Ten through your memoirs they'll take you down with them."

Rocky turned to face his guest. "And they'll use their knowledge of your affair with Robin to destroy your career. You know that don't you?"

Zeke knew how quickly the public's attitude changed when someone it had seen as a respected individual was caught in the scandal of an extramarital affair. "My career is the least of my concerns here, Rocky. But did they threaten to expose the affair as a way to control you?"

Rocky laughed. "Just the opposite. They did everything they could to protect Robin. After all, she was the real asset, she was the one the voters came out to see, she was the one the public admired. I was just a necessary sideshow, so keeping your affair a secret was designed to keep her popularity, not to protect you or me."

Zeke considered what he had been told. "When did they tell you about us?"

Rocky smiled. "For such a worldly guy you sure are naïve about some things. I knew about you two from that first trip to New York she took to go shopping. No, she didn't tell me, but when I took the time to notice I could see that her dour mood had changed; she was happy, content, and it had nothing to do with me. I was buried up to my ass in the bank and I just didn't care. I didn't know it was you until later, when we moved to New York and, well, I finally put two and two together." He turned to look at Zeke. "But, like I said, The Ten wasn't about to expose Robin. She was their gold mine, the edge that would keep me in office. They catered more to her wishes than they did mine. Hell," he said in a tone of exasperation, "I'm just surprised they didn't try and run her for office."

Zeke recalled how Robin had warmed to her political duties on the campaign trail, then relished her role as First Lady. He tried to move the conversation back to Rocky's memoirs. "You know it's going to be extremely difficult to verify all you've given me without tipping our hand, Rocky. They've got all the bases covered. They can claim your accusations are simply sour grapes at not getting your way politically, that you're trying to shift the blame for the Hawkins cover-up. And giving me all those classified documents violates more laws than I can imagine."

"If you're worried about me going to jail, don't," Rocky said. "If that's what it takes to expose these guys I'm willing to take that chance." He turned to face Zeke with a serious expression on his face. "I hate to wax poetic, Zeke, but sometimes, for the greater good, you have to break the law. So what do we do next?"

Zeke took a deep breath and released it. "In order to make this work we need to get one of The Ten to turn state's evidence," Zeke said.

Rocky laughed. "And how do we do that? They all think they're above the law."

"Well, out of all the material you gave me, Senator Adams is the most exposed. If we can prove his involvement he'll be facing years in prison. Maybe we can leverage your evidence into getting him to confirm all he knows in exchange for immunity."

"Turn on all his colleagues?"

"To avoid prison? Absolutely."

"That means you'd have to get the Justice Department involved; to grant immunity I mean?"

Zeke nodded. "I've got several contacts over there; guys who owe me. It will require a fair amount of secrecy, some coordinated release of information, but we'll need someone like Adams to verify all you've given me, otherwise your book will just be viewed as political revenge. Plus," Zeke added, "there's no guarantee you won't be prosecuted as well."

Rocky nodded. "I'm willing to take that chance."

"Well, we're getting ahead of ourselves. We have a lot of work to do over the next few years and we'll need to create a cover that will keep The Ten from suspecting what we're really doing."

"Few years? What do you mean?"

"I've been giving it a lot of thought. First, you'll need to issue a press release that we'll be corroborating on your memoirs; a trilogy that we'll claim will take several years for each volume to be written. The first will be about your childhood and upbringing, the second your time at the bank and on Wall Street, the third your political experiences. That should buy us plenty of time to build our case. Then, while everyone is expecting your childhood memories as the first installment, we release your political expose instead. It will catch everyone by surprise."

Rocky looked at Zeke forlornly. "I want these bastards punished as soon as possible. The longer we wait, the better chance they have of covering their tracks."

"Rocky, we just can't whip all this together over night then drop this bombshell of a story. We have to have an airtight case, proof beyond the shadow of a doubt and getting Justice to cooperate will require some careful string pulling."

Rocky studied his friend. "You're trying to sit on this to protect me aren't you?"

There was an awkward silence, then Zeke let out a heavy sigh. "I won't trade your life for a goddamned story, Rocky, no matter how spectacular. We've got to protect you."

Rocky looked at Zeke quizzically. "No thanks. I don't want any special favors or any strings attached. If you can't agree to that I'll get someone else to write my story."

"Damn it, Rocky, I'm trying to protect you because you're my friend and I don't want to see anything more happen to you. You've been through enough."

"Jesus, Zeke, what have I ever done to be your friend?"

Zeke's shoulders sagged, then he turned to look at his friend. "You forgave me, Rocky. I deceived you, lied to your face, took advantage of your failed marriage, and you forgave me."

"Have I? How do you know that I've forgiven you?"

"Because if you hadn't, I would have been on the same list as Beverly Hawkins."

Rocky's face reflected the truth of Zeke's claim. He looked out across the sand-choked river at the place he had been born and raised. "You know," he started, "when I ran the bank, then worked on The Street, I was in total control of my world." He smiled. "But when I got into politics things changed." He looked at Zeke. "I realized that it wasn't about power and control anymore; I could change millions of lives by what I did in office." He turned and studied the skyline. "I could have made a difference, Zeke. I could have helped so many people. Believe it or not, that was what I really wanted to do, but The Ten was bigger than me, bigger than anything I wanted to do."

Zeke nodded his understanding. It was as open as Rocky had ever been with him. "We'll find a way to bring them down, Rocky. But I'll never implicate you, never let anyone know you provided me with the incriminating information."

"You would do that for me?" Rocky said, his words catching in his throat.

Zeke reached out and put a hand on Rocky's shoulder. "I didn't pull you out of that pond years ago to let you rot in jail the rest of your life."

Rocky shook his head. "You know, in college I never understood why you were my friend. I was cocky, arrogant, a real prick, you know?"

"Some people never change," Zeke said with a smile.

Rocky chuckled. "Yeah, but what I've been through has rubbed the edges off that young kid, Zeke."

"Life has changed us all," Zeke said. "And trying times bring friends closer together, back to where we started."

"Yeah," Rocky said wistfully. "Back to when all things were still possible."

"They still are, Rocky. And we'll find a way to make this all work. As friends." He held out a hand.

Rocky looked at Zeke, realized that their friendship had come full circle, all the way from college through their respective careers, from triumph and unimagined success through humiliation and defeat, to this very moment of reconciliation and peace. Rocky reached out and grasped Zeke's hand. "As friends, then," he said.

* * *

Samuel Trifacante was the Deputy Assistant Attorney General at the Department of Justice and a long-time friend of Zeke's. The two men had worked on several cases together with information uncovered by Zeke that Sam used in his subsequent prosecutions. In addition, Sam and his wife Melinda were close friends with Zeke and Andrea, visiting one another's homes for dinners and parties and spending long weekends at various vacation spots together. Zeke had chosen Sam to pursue his expose on The Ten, first and foremost because he trusted him implicitly, and second, because Sam was a man who could make things happen rapidly and discretely.

The two men were in Sam's DOJ office in Manhattan. The East River sparkled in the early morning sun as it flowed beneath the Brooklyn Bridge, the scene displayed like a painting through Sam's floor-to-ceiling office window.

Sam finished reading the five page summary Zeke had prepared based on the latter's interviews with Rocky and the ex-president's cache of documentation he had provided Zeke. The summary had been written with no names or reference to the organizational positions of The Ten. Sam tossed the summary onto his desk. "This is powerful stuff, Zeke. It's a helluva story, but I obviously can't move on this without a lot more specifics."

"If you agree to my conditions I'm prepared to reveal the identity of all the people involved."

"Mr. X, Mr. Z, etc.?"

"Yes, but my first condition is that the key member, the leader of The Ten, Mr. X, must be given immunity for verifying all that's in that report."

"So, you expect him to turn state's evidence?"

"Our argument will be that if he doesn't, one of his cohorts will, and that leaves Mr. X hung out to dry and in prison for the rest of his life. The alternative, becoming the key witness for the government, means a new life for him."

"You want us to offer him participation in the Federal Witness Protection Program, then?" Sam asked.

"That's his choice, of course, but without it he's a dead man and, above all, he'll want to save his own hide."

Sam nodded his agreement. "And your other condition?"

"I want immunity for my sources. That includes any and all crimes they may have committed in following instructions from The Ten, and their providing me with the documentation I now have that supports my story."

"Does that include classified material, Zeke?"

"Yes."

Sam frowned. "That will get DoD and the CIA involved, but I have ways of keeping them at arm's length."

"When I provide you with the identities of The Ten and supply you with all the documentation I've talked about, you will have the biggest case in the history of DOJ. This will be a landmark prosecution and, if you believe the breadth and depth of the claims in that report, undoing The Ten will fundamentally change the way we are governed in this country and the integrity of our major institutions."

"And the integrity of your sources?"

"Impeccable, Sam. This is a slam dunk if it is handled properly."

Sam looked worried. "Can you tell me if there are any members of the DOJ that are involved in this?"

"The results of my investigation to date don't suggest any DOJ involvement, but I've had to keep my inquiries below the radar so as to not alert anyone that I have the information I do."

"You realize that revealing all this will put you in danger? If The Ten is as powerful as you suggest, they won't take all this lying down."

"I know, Sam, but this involves the welfare of our country; that's a little bigger than me."

"The truth, no matter where it leads."

Zeke drew a breath and sighed. "Yes, no matter what the consequences for me personally."

Sam eyed his old friend and slowly nodded his head. "This will require some tricky maneuvering and delicate timing."

"You've always been capable of both, my friend."

"I will be all over this like white on rice," Sam said. "You can count on DOJ to run with this. Now go prepare your unedited version of the story."

Zeke reached into his briefcase and pulled out another document. "It's already written," he said, handing it to his old friend.

# # #

52

Rocky Wellington sat in his favorite recliner, glass of bourbon in hand, staring out across the swimming pool in his back yard. The sun was setting and shafts of light shined through the stand of trees that bordered the property, creating a mosaic of color on the water, like a child's kaleidoscope. Rocky smiled at the pleasant effect, then swallowed his evening pills, chasing them with a sip of bourbon. It had been another long day of reflecting and regretting.

As he often did, he thought back to his college days; the future full of promise, standing on the cusp of fulfilling his lifelong dream: New York, the Street, the excitement and thrill of wheeling and dealing amongst the big boys. It was where he belonged.

But then the unexpected lure of politics, of being courted and encouraged and feted. It played to his ego, of course, but soon took on a new dimension of importance. He was swept away like a child at Disneyland, agog at this new world of power and prestige and national recognition. He had been an easy mark; a yokel playing three card Monte on the street corner; sure of himself, smug, confident, shocked at the eventual outcome.

Rocky struggled out of his recliner and made his way to the sliding glass doors that led to the pool area out back. He struggled with the latch, finally freed it and slid the door open, stepping into the yard. The warmth of the air enveloped him. He closed his eyes and breathed deeply.

"Are you alright, Mr. President?" the voice from behind him asked.

Rocky opened his eyes and raised a hand towards the Secret Service agent behind him. "Just getting a breath of fresh air, Matt. Thanks."

The agent scanned the yard and retreated back into the house.

The grass was still warm from the heat of the Kansas day and Rocky wiggled his bare toes in the lush growth. Yes, he thought, returning to his memories, he had been played, led along like a lamb to the slaughter. For those with a weaker will, less fortitude, it might have been easy to play the game, do as he was told, enjoy the limelight. But not for Rocky.

He had prospered by controlling the world around him, bending people to his will, doing things his way. But that was in the marketplace where understanding economic forces, financial trends, and monetary policy paved the way to success. But politics required a different set of skills: ruthlessness, faux diplomacy, and blind ideology. Politics had no rules, and, as it turned out, no soul.

Rocky sighed and his right hand unconsciously reached for his glass of bourbon, twitching against the emptiness. It could have been different; he could have valued his marriage, contained his ambition, set his sights at a more comfortable level. But all those who are drawn to power have higher expectations and play by a different set of rules. A wry smile crossed his face as he recalled the supposed rules that had been sidestepped, circumvented or run over roughshod by The Ten.

His thoughts shifted to Robin and the carefree life she now led. There was no romantic residue from their façade of a marriage. She was merely part of his scheme, the attractive wife he would need to succeed on The Street. Truth be told, she was ironically the catalyst to his political career too. No one really gave a shit about his "message," his claim to be the "grand compromiser," able to unite the country. She was the difference: sexy, smart, the envy of women, the fantasy of men everywhere.

But then the ex-president's mind, as it often did each day, distanced itself from such matters and returned to the single event that haunted his dreams. Junior.

Despite the fact that the child had been created for political purposes with a woman he did not love, Junior had awakened Rocky's paternal instincts. Once he stared into those clear blue eyes and held the warm bundle of pink cheeks and tiny fat fingers, once he had witnessed the first steps, the unmistakable utterance of "daddy," Rocky's world changed. It was then that the frustration of being the supposed most powerful man on earth shrank by contrast to the joy and pride and happiness that was his son. As much as Junior had rearranged Rocky's priorities and altered his perspective, the toddler's death undid it all, plunging Rocky into an abyss with no apparent escape.

Continuing his political façade was suddenly repugnant, dishonest, unworthy of the office and what it supposedly stood for. No person in a position of such power walks away, voluntarily surrenders, committing political suicide like he did. He would forever be portrayed as the president who had folded under pressure, who fled office with so much undone, memories of his days as the icon of compromise now dust in the wind.

And so here he was, disgraced, humiliated, a rudderless boat on a stormy sea. To the casual observer, to someone who hadn't been in his shoes, these feelings might be viewed as melodramatic. But in his mind this was precisely how he felt. He took a deep breath and smiled, knowing that revenge was just around the corner. What he and Zeke had pulled together these past two years was a masterpiece; a political blockbuster that would turn D.C. on its head and send a lot of deserving people to jail. Even if that turned out to be his fate too, he had resigned himself to accept it. Existing here, without purpose or hope had been a self-imposed prison as well. But now there was a chance at vindication, exoneration, punishment for the guilty. The possibilities eked out a rare smile.

* * *

The two couples sat on the back porch of Lincoln and Elizabeth's house on the outskirts of Wichita. The Reverend and his wife were hosting Zeke and Andrea for a few days before the latter couple returned to their home in New York. The foursome had just enjoyed an old fashioned hamburger cookout complete with corn on the cob, potato salad and iced tea. The table had been cleared and the smell of a homemade pecan pie wafted from the kitchen.

"The twins are absolutely adorable," Andrea said with a wide, genuine smile. "Zeke and I are overwhelmed that we'll be known as their honorary uncle and aunt."

Elizabeth returned her smile. "When they arrived at the orphanage they caught our eye immediately; only three months old."

"A boy and a girl will be a real challenge, but a real joy I'm sure," Andrea said. "They're so fortunate to be brought into such a loving home."

Elizabeth reached across the dining table and took Lincoln's hand. "I'm the one who's been so fortunate," she said with an adoring look at her husband.

"Boy," Zeke said, "I'm not sure what sort of spell he's got you under, Liz', but I'd like a dose for you know who," he said, shooting his eyes and a nod of the head towards Andrea.

They all laughed, but Elizabeth said, "Now Zeke Porter, if there's anyone in this room who deserves our thanks, it's Andy. After all, she introduced me to Lincoln and married your worthless hide."

"Guilty as charged on both counts," Andy said. "The two best decisions I ever made."

They all laughed and hooted. "It is truly getting deep in here," Elizabeth said, standing. "Lincoln, why don't you and Zeke stretch your legs while Andy and I brew some coffee and get dessert ready?" She held up a hand towards her husband. "Yes, we'll check on the kids. Now go," she added, waving him towards the back door.

Lincoln smiled. "Terrific. Zeke, come let me show you our grand plantation." The two wives headed into the kitchen while Lincoln guided his guest out the screen door and into the back yard.

What stretched out before them were several hundred acres of rolling countryside. To their left stood a cluster of out buildings, a modest barn, and a corral with several horses. To the right two rows of maple trees bordered a small creek that flowed into the nearby Arkansas River. The smell of fresh cut hay and horse manure were a familiar reminder of growing up on a farm for Zeke. "I'm always amazed to see so much green in Kansas," Zeke said. "The land around Exeter was flat and brown for as far as you could see," he added, referring to his hometown.

"We love it here," Lincoln said. "It's quiet and peaceful and will be a great place to raise the twins."

"I don't know squat about being a parent, but it seems like you and Liz have bitten off a mouthful in adopting those kids. My guess is they have already changed your lives in ways you couldn't have imagined."

Lincoln smiled as they walked towards the nearby creek. "They've certainly have," Lincoln agreed. "I've already cut back on my time in the pulpit so I can devote myself to those kids. Liz and I are going to be the best parents we can be. Family is our top priority."

"Good for you," Zeke said, enjoying the shade of the trees and the gentle gurgle of the creek. He squatted down, pulled a handful of grass up and tossed it into the breeze. "Say, are the Thrasher brothers still working out?" Zeke asked, referring to the twins who had attempted to murder Lincoln and against whom he had refused to press charges.

Lincoln smiled. "Yes, they run our soup kitchen and are the first ones to help me with the really physical field work out on the farms."

"Maybe they'll let me do a story on them one day?" Zeke asked, picturing a tale of religious zealotry, forgiveness, and redemption.

Lincoln smiled. "Maybe."

They turned and looked back toward the house. Zeke decided it was time to let Lincoln in on the book he had been working on with Rocky. "Rocky's about to drop a bombshell that will send D.C. into a tailspin," Zeke said matter-of-factly. He told Lincoln about how Rocky had provided him with the data that exposed the group known as The Ten and their organization of corruption and control and how that would all be revealed in Rocky's memoirs.

"So, this book isn't about his childhood as his press release described?"

Zeke shook his head. "That was a smoke screen to cover our real intentions of exposing The Ten by surprise. Rocky was anxious to publish as soon as possible, but I kept delaying things until we had an airtight case and I could be assured that he wouldn't be prosecuted.

DOJ has already taken The Ten's leader into custody and, as predicted, he's turned state's evidence. The rest of the group will be arrested in a matter of days and then the book will be released, telling the story to the world."

"Just in time for the presidential campaign," Lincoln observed.

"That's the plan; the timing should be perfect to shake up the whole country."

Lincoln considered this dramatic news. "Do you think it will ultimately change anything, Zeke? I don't mean to be a wet blanket, this all sounds spectacular, but we've both seen firsthand how forces like The Ten have a way of surviving and returning to power in another form."

"So you remember my articles about the cycles of power?"

Lincoln raised his eyes to the sky as he recalled the details. "There's always a rich versus poor battle, the rich almost always win, but when the poor do win, well, they don't seem to know what to do with their success and eventually, old Mr. Rockefeller or whoever the villain du jour happens to be, wins out in the end."

Zeke smiled. "Well, that may turn out to be the case here as well, but, Lincoln, I owe it to Rocky to expose these bastards."

"It's strange, after what he did to us, that you believe you owe him," Lincoln said.

"Rocky did us both a favor. Left to our own devices we would have both railed against the shootings at the protest march and against the administration's refusal to negotiate with the workers."

"Of course we would have."

"Rocky knew that and he knew that The Ten would retaliate against us. Their actions would have been out of his control."

"So he locked me away for six months and saw to it that you were diverted from Washington politics with his threats. He was protecting us from The Ten?"

"By the time we reappeared on the scene The Ten's attention was on other things. We were both old news."

Lincoln studied the horizon. "I never thought of it that way." He turned to Zeke. "Well, you've both got a lot of courage to open this can of worms."

"It's my job, Lincoln."

"The truth, right? No matter where it leads."

"Sometimes that motto is hard to follow because all too often the truth is so painful."

"I assume you address your affair with Robin in Rocky's book. Aren't you afraid of repercussions from that?"

Zeke sighed. "My only concern was making peace with Rocky on that, which we did. I truthfully don't care what the public thinks. Let them cast the first stone, right?"

Lincoln laughed. "Now you sound like one of my father's sermons. Look," he went on, "from what I understand those two were as much to blame for what happened as you were. There's something to be said for following your heart, Zeke. You may not have been honest with Rocky at the time but you were honest with yourself. And," he went on, "after all is said and done you were the one that was hurt because you cared for her and he didn't."

"Well, it was, for a while, a beautiful experience and I refuse to let people who don't understand the emotions involved turn it into an ugly memory for me."

Lincoln nodded his understanding, turned and stared down into the creek. "When things get ugly for me, this is where I come to think," he said.

"And what do you think about?"

He smiled. "Things pleasant and beautiful."

"Well, you've got what you wished for there, my friend. You have a wonderful family and a terrific life."

Lincoln turned to face Zeke. "Thanks to you."

Zeke shook his head. "Now look, we've been through this before. What happened all those years ago was an accident. What I did was just a reaction, nothing more. What you've accomplished, the wonderful world you've made for yourself was all your doing. I'm no more responsible for your success and happiness than---"

"You are for Rocky's fate?" The gurgling of the creek could be heard clearly in the ensuing silence. "Just because you saved his life doesn't mean you're responsible for how he lived it."

Zeke stared at Lincoln, then both men smiled. "How did you get so damned smart?" Zeke asked.

"It's my K-State education," Lincoln said with a grin.

Zeke picked up a small rock and tossed it into the creek. "Do you think college prepared us in any way for the lives we've led, the experiences we've had?" he asked.

"I think," Lincoln said, "that what prepared us for life was each other. Our friendship, whether we sensed it or not, was strong and it stayed that way right to this moment."

"So you don't hold Rocky to blame for your time in prison?"

"From what you've told me that was The Ten's doing."

"Yes, but it wears on Rocky. I encouraged him to talk with you about it; that you were a forgiving man."

Lincoln smiled. "Actually, Rocky called me several weeks ago and invited me to Walnut Grove. Said he would appreciate the opportunity to explain some things, but our visit would make more sense after the release of his book. At the time I didn't understand, but I'm anxious to lessen his load of regret."

Zeke smiled. "He's lucky to have you as a friend."

Andrea's melodic voice rang out. "Guys, dessert!"

"The call of the wild," Zeke joked.

Lincoln looked at his friend and smiled, then threw an arm around Zeke's shoulders and the two men headed towards the house. "Will you come back for the twin's first birthday party?" Lincoln asked.

"Wouldn't miss it for the world," Zeke said.

#

53

The western side of the U.S. Capitol building was festooned with inauguration banners of red, white and blue. The mood of the throng that spread out on the mall like an invading army was jubilant and boisterous. Zeke, Andrea, Lincoln and Elizabeth enjoyed seats on the podium just two rows away from where the newly elected president and his family were seated. The day was clear, but bitterly cold, temperatures near zero, but without the notorious D.C. wind, it was a tolerable day for the spectators. Indeed, the crowds that had been camped out since the night before were record in number, the popularity of the new president-elect unlike any in recent memory.

Zeke reached for Andrea's hand and turned to smile at her. Their place of honor on the podium was at the request of the new president, a man who attributed his victory to the backlash generated by Zeke's biography of Rocky Wellington. The book exposed the octopus-like tentacles of The Ten and how their stranglehold on the American dream shone a spotlight on the corruption, illegal deal-making, sidestepping of the law, and other nefarious acts that served to rouse a sleeping electorate.

Lincoln too shared the podium for his tireless efforts and personal sacrifices for the workers union, his influence responsible for the millions of votes for the man who now stood before them in triumph. Rocky had been invited to attend but chose instead to watch the ceremony from home.

The oath of office had just been administered by the Chief Justice and the crowd roared its approval. Eduardo "Eddie" Perez, cut a handsome profile as he stepped to the podium. Young, energetic, full of life and hope; Eddie flashed his now-famous smile and the crowd erupted once again. Bareheaded and without overcoat or gloves, he began his inaugural address, his words transformed into the white mist of frozen breath.

As the new president spoke, Zeke recalled how Rocky's book had set the stage for someone like Eddie Perez, third generation son of Latino immigrants, champion of the working man, to rise to national prominence on a platform of political and corporate housecleaning, social reform and a promise to undo the wrongs The Ten had foisted on the country. D.C.'s tectonic plates had shifted once again.

As for the fate of The Ten, as Zeke had predicted, Senator Adams had turned state's evidence, betraying his colleagues in a heartbeat in exchange for immunity and entry into the Federal Witness Protection Program. The majority of his co-conspirators were sentenced to varying times in prison, all forfeiting their positions of power and influence in disgrace.

Zeke knew that most would serve the least amount of time permissible, then retire to a life of comfort and seclusion, fueled by the fortunes they had amassed. Many of those holdings had been frozen by the courts in an attempt to ascertain what portions had been illegally acquired. Previous multi-millionaires would be forced to live like ordinary citizens. How ironic, Zeke considered.

As for his own fate, Zeke's fear that the revelation of his affair with Robin as portrayed in Rocky's memoirs would cast him as a villain were surprisingly unjustified. The public chose to view Robin as the villain, cheating on her husband, then leaving him high and dry at his lowest moment, off living a life of luxury and excess with her multi-billionaire boyfriend. Zeke was seen as Rocky's true friend, asking forgiveness, then working diligently with the ex-president to write his spectacular expose, knowing that the details of the affair as depicted in the book would probably destroy Zeke's future. Nothing, it turned out, was farther from the truth.

Zeke continued his job at World News while his columns and "The Bottom Line" remained as popular as ever. Even with the advent of a new administration and the associated honeymoon of good will and hope, there would still be enough evil and corruption in the world to fill the front page every day. Zeke's world of investigative reporting had never been more in demand.

Zeke's reverie was interrupted by a roar from the crowd as President Perez continued his speech. "The problems facing our country," the president said, "are too complex and entrenched to be solved by past partisanship, secret agreements, and the quest for power and profit. Consideration must be given to the working men and women of our country, to our environment, to trust in our government. My solemn promise to you, my fellow citizens, is to do just that."

The crowd roared its approval and the president nodded his head in vigorous agreement.

Yes, Zeke thought, today is a day of hope and promise, of pledges to undo past wrongs, to always do what is right and just and fair. Sincere words, but words untested by their inevitable clash with reality. The marketplace, Wall Street and the hundreds of corporate fiefdoms were a formidable power, with or without The Ten. Collectively they were a force that had withstood a handful of administrations and charismatic leaders who had promised to dismantle them and subject them to the will of the people.

"Our journey together," Eddie Perez was saying, "will be difficult, but we will be motivated by the knowledge that we are righting a heinous wrong-doing, setting our course for a just land that recognizes all its citizens and treats them as equals despite their economic or social status." The crowd erupted and chants of "Eddie, Eddie" filled the valley of the national Mall and washed over the Capitol building like a warm sunset.

Zeke stared off across the heads of the crowd, across the distant Potomac and imagined he could see all the way to Kansas, to K-State, to the pond where he and his friend's lives had changed that frigid night so long ago. As he often did, Zeke marveled at how three college buddies, each in their own distinct way, had helped shape and influence events on a national scale. Each had achieved fame, been seduced by it, recognized it for its insidious effect on their lives, then discarded it, overcoming a fierce struggle with their egos.

The new president had just concluded his speech and those on the podium stood as he and his family started back inside the Capitol building, all waving to the crowd. The president stopped next to Zeke and held out his hand. "This is the people's day," he said, shaking his hand. "Congratulations to you both." He reached for Lincoln's hand and shook it.

"Thank you, Mr. President," Zeke said.

"Great speech, Mr. President," Lincoln added.

Eddie Perez nodded. "It's all the things Rocky Wellington wanted to do and now, God willing, I'm going to try and fulfill his dream. I hope you four will be my guests tomorrow at the White House when I sign Rocky's pardon."

"We'll be there, Mr. President," Zeke said.

Eddie Perez smiled. "See you all then." He turned and started up the steps.

Zeke looked at Lincoln, both men sensing the magic of the moment. Who could have ever guessed that the survivors of that accident so long could have been responsible for all that now spread before them? Three kids from Kansas. Sounded like the name of a rock group. Zeke smiled.

The crowd kept chanting, "Eddie, Eddie!" How long will this last, Zeke thought? The euphoria, the promise of a better tomorrow, the anticipated accomplishment of great things? Administrations, he considered, shared the same arc that individual lives did; the naïve, hopeful beginnings, dealing with the first disappointment, the realization that life wasn't fair, didn't follow the inspiring words in textbooks or the happy endings in movies. Maybe this time around, things would be different. Maybe this time the nation's dreams would come true. Maybe this time.

* * *

Back in Walnut Grove, Rocky Wellington reached for the remote controller and muted the television. The silent picture showed guests filing out of their places on the podium and heading back into the Capitol building. Time for a lunch of lobster or filet mignon for the select few before the parade started. He remembered his own inauguration, the mandatory protocol, his carefully edited speech, the long afternoon of watching bands and soldiers and floats stream by the reviewing stand in front of the White House. Then the evening of grand balls, dancing with Robin to wild applause, the endless smiles and waves. It all seemed like a movie he had seen long ago, the scenes slightly blurry in his memory.

Rocky reached for the empty mug next to his recliner and struggled to his feet, heading for the pot on the table across the room. Coffee had replaced bourbon in his daily regimen some time ago and he drank it black to get the full effect of the caffeine. He paused at the table, refilled his mug and stared at the black and white picture on the lower shelf of the nearby bookcase. Three young boys smiled back at him, innocent faces, hopeful expressions, a look of youthful exuberance and boundless energy. Lincoln looked like a twelve year old cherub, Zeke with his Zapata mustache, Rocky looking distracted, already plotting his first move with the bank.

He remembered that sunny day of cap and gown, the smiles and handshakes and promises to stay in touch, the picture seeming to fill the room with laughter and noise from all those years ago. The three unlikely friends mugging for the photographer as if they hadn't a care in the world.

Rocky smiled and raised his mug towards the picture of Zeke, Lincoln and himself. "Cheers, fellas." And as he stared at the picture, memories flooding his brain, hot tears streamed down Rocky's cheeks. Like so many, he had made bad choices. Now, as he travelled the paths of would-have and should-have, he recalled what Lincoln had told him, right here in this room just a few months ago.

"Everyone's life has many chapters. Turn the page and put the past, good or bad, behind you. Turn the page and start the rest of your life today."

Corny words you would expect from a country minister, but wise words nonetheless. What Rocky had done in the first chapters of his life might have been disappointing, but there had also been good things, great things actually. And there might just be more waiting out there. But only if he tried. Rocky wiped at his tears with a knuckle, smiled again at the picture and decided that was just what he would do. He would try again.

# # #

EPILOGUE

The unmarked road looked vaguely familiar: two lanes of crowned asphalt that had probably first been paved back in the fifties. Rocky slowed the car down and turned carefully onto the side road, the tires crunching on the gravel bed. "I think this it," he said.

In the front seat Lincoln looked back up the length of the paved road. "We were coming from the other direction, right?" He shook his head, trying to remember.

Rocky moved the car slowly down the gravel road. From the back seat Andrea drank in the plowed fields on either side of the road. "I believe I was out cold, so I don't remember any of this," she said.

Sitting next to her Zeke said, "Well, we were going a helluva lot faster that night; all this was a blur then." He pointed through the windshield. "Here comes the turn," he said.

Rocky slowed the car again, found a flat open area just off the road and pulled the car onto it. They all got out and Zeke led the way around the edge of the field towards the pond. The foursome walked to the edge and looked down into the brown water. They were all quiet, their memories churning. Finally, Lincoln said, "It looks smaller now."

"I guess everything's smaller after fifty years," Zeke said.

"Speak for yourself," Rocky said with a grin and a wink towards Andrea.

The four were attending the fifty year reunion of their KSU graduation class. Unlike most of their classmates, they avoided all the "official" activities, not wanting to draw attention to themselves. They had worn baseball caps and sunglasses to walk around Aggieville, wander the campus, and drive around Manhattan gazing at old haunts from Rocky's convertible. The ex-president had long ago turned down further Secret Service protection, so they were on their own to explore their old stomping grounds unencumbered. Hence this drive out into the countryside east of the campus.

"Could any of you have imagined in your wildest dreams what happened to us after that night here in this pond?" Lincoln asked.

The four paths that led from the frigid water and mud of that night so long ago were well known as each of them had achieved their own slice of celebrity, but it was the later years that were more meaningful to them now.

Lincoln and his wife Elizabeth had raised their two adopted children and took great pride in being "typical parents." Lincoln ultimately retired from the Church of Hope and focused on his four grandchildren and the pleasures of being a casual farmer. He published a number of books describing his philosophy and perspectives on how to help your fellow man.

Andrea and Zeke had also retired from their respective careers, enjoying their roles as grandparents for their son's two children. They had remained living in the city, keeping abreast of local politics and show business via old friends and contacts. Andrea wrote a book about life on Broadway, while Zeke expressed his many viewpoints through the world of fiction, crafting a series of best-selling novels.

Rocky became a bit of a folk hero with the publication of his biography that exposed The Ten and sent many of them to jail. Historians treated his one term presidency with an understanding perspective, given the constraints he had dealt with. But Rocky's pride and joy now was his foundation, named "Junior's Kids", which provided food, clothing and medicine for the millions of refugee children around the world. He became a spokesman for the plight of these displaced and homeless kids, raising millions of dollars for their care and well being.

Zeke picked up a rock and tossed it into the pond, the deep-throated plunk indicating how shallow the pond had become. "I'll ask the obvious question," he said. "If you had these last fifty years to do over again, what would you change?"

Lincoln ran a hand over his bald pate and said, "That's easy for me; nothing. Like everyone else I've had my ups and downs, but I've wound up with a wonderful life, a terrific family and have three of the best friends in the world." He put a hand on Rocky's shoulder and smiled.

"So, you would still want to get shot and spend six months in solitary?" Andrea asked, shooting an anxious glance at Rocky.

"Those were both defining moments for me," Lincoln replied. "I learned the true meaning of forgiveness and those events adjusted my perspective, shaped the rest of my life. No, I wouldn't want to change anything. What about you, Andy?"

Andrea had aged gracefully without benefit of a surgeon's scalpel and could still, as she had shown on several late night television appearances, belt out show tunes with the best of them. She stared down into the murky pond then turned and smiled at the trio. "I'd want to walk across the Brooklyn Bridge a lot sooner than I did," she said, her eyes finding Zeke. "That's when my life really began." She reached out and took Zeke's hand. They both smiled.

"Well," Lincoln said, "that's a little weird, but O.K., Andy. What about you Zeke? Want to walk across that bridge sooner?"

Zeke smiled but then his face turned serious. His full head of hair had turned grey, but he otherwise looked much the same as in his youth. "Seeking the truth as a profession can make you cynical about life; the results are so often disappointing." He squeezed Andrea's hand. "But Andy has shown me how to see the joy in life and to appreciate every moment no matter what is going on all around me. So, yes, I wish we could have walked across that bridge sooner. It would have erased a part of my life I regret and maybe eased the pain I inflicted on a good friend." He looked at Rocky and smiled. Rocky smiled back and winked.

Lincoln turned to the ex-President. "What about you, Rock?"

Rocky toed the dirt at his feet and took a deep breath. He looked out across the neat rows of corn in the field. "Me? Hell, I'd want to change *everything*." He paused, then began, "I would have found some young lady who truly loved me, and we would have had kids, lots of them. I would have transferred control of the bank from my father slowly, allowing the old man to keep his dignity and pride intact. I would have settled into life in Walnut Grove as my parents and their parents before them had. A comfortable life in a small town watching my kids grow up."

Rocky exhaled heavily and went on. "And now, if I had done all that, I too could have been a grandfather, a husband who was ready to grow old with his wife, someone who had traded all the glamour and power and money for a normal, largely uneventful existence." He smiled ruefully. "I would have watched all the events I would otherwise have been a part of with a distant envy and an occasional sigh of regret that I had not lived my boyhood dreams." He paused, eyed each of his friends in turn. "Like most every person on earth." He wiped a tear from his cheek, relieved that he had finally said what he had been feeling for years.

The group stood in awkward silence for a long moment, then Andrea moved forward and gave Rocky a hug. "You still have us," she said, wiping a tear from her own eye.

The foursome moved slowly together forming a group hug. "Our greatest accomplishment is that we have remained friends all this time," Lincoln said.

"I honestly don't know why you guys have put up with me all these years," Rocky said, his voice catching in his throat.

Zeke slapped Rocky on the back. "No good deed goes unpunished, Rock." They all laughed.

"You know," Lincoln began, a serious expression on his face, "not to put too fine a point on this reunion, but it is a notable milestone for us." He shot a sad smile at his friends. "I mean, think of all those classmates who are no longer with us. And what about the others? Isn't it amazing how many are stooped, gray and frail?" He smiled. "Makes you wonder what they think we look like."

They all laughed.

"It's funny," Zeke said. "Most of the time I don't think of being old at all. Then suddenly somebody who was a childhood hero of mine; a movie star, a ball player; one of those people who seems forever young in your memory dies and wow, it reminds me how long ago my youth really was."

"He still reads the obituaries every morning," Andrea added with a shake of her head. "So it's up to me to put a positive spin on the rest of the day," she said, putting her arm around her husband.

"And I like how you do that," Zeke said, pulling her close and smiling lasciviously.

"Alright," Rocky said. "Are we going to have to throw you two into the pond to cool you down?"

Everybody laughed, then Andrea said, "Well, right there in that pond is where I first fell in love."

That comment drew a groan from Rocky and Lincoln. Rocky reached out and took Andrea's hand and pulled her towards the car. "O.K., let's shut this soap opera down before it gets too corny." He smiled. "Now, let's go have a beer at Jake's and tell more lies about how we love getting old."

# # #

Printed in the United States
By Bookmasters